FAILED REDEMPTION

OTHER NOVELS BY R A JORDAN

THE WALLS SAGA

Time's Up
England's Wall
Laundry
Cracks in the Wall
Secret Side
A Tower of Strength

CHARITY BOOKS IN AID OF NHS CHARITIES

Match Day Murder
The Family Lie

FAILED REDEMPTION

A John England Story

R A JORDAN

Matador
Unit E2 Airfield Business Park,
Harrison Road, Market Harborough,
Leicestershire. LE16 7UL
Tel: 0116 2792299
Email: books@troubador.co.uk
Web: www.troubador.co.uk/matador
Twitter: @matadorbooks

ISBN 978 1803132 709

British Library Cataloguing in Publication Data.
A catalogue record for this book is available from the British Library.

Printed and bound by CPI Group (UK) Ltd, Croydon, CR0 4YY
Typeset in 11pt Minion Pro by Troubador Publishing Ltd, Leicester, UK

Matador is an imprint of Troubador Publishing Ltd

MIX
Paper from
responsible sources
FSC® C013604

This book is dedicated to my five wonderful grandchildren, who are growing up quickly.

Sam, Dan, Phoebe, Izzy and Roxy.

I wish to pay tribute to all those who have helped me create this book. Some will know who they are. Others have helped in ways they never knew. Thank you all.

Thank you to all those who have purchased and donated to the NHS Charities Together by purchasing my Charity Books.

Failed Redemption is the next book in the Walls Saga.

'Assassination has never changed the history of the world.'

Benjamin Disraeli: House of Commons 1 May 1865

1

'How wonderful to be back. The view over the city never fails to excite me.'

'Yes, my love, the view is an ever-changing picture. It must be like living by the sea or a harbour. There is always something going on. It's the same here, but it's mainly traffic and clouds.'

'Our trip to Ireland turned out to be more exciting than expected. Your proficiency with a pistol managing to save us was exceptional. I thought you had killed the man.'

John and Fiona were back in their penthouse suite in Peters Tower in Manchester. After living in the countryside for so long, John found it difficult to get used to living in this beautifully furnished apartment. Sienna, his wife, tragically killed in a car accident, was responsible for the furnishings. She would never have imagined that John would one day live here. The view from the bifold windows was awe-inspiring.

'You know, everyone who comes here walks immediately to the window to enjoy the view over the centre of Manchester. We are high enough to see the Pennine hills, Fiona.'

'It was a great trip, John, full of unexpected happenings, but it is good to be home,' said Fiona, John's new companion and lover.

'Well, we certainly got more than we expected. Coffee?'

'Yes, please, I will put the washing machine on. Can you let me have your clothes that want washing, John?'

'Sure, I will dig my stuff out as soon as I have had a quick squint at this small pile of mail, mostly rubbish.'

John pulled the waste-paper bin closer to his desk. The junk mail was destined to be sent there. There were only three letters of interest. One from Andrew at Bennetts saying he needed to speak and arrange transfer of funds to wherever John decided. The second was a report from the letting agent, Angela, confirming the current situation in the block. The last was a statement from his credit card company, which had been hit hard due to the additional time in a hotel in Ireland and the unexpected flight home.

John set the coffee machine working.

'You know, I am always fascinated by this machine.' Speaking aloud, he loaded the device with a new cassette, ensuring water was in the tank, pressing the 'go' button and watching the aluminium cup fill with coffee. 'I am sure one day it will overflow. I am puzzled how it knows? Here is your coffee, sunshine. I will get my dirty washing for you now,' giving Fiona a peck on the cheek as he stood up to get his bag with his clothes. Fiona added John's dirty washing to the pile Fiona had already made in the utility area.

'You know,' said John, 'I had always thought that Krups, who manufacture the coffee machine, were part of the massive Krupp organisation in Essen. They were colossal steel producers and manufacturers of armaments for the German Army. It wasn't until I searched the internet that Krups, founded in 1846, made weighing scales, coffee machines and hairdryers. They are nothing to do with Krupp, the steel maker. Thought you would like to know that!'

'You are a fountain of knowledge, John.'

'I have an enquiring mind. The good news is that Angela has sent me a message advising me all the flats are fully let. 803 has had a new tenant for two years. An Italian has taken 801 where the fire was.'

John continued reading and looking at the attachments giving details of the tenants.

'My God, Fiona, the new tenant in 803 is Brandon Phelan. That is not a British name; could he be related to the Phelans from Dunmore Hall?'

'Oh no, John, we have surely seen enough of them. Has he come here on purpose, do you suppose?'

'I will go and see Angela; look at his file. What can I do if he is related to the Irish Phelans? I don't know. He will know why he has come. I would also like to know why he is here, but he is unlikely to reveal the true reason.'

***

'Angela, it's John.'

'John, did you have a good trip?'

'Yes, I suppose you could say that. I will tell you all about it when I call in. Would within the hour be acceptable? I need to see the tenant files on 801 and 803. They moved in while we were away.'

***

'Is everything okay, Fiona? I need to pop down and see Angela. Do you need me to get anything while I am out?'

'Thanks, John. It all depends on what and where we eat tonight?'

'We could go to the little bistro down the road, which looks intriguing?'

'That will do just fine, so no, is the answer to your question. See you later, darling.'

***

'Angela, sorry to bug you as soon as I get back. I need to know where Mr Phelan is from, his previous addresses and his job in Manchester.'

'That's easy enough, John. I have the files here.'

'Good, I will read the contents. I may need copies. Angela, Brandon Phelan is of great interest to me. Let me explain. As you know, Fiona and I accepted an invitation to sail to Cork in southern Ireland with our old acquaintance, Goose. He had just purchased his new boat; the trip to

Cork was effectively a trial sail. I knew before we left that I was to meet a man who had been demanding money from me on behalf of his brother, Michael Fitzallen. The amount was three million pounds. That was the sum his brother lent to my sister-in-law, Sandra Wall. There was an agreement that Michael would receive half the rents from the block, and on the sale of Peters Tower, he would receive his money back. There was a clause that made the agreement void. The agreement would end if Michael committed a crime that put him in jail for ten years or more. Michael would forfeit the right to share rents and for his capital to be repaid.

'Michael did commit a crime. He murdered my sister-in-law, Sandra; a solicitor drafted the agreement. All the problems we have had at Peters Tower with the fire here and the fire I had at my farm in Tarporley were down to Sean Fitzallen, Michael's brother, trying to get his hands on the money for his brother.'

'Good heavens, but it still does not explain your concerns over Brandon Phelan,' enquired Angela.

'Yes, well, it goes back a long way. Michael Fitzallen was in partnership with another guy and their financier, Niall Phelan, who lived at Dunmore Hall. Cutting the story short, Phelan double-crossed Michael Fitzallen and moved all the partnership profits to his bank account in Ireland. It was well more than three million, nearer four million pounds. Goose, who we have just been with on his new motor yacht, managed to recover most of the money for Michael. Niall Phelan was killed in an explosion in his laboratory at Dunmore Hall.

'We have managed to see an end to Sean Fitzallen, who fell overboard from Goose's boat and drowned. It now seems that the Phelan part of the organisation is trying to get their hands on the money.'

'What a tangled web, John. What are you going to do?'

'I intend to uncover the true intentions of Brandon Phelan following the failed retribution attempt by Sean Fitzallen. I need a full copy of this file, please, Angela.'

John took the new papers, carefully secured in a manilla envelope, back to the penthouse.

2

'Fiona, can you spare me some time to consider our future moves relating to the Phelan family? It involves attempting to recover money taken from Michael Fitzallen by Niall Phelan and then lent to Walls Holdings to pay off the bank.'

'Yes, darling, it all sounds dire. When do you want to trawl through the implications?'

'Well, let's put it all aside and deal with it tomorrow. I would appreciate your view on the overall situation. My brain will hurt if we do it today. I may not sleep if I try to work it all out this afternoon.'

Following an excellent meal at the local bistro, a bottle of wine and a good night's sleep, both were ready to try and make sense of the Phelan and Fitzallen mysteries.

'Fiona, can we get started?'

'In a moment, John, I am just loading the dishwasher. Marmalade loves to stick on plates. Here is fresh coffee,' she said, joining John in his office, which had previously been the third bedroom of the penthouse. John's desk was covered in printed sheets of paper. The sort that spews from the printer when you need to obtain information from Wikipedia.

'Okay, I have decided to delve back into history. There could be issues from the past that have led to the terrible consequences we have experienced.'

'Okay, John, you will know the Phelan family then.'

'To get the background, I needed to go back to when Ireland had declared its neutrality before World War II. They were not for or against the Germans but could not compromise their new neutral status by helping either side in the conflict. That, however, did not stop fifty thousand Irish men and women from joining British forces to fight in the Second World War.'

'That's surprising. I didn't know that!'

'Yes, it's amazing. I didn't know that either. First, I worked back using a family tree investigation site. I have the date of birth for Brandon Phelan and an address in Ireland. Would you believe he uses Dunmore Hall as his address? We know all about that from our trip. That's where you shot an Irishman! What a commotion that caused. Luckily you didn't kill him. My masterstroke has been looking at the family tree, which has revealed many names and ancestors associated with Dunmore Hall. Look here,' requested John.

John rolled out a Sellotaped roll, made up of many sheets of paper, making a family tree.

'I have gone as far back as I believe necessary. I have

covered a time when Ireland was bound up with England and then split, leaving the six counties still part of the UK, now known as Northern Ireland or Ulster.

'The first inhabitants of the Hall I have chosen to start with are Niall and Mary Phelan. Niall was born in 1917. Mary was born in 1920. They had one child, Shauna Phelan. The exciting thing is what came next in 1939 when the UK declared war on Germany for invading Poland. Germany had anticipated the declaration of war and sent several spies to Ireland. The Germans believed Ireland would be an excellent place to get information on the UK's intentions.

'On reading the accounts of what happened, a contingent of German intelligence operatives landed on Irish soil early in 1939. As far as could be ascertained, there were eight or ten spies. It looks probable that these individuals were landed on the beach in the loch at the back of Dunmore Hall.'

'Wow, how exciting, John. You could have the makings of a war mystery story here.'

'Yes, you are right, except this was real. The Irish Directorate of Military Intelligence managed to pick up nine of these spies. Six were hanged for breach of new Irish legislation protecting its neutrality, and three died from a hunger strike.'

'What happened to the tenth person, John?'

'Well, my love, you are right; there is a missing person if the original count is correct. However, there was a further "delivery" of people onto the shores of southern Ireland that year. It appears that U-boat 35 sank a Greek freighter in the western approaches. It was delivering iron ore to the UK to support the munitions industries. It was the 16th of October 1939 when this incident occurred. The U-boat picked up twenty-eight Greek sailors. Once again, the loch at the rear of Dunmore Hall was the preferred location for landing the sailors. The U-boat had disappeared when Irish coastal defence aircraft had been scrambled.

'Somehow, they think Albert Heinz was amongst them in the new landings. He was either a spy with the first "delivery" or a member of the crew of the Greek freighter. The name would lead me to believe he was the missing German. However, he could easily have been in the Greek freighter or as part of the U-boat crew. We will never know.

'The significance of Albert Heinz is that he spoke perfect English. He was not in uniform. He had been discovered on the beach, covering a hole in the sand. He admitted to hiding a radio set, which would suggest intelligence gathering if nothing else.

'He was taken to the Hall for questioning; he seemed a reasonable enough fellow to Mr Niall Phelan. As he needed some extra help in running the estate, Phelan employed Heinz to help run the estate and the buildings of Dunmore Hall. Heinz was delighted to get a job. He insisted on just being called Albert. His surname would have marked him out as German immediately.

'Niall's family consisted of his wife, Niall Junior and Shauna. Just the four of them. Shauna would have been about twenty-four years of age when Albert started to work on the estate. Shauna and Albert became romantically involved. She was a pretty girl, and Albert had all the characteristics of the Aryan race. According to Shauna's description, blond hair, sculptured face, tall and slim, very good-looking, at any rate.

'Oh, John, that sounds like a Mills and Boon story. Do you mean they hit it off? Did they get married?'

'Yes, my love, that is what happened. After they married, Albert Heinz, conscious that his name was not ideal with a war going on between UK and Germany and other conflicts breaking out worldwide, thought it would be preferable to melt into the background in Ireland. Albert Heinz changed his name to Albert Phelan. An instance where the bride did not have to change her name when she married.'

'You have to tell me what happened next; a baby arrives?'

'Correct, Sean Phelan was born in October 1943.'

'I think I can guess the rest?'

'Oh really, Miss Detective? Go on then.'

'I think Sean marries someone, and they have two children, Niall Phelan and Brandon Phelan?'

'Correct, Niall was born in 1976 and would now be forty-two, but the bomb delivered with the fake drugs by Goose on behalf of Michael Fitzallen killed him when he was thirty-eight. Brandon, born in 1978, is now forty and the tenant of Apartment 803.'

'So that is very interesting, John, but what conclusions can be drawn from all this?'

'Great question, darling. You don't know, and how could you, that Sean Phelan's father-in-law was a top operative in the IRA. That would have been during the war. The IRA hoped that the Germans would be victorious, which could have led to the unification of Ireland. That was and, as far as I know, is still the intention of the IRA today.'

'Well, John, while that was all very interesting, I am not sure how it helps you understand the reasons behind Brandon's visit to Manchester.'

'As always, you are right, my darling, but we know a great deal more about his ancestry which may still have implications for today. My reading of the Irish is that they are incredibly keen to remember historical events, especially those which impacted Irish history and the independence of the island of Ireland.'

'Okay, John, surely our minds should be on travelling to Palma Mallorca to join *Brave Goose* and its crew. Goose has insisted we join them.'

'As always, you are correct. Let's get booking a flight.'

John booked a one-way flight to Mallorca on Monday 25th June. He was not sure when they might return.

'You know, John, in so far as the cash is concerned, we haven't discussed Michael and Sean Fitzallen's connection with Phelan.'

'You are right, Fiona. There isn't much more to say other than Michael Fitzallen provided the three million to Sandra. In return, he was to receive half the rent from the tower and half its value should it ever be sold, on the understanding his share would never be less than three million pounds.'

'That all sounds perfectly reasonable, John.'

'It does until you factor in two things. There was a cancellation clause in the agreement. It brought the agreement to an end, and all arrangements ceased if Michael Fitzallen was to commit a serious crime that put him in jail for at least ten years.'

'So is this the guy who killed Sandra?'

'Correct. Michael killed Sandra Wall. That action cancelled the agreement. Michael was no longer entitled to get his money back. All the subsequent actions have been to try and persuade me to pay back all or most of the money. That reminds me, I am supposed to have spoken to Andrew at Bennetts. I must phone now.'

'Andrew, it's John, you sent me a note about money. What do you need to know?' John held the phone handset between ear and shoulder, waiting for Andrew to respond. As he did so, John tidied up all the papers he had used to understand the Phelan connection.

'Well, my dear fellow,' Andrew started his announcement, 'you are this morning richer than you expected to be.'

'Oh, you had better continue.'

John put a pad of paper in front of him, retrieved from the top drawer of his desk. There was already a pen ready to note down the salient points.

'I cannot take credit for most of this. Your very clever insurance broker, Ian Birch, has been of invaluable assistance in undoing the benefits and claims on your various insurances. There is quite a list, John, but let me start with the sale of Long Acre Farm, then the compensation awards, then the life policies.'

'Andrew, let me stop you there. I am not keen to know the details of compensation and accident claims. The information will only bring back, as it is now, memories I am trying to leave behind. Never forget, of course, but the detail will be too raw. What is the bottom-line number?'

'John, I fully understand. It is two million, six hundred and eighty-two thousand, seven hundred pounds. All fees have been accounted for with disbursements and VAT paid.'

'That is significantly more than I had expected. Knowing you and Graham, a discount has been applied to your fees. So, my instructions are to send two million five hundred thousand to my bank. The accounts department has the details. The balance is bonus money to everyone who has helped sort this mess out. I will leave it to you to apportion the balance, so long as you and Graham get the lion's share.'

'That is extremely generous of you, John. Just for the record, could you kindly email that instruction? You know what the Law Society auditors can be like! In addition to the money, you will own a plot of land on the Sealand Industrial Estate. It used to have the Walls head office and workshops until it was burnt down.'

'Yes, I do recall, Andrew. In due course, can you please send me the registration documents for the sale of the farm and the Sealand plot of land? Thanks for your help, Andrew. Andrew, I will be away for an unknown period from 25th June. We are going on a cruise in the Mediterranean. Not sure when we will be back.'

'That's odd. Normally cruise ships know when they will return.'

'It's not a cruise ship; it's the private motor yacht we were on when we went to Ireland. It is now in Mallorca.'

'Well, if anyone deserves it, it's you, John. Have a great time, and thanks again for the wonderful bonus.'

3

Brandon had moved into Apartment 803 on his own. Little did he know that the previous occupier of this apartment was Sean Fitzallen. He was delighted with his new home. It would be good for him working for a Chinese computer company. The company had its European base in Dublin for tax reasons. The Manchester office was ten minutes' walk from Peters Tower. Perfect even during the rainy season, which he understood to be most days in Manchester. It had not rained since he moved in. The reputation seemed to be inaccurate and unnecessary.

Brandon was an expert in data accumulation. Data was the new gold standard in computing. The more data stored, the more it could be leveraged for profit by people like Brandon.

Brandon and his team were working on the current project collating all the information on every residential property in Manchester. Brandon realised how valuable this could be in all sorts of ways. The main object was to try and value the cost of recladding those properties that were not up to standard and often clad in the same material used on Grenfell Tower in London.

The interested parties in this data were, amongst others, cladding companies, the local authority, the building finance sector, insurance companies, surveyors and building owners and managers. Brandon had to design software that would record the blocks in detail: construction, cladding age, etc. He then had to split each block down by flats and then occupiers.

Obtaining the raw data was difficult. Firstly, Brandon organised his team to list all the blocks and discover how many flats were in each. While that was underway, Brandon designed a website that was a questionnaire. He needed to know the questions to ask. Why not start with his flat?

'Angela, it's Brandon Phelan, 803 Peters Tower. I am working on a computer project that involves collating data on blocks of flats in Manchester. I am not quite sure about the range of questions I should ask. I wonder if you could help me?'

'Ah, Brandon, I would normally say yes in a flash, but my client, your landlord, is careful about data released about the tower block.'

'Is the landlord local? Would he be willing to help me, do you think?'

'I have no idea, but I will ask him if you like.'

'I would be extremely grateful.' Brandon left his mobile number with Angela.

Angela spoke to Brandon, giving him John England's phone number within ten minutes.

'John England,' he said, on answering the phone.

'Hello, I am Brandon Phelan, tenant of Apartment 803. I am working on a database solution in Manchester to link in with multi-storey blocks of flats. It helps the emergency services to identify who is in occupation. As you are the owner of a block, I would be very grateful if you could spare me a moment to discuss the system and get your opinion.'

'I can give you an hour at ten tomorrow morning. The lift card you have will not bring you to the penthouse. Pop in and see Sydney at reception. I will ask him to create a card for you.'

'Thank you, Mr England. I will see you in the morning.'

'It's John, Brandon.'

'Fiona, you will never guess who I have just been speaking to?'

'Well, without a clue, it is difficult to guess.'

'Brandon Phelan is coming here at ten in the morning to discuss a project he is designing. It will be a database of every residential block of flats in the city.'

'Oh, and what does he want from you?' asked Fiona, beginning to bite a nail.

'I don't know exactly, but it is a perfect way of finding out more about him and his plans.'

'Do be careful, John. These people worry me.'

'Don't worry. He is coming here on my territory. Sydney knows he is here. His lift pass expires after an hour; don't bite those lovely nails. The meeting tomorrow will be very safe.'

'Do you need me to stay, John? I had thought I would go shopping tomorrow.'

'Are we short of food?'

'No, my love, we are not. It's a girly shop for clothes. Have you forgotten we are off to Mallorca in two weeks? I have nothing to wear.'

'I thought you had bought some clothes when we sailed to Ireland.'

'Southern Ireland in the spring is quite different to Mallorca in the summer. Less is more, John when it comes to summer clothes in the sun.'

'Ah, I see,' said John, not comprehending the shopping thing.

'Fiona, you get back to reading your new Ian Rankin. I will be fine; enjoy your shopping tomorrow.'

John returned to his office, bemused at the requirement for more clothes.

'Sydney?'

'Yes, Mr England?'

'The tenant of 803 is coming to see me at ten in the morning. Can you please prepare a temporary lift pass with a one-hour window for him?'

'Yes, certainly, Mr England.'

***

The internal phone rang at five minutes to ten; Sydney confirmed that Mr Phelan was about to get in the lift.

Fiona had been gone for more than half an hour.

Phelan was invited in, expressing the same reaction as everyone who came into the penthouse.

'What a view.'

'Yes. Mr Phelan, I don't have long, and your lift pass is for an hour. You said you are creating a database of residential blocks in Manchester to include a list of everyone who lives in the units?'

'That's it exactly, Mr England,' Brandon stated with an Irish lilt to his voice.

'Well, first off, would you like a cup of coffee?'

'Yes, I would.'

'My name is John, so may I call you Brandon?'

'Thanks, John. This database is not just a snooping thing. It will be a safety feature and a facility to know at a glance who is in occupation.'

'That sounds intriguing, Brandon. Tell me more.'

'Well, John. Every occupier, be they owner or tenant, will have a unique door handle that allows their signature by finger recognition to tell the system if they are in occupation. So in the event of a fire, it is easy to understand who is in the block – invaluable information to the fire brigade.'

'Very clever, Brandon. So will the in and out information be held on-site or at a central base?'

'Both John. The central database will be held by us, my firm, but in a 999 call, the fire station can use a code to download the up-to-date information. The occupancy information is sent to a computer in the fire engine. This gives information about who is in and where they are in the block.'

'Does the fingerprint information link with the names of the owners of the fingerprint?'

'Yes, that's the idea.'

'Well, immediately, I can see an issue. Firstly, Data Protection legislation will prevent other landlords and me from divulging the names of occupiers. It will not know who visitors are, so that the numbers will be inaccurate.'

'We will know how many people are on the property, but not necessarily their names if they are guests.'

'Brandon, the scheme seems to meet a need, but there are legal issues. However, I am afraid I cannot let you have the details of the tenants. The data is protected under Data Protection regulations. If you can think of another way of checking the number of people in a flat at any time without drilling down to their names, that might work. It will have to wait if you need any further information, as I am about to go away.'

'Okay, John. I will look at that aspect. Are you going anywhere nice?'

'We are going to Mallorca.'

'Have a great time. May I contact you on your return?'

'Well, yes, but I am not sure when my return might be.'

'Okay, well, here is my card. When you are back, would you be kind enough to let me know when I might come and discuss this further with any amendments we may have made?'

'Yes, but I am a busy lawyer, so I cannot say for sure when that is.'

John stood up and walked to the door, by his body language inviting Brandon to leave, which he did. The lift pass was about to expire, so no matter if he didn't hand it back. John suspected he wouldn't do that. Brandon would travel down to the eighth floor and return to his apartment.

Once in his apartment, Brandon made some notes about what he had discovered. Then he started to write a letter to Michael.

Michael Fitzallen
HMP Strangeways
Manchester

I visited the landlord this morning. He does live a lavish lifestyle in the penthouse.

I had a scheme to consider assisting the fire brigade in knowing how many people were present and where they were in the block. He was interested but no further. He is about to go on holiday to Mallorca, and he has no return date in mind.

I will see if my contacts in Calla Ratjada can set up a welcoming party for him and his girlfriend. I will write again, Michael.

Brandon

4

'Is that Goose?'

'Yes, hi John. When are you coming over?'

'We have a flight in the morning of 25th June. A Monday, so we should be at Palma Airport around noon. How do we find you?'

'I will make it easy for you. Take a taxi and go to the Real Club Nautico de Palma de Mallorca, the Royal Yacht Club in Palma Mallorca. *Brave Goose* will be moored on the club jetty on the south side.'

'Wonderful, all understood, we should be with you about one in the afternoon.'

'Great, in time for lunch.'

'Is there anything we can bring you, Goose?'

'No, just yourselves.'

'Looking forward to coming, bye.'

Fiona arrived back at the penthouse at just after four in the afternoon. Her arms were full of the carrier bags so beloved of boutiques and fashion shops.

'What on earth have you bought now?' enquired John.

'John, you don't understand. Girls have to look pretty, especially when staying on board a superyacht.'

'It is just as well I spoke to Goose after you left. Otherwise, I dare not think what you might have purchased.'

'Why, what has Goose told you?'

'Just where we can find *Brave Goose* when we get to Mallorca.'

'And where is that, John?'

'Well, *Brave Goose* will be moored on the quay of the Royal Yacht Club in Palma.'

'John,' screeched Fiona, 'that is mega. I have nothing to wear at a Royal Yacht Club.'

'I am sure you have. Just don't wear high heels, preferably deck shoes.'

'Okay, as you say, but if it is uber-smart when we get there, I may just do a little more shopping!'

On arrival at Palma Airport, which was significantly larger than either of them expected, a taxi was hailed at the front of the rank. Hardly any other passengers on the aircraft went to the taxi rank. The various tour operators lined up coaches for the majority.

A majority of taxi drivers were fluent in English, so the instruction to the driver to take them to the Real Club Nautico de Palma de Mallorca was easily understood. Like all the others on the rank, the taxi was a white Mercedes saloon. *Goodness knows how many miles it had travelled*, thought John. The seats had been well 'sat in' over its life.

The driver was accommodating, taking their baggage and filling the boot with John's bag and the three bags Fiona had brought.

They were both taken aback by the magnificence of the exterior of the Royal Yacht Club. Inside it was relatively sparse, but the cool marble floors and walls made the atmosphere far more bearable given the heat.

'Good afternoon, senor. Are you joining a boat here?'

'Yes, *Brave Goose*.'

'Yes, sir, I know exactly where she is moored. I will take all your bags, sir.'

John thanked the taxi driver and gave him the fare demanded and a tip.

'John, it was good advice to wear deck shoes. If I had worn heels, I would have sounded like a carthorse walking along this long corridor in the club house, with a marble floor.'

Large glass windows let streaks of sunlight in on one side of the gallery, lounges, and various meeting and dining rooms with views onto the harbour beyond the opposite side to the sunny windows.

Following the porter, John realised this would require a tip. All he had was a five-euro note.

'Have you any cash, Fiona? I only have a note.'

'No, darling, I only have notes, a five-euro note should do the trick. Do you want it?'

'No thanks, I have one.'

He hoped that would be sufficient. At the end of the corridor, they burst out of two glazed doors into the heat of the midday sun. They walked to the end of the quay, against which *Brave Goose* was moored.

The porter placed all the bags carefully at the end of the passerelle, just as Jose appeared on deck. Jose had told the porter to leave and not request a tip in Spanish. John had by then given the porter the five euros. Jose was coming down the passerelle to greet the guests.

'Sir, madam, how good to see you again. Would you please go on board? I will bring your bags up to the deck and then your cabin.'

No sooner had John and Fiona appeared on deck than Goose was there.

'My dear friends, how wonderful to see you again. You managed to find us, then?'

'Goose, it's good to see you. This is a wonderful place to moor.'

'Goose, it's wonderful to be back on *Brave Goose*. Thank you so much for inviting us.'

'My dear Fiona, it is my great pleasure. Everyone on board was excited to learn you would be on board again.'

Sally and Noel joined the welcoming party.

'I hope you have not had lunch. I have lunch prepared, and it will be ready on the quarterdeck in fifteen minutes if that is in order?'

'That sounds wonderful, Sally,' said John. 'We will go and freshen up and be back here.'

John turned to Fiona on their way to the cabin to enquire if she needed any further shopping.

'You know very well my answer,' Fiona replied to John with a broad grin on her face. 'The lack of ostentation in the Royal Yacht Club is a bit of a disappointment. I have exactly what I need for our stay.'

'That's good to know. I will use this small chest of drawers and three coat hangers. All the rest is available to you, my love,' advised John.

Once John had unpacked and stowed his clothes, he left Fiona to join Goose on the quarterdeck.

***

The taxi returned to the airport, stopping at a local *tabac* to buy water. He also made a phone call.

'Yes, it's Carlos. The delivery has been made. A large motor yacht, *Brave Goose*, dark blue hull. Destination currently unknown.'

He hung up, took a swig of water, and drove to the airport to join the end of the taxi rank.

***

Fiona eventually joined the men for the promised drink. She now wore a flowing coral-coloured silk dress and no shoes. She gave Goose a big kiss to thank him for the invitation.

'Now that is a welcome. I hope you have a relaxing time with us this trip, unlike the stress you suffered on the previous trip to Ireland. I am not sure how long you can stay, but I hope it is a good length of time. I want you to enjoy the benefits of sailing in warm waters, with no tide, so we can go when and where we like.'

'That sounds wonderful, Goose. Have you a plan in mind?'

'Only generally, John. It is very flexible. As we are in the port, you must visit the Cathedral of Palma. It is only a short walk. It is magnificent inside – one of the religious buildings that make you feel quite religious once you are inside. Then when you are ready, I propose we sail to Ibiza and spend a couple of days there. It's a lovely town to walk around, and it is a party place at night. I thought that might be of interest?'

'That sounds perfect, Goose. When I met this wonderful man,' she gestured towards John and hugged him, 'I had no idea we would be able to travel the Mediterranean in such luxury on your wonderful motor yacht. Thank you, thank you,' said Fiona.

'Well, Fiona, I have only filled four days. I propose we sail on to Formentera, which is nearly connected to Ibiza, but it is a desert island. The sandy beach is almost ten miles long. A perfect place to moor, swim and sunbathe. Mind you, we will not be the only boat there.

'Once we have had our fill of Formentera, we will sail to the Cabrera Islands, which lie to the south of Mallorca. That will be a good day's sail. Time to read a book. The plan may change as circumstances change or the weather.'

'Great,' said Fiona, 'John will be able to finish his Ian Rankin. I will read my magazines. I am happy to leave them on board for others.'

'Kind of you, Fiona, but no one else has been invited on board. You are my special guests.'

'Wow, we are so lucky!' exclaimed Fiona, looking at John.

'Well, after Cabrera, I thought we could sail up the east coast of Mallorca, stopping in a few places that have exceptional restaurants – eventually setting sail for Minorca. Then to Barcelona, have you ever been there?'

'No, I haven't been there, John?'

'Just the once on a stag weekend years ago. I am not sure I recall much about the place.'

'Good, John, well, that's a plan.' As Goose finished talking, Noel, the captain of *Brave Goose*, appeared on the quarterdeck.

'Just the man, Noel. Can you grab a notepad?' As he disappeared to the bridge for pad and pencil, Sally, the stewardess, arrived on the quarterdeck to enquire if other drinks were required and if everyone would be eating onboard tonight.

'No, we won't be eating on board tonight, thanks, Sally,' said Goose. 'Have you a pad and pencil, as I am about to run through the route we will be taking with Noel. You may like to take note regarding catering.'

Sally and Noel arrived back at the quarterdeck table. Goose invited them to sit down.

Goose explained the route he had just outlined to John and Fiona.

'We will not be eating dinner on board when we are in Ibiza town. We will be on board for dinner in Formentera, possibly two nights. We will need supper on the trip to Cabrera but nothing on the following three nights as we shall be in or near ports that have excellent restaurants.

'After that, we shall be off to Minorca and then

Barcelona. We can discuss culinary issues as we get nearer there, Sally. Is everything all right with you, Noel?'

'Yes, sir, I will book a berth in Botafoch Marina on Ibiza. Jose earns his corn in these exchanges. I will launch the ship's boat for visits and shopping ashore when we are at anchor. I intend to call the food delivery team in Palma to deliver tomorrow before we sail. I will chat with Sally to find out what we need to order.' Sally smiled in agreement. Noel and Sally left to work out their requirements.

'Well, that's all settled. We can look forward to a slap-up dinner tonight. It's in a restaurant not far from the Cathedral. A short stroll. Will that be all right with you both?'

'Yes, fine,' was the unanimous response.

The afternoon was occupied with sunbathing, reading, and a Spanish-style siesta.

'Everyone eats late here in Spain, so I have a table for three, at nine-thirty. It will mean we will probably not be back on board until midnight.'

'That will be wonderful,' John responded. 'We will go and change for dinner now, Goose, see you later.'

We will leave the ship at eight, as I will first take you to Abaco for pre-dinner drinks. To say it's a bar is to undersell this place. It's like nothing else I have ever been to, and I hope you both like champagne.'

'Let's go and get ready for the evening activities,' John suggested to Fiona.

'It must be the warm weather, but I feel very romantic, Fiona.' His lips brushed her ear, raising goosebumps across her skin. She sank into his body instantly, the hard planes of his muscles enfolding her. Their lips met. Their holiday had begun.

***

'Come on, hun, it's eight o'clock. Time we were on the quarterdeck.'

'Wow, you make an old man feel delighted, Fiona, you look beautiful in that powder blue dress. You look wonderful. Can you manage to walk to the venue?'

'Thank you, Goose. Yes, we are both ready for the evening's adventures.'

John confirmed he was certainly ready for the evening.

'You don't look too bad yourself, John,' said Goose. 'White trousers and a white cotton shirt make you look like the owner. All I can manage is my rather drab outfit of beige trousers and a blue shirt.'

'You look the part, Goose,' said Fiona.

The three of them left *Brave Goose* via the passerelle. Fiona now sounded like a carthorse going up the passageway linking the club's front with the harbour.

'I had forgotten that I would clip-clop down this marble floor.'

Her sound attracted the attention of mainly male members who were drinking in the bar. Fiona looked like a fashion model, straight out of a magazine. They walked through part of the old town towards Abaco.

Goose led them through the wicket door set to a pair of enormous barn doors. If this were the entrance to a bar, it would be the most unique entrance ever. The small door opened to a magical world of fruit, stone paving, staircases, and numerous small tables adorned with flowers and a candle – a display of fruits, drapery and embellishments entirely over the top.

'John, this is just amazing. Goose, you are so clever to find this place,' said Fiona.

'It's a special place, Fiona.'

'Can I help you?' requested a beautiful girl dressed in a rather revealing Spanish traditional costume.

'Yes, I have reserved a table for three about now. My name is Goose.'

'Would you like champagne or Spanish sparkling wine?'

'Which would you prefer?' Goose asked his guests.

'The Spanish, I think,' said John.

'I will go with the majority,' Fiona commented.

'We will have the French champagne, Veuve Clicquot if you have it?'

'We do, sir. Just three glasses?'

Goose nodded, and the young lady retreated to fulfil the order.

'This certainly is a unique location, Goose. I have never been to such a place.'

'Me neither,' chirped in Fiona, 'it is fabulous.'

Fiona was awestruck. She found it difficult to explain what she was seeing. A living cornucopia of fruit and vegetables cascading down staircases, adorning fireplaces, piled with pineapples, avocados by the ton, and other fruits of every variety. In between were small metal tables and chairs. Candles lit the room. Swags of fine drapery, beautiful women floated around the space. One of them, their waitress, delivered three cut-glass flutes and a bottle of Veuve Clicquot in a bucket of ice set on a stand. The cork was popped, the golden liquid filled each glass with a flume of bubbles.

They chatted and supped the champagne.

John agreed with Goose's choice. It was a superior product to the Spanish equivalent. However, he was confident the cost would be significantly higher.

'Have you any more surprises in store, Goose, as this is just unreal?'

'No, Fiona, I cannot beat this. But as we are in Palma for the night, it was too good an opportunity to miss.'

Goose was about to drink champagne when he received a tap on the shoulder.

'It's Goose, isn't it?'

Goose swivelled around to greet the unexpected visitor. Goose had no idea who this person was for a moment or two.

'Sorry old chap, but my brain will not remind me of your name.'

'No worries, it was a long time ago.'

'What was a long time ago?' requested Goose of the unexpected visitor.

'My name may not ring any bells with you, but I supplied you with some explosive devices for your yacht when you were in Puerto Banus. I heard that they were put to good effect in sinking your motor yacht.'

'Yes, I recall now, you are Pedro?'

'Correct, so what brings you to Mallorca?'

'I am on holiday with my friends John and Fiona,' he pointed them out. Goose was delighted that there was no other vacant chair nearby as he didn't want to spend the rest of the evening with this guy.

'Holiday, ah! You are never on holiday. There must be a reason behind the trip?'

'No, even I am permitted a holiday from time to time.'

'Have you a new boat, Goose?'

'Yes, I have,' he said, not wishing to give away any more information.

'How do you like my little bar?'

'This is your bar, Pedro?' Goose enquired, somewhat taken aback.

'I am a regular here. I am well known here. Let me know if there is anything you need. Here is my card with my mobile number. You never know. You might find a use for some of my services.'

'Thanks, Pedro. I will keep it. We are going for dinner now, excellent bar, Pedro.'

'Where are you eating?'

'Oh, just down the road, so we need to be going, as our table is available from nine-thirty.'

Saying farewell to Pedro and making their way out, Goose hesitated and paid the bill. They all gathered outside and made their way to the Fera restaurant.

John was dying to enquire about Pedro but thought better of it. Goose was not pleased to be reminded of him, as Goose knew Pedro was the person who organised the IED (Improvised Explosive Device), which Goose used to kill Niall Phelan. He didn't want reminding of that, especially amongst friends, who he knew had good reason to be cautious when discussing the Phelan family.

'Goose, this is an amazing evening. Thank you so much.'

'My dear Fiona, for an old man to be seen out with two younger people does my ego no harm.'

The three strolled back to the Royal Yacht Club. Goose showed the security pass. They walked on to board *Brave Goose*.

Back onboard *Brave Goose*, the three sat for a short while on the quarterdeck, admiring the lights of Palma town.

'Brandy anyone?' enquired Goose.

John accepted the invitation, and Goose joined him in an ample glass of Carlos 1 Gran Reserva brandy.

'This brandy is the most mellow and delicious brandy I have ever tasted, Goose.'

'Good, glad you like it, John.'

'Would you like a taste, Fiona?' asked John.

'Yes, please,' she said, with a grin on her face. 'You are right, John, that brandy is delicious.'

Goose got out of his comfortable chair without further conversation and poured Fiona a glass of brandy. He brought the bottle back to the table.

Sitting on the quarterdeck in the soft air of a Mediterranean night was blissful. Fiona was almost asleep when she thought she heard someone walk past the boat, close to the passerelle. The passerelle was still down.

'Goose, it seems irrational, I know, but would it be possible to raise the passerelle while we are asleep? I think I heard someone walk past very slowly just now.'

'Of course, you can, for added security.' Goose raised himself from his comfortable chair again and went to the side of the boat where the passerelle was attached. Fiona was expecting Goose would have to pull some ropes, but no, he pressed a button on the side of the ship, and slowly the passerelle came up to deck height. Goose closed the gate in the bulwark.

'All secure now, Fiona. I am off to bed. Sleep well, you two.' Fiona and John followed Goose as soon as they had quaffed all the brandy.

5

It was eight-thirty when Fiona woke. John was fast asleep. She slipped carefully into the bathroom, put on a bikini and a translucent top, and crept carefully out of the cabin to not wake John.

'Morning Fiona,' said Sally. 'No John yet?'

'No, he was sound asleep, so I left him. It will do him a power of good.'

'Yes, I am sure boats have this effect on people.'

'Not to mention the late-night brandy,' smiled Fiona.

'I did see the empty bottle,' smiled Sally. 'Do you want some breakfast now, or will you wait for John?'

'I will wait for John. I might catch some early morning rays on the boat deck.'

'Good idea.' Sally continued clearing up and then laying the breakfast table and putting out the breakfast sundries on the top of a cupboard on the quarterdeck, which doubled as a practical sideboard.

There were very few people around – no one else on the boat deck. A sunlounger was the ideal seating for Fiona, as she soaked up the sun and then fell asleep.

By ten o'clock, the boat was a hive of activity. Even John had appeared. Fiona retreated to the cabin to change into more substantial clothes ready for the voyage. *Brave Goose* slipped her berth at eleven and progressed slowly out of Palma harbour. Noel was on the flybridge to get the best possible view to avoid small boats, buoys, and debris in the harbour.

Passing Pta de Cala Figuera at the southwest corner of Palma Bay, they set a course of two hundred and forty degrees towards Ibiza town harbour, a distance of sixty miles.

Noel picked up the microphone for the intercom.

'We have just passed the southwest corner of Mallorca, and we should be arriving at Ibiza town by six o'clock this evening. I have notified the marina of our ETA. Enjoy the trip.'

Goose spent most of the morning in his office adjacent to his cabin. John and Fiona settled into sunbathing and reading on the boat deck.

'Travelling at this speed, John is the most relaxing way to travel. Listening to the water hiss past the boat is hypnotic.'

'It is. I love this way to travel. So much better than coming to a hotel. Your home moves with you. It is great.'

Brave Goose closed the entrance to Puerto Ibiza by rounding the small headland with Botafoch light on its southwest finger. Straight ahead was the entrance to Botafoch Marina.

'Hey John, we are almost there. I will put some clothes on and stand and watch how we get this big boat through an entrance that does not look wide enough from here.'

'I will join you. It's this part of boating I would find difficult. I can see why Noel gets cross with people who have not trained to manoeuvre a boat. They can mess up the whole thing.'

Noel made radio contact with the marina office as he closed the entrance to the marina. He received instructions to berth alongside the southerly mole at its inner edge. The marina suggested he entered the marina stern-to.

'What do they mean by that, Noel?' enquired Fiona.

'They want us to go in backwards, making leaving a great deal easier. As in most evenings, the wind has abated, all is calm. This should not be a difficult manoeuvre.'

Noel was on the tannoy again for all the crew. 'Listen up. Please have bow and stern lines handy with heaving lines on the starboard side, fenders for mooring alongside, again on the starboard side, and springs to starboard.'

Fiona was fascinated with the language. The crew were mighty busy, and Noel had slowed almost to a stop while preparations for berthing were made. She was dying to ask what it all meant, but she saved her query for later.

Once Noel received confirmation that everything was ready, he turned *Brave Goose* through one hundred and eighty degrees.

'Okay, everyone, we are reversing in. Please look out for me forward and aft, especially for small boats.' Her stern was now facing the harbour. He didn't touch the wheel. It was all done with the engines. He engaged reverse and slowly, so gently, made *Brave Goose* slide into her prepared mooring with marinaras standing on the quay ready to accept the lines.

Hardly a word of command was spoken; *Brave Goose* kissed the harbourside as the fenders took the pressure of the hull. Lines were thrown. The marineras caught the lines and returned the ends to the ship; a loop around the strong bollards held *Brave Goose* firm.

'Are we all made up?' asked Noel, not shouting but loud enough to be heard.

'Yes,' came the response from fore and aft. The engines were stopped. Jose and Jock deployed the passerelle, and all was ready for disembarkation as and when the guests wished to go ashore.

Fiona couldn't help showing her appreciation for a sensational bit of seamanship and gave all concerned a clap.

'Well done, Noel, that was fantastic,' she said, 'I would love to know what all the language meant?'

'I promise I will tell you all about it. Just let me complete my log, and then I will explain everything to you. Okay, Fiona. It is quite simple. Port and starboard are left and right. Then there are heaving lines. They are light lines with a weighted ball to aid throwing distance. The ball is often referred to as a monkey's fist. They are thrown, and the dockside people pull the mainline from the boat and throw the monkey's fist back so my crew can pull the main mooring line back on board. That makes a loop around the bollard. We can control the pressure on the lines by using our winches. That manoeuvre ensures we have a loop around the bollard on the quay. Springs are lines tied fore and aft from the vessel's centre to stop movement fore and aft. Okay?'

'I see,' said Fiona, unsure if she could remember the names but understanding the principles of what was achieved.

'Are you going ashore? It is the Gay Pride carnival this evening.'

'Like Rio?'

'Yes, just like that, it gets extremely busy but very spectacular.'

'John, Noel has told me the Gay Carnival procession is this evening. It would be great to go and watch. It is just like Rio, apparently.'

'Yes, we can do that. I had better find out if Goose has any plans.'

'No, Goose has no plans, but he prefers to eat on board tonight. We are free to go and explore. Let's do that, get a meal and watch the carnival.'

***

John and Fiona left *Brave Goose* at about eight o'clock. They first walked along the quay and out of the marina towards the action. However, they found a small restaurant near the fish quay towards the nightclubs and casino, which must serve fresh fish, John thought. That agreed, they ate a great meal of fresh dorade grilled with garlic, a salad and some chips, washed down with a carafe of local wine.

Live music floated over the harbour. The carnival procession was about to happen. It was nearly half-past nine. The clear night was warm, and the moon was half a moon. Fiona held tight to John's hand and her camera in the other, skipping along to find the carnival. As they turned at the end of the harbour road towards the town and more clubs, the parade engulfed them. A pair of jugglers split them up as they had to make way for the men throwing Indian clubs to one another. Fiona took the chance of having two free hands. She took some photographs. She lost her balance and was caught by an unknown hand which pulled her to the side and into a small doorway. The music played by the travelling carnival was deafening. She called John but couldn't see him. He didn't hear her. He expected to see Fiona on the other side of the road as soon as he could make his way through the procession.

She was nowhere to be seen. John shouted her name over and over again.

'Fiona, Fiona,' John shouted. Nothing.

Once the end of the carnival procession had passed by, the noise abated somewhat. He tried to call Fiona again and again.

'You lost someone, senor?'

'Yes, my girlfriend Fiona, she just disappeared in the middle of the procession.'

'Don't worry, senor. It can happen. She will be back soon as soon as she realises that she has lost you too!'

John was frantic. It was not like Fiona to just disappear. He ran around, knocking on doors and asking people if they had seen her.

John spotted two Spanish police officers sitting in a café drinking a coffee.

'Can you help me, please? My girlfriend has just disappeared in the middle of the carnival procession. I can't find her anywhere.'

'Can you describe her please and what is her name?'

'I can show you a photograph on my phone. Here, look. She is in a pink dress this evening. Her name is Fiona, Fiona Holmes.'

'Can you please send this picture to my mobile, senor?' The police officer typed in his mobile number to John's phone, and as if by magic in moments, the photograph of Fiona appeared on his phone. 'What is your name, sir, and where are you staying?'

'I am John England, and we are both staying on a large motor yacht, *Brave Goose*, she is alongside at Botofoch Marina.'

'That is a huge boat, senor. I watched her come in earlier. It was a master class in boat handling. Your captain is outstanding.'

'Thank you, but what are we going to do to find my girlfriend?'

'I will go to the station now. I will give my friend here a copy of the picture. At the police station, I will send the photo. I will also alert all officers of her disappearance. I am sure she will turn up. Will you go back to your boat, sir?'

'Is that best?'

'Yes, she will probably come back there if she cannot find you.'

'Makes sense. Thank you, officer. How do I contact you if I have some news?'

The police officer handed John a card with the Ibizia police phone numbers and station address details.

'Thank you,' said John, feeling extremely concerned for Fiona's safety.

Within half an hour, John was at the foot of the passerelle of *Brave Goose*. He spotted an envelope taped to the handrail. John was sure that had not been there when they left. It might be something for Goose. John pulled the envelope from the upright and took it on board. John found Goose having a quiet glass of wine on the quarterdeck, reading some papers.

'Had a good time, John? Where is Fiona?'

John explained what had happened. The police suggested that he wait on board to see if she turned up. 'Oh, and this was taped to the passerelle upstand when I came in just now.'

Goose opened the envelope. He was not fluent in Spanish, but he could work out this. It was a ransom note for Fiona.

Goose told John what he could make out, simultaneously pressing the crew bell. Sally arrived almost immediately. 'Can you ask Jose to come here, please? We think Fiona has been kidnapped.'

The news of the kidnapping spread quickly amongst all the crew. Jose, when he appeared, was asked to translate the note.

Don't involve the police. We have Fiona, who is unharmed. Pay to us in cash ten thousand euros, and she will return to you. You have until noon tomorrow. ETA.

'What does ETA stand for, Goose?'

'Euskadi Ta Askatasuna, which means Basque Country and Freedom. They are a group like your IRA in Ireland. They want Catalonia to be separate from Spain.'

'So why would they kidnap Fiona to help in their quest?'

'I cannot say, senor,' said Jose. 'Do you have any connections in Ireland? If so, ETA may be doing this for the IRA.'

'Good God, well, yes, I do have connections there. How the hell do I get ten thousand euros by noon tomorrow?'

'That's easy, John. I have a supply of cash on board as you never know when repairs or fuel must be acquired, and the supplier doesn't always accept credit cards. I can give you the cash. All you need to do is transfer the sum into my bank.'

'That's no problem, Goose. That would be great. How do we contact these people, and should we alert the police?'

'My advice, John, is that you don't tell the police until we have Fiona back. Pay the ransom. It won't hurt, will it?'

'How did these people know we were here and on *Brave Goose*?'

'They have a network. It would be easy enough. They will have contacts in the airport. Your taxi driver to the boat, the restaurant or Pedro could all be involved.'

'So, what do I do now, Goose?'

'Sit tight, John. We will not leave here until Fiona is safely back on board. I suggest, John, we all turn in, and by early morning I am sure there will be another envelope on the passerelle giving instructions on how to get her back.'

6

No one on board *Brave Goose* slept much that night, least
of all, John. He was very concerned for the safety of Fiona.
She might be hurt, or worse, by some thugs who had no
reason to respect her. What could they want other than
the money?

John did not know that Fiona was almost within
earshot of *Brave Goose*. Fiona's hands were tied with cable
ties to an iron bedstead; she could not move. The bed was
in a bare room over a café on the harbourside of the fishing
dock. She was given a drink of water from time to time.

'Hey, you, I need a pee!'

'No comprendo, senorita.'

The thug went out of the scruffy room. She had to pee
in the bed that she was lying on with her hands tied to the
bed frame.

Her guard was a rough-looking Spaniard, with filthy
shirt and trousers, tousled black hair and a deep bronze

complexion. *He has a wild eye*, Fiona thought. He looked to Fiona that he was the man for the job if she was killed. She sobbed most of the night.

At first light, Fiona was manhandled down the stairs. A sack was placed over her head and tied around her neck. She tried to scream, but the tape they had placed over her mouth prevented any sound from escaping.

She was screaming in her head, but no sound could be heard. Her captors lifted her and dropped her into a very narrow space. Whatever it was she was in, stank of rotten fish. Her arms were tight up to the sides. She couldn't stand. She couldn't sit. She crouched, and it was painful. They put on a lid. Could she breathe?

To Fiona's horror, her container tipped onto its side. This was less painful. She realised it was a plastic barrel, and they rolled her along on the road. She could feel every bump and pebble. Then the barrel was rolled over the road and lifted onto a boat. She could hear her captors talking about a 'Barca de Pesca'. Her rudimentary Spanish informed her she was now on a fishing boat.

After a few moments, she heard the engine of the boat start and felt the vibration through the bottom of the barrel. Fiona had no idea where they were going, except she knew they were at sea. Eventually, she heard the crunching of the boat's hull on gravel. The stones of a beach, she hoped. She was right. Two men chatting, coordinating their efforts, lifted the barrel containing Fiona to the side of the boat and dropped the barrel over the side, where it landed with a terrifying splash. Fiona thought she would drown. The depth of the water was less than the height of the barrel, fortunately. The two men were heard jumping out of the boat, still chatting. They then placed the barrel on its side. It floated, then rolled up the beach. Fiona could hear the crunching of the stones under the barrel mixed with splashing water. Then the splashing stopped. The barrel was pushed further up a slope covered with pebbles. Eventually the barrel's lid was removed, to Fiona's delight. She was in an echoey area. She could smell the fresh air as she was tipped out.

Fiona was now tied with another cable tie to a rusty iron ring fixed on the stone wall. The fishermen retreated with the barrel down the beach. Fiona could hear their feet crunch the pebbles. They threw the empty barrel into the fishing boat. It made a booming sound, which confirmed to Fiona that they were about to retreat. Fiona could hear the engine start and the boat 'putt, putt' away. She still had the bag over her head and the tape on her mouth.

***

At seven-thirty, everyone was awake and active on *Brave Goose*.

'Has anyone had any ideas about what could have happened to Fiona?' pleaded John.

There was no response. Jose was redeploying the passerelle, only to discover another note attached to the railing. He raced up to the deck, handing the message to John. He opened it as quickly as he could, then handed it back to Jose for a translation.

Take ten thousand euros in a plastic bag to the Restaurant Pescatore on the quay. They will confirm to me that the money is received. We will then transmit the coordinates of the location of your woman.

'Goose, can you let me have the cash? I will, of course, transfer the equivalent to your bank later today when my mind hopefully will be less stressed.'

Goose disappeared to his cabin, extracting the cash from his safe. He obtained a plastic bag from Sally in the galley, then handed it to John. John was down the passerelle faster than an Olympic runner. He found the restaurant, but in horror, the door was locked. He was banging as loud as he could when a scruffy fisherman came up to him and said in broken English, 'Senor, the money?'

'Si,' said John, not knowing whether to give the money to the man or not. After a moment's hesitation and shaking like a leaf, John handed over the money.

He hoped like hell that it was the right thing to do. John was sweating profusely. He had a parched mouth and could hardly speak. The fisherman ran off down the quay, hopping onto a small fishing boat with its engine running. The boat, the fisherman and the money then disappeared out of the harbour. Sally took a series of pictures of the boat on her camera.

Noel stood close to the VHF radio set on the bridge with a handheld tape recorder.

Fifteen minutes had elapsed; the radio was silent. John was beside himself. How could he have been so foolish to let go of Fiona's hand in the first place, then hand the money over to a scruffy fisherman, against the instructions? And now, no message had been received to give Fiona's location.

'Senor, senor,' shouted a small boy on the quay.

'Jose, can you speak to this child, please?' requested Goose.

A conversation ensued. Jose relayed the essence of the message.

'He says he has a piece of paper for you and was told that he would be rewarded with five euros when he delivered it.'

'Let me give him the money,' interjected John.

John rushed down the passerelle and saw that the small boy did indeed have a piece of paper containing writing. John gave him a ten-euro note. The small boy grinned and handed over the paper. Sure enough, John realised the information giving coordinates was potentially Fiona's location.

Rushing up the passerelle again, he handed the note to Noel, who plotted the position.

'It's only a mile and a half from here. May I launch the RIB, Goose?'

'Yes, yes, get on with it.'

Jose and Jock untied the RIB on the boat deck and deployed the crane lifting the rigid inflatable boat with a hundred horsepower Yamaha engine into the water. Noel and John were ready to jump in, both wearing life jackets. Another jacket for Fiona was loaded onto the RIB, and they were off.

Noel had loaded the coordinates into a handheld GPS, so it was reasonably simple to find the indicated location.

Both men could see the narrow stony beach and a narrow cave at the rear with limited headroom.

'She must be in there,' shouted John over the engine's noise.

John spotted Fiona trussed up with a bag over her head as soon as he gained the entrance to the cave.

'Noel, bring a knife if you have one?'

Within moments of arriving in the cave, they had released Fiona from her binds. She burst into tears and was shaking all over. Her wrists were red from the bindings.

'Oh John, I am so sorry I let go of your hand. I was so frightened. I thought they would kill me.' She hugged John. 'Thank you, thank you, for finding me,' she said as tears poured from her eyes.

'Darling, you are safe now. We will get you back to *Brave Goose* to recover.'

The two men carefully brought Fiona out of the cave into the Spanish sunshine. She blinked and screwed up her eyes. John fished the extra life jacket out of the RIB, placing it on Fiona.

John lifted Fiona into the RIB with ease. He and Noel jumped into the RIB, now afloat.

They left the beach at a sedate pace, back to the harbour and *Brave Goose*.

Back on board, everyone was delighted to welcome Fiona back. She was not ready to explain what had happened just yet.

'Shall I make a brunch in an hour so that you can recover, Fiona, and we can all hear your story?' suggested Sally.

'Excellent idea, Sally,' said Goose.

That was agreed, Sally started her preparations. Goose insisted that the crew join John, Fiona, and himself for brunch on the quarterdeck.

***

'Is that Pedro?'

'Yes, who is this?'

'Goose.'

'Ah, good to hear from you, Goose. What can I do for you today?'

'Well, I am in Ibiza at the moment. I may need a couple of IEDs if you have any, or do you have an agent on this island who could supply them to me?'

'No, I don't use agents, but I could put a couple of deactivated items with the missing bits in a separate parcel. I can put those on the ferry from Palma to Ibiza. You should get them tomorrow morning. You would have to go to the ferry terminal for the parcel.'

'That sounds like a plan. I am in Marina Botefoch now, so the ferry terminal is close. How much, Pedro?'

'A thousand euros each and a contribution to transportation, say, two thousand five hundred. I will email you my bank details. Please send the money today so that I can ship on the evening's ferry.'

'I will, thanks.'

'No worries, just be careful with them.'

'I will, no problem.'

***

'John, I hope you don't mind but here are my bank details. If you could arrange the transfer, I would be grateful.'

'Of course, Goose. I was going to ask you about a kitty or making a significant contribution to the ship's running, fuel, food etc. How much do you think?'

'Well, it all depends on how long you will stay. As far as I am concerned, you two can stay all summer.'

'That is a tempting proposition. Shall we say ten thousand a week?'

'John, that is far too much. Five thousand pounds a week, and we will call that straight unless you want fine French wines, then there may be an increase!'

They both laughed. 'I will send you fifteen thousand pounds now. Just let me have your bank details, and I will make the transfer before brunch.'

Receiving the bank details from Goose, John went to arrange the transfer.

'Jose, there will be a package for me on the next ferry from Mallorca. It will be here in the morning. It will be labelled 'Nautical Spares' and addressed to *Brave Goose* and me. Will you take a trolley, bring the box on board, and put it in my cabin?'

'Si, senor,' replied Jose.

***

'Hi, darling, are you feeling a little better?'

'Oh John, I am so sorry. It's all been a nightmare. I cannot think why or how this happened.'

'Don't you worry your head about it? We found you, and you are back with us. That is the main thing.' John and Fiona embraced for a moment or two.

'I must send some money. I will do it now to continue to enjoy this beautiful boat if that is what you would like?'

'It certainly is, my prince. How many more times are you going to rescue me?' They kissed again, and John then sent the money to Goose's bank account. They both went to the quarterdeck for brunch.

Over brunch, Fiona explained the strange events of the evening of the Gay Pride march.

'John and I had been holding hands. As I wanted to take some photos, I broke our bond. I became disoriented in the centre of the parade and nearly fell, dropping my camera. Oh, where is my camera? I must have lost it!'

'No darling, I picked it up.'

'Oh, thanks, John. Anyway, I was helped to my feet by two men who held me tightly. They rushed me to the side of the road and into a café. Then they pushed and pulled me upstairs. They threw me onto a bed, tied my hands to the bedstead and put tape over my mouth. It all happened so quickly. I was now terrified. I was crying. I couldn't wipe the tears from my eyes, which became very sore. Nothing happened until all the carnival had passed and the first glimmer of dawn percolated through the window. The men returned, undid my bindings, then pulled me downstairs. They placed a bag over my head at the bottom of the stairs. Then they lifted and put me in what I subsequently discovered was a fish barrel. It took no time at all to realise it had previously held fish. It stank. I was rolled over and over on my side and then placed on a boat. The movement of the barrel could only have come from the motion of a small boat.

'Then I heard the engine start, and we left the quay. We must have travelled for half an hour or so. Then I realised the men had run the boat up a small pebbly beach. It has a distinctive sound.'

'We could see where the boat had been. There was a groove in the stony beach and some blue antifouling paint on the stones,' confirmed Noel.

'Well, I was tipped out headfirst from the barrel, and then my hands fastened to a steel ring in the rock. They knew precisely where the ring was. I don't know how long I was there, but breathing clean air was better than being in the fish barrel. Then I heard John and Noel. Thank you both. It was so wonderful to see you. Thank you.'

'Fiona, you have had a terrible experience. Maybe you should always carry the small pistol you had in Ireland when you shot the man at Dunmore Hall. There seems to be a group of people who want to incarcerate you, presumably to try and extract money from you?' said Goose.

'I think you have hit the nail on the head, Goose. Jose, was there any indication that ETA was involved in this episode?'

'Well, I am not sure, but the person I spoke to when I took the money was Catalonian. A quite different accent.'

'Jose, please ring the Guardia Civil, and tell them we have Fiona back. We will be departing tomorrow, so if they need to interview her, they need to come today. I don't expect Fiona has a desire to walk around Ibiza town,' said Goose, smiling

7

Jose returned to *Brave Goose* carrying the parcel he had collected from the ferry. He placed it as instructed in Goose's cabin.

Goose went to inspect his parcel. Two IEDs and four detonators were carefully packaged and secured in rigid cardboard and polystyrene dividers. Two were marked mobile phones, with a phone number on each. The others were pressure detonators. Not fully understanding why he had four detonators, he texted Pedro by WhatsApp, which has encryption to avoid interception of the message.

Pedro. The cakes have arrived with four candles. Is it all right to cut the cakes to use a candle in each piece?

Goose was proud of his message and hoped Pedro would understand.

Goose received an instant reply. It was an emoji of a thumbs-up sign, which meant that his suggestion was good to go.

Goose placed the items in his safe. They would be helpful given the attempt to kidnap and extort money from John. Goose recalled the reason for the effort to obtain the three million pounds used to pay off the bank for Peters Tower. Goose was sure further attempts would be made to recover the money. After all, he had been involved once before in recovering this money. The involvement of ETA in trying to extract money was a helping hand for their sister organisation, the IRA, who also wanted an independent island of Ireland, similar to the desire of ETA to secure an independent Catalonia.

'Sally, you were out and about yesterday. Did you take any photos of boats in the harbour?'

'Yes, Goose. I will get my phone and show you what I have taken.'

The two looked through several photos of the harbour. In front of the restaurant thought to be involved in the plot to kidnap Fiona was a white fishing boat, with blue tops to the gunwale, blue antifouling on the hull below the waterline, and blue barrels with black lids on the deck.

'This could be the boat the kidnappers used to transport Fiona?'

'It looks remarkably like the sort of boat the kidnappers might have used. Look, it has a registration number on the side, IB306,' said Sally.

Goose collected his binoculars from the saloon and went to the boat deck. He scanned the harbour, but this little fishing boat was not in the port. Goose also spied two officers from the Guardia Civil walking their way.

'Fiona, the police officers are on their way.'

'Thanks, Goose,' responded John, 'I will let her know.'

The two Guardia officers came onto the quarterdeck. Sally greeted them, inviting them to be seated and offering a refreshment, which they refused.

'I will let Fiona know you are here.'

Fiona and John appeared soon after Sally had disappeared into the depths of the boat.

The two sat with the police officers. Fiona repeated the events that led to her kidnap and recovery.

'Do you have any indication who the kidnappers might be?' enquired John.

'No, sir, not at the moment. The identification of the boat may help. We can check the records. We will also search the restaurant.' The police officers took down John and Fiona's contact details to advise them on the progress of their enquiries.

***

'Sally, I think it would be fun to have a barbecue this evening. Would that fit in with your plans?'

'Yes, Goose. I will let Jock know as he is the best at the BBQ. Will it be for the full crew?'

'Certainly, shall we say eight o'clock?'

It was agreed that Sally left to prepare for the evening.

***

Goose was mulling over recent events. John and Fiona had a predicament.

Unknown people were trying to recover money lost to them by Phelan buying a fake consignment of drugs. Goose realised he had been responsible for the death of Niall Phelan with an IED with a compression switch. Niall was apparently opening the parcels of drugs like a man possessed when he realised that the contents of the boxes were mainly cement, with a scraping of cocaine on the top. This false consignment of cocaine was delivered to Niall Phelan by Goose in the Irish Sea called the Irish Box.

Niall Phelan's business partner, Michael Fitzallen, had contracted with Goose to recover most of the money Phelan had taken out of the company. Phelan had double-crossed Michael Fitzallen, his business partner. The "drug money" was nearly four million pounds. Goose took the "loose change" of about half a million and gave three million, five hundred thousand pounds to Michael Fitzallen, his client.

As soon as the money was in Goose's hands, following the delivery of the fake drugs, he had headed through the north channel, out into the Atlantic and south to Africa.

'Best to keep clear of coastal patrols,' Goose had suggested to the captain of his then superyacht, *Flying Goose*.

Michael Fitzallen had earned this money; Niall Phelan had taken it out of the company account in Spain to his account in Ireland without consent.

When John and Fiona had come on *Brave Goose* to Ireland earlier that year, they met Sean Fitzallen, acting for his brother Michael. He was still in jail for the murder of John's sister-in-law, Sandra. Sean was on a mission to recover the three million his brother Michael had lent to Sandra Wall to enable her to pay off the bank. Michael received half of Peters Tower and half the rents in exchange for the three million.

He was languishing in jail, realising that the three million loan agreement stopped him from getting his cash back. It was eating away at him.

He wanted to get the money back. Michael and Sean (his brother) both knew the agreement Sandra had with Michael to borrow the three million pounds contained a cancellation clause. The clause made the loan agreement void if Michael committed a crime that put him in jail for ten years or more. All the funds belonged to Sandra and Walls Holdings, the family firm. The murder of Sandra by Michael ensured the agreement was void, and the money became the companies.

Goose felt he had personal involvement with the death of Niall Phelan. How could he help John and Fiona? He was sure part of the vendetta was to get revenge for the killing of Niall Phelan. Goose continued to consider this dilemma. He decided to get some exercise and have a walk around the harbour. Donning a wide-brimmed hat, he set off walking in the hot Mediterranean sun.

John and Fiona took sun cream, hats, and beach towels to the boat deck and sunbathed, read books, and napped for most of the afternoon.

Goose was interested in looking at the boats moored in the marina and harbour with a professional eye. He was fascinated with the small Spanish fishing boats which worked inshore, mainly catching bait. The bait would be sold to longline fishermen who worked on the bigger boats out to sea.

Goose spotted a cluster of small boats in the northern quarter of the main harbour. There were numerous boats, all very similar. On the outer edge of the group moored alongside one another was a boat with larger than average blue barrels gathered on its deck. The unique feature as far as Goose was concerned was the number painted in black on the bow. It bore the same number as the boat Sally had photographed outside the restaurant that had been the kidnappers' first port of call when hiding Fiona.

Several fishermen on the quay tended to their nets that needed mending or floats replacing. In addition, others were soaking remnants of carpet laid on the wooden decks. The fishermen were soaking the mats with water. This ensured the timbers of the deck would remain damp and tight. If they dried out under the fierce sun, the deck planks would open and allow water to enter the void below the deck.

Goose made a careful note of the location of this particular boat. He might need to find it later. He walked in silence on his own, deep in thought.

Sally had arranged all the food for the barbecue. Drink, including beer and wine, had been brought to the quarterdeck by Jose. The beer and white wine were committed to the fridge on the deck.

A side awning on the quarterdeck had been erected on the starboard side to shade the setting sun. The passerelle was retracted once everyone had confirmed they did not want or need to go ashore again.

'That will prevent gatecrashers to our party,' said Jose to anyone who might be listening.

Jock got busy with charcoal, lighting it with fuel in a bottle, which caused a fierce flame to shoot up. The place stank of fuel for a while.

'I have to do this, John so that the coals will go grey, as that is when it is perfect for cooking,' Jock explained. It could take well over half an hour to reach this condition. He was pleased it was a calm night; the coals would simmer perfectly.

John, Fiona and Goose assembled the whole crew at eight o'clock. Sally handed the steaks to Jock and then passed the salad and new potatoes. Noel was on wine and beer duty.

'What a beautiful night,' remarked Fiona.

'It's for moments like this we come to the Med,' said Goose.

'It has been quite a twenty-four hours. At one point, I thought I might never sit here again, Goose.'

'No, you must have been terrified, Fiona.'

'I was,' she replied as a tear trickled down her cheek.

'You know, John, it's strange that the police never enquired how we managed to retrieve Fiona. Also, if we had paid the ransom.'

'You are right, Goose. How can they pursue the culprits without all the facts? I suppose we should have told them what we did and how we did it?'

'You know, John, there will come a moment when we can extract our retribution. These terrorists should not be able to get away with this sort of activity. Who knows what else they will get up to?'

'You are correct, John. The moment will come when we can extract our revenge. So far, we have paid the money and retrieved Fiona. That is an excellent solution, but they should not profit from the kidnap. In that regard, we have failed, but importantly we have recovered Fiona.'

'I am not sure, but I hope you are right.'

After the barbecue, John and Fiona had an early night, expecting to leave Ibiza town the following morning.

8

Brandon was just switching his mobile off following a short call from Spain. He was grateful for the actions his compatriots had taken.

Sitting in the lounge area of the living space in Apartment 803 of Peters Tower, Brandon began to muse on the plan to recover the three million. Michael Fitzallen was desperate to have the money he had worked hard for returned. He would use part of the funds to put Dunmore Hall into a habitable state.

On two continents, Europe and Australia, the police were keen to apprehend Brandon, as they were sure he had been responsible for a series of crimes. Murder, kidnap, extortion – a one-person criminal dynasty. Brandon Phelan was not his natural and given name. No, that could be dangerous. Research into the case on which he was now engaged required a change of identity, in exchange for twenty-five per cent of the takings, less the one hundred thousand fee paid in advance. In all, the job could mean a payment of seven hundred and fifty thousand pounds. He determined it was worth the effort required to hide in full view of the target.

Brandon was an Irishman. He was born in Ireland to a family which was originally German. He had developed an ability to speak several languages and speak in an accent that fitted the task at hand. For now, an Irish accent was acceptable. It was straightforward for him to use his natural accent. He had refined it somewhat to be upper-class Irish.

Brandon had also refined his wardrobe. He dressed as a city Irishman but with country overtones. He could mingle with a crowd and never be seen. His complexion was currently clean-shaven. His beard, should he choose to grow it, was naturally red. It could be dyed a different colour should the need arise.

Some time ago, Brandon had met a man in Ireland, Sean Fitzallen. Sean had explained the circumstances of his brother's loss of over three million pounds. Sean explained who was now benefitting from the funds. Sean had instructed Brandon to act on behalf of his brother in recovering the money. Sean said that Michael was in Strangeways Prison in Manchester.

Brandon had received a short but to the point letter from Sean's wife, who lived in the south of Ireland.

Just so you know, Sean is dead. The authorities say he fell overboard from a British motor yacht called Brave Goose. *We don't believe that. The money has not been recovered. As a good man of Ireland, we need retribution. So far, it has all failed. The deal will be honoured if you carry on to a satisfactory conclusion.*

Brandon took this note to be a contract to fulfil the family's requirements. A task they had been unable to complete themselves. Having met with John England, he realised England was a smart cookie. However, he was a lawyer and would naturally act following the law. That was not a restriction Brandon had. Having discovered the details of all the block's tenants, Brandon knew the letting agents and had met the landlord and owner. He now knew that John England and his girlfriend, Fiona Holmes, were travelling on *Brave Goose* in the Balearic Islands. Last he'd heard, the boat was in Ibiza. The test abduction of Fiona and the collection of ten thousand euros by Brandon's temporary operatives had gone well, and they were well paid for their work.

Brandon now prepared for a major assault on John England to recover the money. Brandon knew he would need a bank account for John England to transfer the money, as the funds would have to be transmitted through the banking system. How to establish a bank account was always the tricky bit. He knew the British legislation on money laundering was so tight that it made it difficult for him to transfer money. Luckily there was a branch of an Irish Bank in Manchester. A call to Sean Fitzallen's wife obtained their bank details in Ireland. This could be the link he needed to create a current account.

Brandon made an appointment to meet the manager of the European Irish bank (EIB), Manchester, which had branches in southern Ireland, London, and every other European capital in the European Union.

Eamon Strang was the manager. The meeting was in a week. Brandon had time to construct his back story and some accounts and prepare to transfer the funds he had received in advance for the job in hand from his bank in the Cayman Islands to the EIB.

***

Brave Goose, now basking in the hot Mediterranean sun, was ready to depart the Botafoch Marina. Noel had been to the harbour office and paid the marina fees and water and electricity. He was thankful that they had fuelled up to capacity in Gibraltar. The price of diesel in Ibiza was twenty per cent higher than the cost in Gib. This summer had all the makings of a long and exciting cruise. Noel was delighted to be away from the berth in Southampton. As with the previous owner, there was nothing more frustrating than just waiting for something to happen. He was generous to a fault and never left *Brave Goose* short of funds, but as he was well over eighty, he had been in no fit state to go sailing again. Noel couldn't believe his luck when Goose bought her.

Everyone on board *Brave Goose* was notified by the intercom.

'Hello, listen up. *Brave Goose* will be leaving port in thirty minutes. The passerelle will be hauled in ten minutes.'

The springs which were fast on the quay were slipped. Jock pulled them onto the ship when Jose took the loop off the bollard. Noel already had the engines running on tick over, ready for immediate use. As soon as the springs had been removed, *Brave Goose* moved fore and aft along the quay a short distance caused by the force of the wind. There was no requirement to use the engines yet. Noel was always one to be safe rather than sorry.

Jose returned on board and hauled the passerelle. This could be used at anchor as a bathing platform or a means of embarking onto the RIB. Jose then took his station on the bow, ready to slip the line. Jock was on the stern, as that placed him closest to the access to the engine room.

There was a light breeze this morning. The breeze was pushing *Brave Goose* hard onto the quay. This would require Noel to manoeuvre to put the stern out into the channel before pushing the bow out. *Brave Goose* had a bow thruster but no stern thrusters. That didn't worry Noel, as he could move *Brave Goose* off the wall with the engines.

'Jose, please place two other fenders on the bow so I can spring off the wall, should it be necessary. Jock, stand by; when ready, I will ask you to cast off and bring the line on board. Please tell me when you have all the line on board.'

'Yes, sir,' shouted Jock.

'Fenders in place, sir,' shouted Jose.

Noel was on the flybridge. Goose, Fiona, and John watched this intricate manoeuvre from the flybridge. The tight confines of the marina made the manoeuvre quite tricky.

'Okay, Jock, take in your line. Jose, hold yours tight and made up, on the ship. Don't loosen it until I say. There will be considerable pressure on the line shortly.'

'Stern line clear,' shouted Jock.

'Fiona, can you please come and help me on the bridge?' requested Noel.

Fiona was a little apprehensive but was happy to help.

'When I say, please push that button which will sound our horn. Sound it for a short while so everyone can hear it, but don't press it again. That signals we are making a manoeuvre to port.'

Fiona was excited at the prospect.

Noel moved *Brave Goose* forward very slowly with right-hand rudder on and the port ahead starboard engine in astern. Both engines were running slow. The bowline groaned under pressure.

'Okay, Fiona, press now.'

Fiona nearly jumped out of her skin; the noise was deafening.

'Okay, that's sufficient, thanks. As you can see, I am short of a hand to do that. Great, really helpful.'

Fiona and the others realised that *Brave Goose* was pushing her stern out into the channel as the horn stopped. At the same time, the bow was being pressed against the bow fender. The bow line had now gone slack.

'Okay, Jose, strike the bow line.'

Noel centred the rudder once the bow line was hauled in and pushed the bow to port with the bow thruster. *Brave Goose* was now in the middle of the channel, taking them out of the marina to the Mediterranean again.

'Well done, Noel, that wasn't easy,' said Goose, who made the compliment. Noel much appreciated it from one who had an experienced eye for such activities.

'Thank you, sir. I am heading for an anchorage on the northern shore of the island of Formentera.'

Fiona was fascinated with the prospect of anchoring off a desert island. Noel warned her not to be too disappointed as hundreds of other boats would be there during the day. Noel had *Brave Goose* on course for the passage between the islands of Ibiza and Formentera. There was an area in the channel only seven metres deep, which would be sufficient for *Brave Goose*. Noel turned the boat to port once through the buoyed channel to open the vista of the large sweeping bay and sandy beach. There were hundreds of boats moored off the beach.

'Jose, can you be ready to drop anchor in a few minutes?'

Jose acknowledged the instruction. 'How much do you want out?'

'We will be mooring in about twenty metres, so we need sixty metres of chain. I haven't chosen my spot yet; when I do, I will let you know exactly.'

'That's a lot of chain, Noel,' enquired Fiona. 'Why do you put so much out for the depth?'

'Well, the principle behind successful anchoring is that you need a third of the chain on the bottom from the anchor before it rises to the boat. The amount I intend letting out will allow the chain to be stretched in the afternoon wind and still leave a third on the bottom. That way, the anchor is pulled horizontally over the sand, its flukes dig in and hold the boat.'

'I see, there is more to this than meets the eye,' stated Fiona.

'You are quite right. There is no compulsion on people putting to sea in the UK to obtain qualifications. In my opinion, accidents are caused by a lack of training, since navigation has been made so much easier by GPS and chart plotters.'

'Do you have to qualify to sail in Europe?'

'Yes, Fiona, you do.'

Goose and John arrived on the flybridge to watch the anchoring activity.

'What's your plan, Noel?' enquired Goose.

'Well, sir, I was planning to anchor just off the first tiny island over there,' he said, pointing to where he intended to go.

'Can we go further round the bay, closer to the main island? I had hoped to go for a walk on the main island later.'

'Yes, sir, no problem. Jose, hold on, we are moving location.'

'Noel, it's Goose! Not sir.'

'Sorry, it is a force of habit. I will try harder.'

They all laughed.

Noel eventually found a suitable spot pretty well opposite the entrance to the tiny port of Sabina. It held a few yachts but mostly fishing boats. The little town had a small hotel, a couple of shops, a few houses and a police station for the Guardia Civil, next to a slipway.

Once anchored, the passerelle was let down the side of the boat and rigged with a platform at the end just above sea level. It was ideal for swimming from and boarding the RIB. That was the next job, launching the RIB from the boat deck.

Jose, Jock and Noel prepared the RIB with grey inflatable tubes and fibreglass hull. The engine was a significant size that would allow water skiing, should that be of interest. The RIB was moored forward of the passerelle to allow swimmers access to the water.

Fiona and John dived into the turquoise blue sea, which was a very acceptable temperature. The end of the passerelle had a fold-down bathing ladder that dropped into the water, allowing the bathers to exit the water easily. John and Fiona were in the sea for over half an hour. They used the freshwater shower on the passerelle to rid themselves of the salt.

'That was fantastic. What a beautiful spot!' exclaimed Fiona.

'It is trendy, as you will see later as more boats flood out from Ibiza.'

Goose instructed Noel that he would like to be landed in the small port after lunch as he wished to walk. He would take a handheld VHF set, so he could recall the RIB after he had done his walk.

As anticipated, Goose went for his walk. He took with him a small rucksack. He looked quite the part with his Tilley hat to keep the sun off, a khaki shirt and shorts, and walking boots. It wasn't a large island but good for a short expedition. He was put ashore in the small harbour. The little town and port looked as if it were closed. It was just gone two in the afternoon. As was the tradition in this part of Spain, everyone took a siesta. Only the English ventured out in the heat of the day.

In the small harbour, moored at the end of a short flight of steps cut into the stonework of the harbour wall, were three small fishing boats bobbing gently on the slight swell that worked its way around the harbour entrance. They were safe here. The middle boat was of interest to Goose. It had a white hull, a small wheelhouse that was so small no man could use it as shelter, painted in the same blue used to paint the cap rail on the gunwale. It allowed such electronic instruments as this little boat required to be sheltered from sea spray. The wheel was also there, but the owner preferred tiller steering. The tiller had been removed from the rudder stock and was lying on the deck. Goose was fascinated by the construction of these little boats. The deck completely enclosed them, so waves coming over the boat would not affect the craft's stability. These boats could also use oars if there were engine failure or the desire to work quietly in small coves. The oars were most often used as a prop for an awning, being held aloft by two poles, one each fore and aft. There was a fork at the top end of each pole. This arrangement permitted the long oars to be stowed and support an awning. The awning provided the essential shade during the height of the summer.

It was necessary to sit forward of the wheelhouse with the oarsman's back to the bow to row the boat. The boat had two hinged hatch covers which had been opened, presumably for ventilation. That arrangement allowed the rower to sit and have a comfortable position for rowing, with his feet in the hatch. This middle boat had the symbol of IB306 painted in peeling black paint on the bow. Goose was sure this was the boat they used to transport Fiona in one of the blue plastic barrels, now stored aft of the wheelhouse. Several of these were strung together on the aft deck. He realised what a terrible ordeal it would have been to be in one of these barrels. There would be very little air, and what air there was would be contaminated with the pungent smell of rotten fish.

Goose sat on the quay with his feet on the first step, pulling a water bottle, a sketch pad, and charcoal stick out of his rucksack. He drew slowly and sat in the same place for over half an hour. No one came into sight; he observed the houses opposite as he sketched them. No one appeared; the curtains were drawn against the fierce afternoon sun in the main.

He considered at a point in time that he could now fulfil his errand. He bent forward and stepped down two steps, so his feet were just in the water. He could easily stretch over to the nearest open hatch cover. With his spare hand holding a small brown paper parcel wrapped in a plastic bag, he managed to gently throw the parcel as far forward as possible so the parcel would end up virtually in the bow of the boat under the deck. He quietly closed the hatch and resumed his sketching.

At about four o'clock, he decided that as he was out of fresh water and had drawn different parts of the harbour, he would recall the RIB to return him to *Brave Goose*.

***

'Have you had a good afternoon, Goose?' enquired Noel as he came close to where Goose was standing, ready to board the RIB.

'I have Noel. I managed to achieve everything I wished to do. Tomorrow, I think we will have a day at sea, and sail to Mallorca. An excellent fish restaurant is just behind the marina at Puerto de la Rapita. Do you think you will be able to organise a berth? It will have to be on the visitors' quay. If they can't accommodate us, we can anchor off and take the RIB into the port. Don't accept a berth inside the port. It is very tight on space.'

'Thanks, Goose. Have you been here before?'

'Yes Noel, I like this restaurant a lot. The day after, we will sail up the west coast of Mallorca. There are several places to stop, with the day after that we will moor in Cala Ratjada. There is another excellent fish restaurant there. I will treat you all to a fish supper when we get there. I have the name of the restaurant with me. I will get Jose to book. Does that sound like a plan acceptable to all?'

There was a unanimous acceptance of the suggestion.

9

'Look folks, would you like to sail to La Rapita tomorrow? It would be a day at sea, as it will be ninety miles or so, and that will probably take ten hours. If we leave the anchorage here at eight in the morning, I think, all being well, we should be off La Rapita by six o'clock in the evening. Once there, we will have to anchor off. We can go ashore in the RIB; there is an excellent fish restaurant outside the marina. I want to be sure, Fiona, that you are up to a day sail?'

'Goose, please don't worry about me. I will be fine. I get flashbacks when I am in bed. They wake me up, so a day at sea where I can sleep all day would be great.'

'I will book a table for nine in the evening. If we get there by six, perhaps Jose, Sally and Noel can take the RIB and stock up on food from the local supermarket outside the port. I recall it had good supplies last time I was here a few years ago.'

***

At seven-thirty the following morning, John and Fiona were aware of the activity on board.

'Had we better get up?'

'Okay, John. I was having a wonderful dream, which I cannot recall, but now I'm awake. I don't think it was a dream. It is all real. Yes, the sun's up, and we are about to set sail; let's watch as we leave. I love this life, John. Clothing is not an issue. Just a bikini, a cover-up, are all I need.'

'Well, Fiona, I never thought I would hear you say that.'

The two dressed quickly in whatever was to hand and joined Goose on the boat deck to watch the departure. The engines had started, Noel was at the wheel Jose was on the foredeck. Goose was looking around with his binoculars.

'Everyone ready to go?' enquired Noel. He phoned Jock in the engine room, who said all was well and Noel could leave as soon as he wanted.

Brave Goose was ready.

'Jose, okay, haul the anchor.' He gave arm signals to Noel so Noel could steer the boat at slow speed in the direction of the chain to assist the winch in pulling up the chain.

A gush of seawater poured out of the anchor port, which cleaned the chain as it came aboard. Not necessary here as *Brave Goose* had anchored in silver sand. The chain was like new as it came back on board.

Goose swept the horizon for the last time as they got underway towards the channel markers to take *Brave Goose* through the gap between Ibiza and Formentera.

Noel set the course on the autopilot for La Rapita, which lay just to the southeast of Palma Bay. Once *Brave Goose* was beyond the channel between Ibiza and Formentera, *Brave Goose* increased speed to fit the passage plan. Goose had retired to his cabin.

John and Fiona climbed down the access ladder to the quarterdeck, where Sally was laying the breakfast table.

Without any warning, there was an enormous explosion from Formentera.

'Good heavens, what on earth could that be?' exclaimed John. Goose appeared on the deck to see a plume of black smoke lift over the small island.

Goose was again looking through his binoculars at the location of the blast. 'It is possibly a small fishing boat that has exploded,' he advised.

'How could that be?'

'Don't know, John, possibly they had some petrol on board for an outboard; I guess that is what has exploded.'

'Yes, that is a possibility. I hope no one was hurt. Should we return to help?'

'It's a good thought, Fiona, but by the time we have got back, anchored and launched the RIB, it would take an hour. There will be lots of other people closer than us to render assistance. I also found a Guardia Civil office on the island so they may take control.'

'We will listen for the lunchtime news on the radio to hear if there is a report on the incident,' said Goose. 'That noise reminds me of when a petrol-powered speedboat was towing two water skiers in a bay in North Wales. Bang, the engine compartment exploded, and both speedboat crew flung themselves off the boat. It, too, sent up a plume of black smoke. It was a fibreglass boat and burnt to the waterline. The two crew and the skiers were unharmed. It was possible in that case there was a hole in the fuel pipe, which sent a spray of petrol into the engine compartment which ignited due to the heat of the exhaust pipe.'

'Wow, that must have given everyone a big fright.'

'It certainly did, Fiona. I saw the remains of the boat being hauled out of the sea later. There was nothing left above the waterline.'

'I hope they were insured,' suggested John.

'That's a lawyer speaking if ever I heard one,' said Goose.

John just smiled.

The sea was amazingly calm. *Brave Goose* hardly moved in the water but achieved nine and a half knots. They were up on their predicted time of arrival.

Most of the day, John and Fiona used the sunbeds on the boat deck, napping, reading, and chatting in a never-ending cycle.

It was about three in the afternoon when Noel announced on the intercom that Mallorca had been sighted dead ahead. A small cheer went up. It should not have been a surprise that they were on course. It was a given that Noel would get them there.

The intercom came into life again. 'Everyone should look out to the starboard side over the bow; I have just seen the spout of a whale.'

Even Jock appeared on deck to see this rare sight. Sure enough, a few minutes later, there was the spout of water from the creature's blowhole, and it dived, giving all those on board a ringside seat to see the fluke of the tail flap and disappear into the depths.

'I suspect we will not see it again. They can dive for twenty minutes or more. The whale will have gone down to the depths after the small fish that only reach the surface after dark. The depth here is about nine hundred metres, nearly a kilometre. The whale will be after the small fish down at the bottom.'

Everyone was awake and alert, thinking there might be something else to see. Sally had brought some lemonade in a jug and glasses for everyone to assist in the cooling down process.

'You are so thoughtful, Sally,' said John. 'I love lemonade.'

Noel switched on the radio as they were sufficiently close to Mallorca to pick up the English broadcasts.

'Here is a news flash,' the radio announcer said. 'Any vessel that was recently moored off Formentera is requested to call Palma Radio and provide information, following an unexpected explosion on a fishing boat moored in the harbour. There are no reports of casualties.'

'Goose, did you hear that? I must call Palma Radio on VHF.'

'Yes, you must. I am glad it didn't explode when I sketched on the quay.'

Noel called Palma Radio. He reported that they had been moored for the night close to the harbour and left at eight o'clock but had been around since seven o'clock.

Palma Radio thanked them for the report.

'You must have a very powerful radio, Noel,' commented John.

'Well, John, the power is five watts on full power. VHF radio works on line of sight. There is nothing between us and Palma Radio. That is why there was such an excellent signal.'

It was five forty-five in the afternoon when *Brave Goose* let go of her anchor in six metres of water outside the harbour breakwater at La Rapita.

'Well, you got that wrong, Noel, you said six o'clock,' commented Goose with a wide grin on his face.

'Sorry about that, Goose. I will try harder tomorrow.'

John and Fiona went for a swim the moment the passerelle was in its boarding ladder mode with the platform and swimming ladder attached.

'Oh John, this is simply heaven. I just love this life. Thank you so much for being my friend and saviour.' The two embraced in the water and kissed. John then pushed Fiona's head under the water with a wide grin on his face.

'You sod, John England, I will have to wash my hair now,' said Fiona with a grin.

***

'Brandon, the boat is now in Mallorca. I am sitting on the quay's edge at La Rapita, reasonably close to Palma. I suspect the three of them will be going out for dinner. They will come ashore in the RIB. There has been a development. A small fishing boat, coincidently the one used to transport Fiona, has exploded in Formentera this morning, but *Brave Goose* had left when that happened. It must be a coincidence. No one was hurt in the blast.'

'Thanks for the update.'

'Brandon, I think *Brave Goose* may be in Mallorcan waters for some time.'

'It may be a good moment for me to come over?' enquired Brandon.

'If my assumption is correct, they will gradually move up the coast and anchor finally in the bay of Pollenca on the northeast side of the island. There are lots of hotels in Puerto Pollenca. Let me know when you are here. Oh, Puerto Pollenca is an easy taxi ride from the airport. They have built a motorway to Pollenca,' said Alvero.

The phone went dead. Brandon hit the internet to fix a flight and a hotel reservation in any hotel that had space in Puerto Pollenca for probably a week. What identity should he use to travel to Mallorca?

***

'Come on, everyone, it's time to go to dinner,' announced Goose. 'It's eight forty-five already.'

Fiona realised there was no elegant way of getting out of a RIB.

'That was more of a struggle than I had anticipated,' she said.

'Well, it's one of the features of boating, scrambling out of dinghies,' commented Goose.

They walked through a well-trod gap in the fence of the marina to a road which, after a hundred metres, brought them to the restaurant Goose had booked.

It was an unusual setting for such a magnificent restaurant – one of three shops built in a row. The middle one was the restaurant. The shops on either side were empty; the restaurant overlooked the sea. The other three units had never been occupied. The fish restaurant was fitted out to a high standard. The steps up to the restaurant had two large areas as part of the steps up to the main restaurant. These areas were also set with tables. By the time John, Fiona, and Goose arrived, the restaurant was nearly full.

The three diners were sitting at a table on the top tier, with a panoramic view of the sea. *Brave Goose* could be seen over the buildings and boats in the marina. The anchor light and display lights had also been illuminated on *Brave Goose*. She looked a picture.

'Goose, this food is wonderful,' said Fiona. 'A real treat. I have never eaten barnacles before, but they are delicious.'

The meal was unusual but beautifully served and had unique and delicious flavours. At the end of the meal, coffee was served.

'Senor Goose, was the meal satisfactory?' asked the proprietor.

'It was absolutely delicious, as always.'

The restaurant owner placed a bottle of Carlos Primera brandy on the table.

'This is the best there is in Spain. Please to help yourselves.'

'John, that kitty we have established will meet the bill.'

'That was a magnificent meal, Goose. I will have memories and tastes to savour.'

They all strolled to the marina. Goose pulled the small VHF radio from his pocket.

'Jose, we are beginning to stroll down to the marina. Can you pick us up, please?'

Jose brought the RIB perfectly alongside the marina wall.

'I will see if I can make a more elegant entrance than I made on exiting the RIB,' announced Fiona.

'That looked exquisite, darling.'

'Thanks, John, it isn't easy in a long dress.'

The RIB returned with its charges, overlooked by an unseen local fisherman, Alvero, as the RIB deposited its load back at *Brave Goose*.

The following morning was slow. Fiona went for a swim before breakfast. Sally and Jose took the RIB to purchase fresh bread, croissants, and some pastries. As the RIB arrived back at *Brave Goose*, Jock came to help bring the food on board.

Breakfast at ten o'clock was a luxury. Fresh coffee, croissants still warm from the bakery, fresh fruit, yoghurt and anything else they might desire was placed before them.

'This is food for kings and queens, delicious,' remarked Fiona.

They chatted and discussed the explosion of the small fishing boat in Formentera.

The weather was bright with a sparkling sea. There was not a breath of wind. The water-skiers were out as it was the perfect place to ski. The three breakfasters sat drinking more coffee for over an hour.

The conversation turned to the next location to moor *Brave Goose*.

'Well, my plan, which of course can be changed should you wish, is to go to Cala Ratjada. I will ring the fish restaurant on the harbour, Ca'n Maya. It is a fantastic little restaurant, but last night was at the other end of the scale. The speciality is sole a la garlic. It can take a day to get rid of the garlic, but the whole experience is terrific. I will treat everyone to a fish supper,' suggested Goose. 'If the weather remains calm, Noel, are you happy to moor outside Cala Ratjada?'

'Mooring in Cala Ratjada can be difficult as it is a very popular stop. There is a visitors' quay. We would occupy half of it, which could upset several yachts, and locals who like to see numbers of visitors, not just a few,' said Noel.

'Have you moored here before, Goose?' enquired John.

'No, not in *Brave Goose*. We can anchor off. The weather is fair. It will be no problem this evening,' suggested Goose. 'If it is rough, then we will not be able to moor off. The location is at a point on the coast where currents meet. It can get very rough here. I have seen waves splashing over the very high harbour wall.'

'Well, let's hope the weather holds. The problem is that if we anchor off, then we will have to leave someone on board. I will see if there are any volunteers. The unusual aspect of this harbour is that all boats go alongside, whereas it is stern to mooring in other ports.'

At that point, Noel rejoined the party on the quarterdeck. 'Goose, I was wondering if your choice of venue for tonight remains the same?'

'Yes, unless you think we could have a weather problem?'

'That is my concern, Goose; there has been a noticeable drop in barometric pressure, which usually signals strong winds in this part of the world. However, as the wind, if it comes, will be from the southwest, there is a reserve location we could anchor in, a small cala behind a headland just before Cala Ratjada. It's called Cala Molta.'

'Okay, Noel, I will accept your forecast, and we shall anchor in Cala Molta, so I am sorry, but there will only be three of us eating on shore tonight. Can you please ask Jose to come and make the phone call for me?'

'Is there time for another swim, Goose?' enquired Fiona.

'There is always time for you.'

'Goose, it is an eight-hour run up the coast. We are unlikely to be at our destination much before seven or eight this evening.'

'That's fine; we will book the table for nine.'

Fiona arrived on deck twenty minutes after she entered the water.

'Two circumnavigations of the boat, fantastic.'

'Okay, my darling, we are off on an eight-hour cruise north.'

***

Alvero Dali, a local fisherman and an ardent supporter of ETA, met with Brandon Phelan in the small café in the marina of La Rapita for a coffee. Many of the local marine workers stopped for breakfast in the café. They usually had a coffee and a brandy. This amused Brandon.

'So, what news, Alvero?'

'The motor yacht is due in Cala Ratjada this evening. According to my contact in the north of the island, Diego, they have a booking for dinner at nine o'clock. I think the weather will be getting worse as the day progresses; there could be a strong south-westerly wind.'

'So the issue is, where will be the best place to snatch our hostages? Have you a place ready to hold them when we get them?'

'Si senor, it is an old finca, in the northern hills of the island. No one ever goes there.'

Good, so we need to snatch them either in Cala Ratjada or possibly in Puerto Pollenca, which I suspect is their most likely next stop, thought Brandon.

'Well, I doubt they will be able to come alongside in Cala Ratjada, so if the wind does get up, the appropriate place to anchor will be Cala Molta, just south of Ratjada. This cala could be the ideal location to intercept their RIB. There is usually only one crew member. You want Goose as well as the couple?' asked Alvero.

'Yes, Goose was responsible for the death of my uncle.'

'This cala is quite busy in the season, but by eight in the evening, there is unlikely to be anyone on the beach by the time we arrive.'

'What happens if the beach is occupied, Alvero?'

'In that case, we cannot do the snatch. The alternative is to get Diego, a taxi driver, to pick them up from Puerto Pollenca marina. I am confident they will berth the boat there. We can then restrain them all after a short distance by driving into Diego's garage, closing the door and having some other patriots help restrain the three. We can chloroform them, which will calm them all down.'

'Sounds like a plan. Let's get going; it looks like *Brave Goose* is leaving now.'

***

'Pedro, it's Carlos. I have just had a message from my friend in the café in the marina at La Rapita. There is a plot to kidnap your friends on *Brave Goose* when they order a taxi for dinner in Pollenca. Do you want to come up, as I will need some help to sort this out?'

'Thanks, Carlos, I am on my way.'

Pedro thought perhaps he should advise Goose. Then he thought better of it. They would not be at Puerto Pollenca until the day after next. It would be appropriate to search out the taxi's garage. Then the home of the driver.

Pedro arrived in Cala Ratjada at seven o'clock in the evening. *Strange*, he thought, *there is no sign of* Brave Goose *in the harbour*. Pedro settled into a tortilla and a San Miguel at a café in the town square. He called Carlos, who agreed to meet him for a beer within the hour.

'Hi, Carlos, beer?'

'Si senor, same as you.'

The barman overheard the order and delivered a glass of the foaming amber liquid.

'Ah, that's better,' exclaimed Carlos.

'I was wondering if we should advise the Guardia about what was going on?'

'No, I don't think that would be a good idea. I guess they will become involved in due course. We need to stop this activity; ETA is out of order. They are acting as agents for the Irish IRA.'

'Mmm, the problem with that is that ETA has many supporters and foot soldiers. If we stir up a hornet's nest, who knows what will happen.'

'Yes, I agree, Carlos, but we do need to do something. I cannot stand by and see three people who have done nothing wrong get hurt or possibly killed because of the greed of an Englishman who is in jail and a brother of a man who was a drug dealer.'

'I see your point. My issue is that if we stir something up, we might not stop it. ETA have far more troops to call on than we do.'

'I agree, my friend, which is why I think a pre-emptive strike in Pollenca will stop something before it starts,' said Pedro.

'Do you know where the taxi driven by Diego, presumably a Mercedes, is garaged?'

'No, but I can find out. Will tomorrow morning be okay?'

'I need to know before the night ends. I need to put the taxi out of action before he comes to it in the morning. I will drive to Puerto Pollenca now. Do you want to come with me?'

'Okay, will you please bring me back?'

'Yes, sure, are you able to come now?'

The two men drove to Puerto Pollenca, in the north of the island of Mallorca. They went to the outskirts of the port. It was mainly scrubland with a few warehouse-type buildings, one providing storage for small boats. Others housed coaches for the tourist trade. Two warehouses stored Mercedes taxi cars. The buildings were mainly used to store and maintain vehicles and boats.

Pedro stopped the car opposite one of the taxi sheds. Carlos got out and wandered over to the only person he could see in the building. They spoke in Spanish.

'Hi, do you know a driver called Diego Agua?'

'Yes, who wants to know?'

'I do. I work for the Mercedes dealers in Palma. He rang today saying he needed a part for his car urgently.'

'So?'

'Well, I came up here with it. My friend was visiting family in the old town and said he would give me a lift.'

'Okay, what's the part?'

'I believe it's an alternator.'

'That would make sense. He has been having trouble with starting in the mornings. I told him he needed a new battery. He said he had a new one recently, but it kept going flat.'

'Well, an alternator would solve that problem if the old one isn't working properly. I was told to bring the old one back. The new one is an exchange item.'

'That can't be done; the car will not be back here before ten tonight, at the earliest.'

'Will you be here then?'

'No, I finish at nine.'

'Will Diego be here at ten?'

'Yes, he should be. He locks up when he is the last in.'

'Okay, I will come back at ten. If you speak with Diego, can you tell him I have the part, and as I brought it up with a friend, there will be no delivery charge?'

'He will be pleased to hear that.'

Back in the car, Carlos told Pedro the story. It was just good luck Diego had called for a new alternator sometime this week.

'So what will we do when we come back at ten?' said Carlos.

'Well, we either kidnap Diego or put his car out of action or both.'

'The problem I see, Carlos, is that he might be able to borrow another car, and what do we do with him if we snatch him?'

'Well, I don't know what to suggest, Pedro. That's the best I have been able to do.'

'I have an idea,' said Pedro. 'We need to make sure that Diego's car is disabled and the rest in the garage.'

'How do you plan on achieving that, Pedro?'

'I have a few useful bits and pieces in the boot. Let's drive up the road and see if we can find a spot off the road where I can assemble some suitable devices. I have in mind that we don't need to meet Diego or anyone else. It will be all automatic.'

Pedro drove his battered Seat car further out of the town of Puerto Pollenca. They found scrubland with a rough track to a tumbledown building. They could park around the back of the building and be out of sight.

Pedro assembled three devices with a mobile phone detonator. He noted the numbers. He wished to demolish the building by coincidence, just like they had parked behind the old building. Pedro walked inside the building with Carlos to try and work out which of the main supports, if blown up, would collapse the whole building.

Pedro decided that there were three main supports, one at the back holding up the roof and a similar one at the front. Taking out another support along the side would certainly collapse the roof down into the garage space.

'Carlos, if I blow the three main stanchions, I think the whole roof will collapse.'

'That sounds like a plan, Pedro. How will you detonate them? Do we have to stay here until much later?'

'No, we can be miles away when the detonation occurs. I need to set the devices between nine and ten. The mechanic you spoke to said he finished at nine, I think?'

'Yes, that's correct. We could go back to the port for another beer for an hour and then come back?'

*****

Goose, John and Fiona were in the RIB, being ferried from the small bay to the south of Cala Ratjada. Jose was at the helm; Goose had the small VHF. The expected wind had not materialised. The wind had gone, and the sea was flat.

'Wow, I can see the problem of mooring alongside the quay,' said John. The harbourside of the visitors' quay was full of yachts three deep.

'Do you want me to come alongside the slipway over there, Goose?' enquired Jose alongside the restaurant.

'Yes, that's the spot.'

'Jose, I will give you a call on the VHF when we are ready to be collected,' said Goose.

Jose zoomed off in the RIB out of the harbour to rejoin *Brave Goose* in the adjacent bay.

After the expected garlic sole and chips, and two bottles of local white wine, the three were enjoying a coffee when a face well-known to Goose appeared. It was about ten in the evening.

'Hi Goose,' said Pedro.

'Good heavens, how did you find me here?'

'I heard *Brave Goose* was in the adjacent bay. I know your habits. I just guessed you would be here.'

'Very clever, Pedro. Let me introduce you to my great friends John and Fiona. Sit down and have a glass of wine or coffee? You may recall we met Pedro in the champagne bar in Palma.'

'No, neither, thanks. I have to drive back to Palma now. I have a friend with me waiting in the car. Forgive me, John and Fiona, but does the name Brandon Phelan mean anything to you?'

'My God, how on earth do you know that?'

'I am your guardian angel. I also know you intend to

sail to Puerto Pollenca tomorrow. I also know you were in Formentera when a small fishing boat exploded shortly after you left.'

'Goose, do you know what is happening here?' enquired John.

'No, not really; I do know Pedro has contacts all over these islands.'

'Pedro, what is this all about?'

'If you have finished your coffee, can we discuss this outside?'

'Yes, sure,' said Goose. 'I will pay the bill on our way out.' Goose stopped to do the honours with the bill, leaving John and Fiona to walk outside with Pedro.

'Pedro, I am perplexed. We have only met once briefly in Palma, yet you know so much,' said John.

'Your friend Goose told me of the attempts to recover some money from you, which is legitimately yours. I have contacts, as Goose said, so I have been monitoring activities. Brandon Phelan is very well connected with the IRA in Ireland and with ETA in Spain, if that is his real name. Both organisations are seeking independence. Ireland to be unified, Catalonia to be separated from Spain.'

Goose joined the little group perched on the edge of a wall, forming the walls to the small slipway.

'Ah Goose, I was just filling in your friends with my connection to you. I gather you propose to travel to Puerto Pollenca tomorrow?'

'Yes, Pedro, that is the plan.'

'Can I suggest you postpone a trip to Puerto Pollenca

for a few days? May I suggest you go to Mahon in Minorca tomorrow?'

'Well, Pedro, ignoring the information source of our movements, we can, of course, do as you suggest. What is wrong with Puerto Pollenca?'

'I have heard of a plot to kidnap you all once you get a taxi to Pollenca Old Town for dinner tomorrow, which is what I suspect you were planning on doing?'

'Damn it, man, yes, but I still don't know how you know. I hadn't made my mind up where we might eat tomorrow.'

'Well, Goose, it didn't matter where you planned on eating. The issue was that a certain taxi would have collected you, and you would all have been whisked off to a hiding place. A kidnap for a significant ransom.'

'You still have not told me why we should not go there tomorrow. Now we know what might happen, we will not take a taxi.'

'I acccpt that now you know, however, the taxi garage is about to have an 'accident' that they were not expecting. That was to ensure no taxi could be used to get you. I am sure the ETA lot would have found another means of abduction. If you are in Mahon, completely outside their intelligence information, no harm should befall you.'

'Fiona and I have already had a taste of kidnapping by taxi. Not recommended, I assure you. When you say the taxi garage would have an accident, what do you mean?'

'The garage is due to fall down tonight. I will be back in Palma when it happens, and so will my friend Carlos.'

'Okay, Pedro. Thank you so much for the warning. Yes, it would be best if we were somewhere else tomorrow. Speak to you soon. Bye.'

Goose called Jose on the VHF for their ride back to *Brave Goose*.

***

Sometime afterwards, all the crew and passengers were safely asleep on *Brave Goose*. A massive explosion broke the silence of the town of Puerto Pollenca. For the few people around the town of Puerto Pollenca, it was clear the explosion was out of town and inland from the port. It was three in the morning. Alarms sounded at the fire and police station on the road out of town that runs to Pollenca Old Town. The explosion must have been heard miles away. Dogs barked, fire appliances roared up the street to the blast's location, which was now a large fire at one of the taxi firms' premises.

The firefighters got to work immediately to quell the blaze. They were concerned the fire might spread to the shrubs around. Before they knew it, they could have had a massive fire in the surrounding thicket and scrub. They were also concerned about secondary explosions from petrol tanks and possible propane gas bottles. Sure enough, within ten minutes of the fire appliances arriving, more explosions came from the vehicles inside the building.

By six in the morning, the fire was out. The firefighters were damping down. A TV news crew had arrived. They tried to interview one of the firefighters, but the inspector in charge had already left the scene. They made up as best they could from the evidence before them as to what happened. 'The consequences of this fire will mean fewer taxis on the streets of Pollenca and Puerto Pollenca,' the reporter handed back to the studio.

***

On *Brave Goose*, people were stirring at eight o'clock in the morning. Sally was busy preparing breakfast and laying the table on the quarterdeck. Jose was hosing down the foredeck and cleaning all the windows; Jock was busy doing his daily checks on both engines, the filters, the oil levels in the engines and gearboxes. The hydraulic levels for steering systems and controls and the anchor winch had to be checked to ensure everything would work when asked.

Fiona appeared, ready for a swim, and asked Jose if the passerelle could be used for a swim.

'Yes, ma'am, it is quite safe.'

Two circuits of the boat would suit. When she returned to the deck, John was already up and sitting at the breakfast table enjoying a coffee.

'Did you enjoy that?'

'I did, John. It is such a luxury to be able to step out of bed and go for a swim.'

'Good, you are just in time for breakfast,' Noel declared as Fiona dripped her way over the quarterdeck to her towel.

'I will be right back. I just need to rinse my hair and dry it. I will be back in two ticks.'

Fiona passed Goose in the saloon. Fiona assured him she would be back in just a moment.

'Morning Goose, another beautiful day.'

'Yes, it is. We are going to sail to Minorca today. It's a good stretch. Mahon Harbour is a vast place and famous. You will enjoy it.'

When Noel arrived, Goose advised him of a change of plan. 'We need to avoid Puerto Pollenca for a few days, so it is best to sail to Minorca and moor in Mahon. Can you see any issues with that, Noel?'

'No, Goose, we can go wherever you decide. No problem. Have you seen the local TV this morning?' enquired Noel.

'No, I haven't, Noel,' advised Goose. 'Why were you interested in looking at it?'

'It can give me good weather information. Just before that, at the end of the news bulletin was a report of a large fire in Puerto Pollenca, at a taxi depot.'

Goose looked knowingly at John, who returned the glance with a grin.

'Sounds quite a fire, Noel. Anyway, as I have said, I would prefer to go to Mahon today.'

'Good morning, everyone. What a fantastic day. We are so lucky.'

A small chorus of 'Morning Fiona' was voiced simultaneously by the assembled company.

'We are going to Minorca today, Fiona. A slight change of plan,' advised John.

'Oh, I don't mind where we go. It is all so wonderful.'

'I am so glad you are enjoying yourself, Fiona. Out of

everyone, you deserve the relaxation and enjoyment of this little cruise.'

'Thanks, Goose, that's very kind. I am perhaps not keen to join in a carnival parade any time soon.'

'Understood. So, what time will you be ready to sail, Noel?'

'In about three-quarters of an hour. We have to lift the passerelle and put the RIB back on the boat deck.'

'Okay, when you have finished your breakfast, can we get going as soon as possible?'

'Yes, Goose, understood.'

10

Pedro was in his hotel bedroom with the TV playing. The local news was full of a taxi garage explosion in Puerto Pollenca. There were pictures of police and fire departments handling the blaze.

'What caused this damage, sir?' asked a TV reporter of the senior police officer at the scene.

'At the moment, we have no idea. Forensics will be here to inspect the remains of the premises. It might be a feud between taxi firms; we will have to see.'

Pedro smiled to himself. He hadn't thought of that possibility – good old police.

Pedro sent a text to Goose to explain what had happened at the taxi storage depot. He wished *Brave Goose* a happy trip.

***

'Noel, can you please show me where we are now? It is a lovely morning. The opportunity to be able to swim off the boat is surely a luxury.'

'Yes, it is a lovely thing to do. I regret that opportunity will not be available tonight, as we will moor in an extensive enclosed harbour.'

'Well, never mind, I am sure there are other unique features in the harbour.'

'There are but let me first answer your question. It's about forty-five miles to Mahon. We have been travelling for half an hour roughly due west, a bit less than eighty-five degrees true. So we are about five miles from Cala Ratjada, in that direction, so I will let you use the parallel rules to plot our position.'

'Wow, that will be fun. What do I do?'

'Take the rules to the course, then move them without changing the angle down to the compass rose on the chart.' Noel was concerned not to get intimate with Fiona, but part of navigation required hands-on help. 'Keep one part of the rule on the centre of the compass rose and read off the course on the circumference of the compass rose printed on the chart. Then read off the angle which is our course to steer.'

'Wow, that's great. How easy is that?'

'Well, there are a few more issues to deal with, but you are correct in its simplest form.'

'So where are we now, Noel?'

'Well, you have the course as a pencil line on the chart. There are several ways of finding out where you are. Let's talk about dead reckoning.'

'Dead reckoning? Sounds like arithmetic!'

'It is, in a way. This instrument here is a log – mileometer on a car. I put the 'trip' into zero before we started. It now reads four point nine nautical miles. Essentially five miles. It would help if you now had the dividers. Measure the distance of five nautical miles off the chart.'

'What do you mean by nautical miles? Is there a difference?'

'Yes, Fiona, a nautical mile is a little longer than a land mile. You will not find a scale on the chart but the vertical scale opposite the area on the chart where you are working. So measure off five nautical miles.'

'Is that it, Noel?'

'Yes, that is correct, now don't move the dividers; put one spike on Cala Ratjada and the other on the course line. Make a mark with a pencil to record where we think where we are.'

'Wow, so that is where we are?'

'Yes, in a way.'

'What do you mean, in a way, we did it together? Surely that is the correct position.'

'No, it is where we think we are, but it may not be correct.'

'Why is that?'

'Well, we are at sea. The sea is not static. It is so much easier on land which is not fluid.'

'Oh, I see, so how do we work out exactly where we are?'

'Well, I have a gadget here called a GPS chart plotter. It plots our position on the globe's surface from satellite signals from outer space. This is how your sat nav in a car works. Well, at sea at any moment in time, we can see exactly where we are. So let's go to the screen that shows the latitude and longitude. Make a note of that on a piece of scrap paper. Then we can plot the position on the chart. You need to note the time we read the position, as we will have moved on by the time we plot the position.'

Fiona plotted the position after being told which scale was on the side of the chart. It transpired the GPS position was a small distance north of the predicted dead reckoning position.

'That is fascinating. Do you have to do this all the time, Noel?'

'No, I take a reading every hour of all the instruments. The chart plotter records our position on a digital chart.' Noel changed the screen on the GPS to show exactly where they were now. 'I just note the GPS position every hour in my log.'

'Thank you so much, Noel, that is great. Thank you. I am glad you explained all that to me. I can see how you know where to go.'

***

Brandon was furious. His carefully laid plans had been ruined. Fortunately, no one was killed by the actions of this Goose chap, who had somehow managed to blow up a fishing boat and the taxi storage unit.

'Diego, it's Brandon. I am in Puerto Pollenca. Can we meet?'

'Si, say the coffee shop and bar on the boardwalk just after the main promenade area. Caty's Bar is the name. I will be there at eleven.'

'Okay, Diego, see you then.'

***

Fiona was busy working out how *Brave Goose* was navigated and getting a lesson from Noel. Safe in his cabin John phoned his bank.

'Julian Franks, please, it's John England. Julian, I am currently in a boat in the Mediterranean off the coast of Mallorca on our way to Minorca.'

'That sounds rather splendid, John. I see your account has received a substantial credit in the last day or two. I wanted to speak to you about that.'

'Well, in a way, that is why I am phoning you. It is a long story. You may recall how an injection of funds paid off the bank loan to leave Peters Tower debt-free?'

'Yes, I recall, but didn't the person who paid the money ended up in jail for murdering Sandra Wall?'

'That is correct. There was a clause in the loan agreement with Michael Fitzallen, who is in jail, that if he committed an offence that put him in prison for more than ten years, he would forfeit all rights to the money and the repayment. In a way, Julian, this was good, but not at the price of Sandra's life. However, Fitzallen and his friends in Ireland called Phelan are very keen to retrieve the three million. That has put my girlfriend and me in danger. We have survived two kidnap attempts in Ireland

and the most recent on the island of Ibiza, where Fiona, my girlfriend, was abducted. I paid ten thousand euros to get her released.'

'So it's not all fun and games in the Mediterranean?'

'No, and the attempt to extract the three million from me is not over. I expect further attempts, and I fear they may succeed.'

'John, that is terrible. What can I do for you?'

'Well, there is significantly more than three million in my account. I may, in the end, have to pay to save our lives. If I get to the point of asking you to transfer three million to an unusual bank, is there anything you can do to effectively transfer the money but stop the receiving bank from allowing it to be drawn down?'

'Well, John, that is a fascinating question. I see what you want to do, but of course, we don't know the receiver bank or where they might be in the world. There are some banks I couldn't get that agreement from. Others would agree to it but not stick to the deal, and mainly British banks that would point blank refuse to co-operate. I need something from you; an email quoting what you want me to do, and a password you will use to let me know it is on your behalf or that of someone else you are asking to make the transfer for you.'

'Okay, Julian, I fully understand. I will create an email and send it to you now. Would you please confirm receipt? I hope we don't have to resort to this, but to save three lives, it will be cheap.'

'Okay, John, look forward to hearing from you.'

***

'Look, Diego, I need a fail-safe snatch of John England, his girlfriend Fiona and Goose, the owner of *Brave Goose*.'

'Well, killing them will not help your cause; you need them alive so John England at least can arrange for the cash to be moved to your bank,' said Diego.

'Correct, so we need a sophisticated snatch, without harming them so we can get England to send the money to your bank. That is not a simple conversation on the phone. He may have to present himself at a bank somewhere to prove it's him, and his girlfriend and possibly Goose as well,' Brandon explained.

'Do you think so?'

'I do. Banks are now clamping down on money laundering, extortion, and other financial transactions. That is why I have opened an account with a legitimate bank,' explained Brandon.

'Okay, senor, I will go away and see what I can arrange. Puerto Pollenca is the port they are bound to come to as it is a Royal Yacht Club, it has the attraction for wealthy people. There are good restaurants and everything else a motor yacht and crew require.'

'I'll take your word for it, Diego. They could arrive at any time so please don't take too long. Let's meet here again when you have your plan in place. Let me know.'

'Si, senor.' Diego finished his coffee and left. Brandon remained, ordered another coffee and thought he might get lunch there as well.

During his stay at Caty's Bar, Brandon phoned Eamon Strang.

'Eamon, it's Brandon. We spoke recently. I expect to pay about three million pounds into my account within the next couple of weeks. Will there be any hurdles to leap to allow that sum to be credited to my account?'

'Well, we will have to refer the receipt to HMRC, which handles money laundering. There will be some forms to fill in.'

'I see,' said Brandon. 'HMRC, who is that? Is it a long-winded process?'

'No, not at all. We can usually get the credit confirmed within five working days of receiving the forms following the money deposit. HMRC stands for Her Majesty's Revenue and Customs; they are the lead authority on approving transactions.'

'What happens to the money before it is credited to my account?'

'We hold it in an escrow account pending authorisation. Once we receive permission, the funds can be placed in your account within an hour.'

'Okay, well, we will have to see how it all works out. Thanks, Eamon.'

When Eamon had gone, Brandon started to think hard about how to arrange this transfer without causing any suspicion. It looked as though John was the person who he needed to have available to complete forms and transfer the money. Fiona and Goose would have to be kept safe as security for the secure transfer of the money. How to arrange this was the issue.

Brandon knew he would have to kidnap Goose and Fiona yet keep John England available until his bank had received the money.

11

Brave Goose was entering the vastness of Mahon harbour, Minorca. It was an exceptional sight for anyone who had never been to Mahon before. The vastness of the harbour was laid out before *Brave Goose*. Standing on the flying bridge at the forward end of the boat deck gave a spectacular elevated view of the harbour.

'It's like looking at a three-dimensional plan, but it's real,' remarked Fiona.

The sun was at its zenith. The cloudless blue sky allowed the sun to reflect on the wavelets in the harbour, picked up by a slight breeze. Fiona was in raptures at the sight.

'John, you should wear a hat. You will get burnt quickly by this harsh sun. I am just going to my cabin. Shall I bring your Tilley hat, darling?'

'Yes, please.'

'When you come through the saloon, can you please bring my hat as well, Fiona?' requested Goose.

'I will.'

Fiona was back in no time with a baseball cap for herself, John's Tilley hat, and Goose's hat, similar to John's. She also picked up Noel's baseball cap with an America's Cup symbol on the front.

'Look,' Fiona said, pointing to an island and buildings on the starboard side. 'What use could those low buildings have? Must be ten or more, surrounded by a perimeter wall. The entrance must be through those gates hung on the sculptured gateposts.'

Noel answered the question. 'It was constructed in the eighteenth century as a hospital. Ships would allow the ill or infectious crew to be offloaded here before travelling or mooring. It prevented infections being spread further afield in the town or the naval dockyard.'

'That's clever.'

'That maroon-painted house standing up at the end of the harbour must have quite a view,' observed John.

'I believe that house is the one Lady Hamilton occupied, the house facing it over on the port side was the house Nelson occupied when he used the harbour for the Mediterranean fleet. Mahon is the largest harbour in the Mediterranean.'

'I guess Nelson found a way of travelling regularly over the harbour to the red house?' remarked John.

'Over on the starboard side,' pointing with his hand, Noel said, 'is the naval dockyard that Admiral Byng built in 1708. Mahon and Minorca themselves were British possessions in the eighteenth century. You will find many houses built in the Georgian style, many with sash windows. It's quite weird walking around this town and finding English-looking houses.'

'Well, I would love to walk around. It looks a fascinating place,' remarked Fiona.

'Well, I plan on refuelling at the fuelling dock before mooring alongside; we have used about a third of the fuel we took on in Gibraltar. The fuelling facilities here are excellent. They have fifteen-centimetre hoses so that they can fuel up quite quickly.'

Noel gave the orders to Jose and Jock regarding lines and fenders. The fuel dock was on the port side of the harbour before the main quay for the town.

'How much fuel do we need, Noel?' enquired Goose.

'I would like to fill her up, sir. We have used about a third of our capacity. Probably fifteen thousand litres. That will be about ten thousand pounds, sir. Is that in order?'

'It will, but my name is Goose!'

'Yes, I know, Goose, I am so sorry. It's ingrained. Please don't think I don't want to call you Goose, but 'sir' is the greeting I have always used for my owners.'

'Yes, I know, and I appreciate it, but we are a happy family on here. I want to keep it informal.'

Having come alongside, Noel instructed Jose to put water on the decks port and starboard around the filler caps for the fuel. Noel leaned over the side and asked Jose to instruct the docker that they needed fifteen thousand litres, half in the starboard and half in the port tanks.

'Sir, the man says they have two hoses and fill both sides at once.'

'Excellent, carry on.'

'Why do you pour water on the deck around the filler caps, Noel?' enquired John.

'If we spill diesel on a dry deck, it will seep into the wood and leave a stain that is very difficult to remove. Wetting the deck prevents diesel from going into the wood as it will float on the surface. We can wipe it off. When dry, there will be no stain.'

'All clever stuff, Noel. I am learning every day.'

'So am I,' remarked Fiona.

Despite the significant volume, the tanks were full in half an hour.

Brave Goose moved back out into the channel and made fast alongside the quay in three metres of water outside the Mahon Yacht Club.

Jose rigged the passerelle ready for those who wished to go ashore.

'Do you mind if we go ashore, Goose?'

'My dear girl, this is as much your trip as it is mine. Please treat *Brave Goose* as if she were your yacht.'

'Thanks, Goose, I will just change my shoes; John and I will go and have a mooch around.'

As John and Fiona walked around the harbour walls, a huge cargo ship was just completing its docking on the commercial vessel quay. Then almost before the vessel had been tied up, a rope ladder was lowered over the side, along with a long plank supported by rope at each end.

As John and Fiona came up to the ship, a man in overalls came down the rope ladder. Somehow, he stood on the plank. A bucket was lowered to him. The bucket contained white paint. The painter began repainting the letters of the ship's name on the side of the hull. Looking at the man, the letters must have been twelve feet tall.

'Goodness, John. That looks like a crazy operation to me. He has no safety gear, not even a lifejacket. If he falls, he will die.'

'I agree, darling. He certainly can't step back and admire his work.'

'You are silly sometimes, John,' Fiona said with a big smile on her face, realising John was pulling her leg.

They walked on, having been entertained by the ship's painter. The next place to attract their attention was a bodega. Behind large oak doors was a cave-like opening, lined with barrels eight or ten feet in diameter. As they looked, an elderly lady dressed in a dirty smock and a headscarf beckoned them to come in. She offered them wine to taste in tiny shot glasses.

'Hey, this red is quite acceptable,' pronounced John.

'Yes, I like it,' confirmed Fiona.

'How much?' asked John.

The old lady held up ten fingers, then five. John assumed it was ten euros for five litres.

John gave the thumbs-up sign. The old lady picked up a glass carboy contained within a straw jacket. She began to fill it. John proffered a five-euro note. She smiled. 'Gracias, senor.'

'What will this taste like when it's been on board and bounced around for a bit? Who can tell? I am pleased with that purchase.'

They walked on. The next part of the tour required them to walk up a flight of stone steps to the town itself.

'Hey, this wine is heavy. Let's drop it back at the boat.'
Fiona agreed.

Goose welcomed them aboard, enquiring about the contents of the carboy.

John poured out three glasses.

'This is quite acceptable, John,' confirmed Goose.

'It was costly,' advised John with a grin on his face.

'Go on, how much?'

'Five euros for ten litres.'

'That is amazing, fifty cents a litre. Let's wait until the morning to see how we feel!' Goose suggested.

'You are right, Goose. It could be a headache mixture.'

They all laughed.

As it was only late afternoon, John and Fiona resumed their wanderings around Mahon. After an hour, they passed a small café, so they decided a small beer might be the thing to cool the body in the Spanish heat. The waitress brought 'dos St Miguel' beers.

'Perfect,' said John. 'This beer always tastes much better than it does out of a can at home.'

On the adjoining table was another couple who sat down close to them.

'You are so right. It's like Guinness in Ireland. It has the real taste there,' said the man at the next table, who couldn't have helped hearing John's comment on the taste of St Miguel.

'Are you enjoying Mahon? Do you come from Ireland?' enquired John.

'Yes, we like it here. The town is fascinating, with good shops and restaurants. It's our first time here. We have rented a villa near Mahon. We decided to come over here for a walk around, a drink and later a meal. Are you from England?' said the man.

'Yes,' responded John, 'Manchester to be exact. And you?'

'Well, we do come from Ireland, as you surmised. It's much easier for us, as we use euros at home, so we don't have a currency exchange rate to be concerned about.'

'Yes, I can see the attraction. I am John, my partner, Fiona.'

'I am Heinz and my wife, Marie. We live in the south of Ireland at Dunmore East.'

'That's extraordinary. I knew someone once who had a connection with Dunmore Hall, is that close to you?'

'About a twenty-minute drive away. That's where my grandfather worked when he first came to Ireland.'

As John had investigated the comings and goings at Dunmore Hall, he recalled that Heinz's Christian name was the name of the German who landed in the loch behind Dunmore Hall in 1939. He nearly blurted out his knowledge but thought better of it.

The beers had been consumed. 'We had better return to the boat and discover what else is to be done today. Enjoy your holiday.'

John and Fiona left the couple behind. Fiona was bursting to ask John why he had not discussed Dunmore Hall and all he knew about it and the family.

Once back on *Brave Goose*, Fiona questioned John.

'It could all be a coincidence that someone we meet having a beer in Mahon has a close connection to

Dunmore Hall. On the other hand, with the carnival and your kidnapping in mind, I wouldn't be at all surprised to find their surname was Phelan. And who knows where that conversation might lead.'

'I understand, John. Perhaps we should let Goose know and ensure the passerelle is raised tonight.'

'You are right, clever girl. Let's discover what is going on this evening.'

***

'Hi, it's Heinz. Can you talk, Brandon?'

'Yes, go on.'

'We just sat next to John England and Fiona having a drink at a harbourside café in Mahon, Minorca.'

'Ah, that's where they are. We couldn't understand why *Brave Goose* had not arrived in Puerto Pollenca. Have you seen *Brave Goose*?'

'Yes, she is moored around the corner from us. I think she has refuelled.'

'That is interesting. It would indicate they are expecting to travel some distance.'

'They didn't say where they were going.'

'Okay, Heinz, thanks for the info. Minorca has no other ports to accommodate *Brave Goose*, so I bet they are done with Minorca. I expect they may well head for Barcelona. I will relocate and go to Barcelona and meet up with friends there. Enjoy your holidays.'

***

'Goose, have you a moment?'

'Yes, John, what can I do for you?'

John explained their chance meeting with Heinz and his wife.

'I don't think that was a chance meeting; Heinz made it happen. It sounds as though he is part of Brandon's network of informants. Did you tell them where we are going next?'

'No, we didn't stop to talk very much. It seemed like the more we chatted, the more information we might inadvertently give away.'

'Good,' said Goose. 'Best to leave them guessing. They probably think we have now left Mallorca. Our next port of call would be Barcelona. There are no other ports on Minorca that can accommodate us.'

'So where will we go next, Goose?' enquired Fiona.

'I think Puerto Pollenca in Mallorca would be best.'

'Great, it sounds like a fun place,' Fiona said, excited at the prospect.

John retreated to their cabin. He made a call to Jon Kim.

'Jon, I am sorry to bother you, but we have a potential problem in Spain.'

'Is that where you are? Holiday, I assume?'

'Yes, we are on Goose's motor yacht.'

'So, what is the issue?'

John explained what had happened and what he feared might happen in Spain.

'I see. Well, I will have a word upstairs, and I will see what we can do with our Spanish friends. I will call you back in due course. Will this number do, John?'

'Yes, Jon, thanks.'

12

Brandon was considering what best to do when his phone rang.

'Yes?'

'Is that you, Brandon?'

'Yes, who is this?'

'You don't know me. I am a friend of Diego Agua. He is from Palma Mallorca. I understand you need support when you come to Barcelona, is that correct?'

'Yes, that's a way of putting it. It isn't ideal to discuss this on the phone. Can I contact you when I get to Barcelona?'

'Yes, Brandon, sure. You have my number.' The phone went dead.

'Heinz, it's Brandon.'

'Hi, what can I do for you?'

'Can you let me know when *Brave Goose* leaves Mahon?'

'Yes, sure.'

'When you see the boat go, can you please tell me which way it turns out of the harbour? Left or right will do.'

***

On *Brave Goose*, there was a meeting in progress: Noel, Goose, John and Fiona.

'Look, folks, the kidnapping of Fiona at Ibiza was just a warm-up for what is to come. It would seem that the IRA have made contact with ETA to try and recover the money they allege is due to the Phelan family and to Michael Fitzallen, who is in prison in Manchester. I think he is the ringleader of all this. I am sure that the Ibiza incident was the start, not the end of the attempts. We are being observed wherever we go.'

'I agree with you, Goose. The meeting with Heinz and his wife was no accident. They will have seen us leave the boat, sat next to us, and started a conversation when appropriate. I have spoken to Jon Kim, my police contact in the UK,' said John. 'If anyone can come up with a plan, Jon Kim will. He said he would ring me in a day or two.'

'I think we should remain here until we hear from Jon Kim. We can then make a plan.'

'I agree, Goose,' said John.

***

Heinz and his wife observed *Brave Goose* from time to time from the raised area above the harbour leading to the town centre.

'*Brave Goose* is still in Mahon, Brandon.'

'Thanks, Heinz. I don't suppose you have managed to discover how long he intends staying?'

'No, I have asked the harbourmaster and the yacht club. They either do know and will not say, or they just don't know.'

'This makes life a little tricky. I don't have any plan I could activate in Minorca. I need him back ideally in Puerto Pollenca or Barcelona. These are both locations where I have facilities to make life difficult for *Brave Goose* and her occupants.'

'I understand. As soon as I know, I will let you know.'

Brandon was at a loss as to know which plan to implement. He needed *Brave Goose* elsewhere. Mahon was not ideal. Brandon reviewed his plans in Puerto Pollenca, Pollenca Old Town, and Barcelona. He needed to secure three people, possibly more, if he found resistance from the crew.

***

'John, it's Jon Kim.'

'Hello, my dear friend. I am so sorry to put you to so much trouble on our behalf.'

'Don't you fret about that. Anyway, I need some more information from you so that we can put a plan together.'

'Fire away, Jon, what do you need to know?'

'Well, the Spanish police need to know where you are now. What are your next ports of call and when?'

'Ah, I will need to discuss with Goose and the others.

I will ring you back in half an hour. Before you go, do you know what is planned?'

'The general idea is surveillance. Plain clothes officers will keep *Brave Goose* under supervision while in a harbour. I will give you a phone number to call to advise the Spanish of any plan changes. In addition, call this number to report on your course to the following location. You can't do this over VHF, as the world can hear that. The number you will get is an encrypted phone line. Conversations take a bit longer this way but avoid phone hacking. You will be asked for navigation details. The Spanish coastguard will be alerted of your course and destination.

'I have been assured that unless a code word, which will be given to you, is used, then the call will not get through. The coastguard will keep its distance and out of sight; however, they will be close enough to come to your aid.'

'That all sounds terrific, Jon. I will ask Noel, the captain of *Brave Goose*, to make the call on the number we will be given.'

Jon Kim left, expecting a call within the hour.

John England asked Goose, Noel, and Fiona to join him. He had some important information for everyone.

All four were seated around the table in the saloon. Despite it being a beautiful day where the quarterdeck would be ideal in normal circumstances, John was anxious not to allow stray words to be picked up, thereby giving information to those who would do them harm. It was an assumption they were in danger.

'The events at Ibiza are sufficient to indicate that the main prize the Phelans and Fitzallen in prison all covet is the three million pounds. I have received a call from Jon Kim. The next call to him will provide us with the unique encrypted phone number for the Spanish authorities. They also need on the next call our following destinations, and when. When we are underway, you are to call the number, Noel, with details of our course. We are to be shadowed by the Spanish coastguard.'

'Why don't we stick to our plan, John?' said Goose. 'Puerto Pollenca and then Barcelona. Shall we say we will leave here the day after tomorrow? If Fiona and John want to go swimming, take the RIB around from the entrance to this harbour. There is a beautiful little bay, Cala St Esteban. There is a lovely sandy beach from memory.'

'That would be fun, Goose, if you trust us with the RIB.'

'Yes, of course. Take the handheld VHF and keep in touch. Noel will give you a crash course on how to use the radio. Have you the number, John, for Jon Kim?'

John wrote the number on a pad and handed it to Noel.

Noel would make the call, but first, he instructed Jock and Jose to launch the RIB and check the fuel. 'Jose, can you give John some instruction on how to use the RIB?'

'Why don't I go and ferry John and Fiona in the RIB, Noel? I will be available to come back at any moment if needed. I can leave handheld one VHF with John. I will take the other handheld two and keep it in the RIB.'

'Good idea, Jose, you carry on. I have things to do,' said Noel.

John and Fiona went to get ready to go to the beach. A bag with towels, sun cream and a book. The trip around the corner at the entrance to Mahon harbour was exciting. The RIB flew through the water. Fiona caught the odd spray.

'Hey, why don't you get sprayed, John?'

'I know on which side to sit.'

They were both sitting on the sponsons of the RIB. Jose was on the same side as Fiona, so they got wet from spray when they passed over the wash from other boats.

In the bay, they motored sedately to the end, allowing John and Fiona to decant onto the beach, paddling the last metre or so.

Jose decided to check the VHF signal; due to the cliffs at each side of the inlet, he thought the signal might be compromised.

'Test message to *Brave Goose* from *Brave Goose* mobile one,' said Jose into the microphone of the handheld VHF set.

There was no response. As Jose thought, the signal did not work so low down in this inlet. I had better stay with you,' said Jose. 'There is no signal here due to the height of the land on either side of the inlet.'

'There is no need to do that, Jose; I am sure you have other things to do. We have our mobile and *Brave Goose*'s phone number, and we have Goose's mobile. When we want to come back, we will call.'

'Okay, that's fine by me if you are happy with that?'

'We are, no problem, see you later, Jose.'

John and Fiona found a convenient place in the rocks at the back of the beach. It was in the sun but out of the breeze. The towels were laid, books and a water bottle were retrieved from the beach bag. Fiona decided this was the best spot to get the maximum body bronzed. She removed the top of her bikini and started to smother herself with suntan cream.

The sun cream delivery was too much for John to watch. He took over the massaging of sun cream, much to the delight of Fiona. John was delighted to help. Fiona reciprocated, and John was then made impervious to the worst of the sun's rays.

The two of them enjoyed one another's company, eventually falling asleep in each other's arms. John leapt up after about twenty minutes, which woke Fiona.

'Whatever is the matter?' Fiona exclaimed.

'I have a cramp in my arm.'

'Why is that?'

'Too much weight on my arm.'

'What a cheek.'

Neither of them had noticed two men standing close by. They were looking at the two of them.

'Oh!' said John. 'What do you want?' He was thinking these two men were hawkers selling something.

'No, senor, we do not sell anything. We want you to come with us.'

'We have no intention of coming with you. We are happy here.'

'Senor, no is not the answer. We demand you come with us now.'

'And if we don't come?'

'Then we shall force you to come.' At that moment, John recalled all his Krav Maga ' training. These two had the advantage. John was sitting down with only swimming trunks. They had shirts and trousers, and more importantly, were wearing boots.

John stood up, to find he was a bit taller than the main man who had done all the talking. The silent guy was a bit shorter still.

'So you need to explain why we should come with you. We are very happy here, or we were until you two turned up.'

'Senor, my orders are to take you to my boss.'

'Oh, you have a boss, who is that?'

'I cannot say.'

'Well, we are not coming.'

Fiona had gathered all their belongings and wandered a little way off, phoning Jose as she did.

The talker approached John, intending to grab his arm. John was having none of this. He hit the man as hard as he could with his elbow into his throat. John then punched him on the nose with a very hard blow from his clenched right hand. He yelped like a dog and fell to the ground, hitting his head on a stone. He had caused a significant cut to the back of his head, which bled profusely.

The smaller man decided he was not here for a fight. He began to run off the beach. The man on the ground called for assistance. The smaller man returned to assist his friend. They legged it off the beach. The hitman found breathing difficult due to John's blow to his throat.

'John, are you okay, darling?'

'Yes, I am fine. I am better than the guy I hit. They were not very good at their job, running off like that. Did you get through to Jose?'

'Yes, he and Jock are on their way at full steam.'

'Good, well, I think sunbathing is over for the day. I could do with a drink.'

'Me too, what a terrible thing. Where did you learn that trick, John?'

'Oh, I have been doing Krav Maga training for a while. So far, it seems to work.'

'It does. Where did you hear of Krav Maga? I am glad you have stuck to the training. This is surely all part of the attempt to get the money from you?'

'Oh, James, my estate agent who sold the farm for me, involved me in training. That reminds me to find a training gym in Manchester. It's too far to go to Chester. Krav Maga is a self-defence method used by MOSSAD, the Israeli secret service. You are right, I am sure. We need a plan to outsmart these thugs.'

As John discussed the implications for the rest of their holiday, Jose and Jock came whizzing down the cala in the RIB.

'Are you both all right?' a concerned Jose shouted before the RIB had come to a halt.

'Yes, yes, we are fine.' Fiona hopped into the RIB; John followed. Jose skilfully reversed the RIB and turned to go out of the bay.

It wasn't possible to have a meaningful conversation in the RIB due to the engine's noise. There was quite a welcome party awaiting their arrival. The starboard side passerelle had been deployed to form a landing area for the RIB.

The four in the RIB arrived at the side of *Brave Goose*, leaving the RIB by way of the starboard side of the boat. A welcome party on the deck comprised Goose, Noel, and Sally. They all spoke at once, desperately wanting to know what had happened.

'Well, if Fiona and I can have a drink and a sit-down, we will give you the full story.'

His mobile rang as John pulled out a chair to sit at the quarterdeck table.

'John England,' he said in response to the call.

'John, it's Jon Kim. Have you a moment? I need to run some things past you.'

'Can I ring you back in ten minutes, Jon? I will tell you all about our latest encounter when I call you back.'

'Now, Fiona and I were having a quiet afternoon sunbathing and reading a book when, about an hour after Jose had left, out of nowhere, two rough-looking men appeared. They stood behind us. They were speaking in broken English, demanding that we go with them. They became ever more insistent. I stood up, and the taller one approached me as if to grab me by the arm. I hit him twice. He fell back onto the beach, cutting his head on a stone. Blood was everywhere. Anyway, they ran off the beach after that.'

'Can you describe what they looked like, John?'

'I can,' said Fiona, 'I have photographs of them both on my mobile.'

'You what?' exclaimed John.

'Well, I was about to phone Jose for help, so I took their pictures, in case it might be helpful.'

'You clever thing, well done,' exclaimed John as Fiona passed her mobile phone around for everyone to see the intruders and see who they might be.

'Thanks for the beer, Sally. You are a mind reader. I need to phone my police contact in the UK to see what he has to suggest.'

'Jon, it's John England. Sorry I couldn't just talk when you rang.'

'Are you all right, John? You sounded as though you had been in some trouble.'

John explained everything that had happened on the beach.

'Let me explain what we can put in place for you, and from what you say, the sooner, the better,' Jon Kim announced.

13

'Diego, it's Brandon. Any news? I have not heard from you for days.'

'There has not been much to say. *Brave Goose* is in Mahon on Minorca. Two of the targets went to a secluded beach for swimming and sunbathing. Two of my temporary helpers went to try and get them off the beach and take them to a 'safe house'. They met with violence from England. My guys left the beach in a hurry.'

'That sounds like a botched job to me.'

'They didn't expect violence and didn't go prepared.'

'Exactly, a botched job. What now?'

'We expect *Brave Goose* will sail to Barcelona. They have a berth reserved.'

'Have you any men in Barcelona?'

'As the capital of Catalonia, there is no shortage of ETA men to accept the challenge.'

'What do they want for their trouble?'

'Money, not sure how much. I guess it depends on how much they manage to extract.'

'Well, I hope they are better at it than your men in Mahon. Don't forget we want Goose as well.'

'No, I understand that, but they rarely travel around together. Goose prefers to remain on board.'

'Well, he is wanted for the murder of Niall Phelan, so an eye for an eye applies here.'

'I understand, Brandon. The big issue is access to the boat. They moor in public places. We cannot just invade the ship, with a team, in full sight of public and security.'

'Maybe we will have to look at an ambush at sea?'

'That would not be easy. I suspect *Brave Goose* could outrun most of our fishing vessels.'

'Diego, if the Iranians can capture an oil tanker with a large speedboat, we should be able to do the same with *Brave Goose*.'

'That is a possibility. I will look into what sort of boat we can obtain. It may be the best method.'

'Okay, don't fuck up next time. Make it work whatever you decide.'

Brandon hung up, wondering if the activity he was involved with would work. The technical difficulties of moving a few million pounds to a new bank account would, in regular times, be complex. To have a prisoner who does not want to co-operate would make it even more difficult.

***

'John, you will realise it is complicated for the Manchester police to intervene in criminal activity in Spain.'

'I understand, Jon. We shall have to try and sort things out ourselves.'

'It's not as bleak as that, my friend. I have connections. I have spoken with the Spanish Interior Ministry, and they put me in touch with their equivalent of Special Branch. The Grupo Especial de Operaciones (GEO). The GEO is the police tactical unit of Spain's National Police Corps. The GEO has response capabilities and is responsible for VIP protection duties and countering and responding to terrorism. You should be getting a call from them.'

'Wow, Jon, that sounds fantastic. Thank you so much. I can't wait to hear from them.'

John was just about to explain to Fiona and Goose the call's content with Jon Kim when his mobile rang again.

'Senor England?'

'Si, oh yes.'

'I am Inspector Mateo of the GEO. I understand you have reason to fear for your life, if not kidnapping for a significant ransom. Is that correct?'

'Yes, sir, quite correct. Indeed, there has been an attempt to kidnap my partner and me only this afternoon in a small cala outside the harbour in Mahon.'

'Where are you staying, sir?'

'We are on a thirty-metre motor yacht of a great friend. We are currently moored in Mahon. We thought we would return to Mallorca in a day or two and then Barcelona.'

'I understand. I don't want you to speak to me over the phone about why and what your plans are, but if you are going to be in Barcelona I will give you my number. We have a group of five operatives and back-up in Barcelona. We can help you, I am sure.' Mateo gave John his mobile number for the subsequent communication.

'Thank you, Inspector Mateo, I look forward to meeting you.' John ended the call. He had a grin on his face like a Cheshire cat.

'Go on, John, tell us all about what has happened,' demanded Fiona.

'Well, my friends, it looks like we have the crack team of the Spanish police coming to our aid. They are called the GEO. They will help us when we get to Barcelona. They have a specialist team waiting there to help.'

'It looks like we will have to divert to Barcelona, troops,' said Goose. 'Is that okay with you, Noel?'

'Absolutely no problem to me, Goose. Once we get this sorted out, we can then resume our cruise. Barcelona is an interesting place to visit. The mooring at Puerto Vell inside the main harbour has good security and is used to handling large boats.'

'How long will it take us to get to Barcelona, Noel?' enquired Goose.

'About sixteen or seventeen hours, it's about one hundred and fifty nautical miles from here, Goose.'

'Okay, would you be up for a night sail to Barcelona? If we leave here at ten tonight, we should be in Barcelona by two o'clock tomorrow afternoon. Noel, are you happy with that?'

'Yes, Goose. I will get things organised now. Sally, do you need anything from the shore?'

'No thanks, Noel, I can do anything that is required. It's supper and breakfast. I have more than enough for that.'

'Good, well that's all agreed. Let's get ready.'

The rest of the afternoon was spent recovering the RIB and preparing *Brave Goose* for sea and a night passage. Noel made all the calculations and plotted the course.

***.

John phoned GEO on the number he had been given.

'Inspector Mateo, we will be in Barcelona at Marina Port Vell by about 2 pm tomorrow. The name of the motor yacht is *Brave Goose*.'

'Thank you, senor. We will come to the boat at about four in the afternoon. We will check you are there first with the marina office. There will be two of us, to begin with. Look forward to meeting you tomorrow in Barcelona.'

14

'John and Fiona, I thought you would be interested in the mooring method in Marina Port Vell?'

'Oh yes, we would,' answered Fiona, on behalf of them both.

'In Port Vell, they use 'lazy lines'. These are fixed mooring lines for the bow. It is not necessary to drop an anchor here. The lazy lines take up far less space and allow more boats to be moored in a tight space.'

'How do you get the bowlines, Noel?' asked John.

'They are handed over to the crew at the stern. They are light lines, the lazy lines, on the end of which are the larger mooring lines. We bring the main moorings on board and make them ready by bending the lines onto our winches.'

'So what happens at the stern, Noel?'

'When Jose and Jock have the bowlines on, but not tight, they then reposition themselves to the stern to throw our stern lines onto the quay. The marineras put the made loops at the end of the lines onto bollards. The boat end of the lines is attached to the winches, and *Brave Goose* is pulled into the right distance from the quay. Jose and Jock then return to the bow and tighten up the bowlines with the winch. We are then moored.'

'Thanks for the explanation, Noel. Fiona and I will look forward to witnessing the mooring with knowledge.'

'Noel, is this method used on all marinas?'

'Yes, Fiona, certainly in Spain. However, it is mainly for yachts and smaller powerboats. It is rare to have it available for larger boats.'

Once *Brave Goose* was safely docked in Marina Port Vell, a private marina located within the main port of Barcelona, the passerelle was run out from the stern to the dock. The lines had been made up, with lazy lines to the bow, one on each side of the bow. Once easy access to the dock was established, Jock connected the electricity and water supplies from the dock. Once he had completed the connections, he returned to the engine room to ensure electricity was received at the correct voltage and polarity. Water ran into the tanks through the water filter.

Jose established the CCTV camera for the passerelle. The 'Private No Boarding' sign was placed on the entrance to the passerelle, together with the battery-operated bell push; a bell would sound in the crew's quarters when pushed by a visitor.

Two men in casual clothes approached *Brave Goose* at four in the afternoon. Jose went to greet them.

It was Juan Mateo and his colleague, Luis. Jose showed them into the saloon. Goose, John and Fiona soon joined them. Introductions were made, then everyone sat around the saloon dining table. Luis had a small voice recorder to record the conversation.

'I trust you won't mind if we record our conversation. It helps us recall not just the facts, but the emphasis placed in certain areas as we speak.'

Goose was first to speak.

'I have no issues with you recording our conversations, Mateo.'

'Senor, I now presume you are John England, and you, madam, are Fiona Holmes?'

'Correct,' replied John. 'I assume Jon Kim, my friend in England, has provided you with some information?'

'He has, but I would like to hear the full story from you.'

'It is difficult to know where to start, but I think you need the whole story from the beginning.'

John set about giving all the details and reasons for their concerns and troubles. He started with Sandra borrowing money from Michael Fitzallen. He had earned this money with the assistance of Niall Phelan, who turned out to be a drug dealer in Ireland. He had no right to the funds but had access to it. It was acquired from Phelan with the assistance of Goose. Fitzallen lent the money to Sandra as the chief executive of Wall Holdings, the ultimate owners of the tower block in Manchester.

John continued with the exposé of the situation, the latest ending in the kidnap of Fiona in Ibiza, during the Pride Festival procession.

'Quite a story, senor,' Juan remarked. 'It is not for us to state the rights and wrongs of the agreement for the money, but it is our job to try and combat kidnapping.'

'We believe we are likely to be subject to a kidnap attempt in this city,' remarked Goose.

'Yes, sir, it is for that reason that a team of GEO officers are permanently stationed in Barcelona. We cannot know how a kidnap attempt might be made. Just supposing it was made, and they managed to get you to transfer funds to another bank, have you the money to do that?'

'I have, Juan, but I would rather not lose it to criminal activity.'

'I understand, sir, but it is a credible approach and a real threat. We would have to reconsider our position if the kidnappers knew no money was available. As there are funds available, it brings the role of banks and currency exchanges into play.'

'I understand. Do you have a plan, Juan?'

'I do. I have more men to assist if it gets nasty. They will not be far away. I want to embed Luis into your group. He would be dressed as a civilian but would be armed, and have communication equipment with him at all times. Would you have some accommodation on board, sir?' He directed the request to Goose.

'Yes, we have a spare double bunk cabin. I am sure that would be acceptable?'

'I am certain it will be acceptable. As for the rest of the GEO team, we will constantly watch the boat and you wherever you might go. We will have two uniformed officers on motorbikes to assist in this approach. My technical team will want to set up a camera to see who is coming and going, a watch we shall keep for twenty-four hours. May I suggest you withdraw the passerelle every night, once all the guests and crew are on board.'

'As far as I am concerned, that sounds just fine, assuming Goose agrees,' said John. 'Luis can come with us as a friend wherever we go.'

'Fine by me,' confirmed Goose.

'I need to bring my captain in at this point, as the running and security of the vessel is his responsibility. His name is Noel. May I ask him to join us?'

Once Noel arrived, Goose introduced the new members around the table and outlined the threat and the surveillance arrangements.

'I have no objection to any of this, sir. I will be pleased to co-operate in any way necessary. You have outlined the surveillance on land and while we are in port. However, what will happen when we are at sea? If the Iranian forces in speedboats can stop oil tankers, we are certainly vulnerable to an attack at sea. Our cruising speed is nine knots, best twelve. Is there a plan to keep us safe at sea?'

'Good point, Noel,' said Goose.

'Well, sir, when you leave here, what is your next port of call?'

'We had thought we would go to Puerto Pollenca, on Mallorca.'

'If you book in advance, you should be able to get in on the end of the visitors' quay. I will leave you with my details to keep in touch regarding your movements. As to seaborne security, we will have a fast fifty-foot speedboat.

In addition, the Guardia Civil have waterborne units which can move at speed and will come to our assistance. We can neutralise any attempt to intercept you.'

'That would be reassuring,' said Noel, 'but how can we communicate with your seaborne troops without using VHF, which anyone can intercept?'

'Yes, do you have a single sideband set on board?'

'Yes, we do, a Sailor. It's a little dated but an excellent piece of kit.'

'Good, I will give you a certain frequency we monitor. You should be able to hold the frequency in the set in readiness for use.'

Juan handed Noel a card with the frequency on it.

'Thank you. I will program the Sailor UHF set. We hardly use it now due to mobile phone coverage being so amazing. If we were to do an Atlantic crossing, we might use a sat phone, as Portishead in the UK has closed, for UHF traffic. Are you likely to call us on this frequency?'

'Yes, Noel, it is worth having the set switched on all the time until this exercise is over. The UHF frequency is secure. Unless there is anything else, we will leave now. Luis will be back in an hour with his kit.'

All expressed general thanks. Goose, John and Fiona were not feeling as secure as they were when they hadn't known what might happen.

'Well, despite our concerns, we have a few more people on our side,' remarked Fiona.

Goose rang the call button; Sally appeared within minutes.

'Sally, we shall have another member with us for a while. His name is Luis, and he will use the small bunk cabin. He needs to be treated as one of the guests. He is, in fact, a member of the crack GEO Spanish special forces to help us repel any further attempts on people. He will accompany us wherever we go. Have you sufficient provisions?'

'Yes, Goose, that's fine, no problem.'

***

'Brandon, *Brave Goose* has berthed in Barcelona at Marina Port Vell.'

'Thanks, Diego. What is the plan now?'

'We have a high-speed forty-foot boat at our disposal. We will board *Brave Goose* at sea. Do you want us to bring the hostages ashore?'

'Yes, I do, but where, is the issue. I need England to be able to make a landline call to his bank.'

'Do you want this to be done in mainland Spain or Mallorca?'

'I guess it will depend on where you manage to intercept the boat. Ring me if you are closer to Spain than Mallorca, you can take them there. The best place would probably be Reus. The problem is that it is inland, and the coast is full of holidaymakers. Reus is, of course, the seat of the original location of the first attempt to get Catalonia separate from mainland Spain. There are many ETA members in the city. If we could get them there, it would be ideal.'

'Understood. I think the number of tourists along the coast will be a problem. There are several coves on the north coast of Mallorca. If it's rough, we can use Pto Soller. That too will be busy, but it could work if we transfer our cargo in the middle of the night.'

'Yes, okay, that suits me fine as I am here in Mallorca. I will check with Alvero if he still has a safe house we can use. We need it to have a phone. Good luck, let me know when you are setting off for the interception.'

***

'John, it is Jon Kim.'

'Okay, thanks for the contact with the GEO here in Spain. We are in Barcelona now.'

'Be careful. Barcelona is the seat of the attempts to achieve independence from Spain. Some of their politicians are in jail for their attempts!'

'We will. Any news from your end, Jon?'

'Yes, quite a bit, but I don't want to share it all on the mobile. We know nothing that can hurt you, a lot that will help the GEO.'

'Okay, very intriguing. We will let you know how we are getting on. We are not sure when or how the attempt for the 'big' kidnap will occur.'

'Luis, can you spare me a moment?'

'Yes, John.'

'I have just heard from my contact in the police in Manchester. He has told me they have a certain amount of intel, having searched the flat Brandon Phelan occupies in my block of flats. He says he will let you have the information. When you get it, can you share it with me, please?'

'If I can, John, I will.'

No one went ashore on the first night in Barcelona. Sally had to go and do some shopping, but according to the GEO's advice, she went with an escort, Jose, who doubled as interpreter and bodyguard. He also lugged a whole lot of food and drink back on board. He was glad he had taken the folding trolley. They achieved their task without any concern.

The following day, the urge to explore this city was too great. John and Fiona decided to move off *Brave Goose* and explore the city. Luis was nominated to accompany them.

'Before we leave Barcelona, John and I would like to visit the Olympic Stadium and Gaudi's church. Will that be possible, Luis?'

'Yes, that is no problem. I will let base know where we are going in the morning. Do you want to go the easy way or the hard way?'

'The easy way, please,' requested Fiona.

The following morning John, Fiona and Luis met on the quarterdeck dressed for an excursion around Barcelona.

'Okay, folks, follow me. We just have to walk down the quay.'

'You speak excellent English, Luis.'

'That is probably because I am English. I was in the SAS, moved to Spain, mainly for the weather, and joined GEO. We are heading for that tower on the quay. It takes us to a cable car that will deposit us in Montjuic. John, purchase three one-way tickets from the cabin at the base of the tower.'

They waited for the cable car to return from Montjuic.

Luis, John and Fiona waited to enter the lift, which would descend the tower with passengers from the gondola when it arrived back at the port. Sure enough, the gondola discharged its four passengers who came down to the port in the lift. The three entered the lift. Just as they were shutting the latticework metal door, a man rushed into the lift. It wasn't obvious where he had come from, but he was in the lift. No one spoke. Once the lift reached the top, all four people transferred to the gondola for the cable car ride over the port up to Montjuic and the Olympic stadium.

Usually, John and Fiona would be chatting like mad, pointing out features, in particular the aerial view of *Brave Goose*. No words were exchanged. Who was this lone man?

The gondola began to sway halfway along its journey. It was blown by the wind coming from the east. Fiona held John's hand tightly. She was frightened.

Stepping out at Montjuic, the unknown man rushed out and ran up the road. The unanswered question lingered in the minds of the three from *Brave Goose*. If indeed he had instructions to cause injury, he would have acted in the gondola. Nothing happened.

The three walked up to the Olympic Stadium, which was substantially larger than either John or Fiona had imagined. They walked up to the pinnacle where the Olympic flame burnt for the duration of the games. Once they had experienced the aura of the stadium, all three gradually descended into the heart of Barcelona. Luis was helpful as he knew a great deal about the city and its layout.

'Look from here, you can see Gaudi's La Sagrada Familia, which is still being constructed. The problem is that there were no plans for the church. It was a design in Gaudi's head.'

'It's magnificent. I would love to go inside. Would you like to go, John?'

'Yes, we will get down there in due course. It was on the itinerary for today. We will need to find somewhere for lunch. Do you know of a bar where we could get tapas and a beer, Luis?'

'Yes, let's keep going down the hill. I know of a very traditional tapas bar.'

They all agreed and followed Luis to this most iconic of tapas bars.

The interior walls were covered in colourful ceramic tiles, as was the front of the bar. The bar top, made of marble, was strewn with dishes of the most fantastic tapas Fiona had ever seen. There were, of course, croquettes, the dish by which a tapas bar is measured against its rivals. Anchovies, potato salad, prawns, salad items, squid; far too many items to take in. The patron chose a selection of tapas for each of them. A very dry white wine washed the food down.

A leisurely lunch was interrupted by a man who came in off the street, causing a commotion. He was demanding money from the patron. Luis stayed seated, at least at first. The man was the same man who had been in the cable car earlier.

The conversation was all in Spanish, but mainly Catalan. It transpired that ETA was running a protection racket, and he was the debt collector. Luis excused himself. Fiona was convinced he was going to tackle the man. Instead, he went to the toilet. Luis, now in a secure location, called the base, gave his location and explained what was happening. Police attendance was requested.

The man left without collecting any money but threatened to return. Two armed Guardia Civil officers arrested him. Luis did not want to break cover, as the news would be back to the potential kidnappers in no time.

'There is never a dull moment around here, Luis.'

'No, I suspect that was an act to see if an undercover police officer accompanied you.'

'Don't say anything. The patron may be part of the ETA team.'

'Good thinking.'

'Let's go to the Gaudi church now. It's quite a distance away. I will get a taxi,' said Luis.

'May I have three tickets to visit La Sagrada Familia, please?'

'Yes, sir, that will be seventy-eight euros. You can also make a donation, which will enable you to look around now, rather than waiting to join an official tour in two hours.'

'Okay, here is one hundred euros. Will that allow us in now?'

'Hardly, sir.'

'Okay, here is two hundred euros.'

'Thank you, sir, please go straight in, enjoy your tour. Here are your tickets and complimentary brochure on the church.'

'This is quite awe-inspiring, John. It is a great building. I wonder when they will finish it?'

'Good question. Let me read you the first bit of the brochure. Antoni Gaudi started construction on 19th March 1882. He was given a substantial donation towards the building costs. Rather more than I have donated, I suspect. The gift made Gaudi change his mind from building a gothic revival church to a more innovative temple design. Construction was halted during the Spanish Civil War. Gaudi died in 1926. They think the church will be completed by 2026, one hundred years after Gaudi's death. Pope Benedict XVI consecrated the church in November 2010.'

'Fascinating, John. They will have to get a move on to get it finished by 2026.'

'I agree, Fiona.'

All three left the church after an hour. It was a short visit. It was either that, or they could be there a whole day.

The three returned to *Brave Goose*, where John and Fiona decided to have a siesta on the boat deck before the evening activities began.

15

It was half seven in the morning when John heard movements on board. It sounded as though the team were making ready to depart.

John was curious to find out what the plan was. He bumped into Luis first in the saloon.

'What's the plan today, Luis?'

'The intel we have, John, is that ETA has decided to make a raid at sea, due to the amount of pedestrian traffic, bikes, motorbikes, and cars in this area. There will be bulletproof jackets issued to everyone shortly. It will signal our departure.'

'I assume you anticipate a firefight?'

'Yes, you and Fiona should be safe. They need you to transfer money, and Fiona as their security, to ensure you do as requested. As for the rest of the crew and Goose, they will not worry if they take anyone out, so to be safe, we are issuing the vests.'

'How do you expect they will get on board?'

'I expect a lot of rounds being put into the air and across our bow from a fast speedboat to make us stop.'

'What will be our initial response?'

'Not to stop. We will cause damage to a small craft, but we will not be able to match them for speed.'

'Is it possible for a small powerboat to stop a boat like this?'

'Well, John, the Iranian guard just captured a tanker using a speedboat. *Brave Goose* is much smaller than a tanker. We can't take a chance.'

As they discussed the day's anticipated events, a UPS delivery brought two large parcels. Jose collected them at the end of the passerelle and brought them one by one into the saloon. John picked up the second parcel, thinking he would check the contents; the parcel was very heavy. He checked the other parcel, which was much lighter.

'Why is one package so much heavier than the other, Luis?

'Oh, the heavy one has some additional equipment in it.'

John didn't press the point. He returned to his cabin to explain to Fiona what might happen today.

'Oh, I am terrified, John. Should we remain on board?'

'Yes. We will be safer here. We would be too easy to pick up wandering around Barcelona. Anyway, there is a plan to combat these people if they try anything.'

'Okay, darling, it's not the restful holiday we had expected!'

'No, my love, but if we can stop this nonsense forever, it will be worth doing. Just before we leave, I have this for you.'

John handed Fiona a small jewellery box.

'Oh John, what is this?' For some reason, she thought it might be an engagement ring.

'Open the box and see.'

Fiona did as she was asked and found a beautiful art nouveau-designed gold, diamond and amethyst pendant on a thin gold chain.

'Oh John, this is beautiful. Is it for me?'

'Yes, my darling. I must tell you I bought it for my wife. It came back to me from the police as it was part of her effects they recovered after the car accident. Do you mind wearing it?'

'No, I don't mind, how could I, but should I wear it?'

'Yes, I can't love my wife anymore, but I love you now, so I would be very pleased if you did wear it.'

As they were discussing John's gift, the main engines started. Jose withdrew the passerelle. *Brave Goose* was free of the berth; she began her majestic way through the intricacies of the harbour to finally emerge into the Mediterranean Sea.

'If you look to port along the shoreline a little, a smaller marina is now used mainly by yachts,' said Noel. 'That was part of the infrastructure for the yachting events at the 1992 Olympics.'

'John, can you do the clip for me? I won't be taking this off. It's beautiful. Thank you.' Fiona gave John a hug and a big kiss.

As they neared the exit to the harbour, a Guardia Civil patrol boat was holding station at the entrance. The skipper of the patrol boat gave them a wave as they passed. He was expecting to see them later.

Noel set course for the most northern point of Mallorca, Formentor Head. A speed of nine knots was established, with the throttle levers set to maintain the speed. The autopilot was engaged so that the GPS chart plotter could instruct the helm to change course if required. Noel had the two radar scanners running. The ranges were set, one at thirty nautical miles, the other at five miles. They were allowing long-distance reconnaissance. A boat in the distance should be spotted. At five miles, more detail would be possible.

Noel explained. 'Five miles is roughly the distance to the horizon without any other feature showing. If there were a mountain range, as there is on this side of Mallorca, we would probably see them at about thirty miles distant, assuming good visibility.'

Luis established himself on the flybridge, in a prone position. He had an alarming array of firearms.

John and Fiona had made their way up to the flybridge.

'So those were the 'additional items', Luis?' John enquired.

'Yes, I hope I don't have to use them.'

'So do I,' John confirmed.

At fifteen miles out of Barcelona at ten o'clock, Noel reported the sight of a fast-moving boat dead ahead coming out of Mallorca. It was on a reciprocal bearing and twenty-five miles away. Noel related this to Luis.

Luis came to use the Sailor SSB radio to call the GEO contact in Barcelona. He relayed the information Noel had given.

Shortly after the radio call, a fast-moving boat was identified on the radar on the same course as *Brave Goose*, coming from Barcelona.

'That will be the Guardia patrol boat. Due to the distance apart, the fast-moving boat coming towards us from Mallorca, now twenty miles away, will not be able to see the Guardia patrol boat on their radar, assuming they have one and know how to use it. The two high-speed vessels are thirty-five miles apart. I would be surprised if it could see us. If it is a fast speedboat, it will be lower than us and have limited radar coverage,' advised Luis.

Luis requested Noel to make the pre-arranged announcement.

'All passengers and crew. This is Noel, the captain. Please put on your bulletproof vests immediately. We have a possible engagement with a vessel coming from Mallorca at speed.'

John and Fiona retreated to their cabin, putting the vests on underneath a sweater. The weather was somewhat misty, which had the effect of reducing the temperature.

'Darling, will we be all right?' said Fiona, grasping her new pendant tightly in her hand.

'Yes, my love.' Realising Fiona was in tears, he held her tight. She was shaking with fear. 'You must be strong. We can get through this.'

'You forget I have been kidnapped once. It was terrifying. I don't want to be kidnapped again.'

'I know. Please be calm and strong. We are together, that is the main thing. These people will be caught, I am confident.'

They both moved out onto the quarterdeck. Fiona was gripping John's hand so hard it went white. Her other hand was still grasping the pendant. John eased her pressure slightly on his hand with his other hand.

'Don't leave me, John!'

'No, I promise. Let's watch what happens. Luis will shoot at them if necessary.'

As time went by, John and Fiona knew that when the Mallorcan boat was close, they would retire to their cabin. Until then, they were on the bridge with Noel and Goose. All four of them were watching the radar screens intently.

The engine noise had masked the whirring of helicopter blades above and to the south of their position. It was hardly visible in the mist. If they had been able to see it, they would have seen the word POLICE written large on the helicopter's side.

An hour after the first sighting of the Mallorcan speedboat, it was now about four miles away. The Guardia patrol boat had slowed and remained at five miles distant and on the northern side of *Brave Goose*'s track.

Luis had repositioned himself to make a shot in a more forward direction. This meant he had to position himself on the side deck of the flybridge to starboard by the control binnacle on the boat deck. The two boats should pass as dictated by international regulations at sea. The oncoming vessel, being the faster, should move to starboard so that the boats would pass port-to-port. Noel made a slight adjustment to the course of *Brave Goose* to starboard in case the oncoming vessel did not do what was required.

Two miles apart now. John and Fiona were peeping through the porthole in their cabin to see what was happening as best they could. Goose was doing the same from the safety of his cabin. Only Noel remained in full sight, remaining on the bridge in complete control of *Brave Goose*.

Noel picked up the VHF microphone and altered the frequency to Channel 16.

'Vessel on my bow on course for Barcelona, please alter course to starboard.'

There was no reply.

Jose appeared on the bridge and suggested he make the announcement again in Spanish. He did and then passed the microphone back to Noel. The oncoming boat had not reduced speed and was on a collision course for *Brave Goose*.

Noel reckoned it was less than a mile away, so he increased speed to twelve knots and altered course by forty degrees to starboard. *Brave Goose* swung round and leaned about twenty degrees to port. Luis was holding on as the boat tipped.

'Sorry, Sally,' said Noel as a screech came from the galley.

The speedboat was now very close. If anyone thought to look, the helicopter was much lower now and filming the incident.

Noel sounded the ship's horn five times; the international signal for 'your intentions are not clear'.

The large speedboat could now be identified as a Sunseeker, probably forty-five feet in length. They were not flying any flags, so the country of origin was unclear. Noel's manoeuvre of *Brave Goose* presented the rear port quarter of *Brave Goose* to the Sunseeker, which had not slowed down. At the last minute, the Sunseeker altered course, avoiding *Brave Goose* by about a metre. It splashed through the large wash that *Brave Goose* was making, causing the Sunseeker to take on a large amount of water. It now slowed to a virtual stop, although it still had some movement as it had been travelling so fast. Noel brought *Brave Goose* to a halt.

As he did so, there was a great deal of shouting and swearing coming from the Sunseeker.

The Guardia Civil patrol boat joined the collection of vessels and came alongside the Sunseeker. Two police officers boarded the Sunseeker. At that moment, the shouting and swearing stopped.

The helicopter did a circuit of the scene and travelled back towards Barcelona.

Luis was now on the bridge. The Sailor radio burst into life. Luis picked up the handset to receive the message.

'All clear, you can all relax. The man is a novice boat owner who recently purchased the boat from Sunseeker in Cala Dor. He had not been keeping watch. He had been below with his girlfriend!'

'I hope he gets into trouble and sent on a training course,' remarked Noel.

'Yes, here in Spain, he will probably have the boat confiscated until he gets qualified,' remarked Luis.

'Good,' responded Noel. 'That should happen to all idiots who think they can drive boats.'

Noel obtained clearance to continue their trip to Mallorca. Everyone breathed a sigh of relief. Everyone removed their bulletproof vests. The trip continued.

***

'Brandon, it's Diego.'

'Hi, how are you doing?'

'Well, we have discovered that they are extremely well protected. I suspect an armed GEO officer on board *Brave Goose*, plus a helicopter, and Guardia Civil patrol.'

'The exercise was worth it. What is the plan now?'

'Well, we have successfully executed the first part of the plan. *Brave Goose* continues on its course for Formentor Head. We assume the destination is Puerto Pollenca. They will be relaxed, believing the attack was repelled. We have the second phase already in progress. A larger fishing boat is laying a two-mile-long shallow floating net across the sea. It covers the course being sailed by *Brave Goose*. The net is ten miles from Formentor. They are bound to pick up the net in their propellers and grind to a stop. We will move in then.'

'Well done, Diego. Will you take John and Fiona to the finca?'

'Yes, it's all arranged; we have a van waiting at Puerto Soller on the disused naval quay.'

***

Sally brought a plate of biscuits to the quarterdeck and flasks of tea and coffee. Goose invited Jock, Jose, Sally and Noel to come and join in the snack.

'When we get to Pollenca, I guess we will get a visit from the Guardia and discover what was going on with the speedboat. I don't think it was anything to do with the suspected attack on us,' said Noel.

Goose was circumspect as he was sure they were still in the firing line.

'Oh Goose, I hope not. This holiday is going all wrong due to us being on board.'

'Hey, don't worry, we can deal with this. I need you to be strong,' said Goose.

'The opposite is the case,' replied Fiona.

'I have two pizzas ready for the oven. I used to have a salad, but Noel's manoeuvres put that on the floor,' announced Sally. 'Will that be all right for everyone?'

A chorus of 'yes' came straight back.

Noel returned to the bridge. Luis returned his machine gun to his cabin.

The sun had broken through the misty cloud. The temperature was rising. The sea was like glass. Noel repositioned himself to the flybridge, which gave him a better view of the sea ahead. He always had his high-powered binoculars with him, scanning the sea from side to side. He could see a small buoy with a flag to the south. To the north, there was a fishing boat. Noel realised that there could be a mile or so of fishing net down, but they usually sat two or three metres above the seabed. The fishing boats were like a spider waiting for a fly to hit the web. The spider would then pounce on the fly. As they were in an area where the sea depth was over seven hundred metres, he saw no problem if they did motor over the net. It would be so far below the boat as to cause no issue.

There were surprisingly no other boats visible. Noel checked the AIS system, which gave details of ships and larger boats like *Brave Goose*. The only vessel with AIS running was the Barcelona to Palma ferry, well north of their position.

Noel began to feel relaxed. They had successfully overcome the attempt by the speedboat to collide with them. He didn't anticipate any further issues.

No sooner had he begun to relax, than *Brave Goose* juddered to a halt. Noel immediately put the engines into neutral to avoid damaging the gearbox. What had the boat picked up in the propellers?

Everyone on board eventually arrived at the stern or on the rails to port and starboard. It didn't take long to work out. It was a large fishing net.

'My God,' said Noel, 'that will take some fixing.'

'Is it a diving job, Noel?' enquired Goose.

'No, Goose, we have equipment on board to deal with this. I will get Jose to join Jock to access the propellers inside the boat. If I say, we will lift some plates which give us access – you might imagine we would sink. Before my time, the previous owner had installed two square inspection tubes. These are welded to the hull. There are two openings over each propeller. There are sealed covers on each tube, one at the top and another as we open the hull over the propellers. We can open both and turn on the underwater lights which light the propellers. With special knives on poles, we can cut away the nets. No water enters the boat except for a few splashes with the knives.'

When Goose and Noel arrived in the engine room, Jock and Jose cut the net away. They could work on both propellers at the same time.

'That is very clever, Noel. A feature I didn't know we had.'

'Yes, Goose, we have had to use them on a few occasions. There is, I regret to say, so much rubbish in the sea, especially the Mediterranean.'

On returning to the deck, leaving Jose and Jock to their work, Noel noticed the fishing boat was considerably closer and steaming their way. Was the spider coming to eat the fly?

'Luis, can you call on the SSB radio? I think this may be the real attempt to board us. I suspect the speedboat made us feel relaxed once dealt with. It worked!'

Luis gave *Brave Goose*'s position. The fishing boat was too far away to identify.

Within ten minutes of the call to GEO, the fishing boat was in hailing distance of *Brave Goose*. It had slowed.

There was a fisherman on the bow, shouting and screaming that they had damaged his nets, or so Noel assumed.

Noel, who was not a Spanish speaker, couldn't solve his problem. The problem was on *Brave Goose*. Realising the fishing boat was proposing to come alongside, Noel ran and placed as many fenders as he could to cushion the blow from the side of the fishing boat, which, looking at the state of the vessel, had no concerns about crashing into the side of *Brave Goose*.

As soon as he was alongside, a man jumped onto *Brave Goose* holding the bow line of the fishing boat. He made fast to *Brave Goose*. He then ran to the stern and caught the fishing boat's stern line.

Two men appeared on deck holding shotguns as soon as they were tied up alongside. They jumped onto *Brave Goose*. The first man on board pulled a pistol from his trouser pocket. One of the shotgun men spoke in English.

'Hey, all the crew go below to the engine room.' He insisted that Noel and Sally go below.

Picking up a long-handled deck scrubbing brush, the shotgun man wedged the door to the engine room shut.

'Which one is Goose?'

John, and in particular, Fiona, was terrified. She was holding John's hand and her pendant; once again, her grip on John was so tight her hand turned white.

'This is very ugly, John.' Fiona still held John's hand tightly. She didn't want to let go.

'I guess you are Goose?' said the armed fisherman. 'They said you were small and bald with a piggy face and round glasses. You are the man who killed Niall Phelan.'

'No, I didn't kill him,' a very frightened Goose spluttered out.

The man with the shotgun motioned the first man on board with the pistol behind Goose. Nothing was said. The pistol man shot Goose twice, once to the back of each leg.

Goose crumpled in a heap on the deck, crying out in severe pain. Blood started to flood the clean deck.

'Hey,' the boss with the shotgun said, 'it was what we learned from the IRA, kneecapping. Good hey?' he laughed.

Luis, who was on the port side deck keeping low, shot the pistol man in the back. Two shots saw the end of the man. Immediately the boss opened fire on Luis straight to his head. Luis was killed instantly.

Fiona was screaming and crying all at once. She had never witnessed anything like this.

'God, stop, stop, you are murderers. Stop it now,' she screamed.

The man with the shotgun shouted at John and Fiona. 'Get on the fishing boat, now.'

They did as instructed. It wasn't easy. They had to climb over the rail of *Brave Goose* and then drop onto the untidy deck of the fishing boat.

'Let me catch you, darling, the landing on this side is not good.'

Fiona landed on the fishing boat, clutching John with all her might.

Once on board, the boss joined them.

'Now one after the other go down the ladder to the hold, NOW!' he shouted. Fiona screamed at his instruction.

Another man already in the hold grabbed Fiona as she came down, hitting her hard with a cosh on the back of the head. She crumpled like a puppet whose strings had been cut.

John followed. He suffered the same fate while his hands were still holding the ladder. He fell the last three steps onto the floor of the hold.

The crew member in the hold tied their hands together in front of them. He covered their faces and noses with a cloth soaked in chloroform.

The fish hold man climbed up the steps and closed the hatch. Jumping onto *Brave Goose*, he took the place of the dead pistol man. He collected the pistol from the dead man's hand and kicked Goose as he went past. Goose was groaning, near passing out with the massive blood loss and extreme pain.

The fishing boat was untied. It set off in a northerly direction, with John and Fiona on board.

'They have gone,' said Noel. 'We have to get out of here.' Only he found the door to the engine room was jammed shut.

'Let me see if I can open it.' said Jock. His immense size and weight smashed the handle of the deck scrub in one go. They were all able to escape. Then they saw Goose. He was in a terrible state. Sally rushed for the big first aid kit and tried to help him become more comfortable.

'Jose, can you help me, please? I need to lie Goose down on his back. Here, put this mask on his face and hold it there.' Sally turned the tap on the small bottle of Entonox. 'That should help with the pain.'

Sally couldn't do anything about the bullet holes in Goose's legs, but she could try and stop the bleeding. Using a crepe bandage, she made two tourniquets, one for each leg, which helped stem the bleeding. Sally then dressed the entry and exit wounds caused by a bullet in each leg. It was only then that she noticed that the shots had embedded themselves into the teak deck, having passed through Goose's legs.

A JOHN ENGLAND STORY

'Have we released the fishing net, Jose?'

'Yes, Noel, we had just finished it when the fishing boat arrived. The quick action of going to neutral avoided a very tight twist of the net on the propeller and the shaft.'

Noel was on the SSB radio to GEO. He explained what had just happened, including Luis being shot in the face with a shotgun.

'Yes, I am afraid he is dead.'

The officer taking the call at GEO was furious.

'I will launch a major operation to find your friends and also get the people responsible for killing my man.'

'Well, Luis managed to kill one of their men, who is dead on the deck.'

'I will helicopter some operatives to you now. We shall recover your friend who is injured and to take him to hospital. We will also drop body bags for the two dead. We will collect them later. Two operatives will be with you and will stay with you until this is over.'

Noel thanked the officer.

Noel was considering what to do. Next, he decided to see if *Brave Goose* could move. She did. He backed her off the area of the fishing net.

'Sally, how are you managing with Goose?'

'Noel, it's not good, and we have two bullets in the deck.'

'Don't worry about the boat. It can be fixed. Might I suggest you elevate his legs, give him some cover with a blanket?'

'Two good suggestions, Noel, thanks.'

'I am returning to our course to Mallorca and Puerto Pollenca,' Noel notified GEO. He radioed the Spanish coastguard with his position, a message that was also picked up by the helicopter.

Brave Goose was able to make speed; nine knots was quickly established.

'Jock, is everything okay with you?'

'Yes, boss, I want to close the inspection hatches. Can you stop, please?'

'Yes, will do.' Noel brought the engines to neutral, stopping the boat within a few minutes. Jock then was able to close the bottom and then the top hatches.

'Sally, there will be a helicopter recovery of Goose, quite soon, they will get him to hospital. There will also be two GEO operatives joining us, who will put both dead men into body bags which will be recovered later.'

'That's good, Noel. Is there any action on finding John and Fiona?'

The radio burst into life, which required Noel to deal with it. Sally had brought a blanket to cover Goose and a pillow for his head. She had put both legs in inflatable splints and taped them together. She lifted them onto two of the large pillows from the saloon.

'Can you hear me, Goose?'

'Yes, Sally.'

'How do you feel now?'

'Much better, the pain has nearly gone.'

'Good, you will be taken by helicopter to hospital.'

Goose just gave a weak smile, which thanked Sally for all her work.

'Brave Goose,' Noel replied.

'Were you able to see which direction the fishing boat

went when it left you with John and Fiona on board?'

'Yes, it went north. I would expect that it may go to Puerto Soller. The disused naval base there would be ideal for transferring the people to a van.'

'Okay, thanks.' The GEO officer switched off the radio.

***

At the Barcelona base, the senior officer of GEO, Juan Mateo, who had visited *Brave Goose* when she was last in Barcelona, was putting various actions into effect. The helicopter rescue was the first to be actioned. It was already in the air. The second action was to alert the Guardia and Policia Local to the imminent berthing of a fishing boat, to offload two kidnap victims in Puerto Soller. The police had to be very careful as the vessel crew was armed. They had already killed one GEO officer.

The third item for GEO to attend to was to alert the coastal patrol north of Mallorca and south of the fishing boat. It was to be intercepted with caution.

Mateo called Noel on *Brave Goose* again to alert Noel to his actions. The two GEO officers would be on the second visit of the helicopter.

***

'Brandon, just to let you know, we have successfully caught John and Fiona, your hostages. Shortly, they will be transferred to the finca. We will be offloading the 'cargo' in Soller using the disused naval quay.'

Brandon just acknowledged the call. As he was close to Soller, he decided to go to the port, sit in a café opposite the naval quay, and watch the action.

After an hour, the fishing boat appeared at the entrance to the harbour. As always, there were numerous yachts and boats anchored throughout the horseshoe-shaped bay of Soller.

Slowly the fishing boat turned, making fast to the quay of the now-abandoned naval base. A white van was on the quay. It altered its location to be alongside the fishing boat.

'Okay, guys, get the two up here quickly. Just one at a time.'

'Alvero, we can't wake them.'

'We will have to lift them out.'

'I don't think we will get them up the steps; we will have to use the winch.'

'Okay, just get on with it,' Alvero shouted. 'We have been here far too long.'

Two of the deckhands opened the main hatches to the fish hold and swung the crane's arm over the hatch opening, lowering the hook and chain to the base of the fish hold.

'We need a sling, Alvero. We can't put a chain around them. It could kill them.'

Alvero was swearing his mouth off. He kicked a tarpaulin down the fish hold, telling them to secure the first body in it.

Fiona was the first choice as she would be lighter. She was wrapped in the tarpaulin. The hook was put through holes made for rope ties in the canvas. The ends of this now canvas tube were made secure with rope closing each end.

'Okay, Alvero, hoist away.'

The driver of the white van opened the side sliding door, ready for the cargo to be loaded directly into the van by the crane. Once inside, the canvas was untied, and Fiona was rolled out unceremoniously onto the van's metal floor. She was still unconscious. The chloroform was still working.

The crane was repositioned over the fish hold. The process was about to be repeated.

'Stop! Put up your hands!'

The van and the access to the naval dockyard were suddenly swarming with police. Guardia and Policia Local. The van driver was the first to be apprehended, and cuffs were placed on his hands. The police took him to their van and locked him inside.

Tourists nearby and on yachts moored in the harbour suddenly realised a major police operation was underway. Two ambulances arrived on the quay. One of the paramedics went to treat Fiona. She was still unconscious and removed from the white van on a stretcher. The ambulance sped away under blue lights and a siren.

The siren brought the attention of the whole port to the activities on the old naval quay.

Armed police had boarded the fishing boat and arrested Alvero and the two deckhands in the hold. They were pushed and shoved up the ladder out of the hold. They were all cuffed and taken to the police van, which departed at speed under escort and blue lights and sirens.

Every boat in the harbour had people on deck watching as John was placed on a stretcher. The police used the fishing boat's hoist to lift him out of the hold. He was moved to the next ambulance and followed Fiona out of the port to the hospital.

The excitement at the naval quay created quite a buzz amongst the tourists. It was the main topic of conversation for the day, except for one man. Brandon Phelan realised that his efforts had failed. He might as well return to Manchester and decide what other plan he could contrive to extract the money from John England.

***

On board *Brave Goose*, a helicopter was just arriving. A man was lowered onto the foredeck of *Brave Goose*, together with a stretcher.

As soon as he had unclipped himself from the high line and removed the tether for the stretcher, Noel and Jose went forward to greet him and bring the stretcher to the quarterdeck.

'Where is the patient?' enquired the medic.

'Follow me. Jose, bring the stretcher. He has been on Entonox, and the stewardess, Sally, has placed tourniquets on his legs, packed the bullet wounds and placed his legs in splints.'

The medic introduced himself to Sally. 'You have done an excellent job here, Sally. We will get him straight to the hospital. What's his name?'

'The name he likes is 'Goose'; however, his real name is Julian Lenwell. He is a British citizen. I am afraid I cannot get his passport, as only he knows the combination to his safe.'

'What is the gas he is breathing, Sally?'

'Entonox, we carry several bits of first aid, including a defibrillator.'

'That is excellent, Sally; let's get him to the foredeck. When the helicopter is called in, Noel...'

'Yes, I know, you would like me to steam into the wind?'

'Have you done this before?'

'No, thank goodness, but I have trained for these scenarios.'

'I can see why you two were chosen to crew this charming motor yacht.'

'Thanks. Are you ready to call the chopper in?'

'Yes, Noel. We will come back to this location to collect the two bodies. Can you put a label on each while we are away? We need to know who is in the bag.'

That was all agreed. Noel got *Brave Goose* underway to allow the helicopter to hover over the foredeck and lift Goose to the hospital.

'Now, folks,' Noel addressed the crew, 'I have been wondering what to do next.' No sooner had he said that than a Guardia Civil coastal patrol boat hove into view, coming from Barcelona.

The patrol boat came alongside. Noel throttled back to a stop. The commander of the police vessel spoke to Noel.

'Hi, are you the vessel that was stormed earlier?'

'Yes, we are, be careful about moving on this course towards Formentor. We caught a two-mile-long fishing net set on the surface. That is how they stopped us.'

'Good, we are here to collect the net. Are you all okay?'

'Yes, we are waiting for the chopper to return. We have two dead bodies in body bags to be sent back to Barcelona. I am afraid one was an officer of GEO.'

'I can take them, if you prefer?'

'I do prefer; can you advise the authorities you have them?'

'Yes, certainly. What is your next destination?'

'I think we will be going to Puerto Pollenca for twenty-four hours. Hopefully, we will be reunited with the two guests, kidnapped and rescued by the police in Soller, by all accounts.'

'Okay, and after that?'

'I will go back to Barcelona, as the owner was taken there by helicopter a little while ago, for treatment to two gunshot wounds. We will be in the best place to visit him if nothing else.'

'How did you know what happened in Soller?'

'I spoke with GEO, who called me to say the guests were safe and recuperating in a hospital in Mallorca. They also told me that the kidnappers had all been arrested.'

Jose and Jock were tasked to place the fenders on the starboard side to allow the patrol boat to come close alongside. Jock and Jose carried the body bags to the patrol boat and handed them over one by one.

'Before you proceed, let us pull part of the net away so you will have safe passage.'

They all thanked one another. The patrol boat removed a large net section, allowing *Brave Goose* to continue to Formentor and Puerto Pollenca.

Noel called Real Club Nautico Puerto Pollenca and requested a mooring for two days. He gave the details of *Brave Goose*. After a brief pause, the helpful lady on the other end enquired if they were the boat that had been attacked today.

'Yes, how on earth did you know about that?'

'It's been on TV news all afternoon. Yes, you certainly can have a berth. You have been through enough today. Would you like me to reserve a table for you in the restaurant?'

That was all agreed. Jock and Jose removed the chairs off the quarterdeck and closed the saloon doors. They then started to hose down all the bloodstains on the deck. They couldn't use the deck scrub, so Jock cut the stub of the handle off and used the head as a scrubbing brush.

Sally put away all the first aid kits, noting what had been used, as she would order more supplies.

They berthed in Puerto Pollenca at five-thirty in the afternoon. They all agreed they didn't want another day like that. The passerelle had been extended and the paperwork completed. Noel went to the office to pay a two-day mooring fee. The payment was refused.

'Pay us when you leave.'

Brave Goose was the largest boat in the harbour.

16

Brandon was back at Peters Tower by mid-morning two days later.

'Morning, Sydney.' Sydney gave the nod. He was busy sorting out the mail.

'Mr Phelan,' said Sydney, 'there is some mail here for you and a parcel. We keep them under the desk here.'

Sydney handed the post and the parcel to Phelan, who already had a few letters from his box.

'Thank you, Sydney.' Phelan took the lift to the eighth floor.

Once inside the flat, he couldn't wait to open the parcel, a wrapped box, without printing outside. It had been posted in Northern Ireland. There were no customs checks on that postal route. That was clear from the stamp. Once he had fought his way through layers of bubble wrap and the final layer of a greaseproof paper-type wrapping, he was delighted to find what he had expected.

The gun fell easily into his hand. A new Smith & Wesson MP380 with an eight-round cartridge. It was precisely what he had requested. There were fifty rounds in a small box and a shoulder holster. He was delighted with the gun. He couldn't wait to put it into action.

***

'Jon Kim?'

'Yes, who is this?'

'Juan Mateo from the GEO in Barcelona. I thought you would like to know what has been happening here.'

'Oh yes, I would, carry on.'

Mateo set about telling Kim all the details of the attempt to kidnap John and Fiona, the kneecapping of Goose and the arrest of all the operatives involved in the attempt.

'Are John and Fiona safe now?'

'Yes, they are. They had been chloroformed and went to the hospital to recover. I guess they will be released sometime today.'

'Thanks, Juan. I am sorry you lost a man. I expect I will hear from John in due course.'

There was a knock on Kim's office door at GMP. A constable was carrying a brown envelope which was for Jon.

Jon was not used to receiving internal mail. He was keen to open it. It was a document in a folder headed 'SECRET'. He was even more curious now.

HM Customs had intercepted a parcel addressed to Brandon Phelan, whose address was given as Apt. 803,

Peters Tower, Manchester. The complete message read:

HM Customs at the postal service of Northern Ireland have intercepted a parcel addressed to Brandon Phelan. On investigation and X-ray analysis, the package contained a Smith and Wesson handgun with a capacity of eight rounds. It is a semi-automatic gun. With it came fifty rounds of ammunition. We have exchanged the rounds for blanks with the same visual appearance as the live ammunition.

Jon was concerned with this development. Grateful, of course, to HM Customs, but what to tell John was the issue. It was apparent to Jon that following the failure to kidnap the pair in Spain, a further attempt had to be made to recover the three million, which Phelan believed was rightly his family's inheritance from Niall Phelan.

Jon was confident that as soon as John and Fiona arrived back, an attempt to meet with John would be made as quickly as Brandon could arrange it. Jon was sure Phelan would try and get the funds transferred by John at the point of a gun. Strangely there would be no point in killing John as, without him, the transfer could not be made. Fiona was the person at most at risk. If Fiona didn't turn up, there would be no opportunity to hold her hostage while John was sent to his bank to sign forms to transfer the money.

Given the trauma the two had experienced in Spain, Jon would not reveal the plan to get the money from John. Jon would have worked out a plan to foil Brandon Phelan on their return.

***

On *Brave Goose*, there was a lot of cleaning and further deck washing going on. Noel had found a carpenter to come and repair the varnished timber surround to the frame surrounding the doors to the saloon and making good the teak deck where the bullets had embedded themselves. Several lead pellets had penetrated the wood and split timber shards from the edge. Sally had taken the opportunity to visit the shops in Puerto Pollenca. She was fortunate to find a small supermarket in the back streets of the town that would deliver all her purchases at no charge.

Wow, she thought, *that is a great help.* Her list was long and heavy. She decided to buy far more than she had written on her list. The delivery made all the difference. Cases of bottled water and several cases of wine were on Sally's list. She needed quantities of food, flour for baking, some spices and fresh bread, which the supermarket offered to deliver fresh each morning. *Brave Goose* was in port.

'Hello, I'm back.' Her shopping trolley was empty.

'Did you hit a problem? You haven't bought anything.'

'Ah, that's where you are wrong, Noel. You will see in a moment. There will have to be a chain gang to get all the shopping on board.'

A small red van arrived at the barrier with the supermarket's name emblazoned on the side. It was allowed through by the security guard. They were permitted onto the quay, as they were provisioning *Brave Goose*.

Noel inspected the van's contents and asked the driver which boxes were for *Brave Goose*.

'All, senor. Your lady was an excellent customer.'

Noel called Jose and Jock. The supermarket had sent two people: the driver and an assistant. The four men started to unload the van and placed all the shopping on the quarterdeck.

'Blimey Sally, you certainly have managed to replace and restock. Are you expecting to be on board for some time?'

'Yes, Noel. I have also bought additional wine and a bottle of Carlos Primera. It is surprising with three people the amount of food and wine needed and the four of us, seven people. A lot of food and drink is required.'

Noel gave the driver and his mate a five-euro note each to say thank you. There was now the issue of storing everything. Sally took all the frozen stuff first and placed it in the freezer, then the cold items for the fridge. Noel took the wine and brandy to the wine rack in the saloon. White wine was placed in the wine cooler in the saloon.

Noel was just finishing loading the wine racks when his mobile went off.

'Hello, Noel speaking.'

'Noel, it's GEO in Barcelona. I have been asked to ring you to ask where you are. John and Fiona are about to be released by Palma hospital. They need a taxi to wherever you are.'

'We are on the visitors' quay in Puerto Pollenca. We are looking forward to seeing them. Have you any news of Goose? We thought we would return to Barcelona tomorrow to be close by when he is released from the hospital.'

'Sorry, I don't know, but I will ring them for you and call back.'

'Listen up, everyone. I think John and Fiona will be back with us in about an hour or so. They are being released from the hospital now.'

Everyone on board was delighted. A final push to stock the boat and a final clean round was undertaken. Sally went back to the shops, returning in twenty minutes with an armful of flowers.

'These are spectacular, Sally. What a great idea. Will you put some in their cabin as well?'

'I will, Noel. Some for the quarterdeck, some for the saloon, and their cabin. Just to brighten the place up after the terrible events of a few days ago.'

'Sally, I think we should take the opportunity to dine onshore. Let's book a six-person table in the restaurant, say eight o'clock. I will go and do that now.'

'Okay, Noel, I don't have any food that will be wasted. I guess John and Fiona might like to spend tomorrow at anchor so that they can swim. How about Formentor Bay?'

'Great idea, the day after we can go to Barcelona. I will book that when I have spoken to John and Fiona.'

Noel went to the yacht club to book a table in the restaurant for six people at eight-thirty.

Noel was back in twenty minutes.

'Look, folks, let's put on a show for John and Fiona. Can we all dress in khaki shorts and *Brave Goose* polo shirts, the white ones? We will all look smart, I am sure, and they will appreciate our effort.'

Twenty minutes later, a white Palma taxi arrived at the foot of the passerelle. John and Fiona got out.

'Hello everyone,' called John. 'Noel, could you please pay for the taxi? I don't have any cash on me.'

'Certainly, John.' Noel went to the quay and paid the taxi with a tip.

Fiona walked up the passerelle to the quarterdeck, bursting into tears when she saw everyone looking so smart and the place all clean and sparkling with fresh flowers. Fiona embraced Sally.

'Thank you, thank you, you are all wonderful people.'

John and Noel joined everyone on deck.

'What would you like most?' enquired Noel.

'A shower and a change of clothes.'

'If you let me have all your clothes, I will wash and iron them for you.'

'You are so kind, Sally.'

The two went to their cabin, showered, and dressed in fresh shorts and T-shirts.

'John, you are wonderful. I hope the police make sure the kidnappers and murderers get their just desserts.'

'Yes, darling, we need to put all that behind us. Let's try and forget it and look forward to more fun on *Brave Goose*. We also need to go and see Goose. He must be in a bad way.'

'Yes, John, you are right. I am worried about Goose. He may never walk again.'

'Well, don't let's get too far ahead of ourselves. We should try to go and see him. I guess he would have been taken to Barcelona, which is where I imagine a helicopter would have come from.'

'Hello, you two, it's great to have you back. Have you had anything to eat so far today?'

'Thanks, Sally, we had a very light breakfast and were then released.'

'So, would you like some lunch?'

'Yes, I would. I am hungry,' said John.

'Me too,' added Fiona.

'I have some fresh ham; I can do an omelette, tortilla as it's known here, with a salad and fresh bread? Maybe some white wine or a beer to wash it down? There is also fresh fruit for pudding.'

'That sounds wonderful. Have you any cheese, as I would like a ham and cheese omelette?' replied John.

'I would go along with that, Sally. It sounds wonderful. Will everyone join us? We have so much to learn and to tell you.'

After a very excellent lunch and a glass of cold white wine, the conversation continued, with each side learning of the problems that occurred to the other.

'We were anaesthetised with rather too much chloroform, which made it difficult for the kidnappers to get us out of the fish hold, which is where we were kept until we arrived in Puerto Soller. We understand from the ambulance crew, who eventually came to our rescue with the police, that we had been wrapped in tarpaulin and hoisted up through the deck hatch by the crane that usually lifts boxes of fish.'

'That all sounds too extreme. Poor old Goose is in a hospital in Barcelona. We thought we would spend a day or two here to suit you; one of the days before we go to Barcelona, we could be at anchor so you can swim off the boat. There is a lovely swimming pool by the clubhouse if you feel like a swim. Possibly tomorrow. I have booked a table for us all in the restaurant at eight-thirty. It's to thank the crew for all the extra work they have done in the last day or two. I hope that plan is okay?'

'Sounds great to me, Noel. How about you, darling?'

'Anything that is serene and relaxing, I am with you all the way.'

'That's good, thanks, Fiona. We will try to make it as serene as we can. The plan when we leave here is to go back to Barcelona. You or we can visit Goose. He will be getting fed up being in a hospital about now, I suspect.'

'I think you are right, Noel. He may have to be in a wheelchair for a while. My thought is how can we get him on board with the wheelchair,' John commented.

'Yes, that has crossed my mind. I am not sure a wheelchair will fit up the passerelle. We could rig up a hoist to get him onto the quarterdeck, and then he is virtually free to get around.'

'The choice of the wheelchair will be important. I assume the deck crane is in your mind for the hoist. Will it feed down here?'

'Yes, John, I think it will. We can test it before we leave.'

'Good idea. I think I will join Fiona on the boat deck for a sunbathe and a snooze.'

All the crew decided to have a rest. It had been a very stressful twenty-four hours.

***

Juan Mateo phoned Jon Kim as he had some news for him.

'Jon, my sources have advised me that a man known to my intelligence team is currently using the name, Brandon Phelan. His current address is Peters Tower in Manchester. We are sure he was the mastermind behind the recent abduction of John and Fiona.'

'Thanks for that, Juan. Yes, we know of him, but we have so far been unable to connect him directly with anything.'

'One of our observers saw him in a café at Puerto Soller, watching as the bodies were hoisted from the fishing boat and placed into a van. It was at that point we swooped and got everyone involved. At that moment, he left Soller. Most tourists stopped and watched; that's what they do. He was conspicuous by his absence, you might say.'

'What is fascinating is that Phelan is a tenant of one of the flats in the block John England owns. John lives in the penthouse apartment. I suspect Phelan moved in there to be close to his target. It's tough to work out what he might do next. We have an idea, but there is nothing for Phelan to do now in Spain.'

'Jon, if we hear of anything, we will, of course, let you know. The people we have in custody are murderers. They killed one of my operatives. They have been charged and are expected to appear before the court for a preliminary hearing within a week.'

'Thanks, Juan. I will mount surveillance activity when Phelan returns to the UK. If we discover anything that might be of interest to you, I assure you I will let you know.'

When Jon had finished the call, he called the deputy chief constable to fix a meeting. Jon needed to set up surveillance on Brandon Phelan, starting as soon as he set foot in the UK.

***

The following day on *Brave Goose*, all was set, ready to return to Barcelona.

'John, I don't feel very well,' announced Fiona while sunbathing on the boat deck.

'Oh, darling, what is the problem?'

'I have a headache which won't go. On occasions, I feel sick and light-headed.'

'Do you want to go straight to Barcelona? You could see a doctor there?' suggested John.

'I don't think I need to see a doctor. It's all the issues we have suffered while we have been here. It has been mostly marvellous, but the two kidnap attempts have been horrific. I can still taste the chloroform in my mouth.'

'It could be the chloroform that is giving you the headaches. I had a bad head soon after we were doped and all of yesterday. Don't forget we also had a bash on the head.'

'Yes, I am sure you are right, John.'

'Some relaxation is what is required. Sunbathing here will help.'

'John, Fiona, sorry to interrupt, but as we are all set, we thought we would have a day sail to Barcelona. We will set off within the hour, if that's okay with you?'

'Yes, Noel, that's fine by us. What time do you expect we shall be back in Barcelona?'

'Well, it's two o'clock now, so if we are away by three, we will be in Barcelona by about six or seven in the morning. I propose going slowly. We will be very economical at about eight knots.'

'Let's go, and we will stay here if that's okay, Noel?'

The crew of *Brave Goose* burst into life with Sally clearing up after lunch and ensuring everything was stowed safely. Jock and Jose went about their standard procedures, making ready for the departure. Noel went to the yacht club office to pay the mooring fees.

At three-thirty in the afternoon, *Brave Goose* slipped her mooring on the quay of the yacht club in Puerto Pollenca. It was a quiet afternoon, with very little wind, bright sunshine, and light clouds. The initial course took *Brave Goose* around the headland, forming the enclosed area for the port of Puerto Pollenca, then onwards to the Formentor headland.

Sailing along the Formentor headland, Noel pointed out the black-coloured birds soaring overhead. 'Those are Eleonora's Falcons. They are very rare, and there is a colony of them on Formentor Head.'

John and Fiona were fascinated by these majestic birds, hardly flapping their wings. A unique sight. Once they had locked onto the birds, they both lay back to observe them from the horizontal sunbeds.

'This is just the boost we needed, John. I love nature. These birds look prehistoric.'

'You are right, my love. They do look exceptional. I don't suppose they will come anywhere near us.'

The two sunbathers said little as *Brave Goose* rounded Formentor head and made a course directly towards Barcelona. It wasn't long before both were asleep.

***

Brandon Phelan arrived at Manchester airport at ten o'clock in the evening. He was surprised that he was asked to wait at the Border Force counter as the officer took his passport into an office behind his desk. He was held waiting for what seemed ages – ten minutes. The officer returned to the desk without Brandon's passport.

'Sorry to keep you waiting, sir, we are just completing some additional checks. Come through the gate and wait in one of the chairs over there.' He indicated towards a row of low unoccupied chairs.

'Yes, I have things to do. I don't want to wait here all night.'

The officer smiled a thin, disingenuous smile. He returned to checking passports for those passengers who had been waiting in the queue. The officer knew quite well what was happening. The passport Brandon was travelling on was a fraudulent one. Brandon knew that, but so far, he had escaped detection.

'Looks like the UK are more efficient than I had given them credit for,' he muttered to himself. Half an hour passed. Another officer came out of the office, requiring Brandon to accompany him to an interview room.

'Mr Phelan, this is your passport. Can you confirm that, and the details it contains are correct?'

'Yes, it is my passport. If the details are incorrect, it will only be my address, as I have recently moved to Manchester from Ireland where I was working for a while. Why, what is the matter?'

'We do random checks, sir, on passports to ensure we can reduce the number of fake passports in circulation.'

'Oh, I see. Do you need my address?'

'Yes, please, sir.'

Brandon provided the officer with his new address at Peters Tower in Manchester. He was then allowed to go with his fake passport.

'Greg, that was an interesting interview. He must think we are stupid not spotting that his passport was a fake when I told him we were on the lookout for fakes.'

'Yes, sir,' replied Greg, who worked in the passport authentication department. 'I managed to get the microchip inserted, sir, as you instructed. I doubt he will be able to discover it.'

'Well done, Greg. I will pass the information on to the GMP and the reference for the chip. It will assist them in their surveillance of this man.'

***

It had just gone nine o'clock the following day when Jon Kim arrived at his office at GMP headquarters. There was a confidential envelope on his desk. He was delighted to see on opening it that Brandon Phelan was now traceable. He sent a short text on WhatsApp to John England, letting him know Brandon Phelan was now back in Manchester.

17

'Look, a Guardia Civil patrol boat is coming towards us,' said Fiona. 'Do you think they want to speak to us, Noel?'

'I don't know. We shall find out any minute.'

The patrol boat switched on its blue flashing light, and a crew member on the bow held up his hand, indicating they were to stop.

Noel made *Brave Goose* stop by applying some reverse.

'Senor, welcome to Barcelona.'

'Thank you,' called out Noel in reply.

'Senor, please follow us.'

'I have a mooring booked in Marina Port Vell.'

'Si, senor, follow us.'

'I hope they are taking us to the marina berth. I assume they think we might not know the way,' commented Noel.

'Look, John,' said Fiona, 'there is a huge warship on the dock.'

They moved further into the harbour past the refuelling dock. Then a square-rigged sailing ship was moored on the same side as the naval vessel. *Brave Goose* maintained station behind the patrol boat, both moving slowly.

'*Brave Goose*, this is the Guardia Civil patrol boat,' the VHF radio announced.

'*Brave Goose* Guardia Civil. Channel nine,' replied Noel.

'Senor, we will require you to moor alongside the quay shortly. Please have lines and fenders ready on your port side.'

'Why? I have a berth waiting for me at Marina Port Vell.'

'There is a good reason, sir, please follow our instructions. You will move to Marina Port Vell shortly once we have finished our work when you are port side to on the quay.'

'Guardia, this is *Brave Goose*, understood. Out.'

'That was a bit abrupt, Noel,' said John.

'No, John, it is how you finish a conversation on the ship's radio.'

Noel announced on the ship's intercom that they were to moor alongside the quay.

'Please fender port side fore and aft lines and springs to port. Mooring very shortly.'

Noel brought *Brave Goose* safely and slowly alongside the quay. Once the lines had been made fast, the Guardia patrol boat was also moored, ahead of *Brave Goose*. The officer in charge disembarked.

'Jose, can you please lower the port side passerelle?'

Once access to *Brave Goose* was established, the Guardia officer came on board.

'Hola, senor,' said Noel. 'I am the captain of *Brave Goose*. What is the problem, officer?'

'There is no problem, sir. Another person is joining you. They will be along shortly.'

'Well, I am sorry, we cannot just accept anyone on board. My guests have had a traumatic time. They will be apprehensive if we receive a visitor who is not known to us.'

'I fully understand,' said the officer. 'However, you won't want to refuse access to the person who will be joining you.'

'You say that, but we cannot comment because we don't know who you are talking about. The delay here will stop us from seeing the owner in hospital, which is why we have come especially to Barcelona.'

'Yes, sir, I understand what you say. All these issues have been considered. Please wait here, and all will become clear later.'

The officer left and returned to the patrol boat, leaving the quay and sailing out of the harbour.

'We might as well have a late lunch now. It looks as though we could be here for some time. This part of the harbour is commercial and not an area to go wandering around.'

'I understand, Noel,' said John. 'It is all very cloak and dagger. I think we have had enough of surprises!'

***

Brandon Phelan was not aware that he was under twenty-four-hour surveillance. His flat had been bugged, and his landline tapped. Against the strongest possible opposition, Special Branch had obtained a court order that Brandon's mobile phone conversations should be recorded and sent daily to Special Branch.

There were secret cameras in various locations in the flat. His car had a bug attached to the underside so that the police could track its movements.

Jon Kim and his team were grateful for the support from Special Branch.

***

In Barcelona, late lunch had been consumed. Sally was tidying everything away.

'Jose, can you lift the passerelle, please? I am nervous someone might run up unannounced. Someone, we don't want to see.'

'Certainly Fiona,' he said, realising that her nerves must be at breaking point.

Half an hour after Jose had removed the passerelle, a large white van-type vehicle arrived alongside *Brave Goose*, and a large forklift truck parked behind it.

'Now what is all this?' enquired John.

'Sorry I can't help you, John,' said Noel.

'Senor, we have a large parcel for you. We can send it up over your deck on the forklift. You will have to take it off the forks and let it carefully onto the deck. Please remove all the chairs that might be in the way.'

'That's all very well, but you can't just arrive and insist on loading. We have to know exactly what you have!'

'Well, senor, you will not be disappointed, I assure you. Just wait. You will see what we have for you before it is loaded onto the boat.'

As the van was parked on the port side where the passerelle would be deployed, it wasn't possible for anyone from *Brave Goose* to go and inspect the unknown cargo.

Some people dressed in white were busy on the other side of the van, then the forklift became involved and lifted an item out of the side of the van.

The forklift backed and made to come towards *Brave Goose*. It hoisted its cargo high to pass the load over the rail.

As the load was carefully lowered to just above the rail, the covering of the cargo was pulled back.

'Good lord, it's Goose!' exclaimed John.

'Hello everyone, will you have me back?'

'Yes, of course, Goose, how wonderful to see you. We had better get you carefully loaded on board,' said Noel.

Noel, Jose, Jock and John all took a corner of the plastic stretcher that was balanced on the forklift arms. The men evenly took the weight. The forklift dropped a couple of inches. The men then brought the stretcher on board and laid it on the deck.

'Can you please lower the passerelle so that the nurse can come on board? We have some medicines and a chair for the patient.'

Jose dropped the passerelle as requested, as the van had moved a few metres down the quay.

After the nurse, a man, also dressed in white, brought up a lightweight wheelchair. Then after depositing that, he brought a pair of crutches.

'Well, Goose, you surprised us with this arrival. How wonderful to see you!' said John.

Fiona bent down and kissed Goose. 'Fantastic to see you, Goose.'

'Well, everyone, what a great welcome. It was an unusual request from GEO that we do this, sir. As we now know, Mr Lenwell, or Goose, has had an operation to repair soft tissue and one artery partially severed by the gunshots. However, I am pleased to tell you that there were no broken bones. I understand the first aid he received from Sally has made his recovery so much faster. She did an excellent job,' said the female nurse. 'There are medicines in this bag, Sally. I will go through them with you in a minute. What we can do is to get Goose into his wheelchair with leg supports. He is well on the way to recovery. He has walked a few steps in the hospital, and he should continue with as many as he feels comfortable with each day. I understand you will be moored in Marina Port Vell. I will call a couple of times while you are here, just to check everything is okay. I would expect he will not need the wheelchair after a couple of weeks. His legs, though, should remain elevated whenever he is sitting or sleeping.'

'That all sounds very promising, nurse,' said John.

'Yes, if he behaves, all should be well in a few weeks. Let's stand you up so you can sit in the wheelchair.'

'That bike is making a racket. What on earth is he

doing?' remarked John about a powerful motorbike revving its engine and racing up and down the quay.

'Just showing off, I suspect, John,' said Noel.

All attention was now on Goose. Would he be able to stand?

'Let us help you, sir. We will lift you holding you under each armpit. Are you okay to try?' said the male nurse.

'Yes, let's do it. I am tired of watching life go by in the horizontal.'

'Are you ready?'

'Sorry, what did you say? I can't hear because of the row made by that motorbike.'

'Can we lift you now?' spoke the male nurse in a loud voice.

'Yes, yes, get on with it,' demanded Goose.

The two nurses who had done all the talking assisted Goose to stand. He was helped to move out of the plastic stretcher. He enjoyed standing there, on his beloved teak deck on *Brave Goose* in the sunshine.

At that moment, there was a thunderous shot; the report of a gun going off. It sounded like an explosion, it was so loud.

Goose crumpled in the arms of the two nurses, whose white uniforms were now crimson with Goose's blood, which had showered them like water from a fire hose.

'God, he's been shot!' said the male nurse. 'Let him down carefully, ideally onto his side so we can get to his back.'

'Christ, we are being shot at,' said Noel.

Fiona screamed, 'John, help.' She spun round and went to the rail to be sick, seaward side.

'Goose has been shot in the back,' said the female nurse.

Sally and the two nurses tried to administer first aid to Goose.

Noel went immediately to the SSB radio. '*Brave Goose* to GEO urgent.'

'Yes, *Brave Goose*, what is the problem?'

'The man who had been shot in the legs has just been returned to the boat. As he stood, he was shot by a rifle. The shooter sped away on a high-powered motorbike. I fear this time Mr Lenwell, known as Goose, might be dead.'

'Okay, we are onto it,' said the GEO radio operator.

The two nurses supported Goose as best they could. Sally recovered the first aid kit from her galley. Blood was streaming from the back of Goose. A pool of red soon established itself for all to see on the teak deck.

'He's bleeding from his mouth as well. His lung must have been perforated,' said the female nurse.

Sally started to cut Goose's shirt up the back so the medics could see the wound.

'Let me put a swab on the wound, Sally. Hand one to me,' demanded the female nurse.

Jose asked the forklift truck to move as they were expecting an emergency ambulance. Jose repeated the request in Spanish. The forklift moved away.

Noel was on his mobile to the emergency services, asking for an ambulance and paramedic.

'Shall I give him some Entonox?' asked Sally.

'No, I don't think so, Sally, have you any oxygen?'

'Yes, wait a moment.' Sally returned with a small bottle of oxygen. She rigged a facemask and line and placed it carefully over Goose's nose and mouth.

'Have you a stethoscope?' enquired the nurse.

'Yes, here,' said Sally, producing it from the first aid bag.

The female nurse listened to Goose's chest.

'It's not good, Sally, he has only one lung functioning, and it is getting flooded with blood. His pulse is very weak.'

Jose was waiting on the passerelle when an ambulance roared into sight. He waved frantically at the vehicle to identify the location of the incident.

Jose quickly explained what had happened and where Goose was located. The two medics raced up to the quarterdeck.

The nurse explained as quickly as she could what had happened and the current condition of Goose.

John and Fiona stood on the opposite side of the deck, holding one another. Fiona was sobbing, gripping her now treasured pendant very tightly.

'Whatever next, John? This is a very dangerous place.'

'Well, whoever it is, they are determined to take Goose out,' said John.

The next arrival was a medical car with an emergency doctor on board. Jose directed him to Goose.

'Can you give me a quick assessment, nurse?'

'Yes, doctor. He received one gunshot to his upper body about eleven minutes ago. I have listened to his chest; it sounds like there is flooding in the lungs with blood. We have him on oxygen. We have not tried to look at the wound. We have put a swab on it. As you can see, he has lost a great deal of blood. His pulse is weak.'

'Okay. We need to get Goose to the hospital quickly. He may need a tracheotomy to help him breathe.'

'John, they are going to move him. Should one of us go with him in the ambulance?' Noel asked the nurse.

'No, I think it best to let the medics sort it. Do we know where they are taking Goose?' John said.

'Yes, John, it's the trauma clinic. Luckily it is quite close,' said Noel.

Goose was quickly and professionally moved on the stretcher he had arrived on, down to the ambulance. The ambulance drove off under blue lights and a siren. The doctor left his car behind and went in the ambulance with Goose.

18

'I need to get this boat into its berth at the marina,' said Noel. 'Then we can clean up.'

Noel didn't need to instruct the two men on the crew what to do. They knew exactly.

'Fiona, John, would you like a cup of tea or coffee?'

'Oh yes, please, Sally, tea for me and a black coffee for John. Thanks, do you want a hand?'

'You are always welcome in my galley, Fiona.'

'God, what is going on, Sally? I have never come across a situation like this. Do you think Goose will survive?' said Fiona.

'It looked very nasty. Luckily, we had medics on hand, and the ambulance and doctor arrived quickly. Miracles can happen, but it looked pretty bad to me, Fiona.'

'Let's hope for the best.'

As soon as *Brave Goose* had been prepared for berthing at Marina Port Vell, Noel eased her away from the quay and progressed further into the harbour and the entrance to Marina Port Vell.

'Marina Port Vell, this is *Brave Goose*.'

'Go ahead, *Brave Goose*.'

'We are approaching your marina. May we have assistance, please?'

'Yes, we are waiting for you.'

Noel hung up the microphone again and moved to the flybridge, where he could get the best view.

Slowly Noel brought his charge to a position where reversing was the remaining task.

Noel managed to squeeze between two superyachts which helped in preventing him from blowing off course. Jock and Jose were manoeuvring the fenders so as not to tangle with the fenders on their neighbouring boats.

Within half an hour, Noel had moored *Brave Goose*. Jock had established water and electrical connections. Jose adjusted the fenders on either side. Noel made several entries into the ship's log. Hopefully, the notations would never be repeated.

Coming down onto the quarterdeck, chairs were moved once again into the saloon. Hose pipes were out with the replacement scrubbers to remove all signs of the blood on the deck. Jose and Jock were hard at the cleaning task, without any request. Noel was very impressed by their dedication.

John decided to ring Jon Kim and advise him about the recent incident from his cabin.

'Jon, good of you to pick up. We have had a nightmare here in Barcelona. Goose came back on board and was looking much better. He showed signs of early recovery. He had received only flesh wounds.'

'That sounds miraculous, John.'

'As Goose stood on the deck for the first time, Jon, being supported by the two nurses who had escorted him, a shot rang out from a rifle from the quay. The marksman disappeared quickly on a high-powered motorbike.'

'Wow, is he dead?'

'Well, when he left here, he was alive, just, but it will depend on what the hospital can do.'

'Someone was unhappy that Goose was still alive. They clearly ordered this attempted killing,' said John.

'Okay, John. I will ask Special Branch if they have any information through their surveillance of Brandon. He may have ordered this. I will let you know.'

***

'Brandon, it's Alvero. Goose was shot about half an hour ago. Your orders have been fully obeyed. Just a matter of money for the marksman.'

'Is he dead?'

'We don't know. At best, he will be very badly wounded. He was hit in the back with one round. The marksman had to leave quickly.'

'Okay, I will transfer thirty thousand euro to your account now. Let me know if he dies.'

'Thanks, Brandon. Yes, if I hear, I will let you know. We have to keep low at the moment. The place is buzzing with police and GEO operatives. They would love to get the marksman, in retaliation for the death of the GEO man who was killed on *Brave Goose*.'

'Yes, I am sure. So just keep low at the moment. Any thought of kidnapping John and Fiona is a non-starter with you. I will see what I can arrange when they return here.'

***

It was early evening. Jose and Jock had managed to clean the deck. It was spotless. The deck was drying in the final rays of the sun.

'What shall we do now?' said Fiona.

'Good question, darling. How do you feel?'

'Oh John, I feel nervous. I have a million thoughts rushing through my mind, though I can't snatch and hold on to one.'

'Sally, have you any thoughts about what we might do now?' enquired John.

'No, John, I am at a loss. I will be making some supper for us all. Do you want to eat on board?'

'Definitely yes, I don't want to go onshore today. I feel safe here,' interjected Fiona. 'Can we all have supper together here on the quarterdeck?'

'Of course, I am sure all the men will be pleased to relax after such a stressful time.'

'Great, let me help you, Sally. I need something to do, to take my mind off the events of today.'

So it was that six people, all the crew, John and Fiona, ate supper on the quarterdeck. It was a quiet repast –

everyone alone in their thoughts and wondering how Goose was.

Water was drunk. The wine could wait for another day.

Noel's mobile phone went off, which broke the silence like a lightning bolt onto a church steeple. The port had been quiet. The noise of the ring tone must have been heard some distance away.

'Hello, Noel, captain, *Brave Goose*.'

'Hi, I am Captain Juan Mateo GEO. I have just heard from the hospital.' Noel held his hand up to signal an important message. There was no other noise to quell.

'Yes, senor, what news?'

'Well, Goose is very poorly. He has had an operation. The bullet has been removed. It had punctured his right lung.'

'Yes, senor, I understand. What is the prognosis?'

'The surgeon who carried out the operation, the man I spoke with, says it is better than fifty-fifty. He has been lucky. The first aid on your boat is exceptional. The oxygen saved his life. Without that, his brain would have died, and then so would Goose.'

'That is good to know. I suppose it will be some time before we can visit him?'

'Yes, as soon as I have an update, I will let you know. Are you remaining in Port Vell?'

'We are, senor. Until we can safely take Goose with us, we shall remain here.' Noel's face lightened as he said these words.

Fiona looked cheerfully at John. *Could it be Goose will return to us*? she thought.

'Well folks,' announced Noel on finishing the call,

'our friend Goose is better than could be expected in the circumstances. They say your first aid, Sally, with your oxygen has saved his life.'

Sally went quite red at the accolade she had received. 'It's because Goose said I must buy all the stuff we need for a top of the range first aid kit that I had all this stuff. I need to replace some of it now.'

'Well done, Sally, we are proud of you,' said Jose.

'It looks as though we may be here for some time,' stated John.

'Yes, I think so, John. Let's not make any assumptions for a day or two. The captain at GEO promised to keep me posted.'

Noel visited the office at Marina Port Vell and explained why they would have to remain in the port for as long as it took to get Goose better, or at least well enough to come back on board.

A month's renewable contract was agreed upon, and Noel made the payment for that period.

The following day John and Fiona had a decision to make. Were they to remain in Barcelona, go to Mallorca into a hotel, or back to Manchester?

The pair went on a sightseeing trip around the city, avoiding taxis and motorbikes. Unknown to them, they were followed every inch of the way.

John became aware that they were under observation from a man in the morning and a woman in the afternoon. He didn't mention anything to Fiona.

'Shall we sit at this café and have a beer or glass of wine, darling?'

'Yes, why not? We are on holiday, after all.'

John knew that the woman following them had sat down at a table, away from them.

John made an excuse to Fiona that he would go inside, she assumed for a pee. He stopped at the woman's table.

'Why are you following us?' demanded John.

'What makes you think that?'

'Because a man was doing the same this morning, and when we stopped for lunch, you took over. If you don't tell me what you are doing, I will call the police or worse.'

'May I come to your table? We shouldn't attract attention.'

'Very well.' She came to join Fiona and John at their table. Fiona gave John a withering look, as if to say, what are you doing picking up women when I am two tables away?

'My name is Maria. I am a GEO officer. I am only following you to protect you. I am aware of all the events that have occurred to you. Captain Juan Mateo has instructed me and my male companion, who is off duty now, to cover your movements and render assistance if required.'

'Well, that's good news. I had other thoughts for most of the day, but because Fiona is very nervous about this city just now, I didn't alert her to your presence.'

'I am sorry, sir, we had not wanted to alarm you. We know some forces would like to kidnap you for a significant ransom. My presence is to be in at the beginning of any attempt so that an appropriate response can be provided.'

'Well, it's good to know. However, I feel we should perhaps return to England. Otherwise, we shall involve the GEO in many hours of surveillance, which might not be required.'

'It is a matter for you, sir. Can you please let us know what you decide?'

'Of course.'

'Are you returning to *Brave Goose* now?'

'Yes, we are.'

'Well, I will follow you to the marina and then leave. There are security gates on your pontoon.'

'Yes, I know, I have a card key,' said John.

All three rose from the table. John left a euro note to satisfy the bill and tip. The three moved off to *Brave Goose*.

Walking along the pontoon, John was chatting to Fiona. 'Let us go back to Manchester, darling. We can come back when we hear Goose is being released from the hospital, if that is what happens.'

'What do you mean, John?'

'Well, we have to be realistic. Goose may not make it.'

'Do you think that is a possibility, John?'

'I am afraid so, darling. We have to be ready for the worst.'

'I hope you are wrong, John.'

'So do I.'

***

The following morning, John and Fiona announced that they would be flying back to Manchester in a day or two.

'Ooh, we shall miss you both. You are special guests on board *Brave Goose*.'

'That is kind, Noel. I have things to attend to in Manchester. We will be back in a heartbeat when Goose is back on board. Will you let me know, Noel?'

'Yes, of course, John.'

So it was that Fiona and John flew back to Manchester two days later.

19

'It's good to be back, Fiona. It's funny how you miss a place, even though I have not lived here for that long.'

'I guess it's familiarity. You have all your stuff around.'

As they were about to unpack, yet again, there was a crashing of mail through the letterbox.

'Sydney must have realised we are back. He saved all the mail up for me. I am one of those people who just cannot leave letters unopened.'

'Don't worry, darling. I will pick out all your clothes that need washing while you look at the mountain of post.'

'You are an angel. Considering the issues that we have both faced on holiday, I don't feel at all concerned. Perhaps I should, but a call to Jon Kim, to let him know we are back, is on my list of jobs to do.'

John commenced sorting the post. Large letters and magazines on one pile. Sales letters straight in the bin; the graphics on the envelope told everything. The rest were attacked with the paper knife. The residue was a small fraction of the original pile.

Personal letters, all too few, were separated from the business letters.

The large letters contained a full solicitor's report on all the transactions and a statement of monies paid into John's account. There were, in addition, three professional magazines and one sailing magazine, which immediately attracted John's attention.

'Everything is in the wash,' Fiona announced as she came to sit on John's knee with her arm around his shoulder.

'Why have you got a magazine on boats?'

'Well, my love, I am fascinated by them. I quite fancy buying one.'

'Wow, that sounds great. How would you sail it?'

'I would need to do some training and get a certificate of competence, as Noel kept on mentioning.'

'Hey, I fancy that I could be your navigator. Noel told me all about it.'

'Well, I think there is no time like the present. Let's go to the south coast and have a mooch around. See what is on the market. We might even get a test sail. Deck shoes only, though.'

'What has got you so excited about sailing?'

'Oh, *Brave Goose*, Noel and his team, and of course, Goose.'

'What do you want, a sailing boat or a motorboat?'

'I would love a sailing boat, but they look very complex, and they heel over. It looks like a sport you need to start when you are young. A motorboat seems to have more stability and looks far more comfortable.'

'So, John, where is this boat going to live?'

'Well, I thought as we have enjoyed Puerto Pollenca so much, we should consider that as our home port?'

John phoned Jon Kim to confirm that they were back, and they were probably going to be away for a week in the south of England.

'Fiona, can we do a quick turnaround and go tomorrow?'

'You are a bit serious about this, John. Yes, I can manage that. Can we get a takeaway tonight so that I can finish the laundry and pack for tomorrow?'

'That's good. I will book the Southern Yacht Club and say we will want a double en suite room for a week.'

'A week?'

'Yes, my love, I want to have a good look around.'

The following morning John prepared the Range Rover for the trip. John loaded the bags. He needed to fill up with fuel before hitting the motorway.

Five hours after leaving the penthouse, the Range Rover drove into the car park of the Southern Yacht Club on the Hamble.

'That wasn't too painful. Surprisingly, it has taken us just over five hours, which is roughly the time it would take to fly to Palma and get a taxi to Puerto Pollenca.'

'Is that right? This place looks pretty good. We are right on top of the Hamble River. All the boats on their moorings look so pretty.'

'They do, my love. I will book a table for dinner, and

then we can walk around to see any brokers around here. Will that do, darling?'

'It will. You like to sweep me off my feet.'

It was late in the afternoon when they set off for their walk. The only brokers they found were shut. 'Better luck tomorrow, eh Fiona?'

After a full breakfast, the pair started their search in earnest in the morning. As John was driving out of the car park, his mobile rang.

'Mr England, sorry to bother you, sir, it's Sydney.'

'Sydney, good to hear from you. What can I help you with?'

'Well, sir, Mr Phelan in Apartment 803 has asked me if I could make an appointment for him to meet with you shortly.'

'Sorry, Sydney, I am away. You are not sure when I will be back. That's not a fib, Sydney, as I don't know when I will be back. So I cannot make any arrangements to meet Mr Phelan.'

'Okay, sir, I will deal with it. Thank you.'

Before John could move, his phone rang again.

'Hello, who is this?'

'It's Noel, sir.'

'Hi, Noel. How is Goose?'

'He will recover, but he is likely to be unwell for quite some time. His doctors have advised him not to return to *Brave Goose* but find a home on dry land.'

'Oh dear, that is excellent news, on the one hand, but sad for you and *Brave Goose*.'

'Yes, sir. I spent over an hour with Goose in hospital

yesterday. He was very lucid and full of instructions for me.'

'That's good that his faculties are intact. Will he be confined to a wheelchair?'

'Possibly, John, they have not had him up and walking yet, but he has been able to stand. The hospital thinks he will walk a few steps and be better cared for at home in weeks. There is the rub. His home is *Brave Goose*.'

'Yes, I can see the problem.'

'Well, John, my orders are that I ask you if you would like to purchase *Brave Goose*. If so, Goose knows what you will ask next, and that is the price. He will sell the boat to you for four hundred thousand pounds on the understanding that she is kept in the Mediterranean during Goose's active lifetime. He would like to think he would be able to come on the odd cruise now and again.'

'You will never guess where Fiona and I are. We are at the Hamble. We were just driving out of the Southern Yacht Club to go hunting for a boat.'

'That is staggering, John! I knew you enjoyed *Brave Goose*, but I hadn't realised you were keen to become an owner.'

'I am seriously interested, Noel. I don't suppose she will be sold this week. If we flew out to Barcelona in a week, I assume we might be able to stay on board? I will then give Goose my answer. As a lawyer, I will help Goose find a place in the sun, on dry land.'

'That would be an ideal arrangement, sir, thank you.'

'Well, just before you go, would you Sally, Jose and Jock, be willing to remain as captain and crew?'

'Speaking for myself, John, I would be delighted to stay. I am pretty sure the rest would say the same.'

'Brilliant, I will let you know when you can expect us. Thanks for the call, Noel.'

'What do you make of that call, Fiona?'

'If you can afford it, John, there is no better boat, is there? We know all about her. She is a lovely boat.'

'Okay, I agree with you. So, let's still go to the brokers and see what we can find for four hundred thousand pounds. It will give us a guide as to the deal. Is it a great deal, or is she too expensive? I have no idea. We need to find out.'

John drove the Range Rover out of the car park with a mile-wide smile and a metaphorical spring in his step.

'Let's go and find some brokers who might have boats in the four hundred thousand pounds range. If we can find some.'

'Great idea, John. I am looking forward to visiting many expensive motor yachts,' said Fiona.

For three days, the pair drove between the Hamble, Southampton, Lymington, and other locations. They met with very experienced and helpful brokers everywhere they went, without exception.

'The boats we have seen are a fraction of the size of *Brave Goose*. There is usually room for only one member of a crew. That rather places an obligation on us to run the boat with a deckhand. Not sure I want to do that, darling.'

'Yes, John, we want to have a Noel, Jose, Jock and Sally to look after us and sail the boat without any anxiety. The idea is that we should enjoy it and have a relaxing time.'

'You mean like we have enjoyed it so far!' said John, with a wide grin on his face. 'Have you seen a boat you like, darling?'

'They were all very modern and smart. The only boat close to *Brave Goose* was the twenty-five-metre motor yacht we saw yesterday afternoon. The problem was the price was one and a half million.'

'You are right, Fiona. The benefit of *Brave Goose* is that it beats these others hands down in space and comfort. They go more than twice as fast, but do we need that? And once again, where do all the crew go?'

'What do you think you will do, John?'

'Look, this is a joint decision. If you don't like it, then we will not do it. I don't want a large motor yacht on my own. The important thing to me is that we enjoy it together.'

'John, how did I ever meet you?' Her mouth went as dry as toast, her tone cracked in the still air of the car. 'You are the most amazing man I have ever met.'

John stopped the Range Rover and put his arms around Fiona. They were locked in an embrace, oblivious to anything else. Then a blast on a horn broke them apart when John realised a queue of traffic had formed behind them and couldn't pass. A delivery van had parked opposite them, which John had not noticed.

'Oops. That was all a bit sudden, Mr England, but lovely, my darling. Pity about the traffic.'

'Well, I think a great deal of you. I want you to be my soul mate for as long as possible. So if you are keen on *Brave Goose*, I think we should make plans to revisit her.'

'Despite the issues, I would love to. She will still be in Barcelona, I guess?'

'I am pretty sure she will be. I will give Noel a ring. I also want to invite Geoff Dickens. I think he was the marine engineer who inspected *Brave Goose* for Goose when he bought her.'

'What do you want Geoff for?'

'Fiona, it's like buying a house. I need to be sure I am not purchasing a can of worms. Things I wouldn't or couldn't see. He will know what to look for.'

'Okay, when do you plan on going back?'

'Later this week, if possible.'

'Oh, that quickly.'

'The way you said that sounds as though you had something else planned.'

'It's just that being a partner of a superyacht owner, I am not sure I have the right clothes!'

'Oh, you have, my darling. It doesn't matter what you wear. You always look fantastic.'

'Flatterer. You forget that the kidnapping I have endured twice has played havoc with my clothes. I have thrown them all away.'

'Sorry, I had forgotten all that. How about spending tomorrow in the shopping centre in Southampton?'

'Will you come with me, John?'

John agreed, and, lying through his teeth, said he would enjoy it.

Later that day, John arranged for Geoff to fly to Barcelona and stay on *Brave Goose* to conduct a thorough survey. John and Fiona would fly out the day after.

20

'Morning, Sydney, has Mr England returned from his holiday?' asked Brandon Phelan.

'I am sorry, sir, I don't know.'

'Come on, Sydney, you know everything that happens around here.'

'Maybe I do, sir, but I cannot help you.'

'I will take that as a yes; he has returned home. I will contact him, as he wants to see me.'

Sydney knew differently. John had told Sydney not to divulge anything of John's comings and goings, especially not to Phelan.

Phelan returned to the lifts and ascended to floor eight.

'Mr England, Mr Phelan has been asking about your movements. I have told him nothing, but I thought you should know.'

'Thanks, Sydney. Has any post arrived?'

'Not yet, Mr England. I will bring it up as soon as it comes.'

Brandon Phelan was back in reception to see if his post had arrived. Sydney was not behind the desk. Phelan had a look behind the desk, and in a slot with envelopes and compliments slips was a duplicate of the master lift card. He took it and returned to his apartment as quickly as he could.

Brandon had purchased a card cloning machine and some blank cards from the internet. It wasn't cheap but would be a gift if it did what its instructions said it would.

He placed the Peters Tower security card in the machine, which he had already loaded with a blank card. It took two minutes for the new card to be spat out of the device.

'Great,' Brandon chuckled to himself. As this was the master card, he assumed it would work in either lift to access the penthouses.

'Sydney, I was looking for you earlier. I found this on the floor just to the side of your desk. I thought it best to hand it to you personally.'

'Thank you, Mr Phelan. Kind of you.'

***

'Mr England, it's Sydney. I have a problem. Can I come and talk to you confidentially?'

'Yes, of course, come up now.'

Sydney explained what had happened in reception and earlier.

'So what could he do with the spare security card, Sydney?' asked John.

'He would need a machine that could copy the card. If he had such a device, the card could be copied, giving him access to the penthouse floor.'

'I would be fairly sure he has such a device. He could, of course, be perfectly genuine. Did he find it on the floor?'

'No, sir, that is impossible. There are only two cards. One I have on my person all the time. The other, the one Phelan had, is kept in a safe place at the back of the counter. Unless you had a rummage in the stationery slot, you would not see it. He could have had an opportunity to find it when I was away from the desk delivering penthouse mail.'

'In that case, Sydney, we need to change the lift code and have new cards. Further, I think you should have a safe behind your reception desk so the new card can be held in that.'

'Shall I get that organised, sir?'

'Yes, Sydney, as soon as you can. For your information, Fiona and I are going away again tomorrow. I am not sure when we will be back. If a new card is required, leave mine in your new safe, which you can buy, and I can pick up my card on my return. Get me two cards, one for Fiona. Can you please arrange a taxi for us at seven in the morning tomorrow, to take us to the airport?'

'Certainly, sir. I will deal with all that.'

'Good, thank you, Sydney, for being so perceptive.'

***

'Angela, John England.'

'Yes, Mr England, how can I help you?'

'I just wanted to let you know I am going away again tomorrow. Not sure when I will be back. If there are any issues, you can always contact me on my mobile. Okay?'

Later that day, engineers appeared to alter the south side penthouse secure lift code. New cards were prepared – two for Mr England and two new master cards.

'That was very quick,' Sydney told the engineer.

'To tell the truth, we could have done this from the office, but we needed to give you the new cards and check they worked.'

'Brilliant, I can give these to Mr England now.'

Two men and a trolley loaded with a heavy safe came through the front door as the engineers left.

Sydney instructed them where to put the safe. He also received instructions on how to set the combination. The spare master card was placed in the safe.

Confident that everything that needed doing had been dealt with, John and Fiona met the taxi and caught the plane to Barcelona.

***

'Toby, it's Brandon Phelan.'

'Hi Brandon, what can I do for you?'

'Are you busy in the next couple of days?'

'No, I am pretty free at the moment.'

'Good, can you come to my flat this afternoon? I have a job lined up. It will be very lucrative for you if we pull it off.'

A JOHN ENGLAND STORY

As arranged, Toby rang the bell of Brandon's flat.

'Come in, come in. I have an urgent job.'

'Oh, it sounded as though it was lucrative as well?'

'It will involve holding a person in their flat, the penthouse above me here, while I take her partner to his bank to complete forms and authority for the bank to transfer three million into my account.'

'Blimey, why take him to his bank?'

'Money laundering rules are so tight now that it has to be done between banks and with the authority of the payee in person, and the recipient in person at his bank.'

'I see, so how long will you need me for?'

'Just tomorrow. We will go and secure the two people in the morning, say ten o'clock. Then I will take the man to his bank. We should be back within an hour. Then we have to keep them under surveillance until I hear the money has arrived at my bank.'

'How are you going to ensure they do as requested?'

'That is where you come in. If I don't reappear within a given time, you shoot the woman.'

'If I do that, what will you pay me?'

'Twenty thousand up front with another twenty thousand if we are successful with the money transfer. If not, shooting is required. I will give you another ten thousand. That is because the money has not been transferred, and I am arrested. There is no other money to pay you, except what I have as an advance.'

'Okay, you don't want me to kill her, just a kneecap job?'

'I suppose that would do.'

'So if you are arrested, how do I get my money?'

'I will give you a cheque tomorrow dated in four days.'

'Okay, Brandon. So what sort of shooter do you have?'

'I have two Smith and Wesson MP380 pistols with eight-round magazines.'

Brandon handed one to Toby to see what he thought.

'These are brand new. How did you get these?'

'They came from America, secreted in other items.'

'Very nice. Shall I come here tomorrow? What time?'

'Oh, nine o'clock will do, thanks, Toby. Here is a cheque for ten thousand now. See you in the morning.'

***

At six o'clock in the morning, Fiona and John were ready to go back to Barcelona. They were standing by the front doors to the tower at five to seven, with suitcases prepared to load into the taxi.

At seven o'clock precisely the taxi arrived. At seven forty-five, they were unloading at Terminal One, Manchester Airport.

At midday UK time, one in the afternoon, Spanish time, they were getting into another taxi in Barcelona.

Jose carried their suitcases up to their cabin on *Brave Goose* just before two in the afternoon.

'Hello John, Fiona. Great to have you back.'

'It's wonderful to be back, Noel,' said Fiona. 'What is the latest news of Goose?'

'We heard he was making progress; fingers crossed he will survive.'

'Did Geoff Dickens arrive yesterday?'

'He arrived the evening before so he could have a full day yesterday. He slept in the bunk room cabin.'

'Well done, Noel. Everything seems to be going to plan. Do you know why he is here?'

'I guessed that you are thinking of buying *Brave Goose* from Goose, who is making satisfactory progress. They don't know yet if his spinal cord has been damaged. The bullet was very close.'

'What is the prognosis, Noel?'

'Hard to say. Much depends, John, on the assessment of his spine. His damaged legs are getting better but still very painful.'

'Okay, we will unpack. I won't take as long as Fiona! The benefit of buying the boat is we can leave a load of clothes here, making travelling so much easier. Fiona darling, let's unpack, and then we can sit and have a chat with Geoff.'

'Before you go, do you need some food?' requested Sally.

'You know all the right questions, Sally. We will just unpack, and we will come back for a tea, and a coffee, and some cake or whatever you have.'

'Will be done, John.'

***

In Flat 803, preparations were being made for the morning's activities. Brandon had all his 'props': an Amazon box to shield his face from view (he would pretend to be a delivery driver), his pistol, bank details, duct tape and cable ties.

'Can you please check the magazine on this pistol, Brandon?'

'Yes.' Brandon flicked the magazine out of the gun. The magazine was full. Placing the magazine back into the pistol handle, he pointed out a vital part to Toby. 'Look, here is the safety catch. The magazine is full. Don't unclick the safety unless you are sure you want or might use the gun. All okay? Let's go.'

The two men went to the lift on the eighth floor. Swiping the card through the penthouse reader, the ride went up to the twelfth floor and stopped. They rushed out, expecting they were on the penthouse level. They were not.

'Sod it. The card hasn't worked. They can't have changed the code in the last twenty-four hours. We are stuffed. Unless I can get to the penthouse floor, we cannot access the penthouse.'

'Let's go to my flat and ring England.'

Brandon did as he had suggested, but it was answered by answerphone.

'Sod it, they are out. They have changed the code. I suspect that because I gave the master card back, they changed the code as a matter of course. Sorry, Toby, we are stuffed. We will have to try again. Let me have the gun back. I will let you know when I am ready again.'

Toby left but felt wealthier than he had when he arrived.

Brandon was at a loss as to what to do next. Next time he would ensure England was at home and that he had a card that would be certain to make the lift travel to the penthouse floor.

***

John and Fiona had unpacked and sat at the quarterdeck table, enjoying some cake and a beverage. Geoff came to join them within an hour of them sitting down.

'Geoff, good to meet you. Have you a preliminary report, or do you want to go away and consider it? Will you be putting it in writing?'

'Yes, John, you will get a full report, but because there are so few issues, I can give you a rundown on what needs attention. I stress these recommendations are just that. There is nothing essential.'

'Good, so in essence, if you had the money, you would buy this boat?'

'Yes, I certainly would.'

'So, what are your recommendations?'

'They are all electronic. Mainly the navigation system is dated. You can purchase items that are far more sophisticated.'

'Given that, what would you advise?'

'I think it would be an additional kit as opposed to a replacement.'

'What would that be, Geoff?' asked John.

'I think an integrated screen with all the necessary charts sensors for various bits of information, engine, navigation, fuel etc. I know all that is available now, but the new stuff is very accurate.'

'Okay, Geoff. Thanks. It's good to know that *Brave Goose* is good to go.'

'Definitely. I was scrabbling around to find something

to report. The most obvious issue is that the furnishings and décor are dated, but there is no issue if you are happy with the way they are.'

'How much do I owe you, Geoff?'

'Need to work it out, John, which I will do when back home. Being able to stay on the boat has been a great help. It will not be more than four thousand pounds in total.'

'You have my email address?'

'Yes, I have. I will be away in the morning.'

Noel appeared and sat down when Geoff had left. 'Everything okay, John?'

'Yes. Geoff did mention that some of the electronics are dated, but I think there is no reason to change if everything is still working. What would you do, Noel? Is there a piece of kit you would love to have?'

'No, John, as you say, it may all be a bit dated, but I know it all works. When installed, it was top quality, so there is no need to change any of it, just because there is new stuff available.'

'I would like to go and see Goose if that is possible. Perhaps tomorrow?'

'I will get Jose to ring the hospital for you.'

'Thanks, Noel.'

John was on his mobile again. 'Senor Mateo, please?'

'Speaking, is that John England?'

'It is. I am just letting you know that I am back onboard *Brave Goose*, with Fiona. I don't expect any trouble, but I thought I should let you know.'

'Thanks, John. You have our number and the SSB radio link, so please let me know if there is any hint of trouble.'

'I will, you can be assured.' As John was finishing the call, Sally appeared to clear items away.

'Is everything okay in your department, Sally? Is there anything you want to change or add in the galley?'

'Yes, John, there is one item I would love. It would be a great help. That is a trash compactor.'

'Oh, do they make them for boats?'

'Yes, they do. One bag of trash would hold at least a week's worth of rubbish.'

'Okay, I will get Jock and Noel on the job to get one purchased.'

'Can I ask, have you bought *Brave Goose*?'

'No, not yet, but I hope to be the owner very soon. Will you want to stay on with us as owners?'

'Oh yes, John, that would be wonderful.'

'Well, I am delighted to hear that.'

'I can't wait to have another female on board. It will even up the odds a bit.'

John and Fiona accepted Sally's suggestion to eat on board; John requested that those who wanted to dine with them do so.

'What do you think we should do about the décor, darling? I wonder if there are specialists who handle a refit?'

'Oh, I am sure there must be several who do this sort of thing. It would make her look much better. The furnishings are dated, John.'

'Okay, I will make enquiries.'

21

'Is that Brandon Phelan?'

'Yes, who wants to know?'

'You don't need my name,' the caller said with an Irish accent. 'I am phoning to tell you that Goose is still alive in hospital.'

'So what do you want me to do about it? It is not of interest to me.'

'That's a lie. You contracted with ETA to assassinate him. They failed.'

'You seem to know a great deal. The information you have is flawed. Go back and think again about why I need to know all this.'

'Okay, you play the game you want, but you are now a target.' The phone went dead. The number had been withheld, so Brandon could not trace the caller. *What did he mean that I am a target?* Brandon thought to himself. *That had to be rubbish.*

Brandon then checked his bank balance online. There wasn't a tremendous amount of the one hundred thousand left.

What should I do next, firstly to get my hands on the three million, and secondly to get rid of Goose, he wondered. He decided to get some fresh air, and as it was approaching noon, he would get a copy of the *Manchester Evening News* and have some lunch.

Brandon sat in a corner window seat of the café closest to Peters Tower. He ordered a burger and a coffee. He then was thumbing through the newspaper pages, scanning the day's stories, all the way to the back and the small ads.

Amongst the situations vacant and services were two adverts – one for a massage parlour close to where he was and one a position vacant for a computer expert, urgently required by a finance company in the city.

Once the burger had been consumed, he rang the finance company to see if he could apply for the job. He made an appointment with the MD at four o'clock that day. He was requested to bring a CV setting out his work experience and relevance to the job advertised. He returned to his flat and prepared an appropriate CV.

***

Brandon was standing outside a large Victorian building on Portland Street at ten minutes to four. He thought it had been a textile warehouse. It was now a Chinese restaurant in the basement and the first two floors. Above that was a bookmaker's office, and the finance company was on the top floor. He took the lift.

The old iron gate of the lift door needed lubricating, judging by the reluctance with which it opened. He hoped the rest of the mechanism was in good order.

As he stepped out of the lift to the landing, the dilapidated decorations of peeling wallpaper and cracks in the plastered ceiling were all too obvious. He walked a short way past a private detective's office, which was closed, no light emitted through the opaque glass door. A plastic sign on the hardwood painted door for Manchester European Finance was at the end of the corridor.

Brandon knocked on the door without waiting for a 'come in'. There was none. He went in.

The guy behind the desk was on the phone. He motioned Brandon to sit down. This allowed Brandon a few moments to assimilate the organisation. Organisation was not this guy's middle name. The place was a tip. He was a young man, thirty-five to thirty-eight, white open-neck shirt, slicked-back black hair. The worst part was that he was a chain smoker judging by the size of the full ashtray. He slammed the phone down at the end of the conversation.

'Hi, you're Brandon, eh?'

'I am.'

'Sorry, I had to take the call.'

'No worries,' responded Brandon. 'I shouldn't perhaps have just walked in. I didn't know what lay behind the door.'

'Well, you are here now. My name is Georgios Armani.'

'Very famous name?'

'No, well, the Armani bit is my idea, but I was christened Georgios. Armani seems to have worked so far.'

'Good, I am Brandon Phelan; I am Irish, but I live in Manchester. I work on a freelance basis, as I find not all my clients need a full-time person for computers. I can set up the software for them to use, and I just go in from time to time as they wish to tweak the software. Your advert indicated you required help with your software systems, so I thought I could help without you having to commit in the long term.'

'I didn't know anyone did that, Brandon, so yes, that would be excellent.'

'Georgios, I am available to start straight away. Can you tell me what you do here and what it is you need your computer to do for you?'

'Hey, Brandon, that is great. What are your charges?'

'I charge one hundred and fifty pounds an hour. There is no VAT. If you wanted me to work a full day, eight hours, the fee is one thousand a day.'

'You are the man, Brandon.'

'So tell me, what do you do?'

'Manchester European Finance is a company which I own. We only lend against assets on which we can take a charge; a house, factory, car, or boat, as security for the loan.'

'Isn't that what banks do?'

'It is: banks won't lend to anyone, you need to be a customer of the bank firstly, and not everyone is a customer. A small overdraft may be difficult for some people to obtain.'

'I see, so what checks do you do on people? Or do you only lend to businesses?'

'No, we only lend to individuals. If the money goes into a company, that's okay by me, but the person who may own the company is personally responsible for the loan.'

'Georgios, you must surely make some checks on people.'

'I do, and the more in debt they are, the better customer they are.'

'How do you make that out?'

'Take this example.' Georgios handed Brandon an application form. Attached to it was a personal profile from a credit reference company. 'The applicant had three County Court Judgements so far unsettled. He did have a five-thousand-pound overdraft fully used from his bank and maxed-out credit card. He has a house with a mortgage of twenty-five thousand pounds. He has lived in his house for twenty years. I think that house is now worth one hundred and fifty thousand pounds, possibly two hundred thousand pounds. I will lend him one hundred thousand pounds in return for the first charge on his house. Wow, and he only applied for five thousand pounds. He can clear all his debts and have some left with my loan.'

'That sounds incredibly generous, Georgios.'

'No, generosity doesn't come into it. It's business, good business.'

'I guess you are charging a premium interest rate?'

'You got it in one, Brandon. What I need is for the repayments to be made by direct debit – bank standing orders are not efficient.'

'So Georgios, what do you want from me?'

'I need a system which confirms offers and the terms, and then if they accept, it converts to a loan, and it becomes a loan handling agreement, all on the computer.'

'Okay, I can see what you need. I can do that. The site will also track payments directly from your bank, and you can spot if someone hasn't paid. I can also work out what you have lent out, and the total predicted income against the cost of money. I guess the interest rates have to be adjustable, as if the rates change with your bank, you need to change the amount your borrowers pay you.'

'You're the man, Brandon. When can you start?'

'Georgios, I have already started. I can work on this at my office. I will come back at the end of the week with the draft of the system, if that's okay with you?'

'That would be great. Is there anything else you need?'

'As you mention it, there will be a contract for me which I will email you. Are you able to scan it when signed and return it to me?'

'Si, no problem.'

'Your Italian came out then, Georgios.' They both laughed. 'Are the repayments based on interest-only, or do you calculate them as capital and interest repayments? Also, you say you take charge on assets. How do you record those?'

'Hey, you've got this quick, Brandon. Yes, they pay capital and interest on repayments. A list of assets and our assessment of value would be helpful.'

'Do you have a standard loan agreement?'

'Yes, I do. I can run a copy off for you.' Georgios printed the document and handed it to Brandon.

'As the loan agreement is on your computer can you email me a copy, so I don't have to spend time copying it into my software? Here is my card and CV which you requested. The card has my email address.'

***

He was busy working on the software when Georgios signed an email containing his agreement.

'Great,' said Brandon out loud. 'Five thousand for this week. If I spread it out, I may get two or three weeks out of it.'

'Georgios, it's Brandon. I think this job will take me at least two weeks, possibly more, when I get into the detail. That's going to run at about ten thousand pounds. Are you happy with that? Would you please confirm the source of your money to lend out? Bank, insurance company etc.?'

'That's the other side of the business, Brandon. Manchester European Pension Managers.'

'Oh, you manage pensions?'

'Yes, we guarantee an annuity rate considerably more than the rate their pension providers give them.'

'So, do you need software to handle the pension payments as well?'

'It would be beneficial. I don't always know where I am up to.'

'Yes, I can do that, Georgios. I assume you get a lump sum from the pensioner. I think you agree to an interest rate paid to them. I also guess that you charge a fee. I can create an account showing what money you received, what goes out to the pensioner, the loan to the borrower, and the income it produces. Plus your fees. So the bottom line will be your profit.'

'Fantastic, Brandon, that is just what I need.'

'That will take a bit longer. I will be back as soon as I can with a draft idea.'

'Yes, sure, Brandon. Press on.'

Brandon had obtained some gainful employment and tapped into the sort of business he liked. The collection of debts must be an issue. He guessed there was a 'heavy' somewhere that enforced payment of recovery of the repayments if the borrower got into debt.

Back at Peters Tower, Brandon set about finding appropriate software on the internet. He was amazed to find that several sites were doing similar things. He set about looking at them all and taking the best bits from each.

***

On *Brave Goose*, John and Fiona were about to leave to visit Goose in hospital. Noel came with them, in case Goose needed anything – possibly to give Noel instructions regarding *Brave Goose*. A taxi took the three of them to the central trauma unit of the main hospital in Barcelona.

The three found the room where Goose was staying in the hospital. They crept very quietly into the room for fear of waking him should he be asleep.

'What are you three doing skulking about at the entrance to my bedroom?'

'Oh, you are awake. We didn't want to disturb you in case you were having a nap.'

'Good thinking, John, but I am not asleep. I can easily drop off, so while it's great to see you all, I will not expect you to stay more than an hour.'

'You don't seem to have lost your sense of authority, Goose,' said John.

'No, I can still shout for a nurse when required, although, on the whole, they like me to press the bell.'

Fiona walked to the opposite side of the bed, leant over and kissed Goose on his forehead.

'Now that is the sort of medicine I like. Thank you, Fiona.'

'Are you feeling any better, Goose?'

'Thanks, Fiona, I don't know. I don't feel unwell, but I think I am full of morphine. However, that will not prevent me from doing what is necessary.'

'What is that?' enquired Noel.

'Let me give you the code for the safe in my office on *Brave Goose*. Can you write this down, John, assuming you have the paper and pen I asked you to bring?'

'Yes, all present and correct, Goose. Do you want the pad, or are you going to dictate to me?'

'Firstly John, and Noel, these instructions are for Noel. My safe in the office has a combination lock. 1973 is the code. Unlock the safe and remove the three paper parcels. Handle them carefully. They are explosives. Phone the GEO and explain and ask them to collect them. There are two packs of explosives. The third has the detonators.'

'Were they something to do with the fishing boat explosion?'

'No, John, because these have not exploded!' Goose said with a smile.

'The next job, Noel, is to dig out the sandwich box. It's pretty significant, because it is full of five-hundred denomination euro notes. You are to keep this in the safe. It's the boat's emergency fund for whatever befalls you, and you consider an emergency.'

'How much money is in the box, Goose?'

'Noel, there should be ninety thousand euros. Ten went on springing Fiona from her captors. John has paid me back, but the cash has not found its way to the box due to other circumstances. That's all the information I have for you, Noel. Is there anything you need to tell me?'

'Are the ship's papers in the safe, Goose?'

'Oh yes, that is important. There is a folder with Part 1 registration as a UK vessel, bills of sale to the previous owner, and then to me. I think you, Noel, have the radio licences, the transit log and so on?'

'Yes, I have Goose.'

'Okay, Noel, can you please step outside? I need half an hour with my lawyer.'

Noel went out to the corridor, and Fiona decided it was best if John did the next bit independently, whatever it was Goose wanted to speak to John about. She sat with Noel.

'Now, John, there are three things on my mind. Money, *Brave Goose* and my will.'

'Well, I will see if I can be of assistance.'

'John, I have two bank accounts. One in the Cayman Islands, and another in London. The details of these accounts are in the safe on board in a folder called 'Banks'. Okay?'

'Yes, Goose, I get all that. What do you want me to do about the accounts?'

'I was hoping you could become a signatory and ultimate beneficiary of these accounts when I am gone. Knowing banks, they will need forms to complete and execute under oath and all that, so can you please contact the banks for a joint signatory form, which should be easy enough to get them to move to the next stage.'

'Okay, Goose, that should be straightforward. I may need my partners at Bennetts to do this so that I can be nominated, and they will do the security bits.'

'Fine, no problem with that. *Brave Goose* is the next bit. You need to draft a bill of sale or get a pre-printed one from the Royal Yachting Association, fill it in and put yourself down as the purchaser and me as a vendor for four hundred thousand pounds.'

'Yes, okay, that's easy enough. I will register her in my name once the money hits your account.'

'Good, this is easier than I thought it would be. I guess the will could be the tricky bit.'

'It usually is. But as you don't have a wife or family, it can't be that difficult. So what legacies do you want to provide? Do you have a will at present?'

'No, I don't have a will. You are correct; I don't have a wife. I do have an ex-partner who lives on Cayman Island.

She has a son, my son called Justin. Her name is Carmel, and her surname is Frobisher.'

'Okay, that's not a problem other than finding them.'

'Okay, now the last statement told me there were eight and a half million pounds in my Cayman account. I want to leave two of those million to my son and his mother a million. The rest can stay as I will have to live on something. I plan on buying a finca in Mallorca, where most of the accommodation is on the ground floor. I want to leave a hundred thousand each to Jose, Jock and Sally with two hundred to Noel, all UK pounds.'

'So, who will be your executor?'

'I was hoping you would do that job, John.'

'Okay, that's not a problem, so long as I can charge my trip to the Cayman Islands to the estate?'

'No problem there, Goose, but even when all the bequests are made, there is a considerable sum left. Any instructions regarding that money? That should pay an air fee to the Caymans!'

'The only charitable bequest is to pay for a new Severn Class Lifeboat for the RNLI. That will be a couple of million, I would think. The residue of the estate will go to my executor.'

'Goose, that is terrific. I will have to get a doctor to certify that you are sane and capable of making these decisions. I also suggest you have a lifetime will so that should you become incapacitated and unable to look after yourself, I can make decisions for you and manage your finances, to your benefit.'

'That's a great idea. You have a bit to do, and I am tired

now so that you may go. Can you ask Noel and Fiona to come and say goodbye? Come back and see me when you have the will and other documents. Thanks, John.'

'Are there any other requests, Goose?'

'Yes, John. I want to be cremated, and my ashes sprinkled onto the Mediterranean, anywhere you like.'

'You can be assured, Goose, that, should it be necessary, I will deal with your affairs as if it were you.'

'I am sure you will. I don't think I could have a better executor. You all can go now. I am sleepy.'

22

'Hi Georgios, it's Brandon. I have a working draft of the system for you to consider. I worked non-stop all week, so I would like to show you the software and collect a cheque for five thousand.'

'That's speedy work, Brandon. Give me your bank details, and I will transfer the money now. Can you come around in the morning, say ten?'

That was all agreed. At ten the following day, Brandon appeared at the office of Manchester European Finance. It had occurred to Brandon that this was not a limited company, which is why he had been unable to trace them in Companies House.

'Hi, Georgios.'

'Brandon, my man. You are a swift worker.'

'I don't like to hang around when there is work to be done.'

'Like me, eh!' replied Georgios.

'Look, I have had to make certain assumptions. I think you have to quote the APR interest on all your documents?'

'Yes, that's okay.'

'I assumed you would charge an upfront fee, which could be added to the loan. As such, it would adjust the APR. You can take your fee before passing the net amount to the borrower.'

'Good, that's great.'

'I have also built in a link for the site to look at your bank account where repayments are made. The reference number you give the transaction must be part of the Direct Debit name, so the system will automatically collate the repayment into your account. Daily you will get a page that will tell you who has paid and who has not paid and their arrears to date. It also shows the security for the loan, a photograph or numerous pictures that can be the borrower, the assets, and anything else you think appropriate to have. The value at loan and other details you might want to keep is also recorded, with a space for notes.'

'Wow, Brandon. You have got it in one.'

'The only thing I have not included is an automatic letter or email to the borrower to remind them they are in arrears, the amount and the amount outstanding. I can make it do that if you want?'

'Yes, I guess that would be sensible. Can you have more than one letter, getting more and more urgent?'

'Yes, just let me know what you want the letter to say and the letter heading you use, as I can embed that as well. It will produce all the letters with the letter heading, etc.'

'This is just great, Brandon.'

'Glad you like it. It is important to input the initial information carefully so the system will do it all for you. It even takes account of weekends and bank holidays.'

'Terrific, Brandon. What can I say?'

'Out of interest, you collect debts. I am sure some of your customers don't pay. What process do you employ to collect the money?'

'Oh, it's a hands-on method. I employ two failed heavyweight boxers. They are thick but know enough to collect the money. Their very presence standing at a doorway is enough to make the punter realise that they mess with me at their peril. Do you have a debt, Brandon, that needs collecting?'

'Yes, I do. It's a long story, but the guy who owns Peters Tower where I live owes me three million quid.'

'Blimey, Brandon. That has to have a story behind it?'

'It does. Have you got time now, or shall I bore you with it another time?'

'No press on, my friend, tell me all about it.'

Brandon started with the loan to Michael Fitzallen and continued with the story up to date.

***

Once John had finished taking instructions from Goose, he left him to sleep.

'Okay, you two, let's get back to *Brave Goose*. I have work to do.'

Fiona was bursting to ask John what was said after she left, but realised John was not about to break his confidence.

'We don't have a computer on this boat, do we, Noel?'

'Yes, there is one in Goose's office. I don't think you have been in there. I will need to go in and get some papers for you out of the safe. Come and join me.'

While the two men were sorting out computers and papers, Fiona went into the galley.

'Sally, can I do anything to help? The boys are playing with computers and rummaging for documents.'

'Oh Fiona, you are an angel. Yes, I have lots to do. Lunch is easy. Tonight's meal needs some vegetable preparation. Can you help with that?'

'No problem, just point me in the right direction.' Fiona became engrossed in her chores, as was Sally.

'What do you think about John buying *Brave Goose*?'

'It couldn't be better, Fiona. We will have so much fun, I know.'

'That's great. We are both delighted to own this boat. I suspect we will be the official owners before the end of the week. It is so sad Goose will not be able to sail on her. He will be mortified. I am sure John will want to bring the boat to wherever Goose will live so that he can see her, at worst. At best, all being well, he might get to come on board on a calm day for a little sail around the bay.'

'That would be wonderful, Fiona. So much has happened since Goose bought her. It is so much more enjoyable than being tied up in Southampton.'

***

'Is this the only computer there is?'

'Yes, John, it is an old one.'

'You can say that again, the screen is ages old; I am amazed by its colour, and the computer has no power. I am going to get a new one.'

'Do you know where to get one from?'

'No, I don't. I need to find an excellent shop with someone who can deliver and set the thing up.'

'Jose, can you spare me a moment?'

'Yes, John, what can I do for you?'

'I need to buy a new computer, screen and printer, and other accessories. I wonder if you know of a good computer store, and if you do, will you come with me to help me buy what I want?'

'I am not sure where there is such a shop. I will make enquiries. We can go after lunch if that's okay, and I will have finished my work here.'

'Great, that's a date.'

'John, here are the documents you need for the registration.'

'Thanks, Noel. I will have a good look at them.'

'Julian, it's John England.'

'John, good to hear from you; you are not in trouble?'

'No, that would have required my password, if you recall?'

'Yes, I do, and I am delighted it is not required for this call. What can I do for you?'

'I have just bought a boat, and I need to transfer four

hundred thousand pounds to the vendor.'

'That's fine, John. It sounds as if you have bought something rather splendid?'

'I have, far more splendid than the price might indicate. She is a hundred feet, thirty metres, long with a crew of four and staterooms for eight passengers.'

'Good heavens, John, are you sure you have enough zeros on the end of the number?'

'No, that is the price. I know I am buying well. It passed the survey with flying colours, which I will request online later today when I get a working computer. That is the only not functioning item on the boat!'

'It all sounds like fun, John. As soon as I see your request for the transfer, I will authorise it. Don't worry. Thanks for letting me know; enjoy your new boat.'

'Thanks, Julian.'

'Noel, I should have asked before, is there Wi-Fi on the boat?'

'No, not really; you can get Wi-Fi when we are in most ports. We can connect a wire to the shore connection on the electrical cable box.'

'How would I get Wi-Fi out at sea?'

'That would require a satellite dish, which would be encased in a dome. Look at the yacht next door. They have two domes. One will be Wi-Fi, the other for TV.'

'How do we get this, Noel?'

'A marine electronics company fits these things.'

'Is there such a company in Barcelona?'

'Yes, there is, but it is an expensive exercise.'

'Well, let's see how expensive. I assume they would have to be fixed on the arch with the aerials?'

'Yes, that would be best. There is trunking down to the bridge for the cables.'

'Could a cable be laid to this office for the new computer?'

'Yes, John, there is already a set of USB plugs connected through the boat to the shore. All that would be needed is to connect that cable to the dome via a splitter. So the signal reception can be selected, dome or shore.'

'Noel, that sounds just ideal. Can you find me the company that can install the domes and the connection? We might as well have a TV and ensure the crew mess can also have the signal.

After lunch, Jose and John got in a taxi and went off to a computer shop. They were back onboard *Brave Goose* in two hours. A van followed them to the quay. Two men started to unload numerous boxes. Two hours later, John had a fully working computer: backup, hard drive storage, a state of the art printer/scanner and a slimline colour screen twice the size of the previous one. John used some of the boxes to carefully store Goose's computer and printer and the large number of cables, to be transported to his new home wherever that might be.

'Are you two going to spend the day in this little office, or will you come out for a drink and some sunshine?'

'Sorry, darling,' John replied. 'I have to get this all working. I have a few transactions to fulfil. I won't be long, I promise.'

John made the transfer of funds to Goose's bank. He then created the bill of sale based on the proforma supplied by the RYA and a request to Ofcom to reregister *Brave Goose* and all its equipment to himself and request the registrar of Part 1 registration to note the transfer and requested that the documents be delivered to his home address at Peters Tower.

'Okay, I'm free of computers, for the moment.'

'Good, we can start to consider all the changes we could make to our cabin.'

'Which cabin is that?'

'Sally says we should move to the 'owner's cabin', which will mean we need to empty everything from our cabin into the wardrobes and storage areas in the owner's cabin.'

'It never occurred to me, darling. Have you had a good look around?'

'No, I just know that is something we need to do.'

'Okay, let's have a look. I have been in the office, off the lobby into the cabin. All the wardrobes and drawers are full of Goose's stuff. Oh, I haven't the heart to move all this. There is everything he needs here. Let's not do this until Goose is settled in a house somewhere, and we can then pack all this up and move it to his house.'

'As always, you are right, John. Yes, we should not disturb all this. The office is a different matter. You have your new computer there. What happens when we are at sea? How does the computer get a Wi-Fi signal?'

'Well, little curiosity, you have always put your finger on the main issue. So Noel will get a firm of specialists to install two domes. Look at next door; they have two domes. Inside them are satellite discs, one for Wi-Fi, the other for TV.'

'So we will have two domes?'

'Yes, darling, any day now. They may as well fit them while we are stuck here. Noel and Jock will help with the installation.'

'How exciting, can't wait.'

23

John was sitting at his new computer, setting up the variables and customising the email address and other items when an email popped up on the screen. It was from Sally Moulton, Frobishers solicitors.

John, not sure where in the world you are, but I wondered if you would be able to assist a client of mine. To be brief, they cannot afford the costs of legal advice and representation. They got into financial difficulties when their own business failed, through no fault of theirs. They were reliant on one large customer in the rag trade. When the customer's business hit trouble, the orders stopped overnight.

My clients had a large mortgage on their house, a bank loan and debts to HMRC for VAT. So that they could get all this off their back, they went to Manchester European Finance for a loan. It was over ten years with an APR of twelve per cent variable. There was a fee of ten per cent of the loan, which was added to the loan. The total debt now consolidated to this one organisation is £60,000 mortgage, £20,000 bank loan, £14,000 HMRC, and £10,000 fees to MEF. £104,000. The monthly repayments are £1455.45, and the cost over the period is £70,000 more than they had borrowed.

Manchester European Finance is pressing hard for only one missed repayment, not just the missing payment, for the whole debt. Heavies are regularly visiting the house making all sorts of threats. Can you act for them, please?

Sally

John responded, ensuring Sally Moulton was in his contacts. He emailed her.

Dear Sally,

It's great to hear from you again. I am in Barcelona, and I will be here for some time. I possibly can do something online, but I will need all the information. Can you let me have all that, which must include the loan agreement, the mobile number of the client and all the usual client contact details, and any correspondence with Manchester European Finance?

Who are they? I have never heard of them.

I may be in Barcelona for another month or six weeks. I should be able to hold up matters until I return. Do the borrowers have any income they can spend on satisfying this debt?

That is the best I can do.

Best wishes, John

'I may regret putting in this computer. I have just received an email request for me to act for a young couple who are being harassed for a debt.'

'Oh John, is there no rest from legal stuff?'

'No, darling. I have put myself out there as a pro bono lawyer, so I get all the cases offered that no one else will touch as there are no fees to be earned.'

'You are a good man to help these people. Can you deal with it from here, or will you have to go back?' enquired Fiona.

'I guess we shall have to return one day, but I will do my best from here.'

'Don't let it spoil our holiday, John.'

'No darling, I won't.'

'What I will need to do is go back and see Goose, maybe tomorrow afternoon. I have everything he wants now, but I need some signatures.'

***

'Hey, Brandon, can I put old debts on this system?'

'Yes, Georgios. Just get the start date right, and the computer will list it in date order. Then you need to put the total debt, the interest rate, the amount repaid monthly and the date of the month. You also need to put in the full details of the borrower and the asset on which you have a charge.'

'Okay, Brandon, my man, that is great. I don't have that many to put on, but they need to go on. What happens when one person is in arrears already?'

'The computer will work that out as there will not have been sufficient payments for the date of input. The system will give you a choice, firstly to add the missing payment to the debt and recalculate the debt to a new monthly figure, or it will ask if you want to leave it outstanding so the borrower will have to pay it off, in whatever grace period you give them.'

'So if they don't pay, what then?'

'I don't know what your agreement says, but normally there is a three-month period to see if there has been a repayment or partial repayment, or you go to court.'

'Okay. I wouldn't say I like courts. They are expensive and don't get the results.'

'That is a matter for you to decide. Just be careful. You could be in trouble for criminal behaviour if you exert too much pressure.'

'Yes, so Brandon, you stick to computers, don't worry about me.'

'As you are chasing debts, don't forget you owe me another five grand, and I have finished the job. When are you going to pay me?'

'Don't fuck me about, Brandon. I have yet to see this system of yours work for me.'

'It does work, Georgios, and don't swear at me. I have no worries about going to court.'

Georgios put the phone down. *Oh, sod it, I hope he will not be difficult*, he thought.

***

The marine engineers arrived in a large, long-wheelbase black Mercedes van. The two engineers obtained a pass for the pontoon and approval to work on *Brave Goose* while in port.

'Hi, we are from Marine Telecommunications and TV. Is this the vessel the new kit is for?'

'Yes, it is. Please come on board.'

Jose advised John that the men were here with the new kit.

The engineers were shown the domes' location and the existing trunking and power source for the installation.

'That's fine, boss,' they said to Noel. 'There will be a guy coming tomorrow to set the system up for you. We are just the installers.'

They worked all day and part of the evening. There was some muttering, but in the end, Noel, Jock and John were all satisfied the job had been done well and professionally.

Jock unplugged *Brave Goose* from the shore Wi-Fi system and turned on the onboard system. The dome emitted a few groaning noises as the giro-operated disc inside sought the satellite needed for a good signal. Then moments later, John's computer screen lit up, and he was connected. He had to input the password, and he was away.

'This is great, Noel. I can spend ages here when at sea or anchor doing my work.'

'Good, that's terrific.'

'I have a few emails that have come in, so I'd better get on with some work,' said John, hoping the mention of doing some work might prompt Noel to go.

'Noel, can you organise for Fiona and me to go and see Goose this afternoon, or tomorrow if this afternoon is not acceptable?'

John started to download information from his various emails. Bennetts' solicitors had sent a proforma will, so all John had to do was fill in the blanks. Sally Moulton had sent several documents regarding her clients that a finance company was threatening. There was also a proforma bill of sale for buying *Brave Goose* from the Royal Yachting Association, which John had just joined.

He decided to do Goose's will and the bill of sale first. He printed off the information from Sally Moulton to read later.

'John, will you be okay to go and see Goose this afternoon, say three o'clock?'

'Yes, Noel. That's fine. I will have everything I need by then.'

All three caught a taxi to the hospital. Goose was ready to see them.

John was delighted to see that he was sitting up in bed. Still with tubes attached but looking so much better than the last time they visited.

'Goose, great to see you again, and you look so much better.'

Fiona gave him a big kiss.

'That's the best medicine anyone can have, my dear.'

Once the niceties were over, John turned to the business issues.

'Now Goose, the first document I have is the bill of

sale for *Brave Goose*. I have already paid the funds into your account. I have brought you a copy of the transfer.'

'Well done, John. I guess I need to sign it?'

'That would be useful as I have already made some improvements.'

'So, what have you been up to in my absence, John?'

Before John could respond, Noel told Goose about the new domes on the hoop over the flybridge. They were for TV and Wi-Fi. The technicians, with Jock's assistance, had done an excellent job. Apart from the obvious domes, nothing below would let you know a significant installation had taken place. There was a keyboard for each dome for tuning purposes.

'That sounds like a very sensible addition to me, John.'

'Yes, Goose, it will allow me to work wherever we are.'

'Good, so now you own *Brave Goose*. Good luck, John, and happy sailing.'

'Thanks, Goose. The only thing I need to do is transfer the insurance into my name. There could be a refund for you, Goose, from the insurers. I needed to supply a copy of the bill of sale. I will do the paperwork and transfer this afternoon. I will also register her in my name.'

'Good, so that was easy enough. What now, John?'

'I have a will I have drawn up. If you are happy with the contents, I will let you have a copy of the signed and witnessed document. Do you want to study it for a few days, Goose?'

'No, John, I am happy that you have done as I asked. Where do I sign?'

'Well, hold on a minute. I need another witness.'

John went out of the private room to see if he could find a doctor.

'Is there a problem, sir?' said a nurse passing by.

'Yes, we need to have a chat with his doctor regarding transport when he is allowed to leave this hospital, and what aftercare is required.'

'I will see if the doctor can come and talk to you.'

A bright-faced doctor in a white coat and stethoscope hanging around her neck entered the room within ten minutes.

'I understand you need to discuss Mr Goose's prognosis, aftercare, and required accommodation type?'

'Well, that is correct, as well; however, would you please be good enough to be a witness to the signing of his will?'

'Of course. I have done this many times for patients. It is something that is never covered at medical school, but it should be.'

'Great, thank you.' John asked Goose to sign, and then he witnessed the signature, as did Noel and then the doctor.

The doctor spoke to the three men once all the paperwork was dealt with.

'Goose, you have had two severe shooting incidents, but I am delighted to say you have made a staggering improvement from your injuries. You will find walking difficult in the future. I would suggest the use of an electric wheelchair. This will avoid you having to exert yourself propelling a standard wheelchair. I expect we shall have you out of bed for short intervals this week, and then with the aid of physiotherapy, you should be able to feel a great deal better. I hope we can discharge you in seven to ten days.'

'That is excellent news, doctor,' retorted Goose. 'What do I need to look out for in buying a house? My superyacht, possibly still moored here in Barcelona, has been purchased by my great friend John. He is also my solicitor. The boat was my home, but now I need to be on dry land. Would that be appropriate if I find a bungalow, or an apartment served by a lift? Thanks, doctor, very helpful. One more thing, if we choose a calm day, can I travel by boat to Mallorca? I fancy buying a place in Puerto Pollenca.'

'Yes, so long as you are not stressed and have to brace yourself to stand or walk. I think you should be fine. You have some good friends with you to help you cope.'

'That's all good news, Goose. I need to get your will copied. I will ask Bennett and Bennett in Chester to keep the original always available.'

'I am looking forward to going back to Mallorca. I think the climate will suit me, and for the most part, the port is flat. So it will be excellent for my wheelchair.'

'Okay, Goose, we will prepare for your arrival. We will come and see you again in a few days. Fiona and Sally asked if they could come and see you. Would that be okay with you?'

'You bet! I'd better have the blood pressure machine handy when those two lovely girls come to see me.'

John and Noel left Goose to his TV and a snooze. Goose was exhausted from all the information he had to digest.

'I must transfer the insurance into my name. Can you remind me, Noel? You should have a copy of the policy on board in case it is required by anyone who needs to check the ship's credentials.'

Back onboard *Brave Goose*, John emailed Bennetts about Goose's will and enclosed a copy. He advised them that he would send the original to them when back in England. He also contacted Ian Birch, giving him the details of the marine insurance for *Brave Goose*, requesting he change the name to John as the new owner.

John read the documents Sally Moulton had sent through. The couple were a hard-working pair whose clothing manufacturing business went under when their only customer went bust. Manchester European Finance sought repayment of the whole loan and interest due to Hamilton's missing one payment.

John drafted a letter to Manchester European Finance. John had created an official-looking letterhead and a post box address at Peters Tower.

The Managing Director
Manchester European Finance
Dear Sir,
Re: Nicholas and Jane Hamilton – a loan
I have been instructed to act for the above as their solicitor. I have endeavoured to trace your registered number with the Financial Conduct Authority (FCA). Please provide me with a copy of your registration, both for the company and the principal.

I must warn you that it is illegal in the United Kingdom to operate a finance company without registering with the FCA.

Please provide me with your full registration details and number.

If you attempt to solicit funds from my clients while I act for them, I will not hesitate to report you to the FCA and the police.

Yours faithfully,

John England – Solicitor

CC to Ms S Moulton, Frobisher Solicitors. Mr & Mrs Hamilton.

John felt very satisfied with his work. That should fire a shot across their bow.

Leaving the office, he nearly collided with Fiona. He grabbed her, they kissed.

'Wow, that was a near miss. I must remember that coming out of the office. I could meet someone head-on.'

'So long as it's me you run into, carry on.'

24

'Brandon, it's Georgios.'

'Hi, have you a glitch with the software?'

'No, there is a man who lives somewhere in Peters Tower. He is a solicitor. He is giving me some hassle.'

'Yes, I know him. He is quite a smart cookie. So how has he got under your skin?'

'He is acting for a couple who have borrowed a chunk of money from me and missed a payment. My "enforcers" have been round to collect the outstanding money. The result is a smarmy email from this guy asking for my registration details with the FCA.'

'So why not just give him your registration number? It's on all your emails generated by the system.'

'Yes, there is a number there. You are correct. It's a wrong number. It's only there to give people peace of mind that my firm is legit!'

'Then you have a problem. I would simply ignore the email.'

'Okay, seems like a plan.'

'Be careful what you do with your heavies. This guy has friends in high places.'

'I need the money. I have to try and get it.'

'Well, it's up to you. Where did the money come from in the first place?'

'My sister company, Manchester European Pensions.'

'How do you persuade people to give you their pension pot?'

'Easy, if you guarantee an annuity of, say, eight per cent, people flock to you. They can't wait to get that sort of return.'

'Go on then, what is your turn on the deal?'

'Four or five per cent plus a fee on lending the money out. The funds I lend are all secured.'

'How?'

'The loan in question has a charge on their home.'

'How much do they owe you, and what is the house's value?'

'From memory, I think they owe one hundred and four thousand. The value of their house is probably a hundred thousand.'

'You don't need to rely on memory, Georgios; just look them up on your computer. Their account will show what they have paid and the balance.'

'Of course, it's £101,089.10. That is very accurate.'

'That is what the system does. Easy, isn't it?'

'Yes, that doesn't help me with this problem.'

'Can't help you, I am afraid, Georgios. You will have to think about what to do.'

'If this guy lives in your tower block, maybe I could meet him.'

'Not easy. He is very well protected. Anyway, he is abroad now.'

'How do you know?'

'I need to meet him as well.'

'Okay, so when he is back, and you are going to see him, I will come with you?'

'Okay, Georgios. I will let you know when he is back.'

***

Another week had passed in Barcelona. *Brave Goose* had the crew attending to spring clean the entire boat. Cleaned and polished so that every inch of her looked spectacular.

John had paid the mooring fees up to date. He was unable to say when they would be leaving.

Goose was getting better, but the hospital would not commit to a date when Goose could be discharged.

John spent several hours a day in his office on board. He was currently looking for a bungalow, finca or apartment suited to Goose in Puerto Pollenca. He was now well known to the agents in the area.

'Ah, that's what I am looking for,' John exclaimed. Sticking his head out of his office door, he called for Fiona.

'Here, look at this.'

'Wow, that looks beautiful. It's all on one floor. This

could be ideal for Goose. He would be able to get around easily in his electric wheelchair.'

'Yes, darling, the views are spectacular.'

'My only thought is that it is out of town and a bit remote. Goose is going to want to go to restaurants and bars and do some shopping without having to go miles.'

'As always, you are right. Well, how about this one? It's a penthouse. You know what it is like to live in one of those!'

'I do. It looks fabulous. There are three bedrooms, a large lounge, a dining area, and an open plan kitchen. Two bathrooms. It has a lift to the ground floor. It's on a block one road back from the promenade, so the views are fantastic. He could zoom down in the lift and out to the town in a moment. I think he would love that, John. He could have a telescope or binoculars and watch all the boats. Fantastic.'

The following day Noel received a call from the hospital.

'Mr Lenwell can go home tomorrow. Can you please organise transport?'

'John, Fiona, great news. Goose can come out of the hospital tomorrow.'

'Fantastic. How mobile is he? Will he be brought here in an ambulance?'

'They have asked if we could get a taxi.'

'That would indicate he has mobility. We need to arrange an electric wheelchair for him.'

'Jose, can you please find a wheelchair company who could come out to us to meet Goose and work out what sort of chair he would need?'

'What time tomorrow?'

'I would have thought about four in the afternoon, Jose.'

'Noel, Sally, have you a moment? If Goose is coming back tomorrow, we should sail to Mallorca tomorrow. That will be Saturday. Is everything ready for that? Do we need more fuel?'

'As for food, I am well stocked up, John. There is nothing I need.'

'We have eighty per cent of fuel. We don't need to be concerned about that. The weather looks fair for Saturday, so that is when we should depart. I only have a credit card for Goose's account. I don't have one for you, John.'

'Okay, I will fix that and get it sent to the yacht club in Puerto Pollenca.'

'John, I think I need to organise a mooring in Pollenca for a couple of weeks,' said Noel.

'I will make arrangements for Goose to visit a couple of properties that I have spotted on the internet. Sally, if he decides to buy one, will you be able to help him settle in?'

'Certainly John, Jose can help with furniture.'

'We will all help, John,' said Noel.

'Good, we can all relax and await his arrival. Once he is settled in, Fiona, I will fly back to the UK as I have some legal matters that need my attention.'

Everything went according to plan. Goose was exhausted when he eventually made it to the deck of *Brave Goose*. He was delighted with the wheelchair and agreed to buy the one the firm had brought with them. On Saturday morning, Goose had breakfast in bed. Then he joined everyone on the quarterdeck, sitting in his special wheelchair.

'Goose, I have found a couple of properties in Puerto Pollenca. The first is a finca, on the outskirts of the town. It has a lovely garden. The accommodation is all on the ground floor. The second property is a penthouse just one road back from the sea. The views from the large balcony are fantastic. It has three bedrooms and all mod cons. There is a lift to the ground floor. Would you like to see them both?'

'No, John, I think the penthouse sounds the best.'

John made arrangements for Goose to view the property on Sunday at eleven in the morning.

Brave Goose slipped out of Marina Port Vell in Barcelona en route to Puerto Pollenca; the Mediterranean was flat calm. The atmosphere on board was as calm as the sea.

***

'Brandon, it's Toby Evans. I have travelled back to Spain. There is a chance of work here. *Brave Goose* has just left Barcelona. My sources say she is headed for Puerto Pollenca. They have Goose on board. He now has an electric wheelchair. Do you have any instructions?'

'Yes, Toby. Can you get to Pollenca? If so, try and discover what they are doing there, and report back.'

Toby agreed and took the next ferry from Barcelona to Mallorca, berthing in Palma. He took a taxi to Puerto Pollenca. *Brave Goose* was manoeuvring to moor up on the visitors' quay.

Toby sat at a small table outside the main clubhouse of the Real Club Nautico Puerto Pollenca, sipping a glass of beer. Once moored, the skipper went to the office in the clubhouse.

Toby maintained a position in earshot of Noel and discovered he wanted to moor for at least two weeks. Toby saw the transaction being concluded. A great deal of paperwork and rubber stamping ensued. Toby returned to his beer.

***

'Okay, folks, we are moored here for at least two weeks. John, do you think the credit card will come soon? I had to pay on Goose's card.'

'No worries, let me know how much, and I will transfer the cash to Goose's account.'

'How are you feeling, Goose?'

'You know, John, I feel just fine. I would love to have a trip around the marina.'

'That can be arranged. We could go to the club and have a drink. If you like, we could have dinner there this evening?'

Getting Goose to the quay was the trick. He needed to walk with crutches and then reoccupy his wheelchair. It was a heavy piece of kit. It took John, Noel, Jock and Jose to lift it down onto the dock. Once there, Goose was delighted to sit down. He was doing remarkably well. His legs, of course, had been recovering longer than his lung.

Sally, Fiona, and John accompanied Goose, who understood how to manoeuvre his wheelchair with the joystick on the armrest exceptionally well.

They took a stroll around the marina, ending at the yacht club, which had a handy wide ramp up to the main floor of the clubhouse.

Passing the office, they moved out to the sun terrace. Sally, Fiona and John pulled up chairs to a circular table. Goose moved his chair to the vacant area at the table.

Goose ordered a coffee. The girls ordered tea, and John had a beer.

'Sitting where you are, Goose, looking into town, you can see a hotel just to the right of the roadway to the marina. Further to the right is a block of flats behind the hotel and one storey higher than the hotel. Can you see that, Goose?'

'Yes, I can very clearly, John.'

'Goose, the top storey of that building painted a pale lemon colour, is the penthouse we shall go and see tomorrow.'

'Now, that couldn't be more convenient. I could find a young person to live in and cook for me. Most dinners I can come and eat here. I should join this yacht club.'

Goose had just uttered those words when the waiter arrived with the drinks, a supply of biscuits as well as coffee and teas. Some crisps were placed in front of John with his beer.

'I am sorry, sir, but I couldn't help overhearing that you would like to join the club. As you are disabled, sir, I will ask someone from the office to come and see you. Would it be convenient now?'

'Thank you, that would be excellent,' responded Goose.

A lady from the office who spoke perfect English came to see the group within ten minutes.

'Would you mind if I sat down?'

'Not at all.' John drew up another chair, that was not in use, from an adjacent table.

'Now I gather one of you would like to join the club?'

'That is correct,' said Goose. 'I have recently sold my boat to this gentleman, John England. He is a solicitor and lives in England. I intend to live in Puerto Pollenca and to access the club in my chair. I hope to be able to walk here before long.'

'That is excellent. I can offer you a non-sailing membership, sir,' addressing Goose, 'and I can offer you, sir, a sailing membership. It is more expensive, but it entitles you to a twenty-five per cent discount on your mooring when you visit by boat.'

The two men agreed to join; John wanted Fiona to enjoy the facilities as a member. 'Is that possible?'

'Yes, sir. I need these forms completed; here are some yacht club pens with our compliments. Shall I come back in an hour to collect them?'

'Oh, before you go, what is your name?'

'I am Maria, sir.'

'Thank you, Maria, that is all very efficient. I plan to purchase an apartment close by here, and ideally, as I am a bachelor, and because of my injuries, I need some help. I can offer free board and a salary to a young person who can help me. I don't suppose you know of anyone?'

'That is extraordinary, sir. The young man sitting over there came into the office not half an hour ago looking for a crewing job. I know this is not the same, but he might be interested.'

'Do you know his name, Maria?'

'Yes, it's Toby Evans. He is English, but he does speak Spanish. Am I correct in thinking that *Brave Goose* is your motor yacht?'

'Yes,' said Goose, 'but I have had to abandon all my hopes of sailing due to my injuries, certainly for a year or two. I will have to see how I go on. Mr England is the new owner, Fiona is his partner, and Sally is the stewardess on board.'

'Congratulations, Mr England, you have a beautiful boat.'

'You must visit, Maria. I will be happy to show you around.'

'I will, thank you. I will come back soon. Just one more thing, will you be able to pay for the subscriptions this afternoon? If so, I can give you a temporary membership. You will get a valid membership card once your application has been through the membership formalities, which must be presented to the junta. Don't worry. I am sure it will all go through without any problem.'

'Shall I go and have a word with Toby, Goose?'

'Yes, please, John. If he is interested, ask him to come over and have a chat.'

Ten minutes later, John brought him over to meet Goose.

'Toby, has John explained what I need?'

'He has, sir. I am very keen on the idea. I don't have any lodgings in Pollenca, and I currently don't have a job. I came out here for the summer hoping to do some sailing, which I have done. I love this place so much I don't want to go home.'

'Okay, Toby. Look, we are here for a few days, so why don't you come to the boat tomorrow afternoon and have a good long chat with Goose?'

'Goose?' enquired Toby.

'Yes, that's my nickname. It has stuck over the years. Would you please call me Goose? I find it difficult to respond to my given name.'

'Thank you, Goose. I look forward to seeing you on *Brave Goose* tomorrow afternoon, say, three o'clock?'

'That's it, yes, that will do very nicely,' replied Goose.

The four of them finished their drinks, and once Toby was gone, they all thought he was a delightful young man.

'If he does what you need, Goose, we may have found the very person for you.'

Maria returned with some temporary membership cards and cards for the crew of *Brave Goose*.

'Here are the temporary membership cards, which entitle you to discounts on drinks and meals here. It also allows you to use the pool. The crew cards do the same thing, but I regret they exclude the use of the pool. Goose, this is your card.'

Maria had brought her credit card machine with her and some receipted invoices for a year's subscription and the joining fee, which was the big one. Three thousand five hundred euros, while the subscription was fifty euros.

Maria explained that the joining fee was a one-off charge; the subscription was paid annually.

'Next time you moor here, Mr England, you will be entitled to a twenty-five per cent discount.'

They all paid and appreciated Maria's help.

Fiona and Sally went to the facilities in the clubhouse. They were attracted by the cabinet displaying club merchandise on their way out.

'Hey Sally, look at these fabulous sweaters – what a badge, all in gold. It looks fabulous on the dark blue sweater. I am going to buy one. Would you like one, Sally?'

'Yes, I would. That is very kind of you.'

Fiona bought the crew a sweater each and one for John in the end. She wasn't sure if Goose would like one, so she would ask.

Skipping back to their table, John said, 'What have you got there? We wondered where you two had got to.'

'I have bought you a present, and one each for the crew, and one for me. I would happily buy you one, Goose, but I wasn't sure if you would want one.'

'Very discerning, Fiona, no, club sweaters are not my bag.'

'We had better be getting back. Do you want to come to the club for dinner tonight, Goose?'

'I don't think so, John. I have had a busy day. A light supper and then bed.'

'Okay, I understand.' John went to the restaurant and booked a table for six at nine o'clock.

'Goose, when you are in bed in your cabin, you will be able to watch TV if you would like to.'

'Is that now possible because of the domes?'

'It is, and I am sure Noel or Jock will be pleased to set it up for you.'

25

John, Fiona and the crew went to the yacht club for dinner. They could see *Brave Goose* more or less from their table. It would take only a moment for someone to pop over if required. Goose had the mobile VHF and Noel the other handset. He could call for assistance at any moment.

They enjoyed their meal and felt relaxed that they had Goose back with them.

'This meal is exceptional, John,' said Sally, 'it's a real treat for someone else to do the cooking and the washing up!'

They all laughed with Sally.

***

Toby Evans had noticed that the whole crew were in the yacht club. He realised that Goose would be alone in the boat. He took his opportunity.

'Sod it. I have dropped the handset,' muttered Goose to himself. It had slipped off the bed as he was rearranging himself.

On board *Brave Goose* now, Toby could hear the TV. It was coming from a forward cabin.

He quietly opened the door; he could see Goose was in bed.

'What are you doing here, Toby?'

'I was just passing, Goose, so I thought I would pop in to see if you were okay.'

'Kind of you, yes, I am doing fine. My wound is still very sore.' Goose rolled the bedclothes down and lifted his pyjama jacket to reveal a large plaster dressing over the bullet's exit wound. 'See, this is what I have to put up with, Toby.'

Toby bent over and hit Goose very hard with his fist right on the wound. Goose screeched with pain.

Toby hit him twice more. More blood oozed out under the dressing.

He hit Goose hard on his chin, effectively knocking him out.

Toby covered the half-conscious Goose with the bedclothes and switched the TV off, turning out the light. He left the boat stealthily, hoping he would not be spotted.

John, Fiona and the crew returned to *Brave Goose* about three hours later. They could not hear the TV. Fiona crept carefully towards Goose's cabin door and quietly opened it a little way, just enough to see Goose was covered up and asleep.

'He's asleep. It will do him good,' she said to all the team in the saloon. They said their goodnights and turned in.

Jose retracted the passerelle for safety.

***

'Brandon, it's Toby.'

'Hi Toby, where are you now?'

'I am in Puerto Pollenca. I have had a brief meeting with Goose.'

'You've what?'

'I was having a beer in the yacht club when John England came to chat. I had previously asked at the office if they knew of any crewing jobs. He came to chat about a job looking after Goose and having all paid accommodation and a salary. I have an interview with Goose this afternoon.'

'I don't know what to say. That could be very useful. You will pick up all sorts of information. While we would like to see Goose dead, in the meantime, he could be the source of beneficial information. Hope you get the job.'

'Thanks, but I think Goose will be dead by the morning. The crew were all off the boat having dinner, so I crept on and finished the job for you. What will be my bonus?'

'You did what!' exclaimed Brandon. 'That is a job well done. I can let you have ten grand. Let me have your bank details.'

'I don't have a bank, Brandon.'

'Okay, I will think of another way of getting the money to you. Are you coming back to the UK?'

'No, not now. I have enough cash to see me through when you send me my bonus.'

'Okay, Toby, I will work something out.'

***

Sally was up and about early, visiting the bakery to get some fresh croissants for breakfast.

By nine or shortly after, John and Fiona appeared for breakfast.

'Morning,' said Sally, 'what would you like this morning? A fry up or muesli, flakes, porridge, croissant; you name it, we have it.'

'Well done, Sally. I would love coffee and croissant and some orange juice.'

'Okay, Fiona. John, what can I get you?'

'It all sounds good, Sally. I want some cornflakes, a plate of bacon, egg and tomato, then some croissant and black coffee.'

'Okay, John, how would you like your egg?'

'Fried, I think.'

'No orange juice, John?'

'Oh yes, please, that all sounds wonderful.'

When Sally went to her galley, John said, 'We are fortunate to have Sally. She is brilliant. Just like you when we are at home.'

'I guess Goose is having breakfast in bed. I must find out. Hope he slept well.'

'I am sure he did, Fiona. There would have been a call for help if not.'

Sally brought the coffee. 'Is Goose having breakfast in bed?' asked Sally.

'I tried to wake him, but there was no reply. I suspect he was exhausted by the outing yesterday afternoon.'

'We have an appointment at eleven to see the penthouse. We need to get him going for that.'

There was no sound from Goose's cabin. It was ten o'clock. They were due to meet the agent at the penthouse at eleven. John decided he should go into Goose's cabin and see how he was.

John couldn't see any sign of life. His body was not moving and he wasn't breathing. He shook Goose by the shoulder and said his name.

'Goose, Goose, are you okay?'

Nothing. John rolled him over to find Goose lying in a blood pool. His eyes were glazed over. There was no sign of life. He tried to find a pulse in his neck and his wrist.

'Sally, can you bring your medical kit, please. It's urgent.'

Sally was very professional. She held the stethoscope to his chest. There was no heartbeat.

She undid his pyjama jacket to see that blood had oozed out of the wound made to patch up his right lung. The wound had opened. The blood was now congealed. Goose was dead.

With a tear running down Sally's face, the two of them went back to the saloon.

'Everyone, we have sad news. Goose died in the night. The wound in his back opened, and he has bled to death.'

'Jose, can you call an ambulance? We need to get an official verdict on this.'

Fiona was now in tears along with Sally. The blood had drained from Fiona's face. She was ashen.

'Despite me not knowing Goose for very long, I thought he was a lovely man. He has had a terrible end. The shot to the back was the end. Surprisingly, he was healed when he left the hospital.'

'John said we need to get professional help quickly. How is Jose doing?'

No sooner had John posed the question than Jose appeared.

'John, there is an ambulance on its way.'

John's mouth went dry. He was now thrown into a situation which he had accepted but never thought it would be so soon. John was now the executor of Goose's estate, not just a friend.

'Noel, do you think you could try and contact the agent we were supposed to meet at eleven this morning? Can you tell them the meeting is cancelled? You can tell them why. Fiona, can you find the details of the penthouse? They have the phone number for the agent, and then give it to Noel.'

'Yes, John,' said Noel and Fiona in unison.

As the crew and John were on the quarterdeck, the security guard let the ambulance onto the quay at the gate. They pulled up outside the passerelle of *Brave Goose*.

John hailed the driver and crew of the ambulance. Jose was there to explain Goose's medical situation and history. John showed the ambulance team into Goose's cabin.

The ambulance team looked Goose over, checking pulse and blood pressure.

'Senor, I am sorry, your friend is dead.'

'Jose, can you explain what happened in Barcelona?'

While Jose was busy explaining what had occurred to Goose in Barcelona, his stay in the hospital, and then his release, the other ambulance crew member brought a stretcher on board *Brave Goose*.

The main ambulance man explained he would have to inform the police. Also, there would have to be a post-mortem examination.

John understood what was being said. He just said, 'Okay.'

Within half an hour of the arrival of the ambulance, it was leaving the environs of the yacht club, bearing the corpse of Goose.

There was a terrible sense of loss on board. No one knew what to say or do.

'Did you manage to stop the agent, Noel?'

'Yes, John, they passed on their condolences. The appointment has been cancelled.'

Everyone on board *Brave Goose* wandered around, not knowing what to do or say.

As they were all stunned, a police car arrived at the passerelle. Two officers came on board.

Jose once again was required to explain everything that had happened up to this point. Going back a few weeks to the start of the end, when *Brave Goose* was caught in the fishing nets, John and Fiona were kidnapped, Goose had been shot in the legs. Then he was shot in the back by a motorcyclist. The GEO had been alerted. The hospital in Barcelona had released Goose, believing he was fit to be released.

In faltering but understandable English, the policeman said he needed to see the passports of everyone, the bill of sale to John, the will that Goose had made in the hospital. John provided the documents he had, and Noel provided the passports for everyone else.

The next question was could he see the scene of the crime.

'Jose, please tell this policeman that no crime was committed here. Suggest he contact Juan Mateo of the GEO in Barcelona. I will ring him now on my mobile so that he can speak to him.'

'Juan, it's John England. We are in Puerto Pollenca on Mallorca. Goose died in his sleep last night on the boat. He was fine during the day, but there must have been a rupture of his wound, and he has lost a great deal of blood. I am having difficulty explaining to the police that no crime was committed here. Would you kindly speak to the officer?'

'Senor, this is Senor Juan Mateo, of the GEO in Barcelona,' said John in his pidgin Spanish.

The police officer took the phone. From the expression on his face, it became clear that he understood everything that happened.

When the conversation was finished, the police officer said to John that he understood what had happened. He handed all the passports back and said he was sorry for their loss. He offered to get a company to come and remove all the soiled bedding, allowing the place to be cleaned.

John signalled that Jose would be delighted if the removal company could come.

The police left with a wave. 'Not something you would get in England,' said Noel.

Within a few minutes of the police car leaving, Toby Evans appeared at the passerelle.

'Come on board, Toby.'

John explained what had happened overnight, so that, regretfully, there was no job.

'I understand. I am sorry to hear of Mr Goose's death.'

'Thank you, Toby. Sorry, we can't do business,' said John.

Toby returned to the precincts of the yacht club, ordered a coffee, and phoned Brandon.

'Good, at least he is out of the way.'

'Yes, I met him yesterday. He seemed a charming guy. He was in a wheelchair. So there you are, nothing more I can do here.'

'Toby, can you let me know if John England and Fiona leave for the airport?'

'How will I know that?'

'They will have cases. They will leave in a taxi, all that sort of thing.'

'Okay, Brandon. I need some cash as it is expensive here.'

'I will send some money to the yacht club for you. Let me know as soon as they leave for the airport.'

'I will, thanks.'

***

'Fiona, we need to discuss what we will do now. I suddenly have a great deal to do.'

'Why is that, darling?'

'I am the executor of Goose's will. There is a great deal to do. The first thing I need is a death certificate. Once I have that, I can get started. Jose, can you ring the local hospital to find out where Goose has gone and when can I get a death certificate?'

Jose was as good as his word.

'The post-mortem examination will take place on Monday. Following that, a doctor will issue a death certificate. They will ring when it is available to collect.'

'Thanks, Jose, very helpful.'

John dug out his copy of Goose's will. The issue would be that the instructions to his two banks had not been concluded, so John would have to rely on his will and death certificate.

The death certificate was made available, and a burial certificate for the burial or cremation of Goose.

John hunted for an undertaker in Mallorca. He found several. They said that the firm he had seen was 'expert in preparing the ashes for burial at sea'. Funeral and crematorium were arranged for a week hence. The ashes were encased in an urn that would dissolve in water.

John discovered that it was not legal to put a casket into the water inside a twelve-mile range of the coast. The ashes could be sprinkled, but in the special casket that could be lowered overboard, the ashes would escape within a day or two.

Armed with the death certificate, John went to the office of the yacht club.

'Hello Maria, you will have seen comings and goings, ambulance and police at *Brave Goose* over the previous week. I am sorry to inform you that Mr Lenwell, Goose to his friends, died a week ago. At the time of his death, he had been a yacht club member for one day. As his executor, I would like to request the return of the membership fee.'

'Fully understand, Mr England. I will have to consult with the president. I will not be seeing him until tomorrow, but this will be a priority.'

'Thank you, Maria. Can I ask to have a reception for guests at his funeral in the club?'

'That will be no problem. If you would like to arrange it with the restaurant manager, that would be the best way.

Back onboard *Brave Goose*, John called everyone together.

'Following his wishes, I have arranged that Goose will be cremated a week on Wednesday. The crematorium is just north of Palma. I think there will just be the six of us unless anyone doesn't want to come, or you know of someone who would like to attend. I will arrange a minibus to take us there as far as we are concerned. The casket bearing his ashes will be delivered to us a few days after the cremation. After the funeral, I have arranged a meal for us all at the yacht club.

'Sally and Noel, can you please get some glasses and a

couple of bottles of Goose's favourite wine, and we shall sit around the table here, as I have more to say.'

Sally brought the wine glasses, some crisps and nuts. Noel poured the wine.

'Now, everyone, I am now in possession of Goose's death certificate, so it is appropriate that I read out the part of his will he made a few weeks ago after being shot in the legs. He was in the hospital in Barcelona. I witnessed his signature, as did Noel and a doctor in the hospital.

'As far as I am aware, this is the last will and testament of Julian Lenwell, Goose, to his friends. Various bequests cannot be honoured until I have managed to get some funds into a bank account I can control. The money is mainly in the Cayman Islands. However, despite a delay that will be inevitable, I will need full details of your bank accounts in due course.'

'Why, John?'

'Well, Jose, Sally, Jock and Noel, your ex-employer, Goose, was so impressed with what you did for him during your short acquaintance he has left each of you some money. I will place the money indicated on the slip of paper in the envelope I have given you. You may open it now, but it is confidential to you, so please do not yell out the amount.'

John passed the envelopes around, each with a name written on the envelope.

'Can we open them now?'

'Yes, Jock, but the amount is for you to have as soon as I get the money transferred to the UK.'

After a few moments, the envelopes had been opened. There were shrieks of delight from all recipients. Noel guessed he had been given more than the others, he was delighted.

'I am so sorry Goose has left us. I hope you will continue as crew on *Brave Goose* for as long as possible. Fiona and I are now the joint owners of *Brave Goose*. Fiona wants to learn navigation.'

Fiona looked at John, her face lighting up in amazement. She had no idea she was now the joint owner of *Brave Goose*.

'Did you mean to say I was the joint owner of *Brave Goose*, John?'

'Yes, I did, darling. I just need you to complete some forms, and the registration will be complete.'

John sent a lengthy email with attachments to Andrew Clifford at Bennett and Bennett solicitors in Chester the following day. John was technically still a partner but had waived his right to a share of fees, following his good fortune in the inheritance of Peters Tower and other legacies.

Andrew,

I recently purchased the superyacht Brave Goose from Julian Lenwell, who liked to be called Goose.

He made a will. You may recall you kindly sent me a proforma. It was appropriate as after he was released from the hospital due to the shooting of his legs when we were kidnapped on the high seas, he returned on board Brave Goose. *A sniper took a shot at him when he arrived on the deck. He was shot in the back. He had been in hospital in Barcelona for several weeks. He was released to our care about ten days ago.*

Overnight the wound in his back ruptured, he bled to death.

I am attaching a copy of his will and his death certificate. You will see there are various bequests. Until I can access the Cayman Islands funds, I cannot fulfil Goose's wishes.

Please discuss with the bank in the Cayman Islands, details attached, and take the money and transfer it to your client account. Leave the three million in the Cayman Islands. If you can find a lawyer there who can discover the whereabouts of his son and his mother, that would be helpful.

I am also attaching details of the bank accounts of the four persons mentioned in the will. When the money arrives, can you please satisfy the four bequests?

When you have done that, can you let me know? I will probably be back in England when the money comes through.

Thanks, Andrew.

John
Thanks for the email, John. Are you sure you don't want me to go personally to the Cayman Islands?

Yes, I can try and do all this. I guess it will not be straightforward. I recall we did receive funds from Goose's bank in the past, so we should make progress.

I will keep you posted.
Andrew

***

The yacht club had agreed to return Goose's membership charges. They offered their condolences.

The funeral had been arranged for Wednesday. On that day, a minibus collected John, Fiona, and Brave Goose's crew. It took them on an hour's drive to the crematorium to the north of Palma.

The undertaker was present, and a priest, who, it transpired, worked for the crematorium.

He gave a eulogy in English. Considering that he had never met Goose and only had the notes John had given to the undertaker, it was extremely accurate and moving. Clever man.

Once the service was over, the congregation, all six of them, returned to *Brave Goose*. John invited everyone to come to the yacht club, where a late lunch was waiting for them.

'I would like to toast our dear departed Goose. He was a rogue, a man with a big heart, and an avid sailor. He had sailed many, many miles in his various boats. Fiona and I are delighted to say we are now the owners of this wonderful boat. So, raise your glasses in memory of Goose.'

'Goose,' was the repeated toast.

26

'Noel, in a few days we should receive the special casket with Goose's ashes. Fiona and I need to get back to the UK for a short while to sort a few things out. So what I had in mind, was that we could come with you to Palma, and on the way, we could stop and have a short service for Goose to commit his ashes to the deep.'

'Yes, John. That is no problem at all. Shall I book a mooring in Palma? Do you know when you will be coming back?'

'Not at the moment.'

'Will you want to use Palma as your base? If so, it is a great deal cheaper to buy a year's contract.'

'Yes, that's a good idea. Let me know the cost.'

John went to the yacht club to enquire if any post had been received for him.

'Yes, Mr England. Just a few.'

Maria handed over the post. John advised that at some time this week, they would be leaving.

The post included Noel's credit card. 'That will give him access to the funds he needs for moorings, fuel and so on,' John muttered to himself.

Back onboard *Brave Goose*, John sat with a cup of coffee while he opened the remaining mail. As Noel passed him, John handed him his new credit card.

'Thanks, John. Is there a limit on the card?'

'Yes, Noel, it's one hundred thousand pounds. You should be able to refuel from scratch to full and still have some to spare.'

'That's a considerable sum, John. How is it paid off?'

'It's a charge card, Noel, so my account will pay it off every month. I get the statement.'

'I overlooked getting a card for Sally. Can that be arranged, John?'

While Noel was speaking, John had opened one of the other letters. In one of the envelopes was the card for Sally.

'Is that what is needed?'

'Thanks, John, that's great. I will give it to Sally.'

'Can I have the old cards, Noel, as executor to Goose? I will need to cancel and pay off these cards.'

The other two letters concerned insurance. The first was from Ian Birch, saying he had put *Brave Goose* on cover; the second letter was the insurers sending the policy.

'Noel, before you go, here are two letters you need to keep. One is from my brokers; Ian Birch is your man if there is any issue regarding insurance. Secondly, here is the policy for *Brave Goose* in our names.'

Later in the day, a courier arrived with a rather heavy parcel in a cardboard box.

On inspection, it was the casket bearing Goose's ashes. It had an instruction pamphlet with it.

'Sally, do you think you could get a floral wreath for Goose, as we shall be committing his ashes to the deep? And I thought it would be a good idea to lay a wreath on the spot. Ideally, it should float.'

'Yes, John. They will be open now; I will go and get one. Thank you for the new credit card, and here is the old one.'

'Thanks, Sally, there is a limit of forty thousand on the new one, will that be sufficient?'

'Yes, for sure.'

'I have found a few words to say tomorrow at Goose's funeral. Let's have a final meal here in Puerto Pollenca and make ready to go tomorrow.'

***

At nine o'clock the following morning, Sally returned to *Brave Goose* with a large wreath of beautiful, coloured flowers, a bag of fresh croissants, and two sticks of bread.

'Okay, Noel, I am ready to go when it suits everyone.'

The crew, John and Fiona, were up and about at ten.

'Which route are you taking, Noel?'

'I thought I would go north up to Formentor head and then at an angle until we reach the twelve-mile limit. That will be a position roughly 40'10" North and 3'00" East.'

'Will it be rough there, Noel?'

'Hard to say, Fiona, but it is the most economical way of finding a legal position to deploy the casket and yet the shortest route to Palma.'

As they approached the position Noel had plotted, the mountains on the north side of Mallorca were lit by the morning sun. The wind that was blowing had gone. The sea was still and calm. Noel brought *Brave Goose* to a stop. She had a little way on, but she was still in the water before long.

John and Fiona and the rest of the crew assembled on the port side of *Brave Goose*, looking straight back at Mallorca. Jock held the casket, and Noel had the wreath of flowers. John spoke to all.

'I have been trying to find some words that seem appropriate for our friend and colleague.

When I am gone, release me – let me go
I have so many things to see and do
You must not tie yourselves to me with tears
Be happy that we had so many years
I gave you love, you can only guess how much you
gave me in happiness
I thank you for the love each have shown
But now it is time I travelled alone
So grieve a while for me if grieve you must
Then let your grief be comforted by trust
It is only for a while that we must part,
So bless those memories within your heart.
I will not be far away, for life goes on.
So if you need me, call, and I will come.

Though you cannot see or touch me, I will be near
And if you listen with your heart, you will hear
All of my love around you, soft and clear
Then you must come this way alone
I will greet you with a smile and 'welcome home'.'

Silent tears were trickling down faces as they realised what had happened to their friend and benefactor, Goose.

'Please release the casket, Jock ,and will Sally, Noel and Fiona cast the wreath into the sea.'

'For as much as it hath pleased Almighty God to take unto himself the soul of our dear brother here departed, we commit his ashes to the deep in sure and certain hope of the Resurrection to eternal life through our Lord Jesus Christ. Amen.'

The congregation, such as it was, stepped away from the rail, all thanking John for such moving words.

There was little conversation. Noel returned to his position and restarted their journey to Palma. The wreath could still be seen on the sea for quite some time.

Sally brought a jug of freshly made coffee and a plate of biscuits for all to enjoy. She was still drying away the tears.

'That was a beautiful farewell, John. Your address was very moving. Thank you, John. Please help yourselves to coffee,' said Sally.

'Beautiful John. Thank you.' Fiona gave John a big kiss in front of the whole crew, which earned John a round of applause.

***

As *Brave Goose* made her sedate way through the blue Mediterranean Sea, the crew and owners were quiet in contemplation.

'If you look ahead now, you will see the island of Dragonera, like a wedge of cheese. We shall pass through the sound and then pass the entrance to the port of Andraitx. It is quite a safe harbour in anything other than a southerly gale,' announced Noel.

'Our plane back to Manchester is at two o'clock local time tomorrow. I guess we shall need to leave at twelve to be safe.'

'Understood, John,' replied Noel.

As arranged, John and Fiona went by taxi to Palma Airport for their two o'clock flight with no hold baggage. Back in Manchester, they were on a tram and back to Peters Tower in no time.

'It is so much easier travelling without hold luggage, John. It's very kind of Sally to do our laundry.'

'I agree. I suspect there may be more clothes to transport when we return!'

'I don't know what you mean, John.'

'I guess that there may be more clothes shopping between now and our return.'

'John, you surely are not referring to me?' exclaimed Fiona.

***

'Brandon, you don't know me, and you don't need my name, but you will discover that John England has returned with Fiona. I suspect they will be in their penthouse now.'

'I would like to know who you are and how you got my number?'

The phone went dead.

'Georgios, can I borrow your heavies in a day or two? I have an issue with my landlord, John England.'

'Is he a solicitor?'

'Yes.'

'You can have me and my two heavies. Just let me know when.'

27

John and Fiona went to their local bistro for an early supper.

'I have a great deal of work on Goose's estate and a debt recovery attempt with menaces for a client of Sally Moulton at Frobisher's solicitors.'

'I need to tidy up the penthouse, and I also need to have a further shop, because now as an owner of a superyacht, John, there are standards to be maintained.'

'Good, you have a good time. I have been thinking. I want to explore the eastern Mediterranean, Greece especially. We need to go out again in September as we are nearly into August. The weather can be great then. We could fly to Corfu and get Noel to bring *Brave Goose* to Gouvia Marina, Corfu. We could join her there. What do you think?'

'Oh John, that would be fabulous. How long will we be away?'

'I was thinking a month or six weeks, what do you think?'

'Sounds terrific to me. Go for it.'

John set about booking a return flight for the 1st of September and returning on the 10th of October. Within the hour, the bookings had been confirmed. Then he emailed Noel to tell him of their plans.

'Can you be at Gouvia Marina, Corfu, in time for us to travel out on 1st September?'

Noel came straight back to confirm that they would be there for John and Fiona to join them in plenty of time.

'Thanks, Noel, have a good sail.'

'The holiday is all arranged, Fiona.'

'Fantastic. It can't come soon enough.'

'Jon, it's John England. Out of courtesy, I thought I would let you know we are back in England at the penthouse at Peters Tower. If you need me, you know my number,' was John's message for his detective friend.

John was conscious he had not received any response from Manchester European Finance. He thought it was time to take a shot across his bow. John sent a powerful email requiring a complete response within seven days.

John was about to lift the phone and speak to Sally Moulton when the phone rang.

'Mr England, it's Brandon Phelan.'

'Hello, what can I do for you?'

'I wonder if you would have an hour free this week?'

'Yes. Okay, which day?'

'Oh, Thursday?'

'Two pm at my penthouse. The same arrangement as before.'

'Do you mind if I bring a colleague who has been working on the finer details of the scheme?'

'No objection. See you Thursday.'

'Sally Moulton? It's John England.'

'John, good to hear from you. What have you been up to?'

'The answer to that would take a very long lunch. Why don't we meet? I will bring my partner if you don't mind? I will book a table at the French restaurant at The Midland for noon. Please arrange it so you don't have to rush off.'

'That's great, but something tells me you didn't ring just to invite me out to lunch.'

'Correct. I have been checking the finance company our mutual client has used. It would seem there is no record of this company anywhere. It isn't limited, so I assume either a sole trader or a partnership. Do you have any detail of its structure, further, have you or the client ever received any headed paper or a brochure from this firm? I would like to see what extravagant claims they make for their services.'

'Don't know, John. I will try and find out. Thanks, John.'

Sally mused to herself on putting the phone down. He is bringing his partner. Is that a business partner or a female lover? She hoped it would be the former.

**

Sydney had, as requested, provided Mr Phelan with a time-limited pass for the lift to the penthouse of Mr England.

At two o'clock, Mr Phelan arrived at the reception desk to be presented with his pass for the penthouse.

Phelan took the lift to floor eight, his flat's floor. Then within a few minutes, it started on its way to the penthouse.

At the penthouse, the lift stopped, and all four occupants got out. Phelan and Georgios stood so that only they could be seen from the spy hole in the main door.

John England opened the door and walked back into the penthouse, not realising that three other men were following him. Fiona was about to come and ask if anyone wanted a drink until she saw the back of the men. She quietly went out of the front door down to reception.

'What's going on here, Phelan? I was expecting two people. Why are there four of you?'

'It seems that my friends in Spain have failed to extract the three million pounds you owe my family. So I thought I would approach it a different way.'

'So you have brought a group of heavies with you to extract the money. Very amusing, I must say. Do you expect the money to be in my personal safe, or do you have some other plan?'

'Oh, we are here to stay until the money is transferred to my bank.'

'What makes you think my bank will just transfer millions of pounds to your bank with a phone call? If you think that, then you are more naive than I thought.'

The heavies moved towards John with that response but only stood close to him, making him feel uncomfortable.

'I will do nothing so long as these goons are here. Send them back to wherever they came from.'

'Hey, don't call my men 'goons'. They don't like that language.'

'And who are you?'

'I am Georgios, owner of Manchester European Finance.'

'Oh yes, the goons will be yours. I suppose that is how you go about collecting your debts. The CCTV here will be making some good pictures of your business tactics. The film will be advantageous for me when I get you into court.'

'I can't see any cameras.'

'That's the whole idea. They are secret, so goons like your assistants can't rip them out.'

The heavies moved even closer to John.

'Look, send these men packing, Georgios. I am not prepared to assist you in collecting any money from me so long as these men are here.'

'Yes, send them away, Georgios,' instructed Brandon. 'They are only making things worse.'

The goons removed themselves, and John heard the lift take them away.

John lifted a phone handset and spoke to Sydney. 'The two large gentlemen are on their way down in the lift. They are to leave the premises.'

Sydney acknowledged the call.

'So, Brandon, what is your intention now?'

Both Brandon and Georgios pulled pistols from their pockets.

'So, how are those pistols going to help you?'

'They will help you remember what you have to do. If we don't get the money, then we will kill you. So how will you enjoy Fiona on your new yacht in the Mediterranean when you are dead?'

'Clearly, I won't, but you will still not have the money, so this is a silly situation. The fear of you pulling the trigger doesn't worry me in the slightest.'

Fiona had escaped and was hiding in Sydney's office. She didn't know the phone number for Jon Kim but felt she should phone 999 in any event as these people were intent on getting money out of John.

'So, what now, gentlemen?' enquired John.

'Phone your bank and make an appointment this afternoon to go and personally give instructions to transfer three million to my account,' demanded Brandon.

'Julian, it's John England. I need to make an appointment to transfer a significant sum from my account number 23 555 999. The sum is three million. Can you see me today?'

'Yes, John. I fully understand. Can we say three-thirty today?'

'Yes, I will be at the bank then.'

***

Sydney had received the message that the two strongmen would be coming down. They had not arrived.

'Sydney, I will be leaving here shortly with two other men. I am going to the bank. Have you seen Fiona?'

'Yes, I fully understand, sir, and yes, everything is just fine here.'

'Good, thanks, Sydney.'

'I will need your full bank details, Brandon. Can you write them down, please? Name of the account, name of the bank, sort code and account number.'

'You seem very calm, John. Are you not a little bit afraid?'

'No, I am not. You will not kill me before we get to the bank, as you are so close to fulfilling your task. You will not be permitted into the bank manager's office with me, so what do you think will happen at the bank?'

'You will make the transfer.'

'Of course, then there is no need to kill me then; you will have the money.'

'Hey, Brandon, this guy can double-cross you. He will call the police when we are in the bank.'

'Smart guy, your friend, Brandon.'

'There is only one thing for it. We need your girlfriend as a hostage. Where is she?'

'I don't know.'

'Don't give me that bullshit. You must know where she is.'

'The last time I saw her was in this flat.'

Georgios did a recce of the penthouse. 'She isn't in here.'

'I genuinely have no idea where she is.'

'So what are we going to do, gentlemen? I am going to be late for the appointment at the bank.'

'Well, we are so close to relieving you of the money, I think we should all go to your bank. I will decide what to do when we get there.'

'Okay, how are we going to get to the bank? I will miss the appointment at the bank if we walk. Shall I order a taxi?'

Brandon and Georgios looked at one another and nodded.

'Yes, get on and book a taxi for five minutes.'

John lifted the handset and spoke to Sydney. 'Can you get me a taxi to go to St Ann's Square and my bank in five minutes? There will be three of us.'

'Yes, sir.'

***

'Okay, Sydney, I will try and contact Jon Kim,' said Fiona.

Fiona managed to get to the main switchboard at GMP HQ, but they made it difficult to put her through to Jon Kim. She waited for what seemed an age, then eventually, Jon was on the line.

'Jon, thank goodness. John is being escorted to his bank in St Ann's Square by two men, one of the men is Brandon Phelan, and they are taking John, I am certain, against his will to get their hands on the three million pounds they have been trying to get for ages.'

'Thanks, Fiona, where are you?'

'I am hiding in Sydney's office in the reception of Peters Tower.'

'Stay there. Don't move. I will have officers over there to keep you safe.'

Sydney was gesturing to Fiona as he wanted to speak with Jon Kim.

'Detective Inspector, I am Sydney, the head receptionist at Peters Tower. Two very large and rough-looking heavies arrived, and I think they went to Mr Brandon's flat, 803. They had gone with Mr Brandon and his colleague up to the penthouse. Mr England rang to say the two heavies were coming down. He asked me to see them off the premises. However, they have not come through reception. I suspect they are still in Flat 803. I thought you should know.'

'Thanks, Sydney, just keep yourself and Fiona safe. We will handle this from here,' said Jon Kim.

Within ten minutes of John England and his two companions leaving in a taxi, two police officers entered and met Fiona and Sydney.

'Where are the two heavies who have been threatening?'

'I am sure they are in Apartment 803 on the eighth floor. They look like powerful heavyweight boxer types. You may need reinforcements.'

'Thanks, Sydney. We will call for backup and then go to the flat. Do you have a master key?'

'Yes, I do.'

'Good, we will go in using that. Are you both okay?'

'I am very worried about John England, my partner. I am sure they intend to harm him as soon as the bank transfers the money.'

'Please don't be concerned. There is a welcoming party for the two hooligans when they get to the bank.'

John England, Brandon Phelan and Georgios Armani left the taxi, allowing John to pay the fare. They entered the bank, which looked nothing like the sort of bank the two customarily used. There was no cashier desk. The entrance to the bank was a large reception area with a counter and four receptionists operating phones with computer terminals at each station. Three security guards were standing in various places around reception. The lifts were guarded by automatic glass gates off the main reception area.

'Good afternoon, gentlemen. Do you have an appointment?' enquired one of the male receptionists.

'I do; it's with Julian Franks.'

'And you gentlemen, will you be waiting here?'

'We thought we could accompany Mr England,' said Brandon.

'No sir, if the appointment was with Mr England only, then I am afraid you can't progress beyond here.'

'Can you please ring the manager to see if we can come with Mr England? It is necessary as we have to witness a document.'

'Very well, sir, I will enquire. Yes, sirs, you can go to the fourth-floor reception, but not into the manager's office. To do that, I need to give you a visitor's pass and take your photograph, your names and addresses.'

Brandon and Georgios submitted photographs and the rest of the required information.

John overheard them both give false addresses. Should he shop them now or later?

Eventually, all three were allowed through the glass gates. A security guard then accompanied them in the lift to the fourth floor.

'Is the fourth floor where all the money is kept, with you guarding us like this?' Georgios said to the security guard, who didn't respond.

On the fourth floor, they all alighted, including the security guard. Brandon and Georgios were invited to sit on large leather sofas while Julian welcomed John into his office. The door was closed behind them.

Nothing was said between Julian and John. Brandon and Georgios didn't speak. They realised they were very much out of their comfort zone in such an environment.

Once inside the office, John and Julian had a brief chat. They realised what the two men outside were planning. The money they were trying to extort from John England was safe, and they wondered if they would ever get the money into Brandon's bank.

The phone on Julian's desk rang. He simply acknowledged the message.

28

'Can everyone come to the saloon? I need to discuss issues with you,' Noel announced through the ship's intercom system.

Once all four of them had assembled, Noel advised them that John and Fiona had decided they would like to sail in the Ionian Sea in Greece.

'Oh, that would be wonderful, Noel. I love Greece. The people are so lovely.'

'I agree with Sally,' said Noel, 'it is a wonderful cruising area.'

Jose and Jock were both as enthusiastic.

'That is excellent. They have a flight arriving in Corfu on the first of September. I suspect it will be mid-afternoon before they come. The journey from here to Corfu is a little more than 900 nautical miles. My calculations make one hundred hours at sea – just over four days. We will burn probably fifteen thousand litres of fuel. The thing is, we have time to go slowly and stop three, or possibly four, times. Instead of four days non-stop, it will be eight, so I will work on ten days, allowing for bad weather. Anyone any thoughts on that idea?'

'I think that would be sensible, Noel. It will allow me to ensure the engines are working well.'

'Thanks, Jock, that makes sense. My rough route will be, subject to more research, Palma Mallorca to Cagliari in Sardinia, then Cagliari to Messina, Sicily, Messina to Gallipoli on the heel of Italy, then on to Gouvia Marina, Corfu. That is the nine hundred miles. It's quite a trip but split into four segments. It should be easy enough. The longest will be about twenty-seven hours. A day off after those segments will recover before starting again. We need to leave here on the fifteenth of August to be safe, so we should be at our destination by the 25th. If I book a berth, we can then have ten days to prepare the boat for the owners.'

There was general agreement to this arrangement.

'So, we have a week to prepare for our trip to Corfu.'

'What should I do with Goose's cabin, Noel? We should get rid of all the bedding, including the mattress. We would need to buy new everything. Should I do that in anticipation or wait for John and Fiona to decide?'

'I am sure they have more than enough to keep them occupied. Let's do as you suggest. We should also parcel up all Goose's clothes, spring clean the cabin and move all John and Fiona's clothes to the owner's cabin. What do you think?'

The response was unanimous.

Jose, Jock, and Sally helped remove the mattress and the bedding from the owner's cabin to the quarterdeck. Sally put all the soiled bedclothes in plastic bags, ready for disposal. Where to dispose of everything was the issue.

Noel booked a mooring in Gouvia Marina from 25th August until 2nd September.

Noel was working out the route on the bridge and making copious notes for navigation purposes when his mobile rang.

'Noel, it's Juan from GEO in Barcelona.'

'Juan, you could be just the man I need. But you rang me, so what can I do to help you?'

'The surgeon who operated on Goose was very concerned to hear how Goose had died. He found it hard to believe that the wound had opened and left Goose to bleed to death. He asked me to enquire if anyone could have been aware of Goose having a fall or hitting his wound. Worst of all, could anyone have visited Goose and hit him, causing the bleed?'

'I can't say, Juan. We were all on board all the time. I am sure we would have heard something if he had fallen. No, sorry Juan, we all left the boat, except Goose, to go for a meal in the yacht club. We left him with a handheld VHF, we had the other set, but we had no call for help.'

'Obviously, the body cannot be examined now, but the surgeon is adamant he must have fallen.'

'Well, if he had fallen because of the state of his legs, he would have been unable to get back into bed. So the only possible explanation is that someone came on board and hit him.'

'Do you have CCTV which covers the passerelle?'

'Yes, we do, Juan. I can look at it and email you a copy if there is evidence of a stranger coming on board. I will do that straight away.'

'You wanted to ask me something?'

'Yes, we are in Palma, and I wondered if you would know where we could dispose of all the blood-stained bed covers and mattress?'

'That is easy, John. I will get the forensic department of Palma police to come and retrieve it. If there is foul play, the assailant is bound to have left some evidence. The forensic team will investigate, and when they have finished with it, they will dispose of the items.'

When Juan had finished the call, Noel went straight to the recording machine for the CCTV and played it back to the evening they were in Puerto Pollenca. At ten past nine, a figure with a hoodie came up the passerelle; at twenty past nine, he left, his hoodie off his head. It was Toby Evans. The boy could have come to work for Goose if he had bought an apartment in Puerto Pollenca. Noel recorded the tape and sent it with an appropriate message and identification of Toby to Juan at GEO.

Within half an hour, Juan rang again. He told Noel he had issued an arrest warrant for Toby Evans. The forensic team from Palma would come on board to recover all the bedding.

'Once the bedding and mattress have gone, are we then free to refurbish the cabin?'

'Yes, Noel, no problem.'

'We are sailing to Corfu on the 15th of August, just under a week away. John and Fiona are flying out to meet us in Corfu.'

'I don't see why we should detain you, Noel. If we have a problem, we can always catch you on the phone. Have a good trip.'

A police van appeared at the end of the quay within the hour. Four officers in white overalls came onto *Brave Goose* with very large plastic bags. They methodically placed all the bedding and mattress in the bags and took them away. They also did a forensic inspection of Goose's cabin.

'That certainly saved a job, Noel.'

'It did, Sally. The CCTV shows that Toby crept on board while we were at dinner in the yacht club in Puerto Pollenca. The police think he could have been responsible for the bleed that caused Goose's death.'

'How awful, Noel. Do you think he was part of the gang trying to kill Goose and extract the money from John?'

'I don't know, but it is a possibility.'

Sally went into town and purchased two cheap carriers for packing Goose's clothes. She hoped she could find a charity shop at the same time. She did, in the back streets of the town.

She packed every last bit of Goose's clothing into the carriers back on board.

'I had no idea there would be so many clothes, Jose.'

'Goose was well dressed. If his anorak is going to charity, I wonder if it would fit me. I don't have a warm coat.'

'Sure, Jose, try it on.'

'Very smart. That fits just fine. You have it.'

'Thanks, Sally.'

'There is a price, Jose. You have to help me take this lot to the charity shop. Noel, have you thought about replacing the mattress and acquiring new bedding for the owner's cabin?'

'Sorry Sally, I haven't. Do you want me to come with you to see what we can find?'

'Yes, please. Jose is coming as we have all Goose's clothes to give to the charity shop. I need to go now before they close at noon.'

'Okay, I will come as well. I can carry one of the carriers.'

The charity shop was most grateful for the clothes. Jose enquired on behalf of all three where they might purchase a mattress and bedding.

Then in perfect English, she advised there was a new furnishing shop just on the outskirts of the town in a new shopping arcade.

'They supply all that sort of thing as there has been an expansion in building villas and apartments. I would take a taxi, as it's quite a walk.'

The shop was just what they needed. There was no other customer in the shop, and the owner could not have been more helpful.

'Yes, we need a very comfortable, top of the range mattress and cover, four or possibly six down-filled pillows, then we need cotton sheets and some blankets. Can you help?'

'Si, senorita, we can help you. Please come to the bedding showroom, and I can show you what we have.'

Eventually, Sally found the comfortable mattress she was seeking. 'Can we have this one?'

'I am sorry, all these are for display. I can order you one?'

'How long would it take to arrive?'

'About two weeks.'

'Oh, we don't have that amount of time. It is for a large motor yacht, and we shall be leaving in a week.'

'What have you been using up to now?' enquired the shopkeeper.

'It's a long story, but our owner was shot in the back while we were in Barcelona. His wound leaked the other night badly, and he died. The bedding has had to be removed, so we are replacing everything for the new owners.'

'Are you from *Brave Goose*?'

'Yes, how did you know that?'

'I walked past her the other evening. I also read in the paper about the terrible time you have had. I understand your problem. Yes, of course, you can have this mattress. We will deliver it this afternoon. I gather you need more bedding?'

'Yes, we do.' Sally went through the list. Noel paid the bill and thanked the kind shop owner for her help.

At three in the afternoon, all the bedding and new mattress arrived. All the men on board helped the driver to bring everything on board.

Sally spent the last of the afternoon making the bed and sorting out the bedroom. She also did a complete spring clean on the cabin. She then moved all John and

Fiona's clothes and belongings into the owner's cabin.

'Noel, I know it's not in the plan, but I would love to make some new curtains for the owner's cabin. The existing ones are very drab. They work as curtains but are not very attractive.'

'I don't see why not, Sally. Can you do that?'

'I certainly can. I have seen some fabric and an electric sewing machine in an electrical shop. I could make all sorts if I had the machine. It will also be perfect for me on long passages. Give me something to do.'

'I don't see why not, Sally. Take Jose with you so that he can help with the lingo!'

No sooner said than Sally and Jose were off to the electrical shop and the haberdashers for the material she had seen. They were back on board within the hour.

'That all looks very exciting, Sally. Good luck with your endeavours.'

'I will start when we start our trip to Greece, Noel. Do you want me to rustle up a meal, or shall we go to a harbourside café?'

'Oh, I think we have all done enough today. Let's all go to a café.'

'Thanks, Noel. I will let everyone know.'

'Not long now, folks. In three days, we set off for Sardinia. The weather looks satisfactory, although we might get a bit of wind once past Minorca.'

'It will be quite a trip, Noel.'

'Well Sally, this boat was made for journeys like this. I am looking forward to it. She can take whatever the weather wants to throw at us.'

'Is everything okay in your department, Jock?'

'Yes, Noel, I have a few more filters to clean and then I will be happy to go.'

29

'Shall I ring the police, John? The two men outside are, without doubt, crooks.'

'No, don't do anything. Let me have a bit of paper to allow them to think the money is theirs. When I have gone, you can recall it.'

'As you wish, John. I will recall it as soon as you are out of that door. It might not have left us by the time I request its return.'

Julian retrieved a piece of paper from his printer. It was official-looking, confirming the transfer from John's account to the account nominated by Brandon Phelan.

'I will let the two of them go. I will follow up later. Do you mind if I make a mobile call after they have gone?'

John came out of the manager's office door. He handed the paper to Brandon without a word.

Brandon thanked him and moved to the lift. The two men, Georgios and Brandon, set the lift for the ground floor, catching a taxi on the street, laughing now.

'How easy was that?' said Brandon.

'Easy,' responded Georgios. They both started to giggle like girls.

***

'Fiona darling, it's me. Can you leave the tower as soon as you can?'

'Where are you, John?'

'I am at the bank. Can you get a taxi to St Ann's Square? I will meet you outside the bank.'

'Are you all right, darling?'

'Yes, I am just fine. Hurry now as Brandon, I think, is on his way back to Peters Tower.'

As a taxi came around the corner and was about to stop, John stood in front of it, hoping he had the right cab. He had Fiona waving from the window. John got in, and they embraced.

'Sorry, cabbie, can you take us back to Peters Tower? Thanks.'

'Wish some people would make up their mind,' said the cabbie.

Sydney was behind the reception desk.

'It's good to see you back, Mr England. Those people looked very threatening. The police came for the two heavies and took them away.'

'I see, that will not please Mr Phelan and his friend.'

'Well, the heavy mob were not too happy either, the way they were shouting.'

'Thanks for looking after Fiona for me, Sydney. It was clever of her to escape as the two men came into the penthouse.'

'Did you give them what they wanted, John?'

'Yes and no; they went away with a piece of paper saying three million pounds had been transferred to their account. However, while they were in the taxi, the bank recalled the money, so it never left my account.'

'That's clever, John. It still means they will be chasing the money, though?'

'As always, you are correct. We will deal with the next request when it comes.'

'I don't fancy going out tonight, darling. Have you something in the fridge you could rustle up?'

'Yes, I have, but I bet it is ages since you ate fish fingers?'

John laughed. 'That sounds fantastic. Well done, my little angel and superyacht owner!'

Sitting at his desk in his office the following day, he was removing inappropriate and advertising emails from his computer when a new email arrived.

John

I hope all is well with you.

You will not believe this, but I have received five million pounds sterling into our client account today. Three million resides in the Cayman Islands. The bank says they do know Carmel Landon. They have asked her to attend the bank

*with some ID. Once that is done, they will transfer the three
million to her and her son.*

I need instructions, please.

Andrew

John immediately responded. 'Andrew, that is excellent
news, in a way. I had hoped I would have to go to the
Cayman Islands!'

'It's good of you to ring me so quickly!'

'Well, it isn't every day you have the prospect of
receiving five million. I have yet to close Goose's current
account in the UK. I can now deal with finalising his estate.'

'If you need any help, let me know, John. I will make
the transfer today.'

John did some calculations. The money that was still
in the UK bank would have the payment for *Brave Goose*
in it. So there could be a few pounds in there to bring
out to John's account. He now had the job of organising a
payment to the RNLI.

John found the phone number of the RNLI and rang
to speak to the donations department.

Once he got to the correct department, he explained
he was the executor of a will.

'Good morning, sir. My name is Hazel. How can I help
you?'

'I am the executor of a will, and the deceased, who was
well known to me, has left a bequest for the RNLI. Ideally,
my partner and I would like to come down to Poole and
talk to you and hopefully see your establishment, and as
boat owners, we would love to see your workshops where

you make the boats. Would it be convenient if we come next week?'

'Yes, sir, can I have your details?'

John trotted out all his details and that he was a solicitor and executor of Goose's estate.

'As you are travelling some distance, would you like a room for the night? We have several rooms we let out.'

All was arranged for the following Wednesday. John couldn't wait to speak to Fiona. She had gone shopping.

'Julian, John England.'

'Hi John, has everything calmed down?'

'Yes, Julian, it has. I guess they are brooding about what to do next. They need to hurry up as we are going back to our boat to spend six weeks cruising around Greece.'

'Now that sounds like a proper holiday! I thought the boat was in Mallorca. How long will it take you to get to Greece?'

'Oh, the boat will be in Corfu. I have a crew of four who will take it to Greece.'

'That sounds like the way to do it. What can I help you with today?'

'I am the executor of the estate of the previous owner of our boat. He has made several bequests. His partner and son live in the Cayman Islands, where his money is, or should I say it was. There were two bequests to his partner and son, which the bank in the Cayman Islands is handling, as they know the woman involved. The residue of his estate was to come to me, save for two million, which is to be donated to the Royal National Lifeboat Institution. So there is a transfer coming into my account from Bennetts, who organised the money coming from the Cayman Bank, of a little over five million pounds. I need a banker's draft to the RNLI from my account for two million five hundred thousand pounds. Fiona and I are going to the RNLI next Wednesday. Can you fix a draft for me in that sum?'

'I certainly can. I have checked your account. The five-point one million has arrived. The draft will be no problem. Could you call and collect it, say on Friday morning?'

'I will, Julian, thank you.'

John phoned Goose's bank in the UK and spoke to a manager. He explained what had happened and that John as executor wished to close the account and transfer the funds to his bank account.

The branch where Goose's account was held was in London.

'Well, sir, we need to see your ID, a copy of the death certificate and the will. Once we have done that and it all checks out, we can honour your request, which we shall require in writing.'

'As you have a branch in Manchester, may I submit my ID and other documents there and request that they send you the copies?'

'Yes, sir, that will be fine.'

John collected all the documents he required, including his passport. He scribbled a note for Fiona, saying he should be back in an hour.

***

'Brandon, what are you going to do now?'

'Georgios, it is a puzzle. Your two men are in custody. I don't have any appetite for going through the process again, as it is clear England would wriggle out of the payment again. I need to get some assistance away from this country, but I don't know what, at the moment.'

'This guy England is making my life hell. He has issued papers for me to attend court. He has reported me to the FCA and the FCS, who have threatened me with closure and told me to stop trading. They will be visiting me soon. I think I will have to go back to Italy, and quickly.'

'Oh, well, sorry to hear that. Let me know when you are going and how I can get in touch.'

'I will be going home this week.'

'Where is home, Georgios?'

'Oh, my family home is in Messina in Sicily. I will go there.'

'What will you do in Sicily?'

'I have a lot of cousins and friends who have businesses. They will find a job for me.'

'Mind how you go.'

As soon as he had put the phone down, Brandon realised Georgios had not paid him for the final bit of the software he had created for him. Georgios's phone was engaged when he rang back. He was sure he would not get paid.

'This is great,' Georgios muttered to himself. 'Two hundred pounds one way on Easyjet, and I will be home.' He had to fly from Liverpool, but that didn't cause a problem. A one-way car hire sorted that.

That weekend Brandon received a call from Georgios.

'Hi Brandon, sorry I forgot to pay you in my rush to getaway. Let me have your bank details, and I will send you the money.'

'I am in Sicily. There was a direct flight from Liverpool. It was simple.'

***

'Fiona, sorry darling, I had to go to a bank to sort out Goose's bank account in the UK. The money has come through from the Cayman bank. Next Wednesday, I have made arrangements to go to the RNLI headquarters in Poole. I have arranged to stay Tuesday and Wednesday nights at their HQ. They have rooms to rent.'

'That sounds exciting, John. What do I wear?'

'Casual, darling, and some deck shoes in your bag, as we may get to look at a lifeboat.'

'That is exciting. I can't wait.'

John realised that all calls to Manchester European Finance and his emails were not returned. The heavies who collected the money were no longer available, sent to jail for six months. They were convicted at the magistrates' court for demanding money with menaces.

'Sally Moulton, please, it's John England.'

'John, good to hear from you. What can I do for you today?'

'It's rather the other way around. I have to apologise that Fiona and I haven't taken you out for dinner. We had a somewhat longer stay in Mallorca. I bought a large boat, and subsequently, the owner who had sold it to me died. Before he died, I made a will for him, and I am the executor of his estate. So I have been swamped.'

Realising Fiona was the partner, the prospect of going out for dinner with John and his 'partner' was less attractive.

'Don't worry, John. I knew when you said you would be stepping back. I thought that was an ambitious prospect.'

'My call is about this Manchester European Finance company. I have since discovered that they had persuaded pensioners to allow them to manage their portfolios and guaranteed a six per cent return. He was lending the pensioners' money to people like the Hamiltons, who you asked me to help. The good news is they will no longer need to make any repayments. I am looking at ways to get the capital back to the pensioners. The reason the heavies were involved, as far as I can tell, was that the money lent to your client was the only loan he had made, and he was running out of cash to pay the pensioners.'

'That is quite a story. What are you planning to do now, John?'

'I am running short of time, Sally. I will write to the Hamiltons and give them the good news. I will also write to the four pensioners he has raided for cash and give them the bad news. I am working on a solution. It isn't easy, Sally.'

'I can see that, John, but thank you so much for what you have achieved so far.'

John did as he had promised and created five letters. Four were pretty much the same, giving pensioners the bad news but holding out a vestige of hope that John might recover some funds somehow. The fifth to the Hamiltons was all good news. They had their loan cancelled, and they would have to pay nothing more. They were free to get on with their lives. John sent copies of all the letters to Sally.

'Come on, Fiona, I don't want to be too late getting to Poole. I am not sure what time the RNLI close their hotel.'

'Okay, John, I have nearly finished packing.'

'You know we are only there for two nights?'

'Yes, I know, but as a superyacht owner, I can't just turn up in jeans and a T-shirt, can I?'

'Well, you can, but you always look wonderful in whatever you wear.'

A cocky smirk appeared on Fiona's face.

'Sydney, Fiona and I will be away for a few days; we will be back at the weekend. I am not expecting anyone in the event someone turns up pretending to have an appointment!'

'Have a good trip, sir. All will be well here.'

John and Fiona took the Range Rover for the trip to Poole.

30

As John was driving, his mobile rang. He could answer it by the hands-free facility built into the car.

'John, it's Noel. Thought I should make contact before we set off for Corfu.'

'Kind of you to call. When will you be heading off, Noel?'

'We will leave Palma at 0800hrs on Saturday. We expect to be in Marina del Sole, where I have a mooring booked, during the afternoon of Sunday. We leave there on Tuesday for Sicily.'

'Where is Marina del Sole, Noel?'

'It's on the southern coast of Sardinia. It's a marina close to the town of Cagliari, which is on most maps.'

'Okay, we shall plot your course. Let me have a text to confirm your safe arrival in Sardinia.'

'Thanks, John, I will. Bye.'

'He's a good man, is Noel. He takes as much care of *Brave Goose* as if he owned her.'

'I agree, Fiona. It is very reassuring to have him as skipper. I don't think I would have bought the boat without the crew. It makes life when we are on board so much easier. Furthermore, we can do what we are about to do and join her in a different location.'

'This is it,' said John as he swung the Range Rover through the gates to the RNLI college, with panoramic views of Poole harbour. 'It is a magnificent facility. An excellent building for crews to stay under training and visitors to stay and visit the facilities.'

John and Fiona found their beautiful room with views across Holes Bay in Poole harbour. 'This is undoubtedly Lifeboat central,' said John.

John and Fiona were waiting in reception to be greeted by someone to show them around. However, John had other ideas before the tour.

'Good morning,' said a lady dressed in blue with an RNLI badge. Maggie was the name emblazoned on her name tag.

'I understand you would like a tour of our facilities here?'

'Well, yes, but I have some business I would like to conduct by way of a donation if that is possible.'

'Oh, thank you. Did you say you wanted to donate when you booked?'

'No, I didn't know it would be necessary.'

'It's just that our fundraising team would like to meet you. Can I get someone to join us? Have you an idea how much you would like to donate?'

'Yes, is it essential I tell you?'

'It's just who can come down.'

'Well, it's just two and a half million pounds.'

Fiona thought Maggie was about to collapse. She wasn't sure what she should say other than, 'Please have a seat, I will see who is available!'

Maggie disappeared through some doors marked 'staff only'.

After a few minutes, a gentleman dressed in a suit came back with Maggie.

'Mr England, I am Jeremy, head of fundraising. Please come with me. We can get a cup of coffee in the board room.'

'What a terrific view,' said Fiona. 'It's like people's reaction when they come into our penthouse.'

'It is amazing what a view will do to attract people. The rest of the room is rather splendid, with panels recording the heroic feats of bravery our crews keep carrying out.'

'Jeremy, Fiona and I are new to boating. We had a wonderful friend who liked to be called Goose. His actual name was Julian Lenwell. I suppose he preferred Goose. His last boat was called *Brave Goose*. I am his solicitor and friend. His legacy was for two million pounds to be donated to the RNLI. As Fiona and I now own *Brave Goose*, I thought it appropriate that we donated, so the amount I have for you in this banker's draft is two million five hundred thousand pounds. Goose requested that if it were sufficient to purchase a boat, could it be called *Goose*?'

'My word. May I call you Fiona and John? Thank you so much. The generosity of people like you and the late Mr

Lenwell is what keeps us afloat. I am certain we can find a boat suitable to receive the name *Goose* at some period shortly. When we do, and she is ready to go, we would like to invite you back for the naming ceremony.'

'That would be lovely,' said Fiona.

At that point, a tray of coffee and biscuits arrived. Maggie joined the party.

'Even though you are so generous, I regret we do need to complete a few forms so that we can satisfy the Charity Commissioners that all is as it should be.' Jeremy wanted to be sure that this money was legitimate, and that the RNLI was not involved in some money laundering activity.

'I perfectly understand,' said John. 'Money laundering is an issue. I can confirm I would not be dealing with this estate if I considered for one moment there was any wrongdoing involved.'

'Good, I'm delighted you understand our position. We provide an excellent vehicle for losing unwashed cash!'

John started to complete the various forms provided. It didn't take him long. Just time to drink his coffee, and he was finished.

'What is the name of your solicitor's practice, John?'

'Bennett and Bennett in Chester. I only work as a part-time lawyer. Due to very tragic circumstances, I have inherited a significant sum. I concentrate now on helping people who need the law, but the cost is out of reach. I am a pro bono lawyer.'

'That's how I met John. He is a wonderful lawyer. He not only got me off a serious charge but won me significant damages. He had been seriously injured, so I helped him.

We seemed to hit it off, and we have been together ever since.'

'I am delighted to hear it. Maggie will show you around, and don't hesitate to ask anyone questions. We will take you out in a Shannon Class boat driven by water jets this afternoon. I look forward to seeing you this evening. I gather you are staying a further night?'

'Yes, Jeremy, we are. See you later.'

***

John and Fiona were back in reception at five o'clock, having had a fascinating day.

'Dinner is at seven this evening. I will take you for dinner – can I meet you here in reception then?'

'That will be just fine, Maggie.'

John and Fiona retired to their room for a shower and to freshen up. John put on his blazer. Fiona had on a dark blue day dress with her beautiful pendant.

The two of them were back in reception, as agreed, on the dot of seven o'clock. They were expecting to go downstairs to the Slipway café bar and the Riggers Restaurant, which they had passed during their tour earlier in the day.

Maggie appeared and asked John and Fiona to follow her through the 'staff only' doors and again to the boardroom. They realised that there were more people than before. Four in all. Jeremy and his wife, the chairman-elect – the current chairman was up in London – Bryan and his wife. The boardroom table had been laid for dinner for six.

John realised the RNLI was pushing the boat out. Thanks for the donation.

'This all looks very lovely. I am afraid we didn't come prepared for a formal dinner,' said John.

'You both look the part, come and have a drink.' Bryan was a delightful man. Easy to see why he had been elected.

Bryan spoke to his colleagues and John and Fiona with drinks in hand. He had in his hand two boxes.

'As magnificent donors, we would like to enrol you both as commodore members of the RNLI. There are badges, a certificate and a car sticker enclosed. What you will not get is an annual request for money.'

Everyone laughed.

'So, where is your boat now?'

'I think she is probably approaching Sardinia in the Mediterranean. We are joining her in Corfu. We have been in Mallorca and Barcelona for most of this year. We are looking forward to sailing the Ionian.'

'That is the way to do it. Get the crew to move the boat to the area you want to explore and join her when the grind of the delivery is over.'

'Yes, Fiona and I were saying just that, driving down here from Manchester.'

Over dinner, John and Fiona were able to fill in how they became the owners of *Brave Goose*. They had issues with kidnapping and people trying to recover the funds they were not permitted to have. 'We are hoping we have seen the last of this now.'

The assembled company wished John and Fiona well and an enjoyable holiday in Greece.

***

'Brandon, it's me again.'

'Who are you?'

'Heinz, you know I spoke to you from Minorca. I am in Mallorca now. I have just seen *Brave Goose* leave.'

'Interesting. I don't suppose you know where they are headed?'

'I do, but I am running out of money. I think the information I have is worth at least ten thousand pounds. Supposing you can pay that into my UK bank, that will allow me to give you all the detail you need. Get a pen and paper, and I will give you my bank details.'

'Okay, Brandon, when I see my money in my bank, I will phone again. You haven't got long. Their destination which will be the best for you will be reached in five days.'

The phone went dead. *Could this be the last chance I have to get my hands on the money? Is it worth ten thousand? I am nearly out of cash.*

Brandon decided to do as suggested. It was his last throw of the dice.

Three days later, Heinz was on the phone again.

'Brandon, thank you for the money. *Brave Goose* is on its way to Corfu. In a few days after its first stop in Sardinia, it will make for the port of Catania just south of the straits of Messina in Sicily. I am sure your Irish connections will know of someone who can put up a force to hold the vessel and crew until you get your money?'

'Good work, Heinz. I shall get straight onto it.'

'Wow, this could be a chance,' Brandon muttered to himself.

'Georgios, it's Brandon.'

'Si, hello Brandon, can I help you?'

'Yes, you can. Let me remind you, you still owe me five grand, so this is not a favour. It is an instruction. If it comes off, you will owe me nothing.'

'Okay, what can I do for you?'

'The Mafia, do you have any connections?'

'Hey, I am Sicilian. Everyone knows someone in the Cosa Nostra.'

'Good, *Brave Goose* is going to dock at Catania in about two days. I want her, and her crew, held until John England pays the money. Do you understand?'

'Yes, I understand. I will have a word with some of my cousins.'

'Well, let me know as soon as the boarding has taken place. The crew should be constrained so they cannot leave until we allow it.'

***

Noel was on course, having left Sardinia behind. The course was 105 degrees, almost due east. He had calculated that it would take about twenty-eight hours to get south of Messina to their next port, Catania, on Sicily.

'Hi, Jock, all well down below?'

'Yes, Noel, no problem at all. Is that the course?'

'Yes, we will enter a separation zone through the straits of Messina. Out of interest, let me show you the pilot. In the centre of the zone is a virtual roundabout to allow ferries from the south to get to Messina or the other way around. I can't say I have ever seen such an arrangement.'

'That is certainly most unusual. I agree. I have never seen such an arrangement before. It will be interesting if we meet a ferry.'

'Yes, I intend to keep out of the separation zone and take the inshore route. That should keep us safe.'

'Where in the port are you planning on mooring in Catania?'

'I hope to go against the wall north of the Mediterranean Yacht Club. There are ten metres of water there. The forecast is for northerly winds so that it will be sheltered there.'

'When do you anticipate we will be there?'

'I would say in the early afternoon, which will allow us all to get a good look in the distance to the Aeolian Islands, which has Stromboli, the volcano, amongst the islands. As we go through the strait, we should see Mount Etna. Quite a volcano, really.'

There was a gentle swell from the north. *Brave Goose* was making steady progress. As forecast, she arrived at Catania at two forty-five in the afternoon.

'Jose, can you prepare the fenders on the port side. I will turn through one-eighty, so we face the entrance in case the wind swings around to the south.'

Once moored alongside the substantial quay, the port passerelle was deployed with the CCTV camera and the notice on the gate to stop visitors. *Brave Goose* didn't require any services. They had plenty of diesel, and the watermaker ensured a full tank.

Noel completed the log. He switched off all the navigation equipment and relaxed.

The whole crew were sitting on the comfy chairs on the quarterdeck when a car arrived alongside the passerelle. Three men rushed up the steps. Another car joined and parked behind the first. Once again, three men came on board.

'Hey, who are you? What do you want?' shouted Noel, in a way none of the crew had ever seen before.

'Who is the captain?' demanded the tallest of the men.

'I am the captain,' replied Noel. He looked at the men. They all wore black. Three had long black overcoats on. Noel thought this was over the top. The temperature was over thirty degrees. The reason for the coats was soon revealed. The three men had Uzi machine guns, currently pointed to the deck. Noel realised they could kill them all if they wanted to.

'What do you want?' shouted Noel.

Sally was frightened and started to cry. Jose spoke to them in the small amount of Italian he knew. It isn't so different from Spanish.

'Noel, they say they are here to keep us hostage until some money has been paid in England.'

'That could be ages. Tell them that we will not cause any trouble and not try and leave the boat. Would they like a drink or something to eat?'

'They are happy to hear that. We can go inside and be comfortable if we like. They don't want anything to eat or drink.'

Noel and the rest went into the saloon and sat down.

Two of the 'guards' came with them – one with a handgun, the one in his overcoat and the Uzi machine pistol.

***

In Apartment 803 in Peters Tower, Brandon's mobile phone rang.

'Hi, it's Georgios. We have *Brave Goose* captive and all the crew. There are six men on board ready to kill the crew and blow up the boat if they are told to do that.'

'Bloody hell, Georgios, that is amazing. I will take it from here. I will ring you with instructions on what to do next. I will keep in touch. The next bit could take some time.'

'Mr England, it's Brandon Phelan. I need to come and see you urgently. *Brave Goose* is in Sicily, and I have six armed men holding your crew. If I don't ring them this afternoon, they have instructions to kill the crew and blow up the boat.'

'You had better come up in half an hour. I have to get some things organised, and Sydney will provide you with a pass.'

'No funny stuff, mind. The Cosa Nostra doesn't play games.'

John switched his mobile off to kill the call. He immediately rang Noel.

'Senor, I need to answer the phone. It is the owner of the boat. He will need to know we are okay, before and after he has paid the money.'

'Hi, it's Noel.'

'Are you all okay?'

'Yes, John, but I am not sure how long I will be able to say that. There are six heavily armed men on board and two in cars outside. They have said that money has to be paid. Is that correct?'

'It is, Noel. I am just making arrangements for it to be paid. I will ring you when it is paid.'

Noel held his hands up and returned to his seat. 'My boss is paying the money now.'

John thought carefully for a few minutes. He was not prepared to have the death of four beautiful people on his conscience for the rest of his life. He was now in receipt of extra cash following the death of Goose. Of the five million, he had already spent two million of it and five hundred thousand of his own money.

There was a banging on the door. Brandon was on his own.

'Come in,' John demanded in a less than friendly voice.

'Tell me, Brandon, how have you pulled off this scheme? Do you have contacts in Sicily?'

'Yes, you are not the only one who can organise things, you know.'

'Who is your contact?'

'It doesn't matter. They are well connected in Sicily.'

The penny suddenly dropped with John.

'It's Georgios, isn't it?'

Brandon was not a good liar. He was unable to summon up an answer.

'Don't bugger about, Brandon. It is Georgios, isn't it?'

'Yes, but it doesn't help you very much knowing that.

He has left Manchester and is now in Sicily. You will never find him.'

'I don't intend to try and find him. You might want to find him, though.'

'Why is that?'

'Brandon, Georgios was running an illegal finance and pensions business. He talked old folks out of their life savings. He promised them a good return on their savings but lent the money to people who could not afford to pay the money back. If he were still in England, I was ready to take him to the cleaners. He would have ended up in jail.'

'I still don't understand. Why will I need to find him?'

'Because, Brandon, I will pay you now two million eight hundred thousand pounds. The two hundred thousand I will pay back to the pensioners. You can collect that money from Georgios. Is that a deal?'

'No, I need three million.'

'If we don't have a deal now and you don't accept my ridiculously generous offer, you will be behind bars later today.'

Brandon was doing the arithmetic in his head for what he would get. Indeed, Michael Fitzallen would get at least two million. He thought it had to be a deal.

'Okay, England, I will accept your offer. Here are my bank details. I want to be able to ring my bank within the hour.'

John pressed the link to dial Julian Franks at the bank.

'Julian, I need your real help now and urgently. This is, I promise you, a very genuine request. My crew and boat are being held in Sicily by the Mafia.'

'Okay, John, I understand all that; who is the money going to and how much?'

'The sum is two million eight hundred thousand pounds.' John then read out the bank details for Brandon. 'Can it be in the recipient's bank within the hour?'

'It's the hour thing that is a bit tricky. There will be a fee at either end, usually a thousand pounds, to expedite a transfer of this amount.'

'Look, Julian, it's a life-or-death situation in Sicily. I can just ring the local constabulary and ask them to fix it. Who knows, they could all be in on the kidnap. Just take two thousand from my account to pay your fee and the recipient's bank. Can the receiving bank phone their client as soon as the money has arrived?'

'I will do my best.'

'Julian, this has to happen. There are four lives on the line here.'

'Brandon, I have done my best, as you have heard. Can you please ring your bank, explain the urgency of the situation, and ask them to ring you as soon as the money arrives?'

Brandon did as instructed.

'Drink, Brandon?'

'Have you any whisky?'

'I have water with it or ice?'

'Neither, just as it comes.'

John poured him a good slug of whisky. John didn't join him but set the coffee machine running. He was in the kitchen. Fiona came in through the front door.

She was chirpy, carrying two much smaller bags, but

clothes, nonetheless.

'Hello, darling,' she said. John put his finger to his lips.

'We have a visitor. It's complex and stressful. I will explain later. Do you want a coffee?'

'No thanks, darling, I will go into the bedroom and watch TV for a while.' Fiona fully realised that when John needed space, he should have it and remain undisturbed.

31

'Can I go to the toilet?' enquired Sally.

'Si,' was the reply. She did and was back in ten minutes. 'Anyone like a coffee?' Sally enquired.

All four Mafia men wanted a coffee, as did Noel, but Jose and Jock preferred tea. Sally set about making the beverages under the gaze of a black-suited man wearing shades, even though the sun had gone. He held a handgun, watching as Sally made the beverages.

Noel's phone rang as she poured the hot water into various mugs. Noel answered it without seeking permission.

'Noel, it's John. Are you all safe? No one has been hurt?'

'No, we are under armed guard, but we are just fine apart from the stress that creates.'

'Okay, Noel, keep with it. I am working hard to get you all set free. I am sorry, but it looks like tomorrow morning.'

'That's a long time, John. I hope we will be allowed to sleep in our cabins in that case.'

'Yes, I am so sorry. It takes time. I am working on it as fast as I can. I will let you know of any changes. Bye.'

Noel passed on the bad news to all the crew. 'I hope we will be allowed to sleep in our beds tonight?'

***

'Julian, thanks for getting back to me. Has the money gone?'

'Yes and no, John.'

'Sorry, Julian, but what the fuck does that mean? I have four people very dear to me, held under armed guard and unable to walk around. It is devastating for them. Why hasn't the money gone?'

'The money has left the bank, and I have emailed you with the confirmation.'

'So, what's the problem?'

'To transfer money bank to bank, it has to go through a clearing house. It is the same for all banks. The money was at the clearing house at three forty-five today. However, the clearing house stops clearing items at four in the afternoon five days a week. They had a considerable amount to clear today. Yours didn't make the cut. It will be one of the first to go tomorrow.'

'Oh my God. This is a life and death situation. Is there no one you can appeal to who can sort the log jam?'

'Sorry, John. I can't even recall the money. It's stuck until nine o'clock in the morning.'

'That is ten o'clock in Sicily.'

'John, I wish I could do this some other way, but it is impossible.'

'All right, I will let the crew know.'

'Brandon, did you get the gist of that conversation? The money has left my bank, but because there is an intermediate step, probably run by the government as it is so poor, they stop work at four and recommence at nine tomorrow. I have been assured the money will be one of the first to be transferred.'

John handed a copy of the transfer confirming the payment.

'I have had one of these before. I will wait and see. I will phone you in the morning when I know the money is in my bank.'

'Will you please call off the Mafia at the same time?'

'Yes, I will, John.' Brandon left without a handshake or a 'goodbye'.

As soon as the front door shut, Fiona was out of their bedroom to check on John.

'It's a nightmare, not for us but the crew on *Brave Goose*.'

'Oh, John. Will this be an end to it all?'

'I do hope so, darling. We have all had enough of these people. When Sandra did the deal for the benefit of the Wall family, she could never have imagined for a moment what a pickle it would lead to.'

'You have been fantastic throughout all this. Let us pray that this is truly the end of hostilities.'

'I agree, darling.' They had a big hug and kiss.

'Look, there are still some things I need to do.'

'Okay, I will make supper here. It will be good to have a night in.'

***

'Georgios, it's Brandon.'

'Hi, everything okay?'

'Yes, the money has been sent. It will be in my bank tomorrow. How much will your Mafia guys want to remain overnight?'

'Another ten grand. That's what it has cost me so far.'

'Okay. I will take a risk, Georgios. I am certain the money is in the system. It will be in my account in the morning. You can let the Mafia go.'

'They don't like that name now. Cosa Nostra is what they prefer.'

'Okay, let them go, so *Brave Goose*'s crew can spend a quiet night.'

'Okay, I will sort that.'

***

On *Brave Goose*, the head guy received a call; they all just left as quickly as they had arrived. The two cars raced down the marina road.

'My God, I think that is all over,' said Noel. 'I will ring John and tell him.'

'John, it's Noel. The Mafia men have all left. Just

five minutes ago. The head guy got a call, and they left, speeding down the marina road in their cars.'

'That is great news. What are you going to do now?'

'We haven't discussed it, but I would prefer to remain here and sail in the morning to Gallipoli, our next port. It is not on Sicily!'

'Ha, I guess if it were possible, you would all prefer to go now. I imagine you have all been under tremendous strain. I am sorry for that. I will make it up to you all when you and we get to Corfu.'

'Fiona, I hope we have seen the last of our problems. The Mafia has left *Brave Goose*. They are setting off in the morning to Gallipoli for their next stop.'

'John, what a relief. I dare not think what might happen next, but we surely are free from all this turmoil.'

'Yes, I hope so, darling, I cannot think whatever else might appear, so let's get on with life.'

***

Brave Goose left Sicily the following morning.

Brandon was on the phone as soon as possible to find out if his bank had received the two million, eight hundred thousand.

'Thank you, thank you, that is just wonderful,' Brandon exclaimed to his bank manager.

His gamble had paid off.

Brandon sat down and wrote a letter to Michael Fitzallen.

Michael,

I am writing to advise you that there is two million two hundred thousand in my bank waiting for instructions on where it will be sent.

My commission of six hundred thousand has been deducted. There was a shortage of two hundred thousand, but that was due to an issue caused by Georgios, my Sicilian contact.

He should make up the missing sum, but I cannot help in that area. He now lives in Sicily. He has troops available who I would not wish to take on.

I am leaving the UK today.
Brandon

Brandon wrote another letter to Angela, the letting agent, giving in his notice and that he had already left the flat. He gave no forwarding address.

***

The post dropped through the door as it did most mornings. Fiona collected it. It was all for John.

'Here's the post, John. It is all for you. It is just ten days before we fly to Corfu. God, I cannot wait. We will have a wonderful time, just us. We are so lucky.'

'Yes, darling. We are. I still have to complete the final bits of Goose's estate. I hope to have it all cleared up before we go.'

John had received far more mail than he expected. He started to work his way through it all. There were no rubbish letters, which was a unique event.

There were five letters from individuals replying to John's advert in the Manchester Evening News, advising him that they were customers of Manchester European Pensions. There should only be four. One must be a fraud, John muttered to himself.

In the residue of the mail was a letter from Goose's bank confirming the closure of his current account and the transfer of the balance to John's account.

'Fiona, Fiona, come quickly.'

Fiona burst into John's office. 'Whatever is the matter, darling? Are you ill?'

'No, quite the opposite. I have just had the closing bank statement from Goose's bank and the transfer into my account. You will never guess how much there is.'

'How can I do that, John? I have no clue how much he would have in his account.'

'Well, my darling, he had one million, seven hundred and thirty-six pounds and twenty pence.'

'Wow, what a crazy sum of money.'

'It is all altered by interest, bank charges, etc. So that is the rest of his estate. I guess there will be some tax to pay, but I have no idea how much that might be.'

'What are you going to do with all this money, John?'

'My darling, pay taxes, but most importantly, I am going to arrange for your bank account to be swelled by two hundred and fifty thousand pounds. That should buy a few more dresses.'

Fiona flung her arms around John in sheer delight. 'You are the most wonderful man. I love you to bits.'

'You deserve every penny and more. I will see what is

left after the taxes have been paid. I have put you through traumas. No one should have to have to endure what you have suffered.'

Fiona again smothered John in hugs and kisses.

32

'Sally, it's John,' phoning Sally Moulton, the solicitor.

'Hi John, I thought you had forgotten me!'

'No, I haven't, it's just life has been hectic. I will tell you all about it over that dinner I promised you. Would next Thursday evening, say seven-thirty, at the French restaurant in the Midland, be okay?'

'It certainly would. Looking forward to it.'

'Fiona, I have made arrangements to meet Sally Moulton, a solicitor I know, at the French restaurant on Thursday for dinner at seven-thirty. Will that be okay for you, darling?'

'Oh John, I guess we should compare diaries more often. I have arranged to meet all my girlfriends for a night out. Do you mind if I don't come? We will have lots of time to dine together in Corfu.'

'Likewise, you don't mind if I go out with Sally?'

'Why would I mind? It's not as though we are welded at the hip.'

'Okay, that's a deal, have a good time, hun.'

John returned to identifying the pensioners who were legitimate customers of Georgios's pension scam.

All the responses had phone numbers, so he decided to start and work his way through.

They were George Nichols, Costa Marinella, Diane Roma, Fred Travis and Mavis Thaker, who had indicated they had put their pension pot with Georgios.

'George, it's John England, solicitor. You have responded to my advert. I just need to ask you a few questions. Are you happy with that?'

'Why, what are you going to do? The company has folded, you know. I guess I have lost the lot.'

'Not necessarily.' John went on with his questions, starting with the full name, date of birth, and the amount he had put with Georgios. Did he get a receipt of a letter confirming what he had paid over and the return he would be guaranteed?

The answers were essentially the same with different numbers and fitted the bill until Costa Marinella arrived.

'Costa, I am a solicitor, and you answered my advert in the Manchester Evening News.'

'Yes, you say you can help me with my pension?'

'Only if you had moved your pension pot to Manchester European Pensions for them to manage. Did you do that?'

'Oh yes. Georgios, my cousin, said I would get a great pension.'

'Okay, so how much was your pension pot?'

'No idea, I just gave Georgios the papers. I signed a form, and I get a thousand pounds a month.'

'So how much did you have saved in your pension that went to Georgios?'

'I don't know. It can't have been very much as I had only been saving for five years.'

'What amount did you pay in a month?'

'Fifty pounds, mate.'

'That would be six hundred pounds a year or three thousand in five years. There is no way you would get a thousand pounds a month. That would be impossible.'

'Well, you say that, but that's what I got. He said it was a special deal as I was family.'

'Well, Costa, I am sorry, I cannot help you because you had not paid enough in to warrant any pension of the size you received. You have probably received more in payouts already than you put in. That is just not possible. Sorry, Costa.'

'Are you some sort of hacker who tries to get money from old people? I have read about people like you.'

John just hung up. There was no point in pursuing this conversation.

The four people he had spoken to confirmed they would arrange to call and see him in the next few days and bring their passport or photo driving licence and the documents Georgios gave them.

'Sydney, here is a list of four people who are due to come and see me about the pension rip-off they had become involved in. When any one of them comes, give me a buzz, and I will come down.'

Over the next two days, John met all four pensioners, who went away with a cheque, more or less for the sum they used to have in their pension pot. In all, it had cost John two hundred thousand pounds.

'I hope you have a great night out, Fiona. Be careful and stay safe.'

'You too, darling. See you later.'

John met Sally as agreed at the French restaurant in the Midland Hotel.

'Hi John, I thought you were bringing your partner?'

'I was, but she had already made arrangements to go out on a girls' night. So you will have to manage with just me.'

'I don't mind one little bit. We will have plenty to talk about, I am sure.'

They ordered drinks as they read the menu.

'You said you had been up to your ears in it, John. I hope it wasn't the debt problem my Mr and Mrs Hamilton had that has troubled you?'

'Not exactly, but they have been involved. I can tell you now that their whole debt is written off. No further repayments are required.'

'My God, John. How on earth did you manage that? It sounds like a miracle.'

'I need to go back a bit. When I started to look into the guy behind the finance company and the company itself, he was not registered with anyone. His collection methods were sending in the heavy mob.'

'Yes, I recall you saying that. So how did you beat them?'

'I got them arrested. They came to my apartment with Georgios and someone else. I said I would discuss nothing with Georgios if those two muscle men were around. They left the apartment and were arrested. I have my connections.'

'What always puzzled me, John, was where did this man Georgios get the funds from to lend out?'

'He persuaded pensioners that he could offer double the return on their pension pot than they were getting from their pension company. Four people fell for the oldest trick in the book, a great return no one else could offer. His excuse was that he was small, didn't advertise, so he cut all the costs out and could offer great returns.'

'Yes, of course, people get taken in by that. Was it that money, or part of it, that he loaned to the Hamiltons?'

'Yes, but there was no chance the Hamiltons could pay the rate Georgios was charging, so the repayments stopped, and so did the payments to the pensioners.'

'So the pensioners have lost out?'

'No, I have refunded all their money.'

'John, you sound like a conjurer pulling a rabbit out of a hat.'

The head waiter appeared, requesting their order. There was some discussion between them to finalise the order and the wine. The waiter went away happy.

'So go on, John. How did you pay the pensioners back?'

'It goes back a long way. The guy who murdered my sister-in-law, Sandra Wall, had lent the three million pounds in the first place. The binding agreement had a clause that ensured Michael Fitzallen lost all rights to the money if he committed a crime that put him in jail for more than ten years. Well, that angered the Irish Fitzallen and a guy called Niall Phelan, who was the owner of the money until he was conned out of it by Goose, acting for Michael Fitzallen. The ownership of the money always was an issue, as Fitzallen earned money from property development, so when Phelan took the cash from the joint company account in Spain, Fitzallen was furious. Goose got him four million back from Phelan. Too complex to go into now.'

'What a tangled web?'

'Sally, it gets worse. Obviously cooling his heels in prison, Fitzallen was becoming fixated with getting his money back. It would presumably give him something to look forward to when he got out of prison.'

'Yes, I see, John, there can't be too much to think about in prison other than what you want to do when you get out.'

At that point, the starter arrived – pacific prawns with garlic mayonnaise.

'Sally, I have done all the talking. I hope I am not boring you.'

'Boring me, John, certainly not. It's like being read a good crime novel.'

The empty starter plates were whisked away.

'Okay, do you want me to continue?'

'Ooh, yes, please.'

'Fitzallen had a brother, Sean. He was in touch with Goose at the suggestion of his brother Michael that Goose might be just the person to get the money out of me.'

'Two turbot Milanese?'

'Yes, that's correct, we will need some more white wine,' instructed John.

'This looks beautiful, John. Thank you. Can you carry on with the story while we eat?'

'I guess I can, but there will be gaps in the conversation as I enjoy this lovely fish.'

'Anyway,' John continued, 'Goose did not see himself as the debt collector for the Fitzallen family. We dined together, and in the end, after many ups and downs, I became Goose's solicitor, wrote his will and became his executor. Attackers had injured him at sea.

'He spent some time in a hospital in Barcelona. He was shot in the back when he was released from the hospital. The assassination attempts were because he had killed Niall Phelan when Goose supplied Phelan with a bogus supply of drugs. One of the larger packets included a pressure fuse. When Phelan opened the packet, it killed him.

'The Fitzallens employed a man called Brandon Phelan. It was a false name, no connection. It was to put me on guard as this man took a tenancy of one of the flats in Peters Tower when I was away.'

'John, there can't be more to this story, can there?'

'Yes, I have missed bits out, like how I met Fiona and how Sean Fitzallen died by falling off Goose's boat in southern Ireland.'

'Go on then.'

'Well, Goose left a considerable sum of money, I managed to dispose of the funds to settle the legacies he specified. I had to pay back the three million to Brandon Phelan on behalf of Michael Fitzallen. We held Goose's funeral at sea from the deck of *Brave Goose*.

'The man who ran the scam on the Hamilton family and the four pensioners, Georgios Armani, is a Sicilian. When *Brave Goose* docked in Sicily, Georgios had mobilised the Mafia to hijack the vessel and hold the crew hostage until I coughed up the money. The money left to me by Goose covered the amount due. However, as Georgios was involved with Brandon Phelan, I thought it would be only justice if the three million were reduced by two hundred thousand to pay back the pensioners. That would put Georgios and Brandon at odds because Giorgio would lose his share of the commission that Fitzallen said they could have if Brandon collected the money. Fiona and I will be joining *Brave Goose,* when she gets to Corfu.'

'What a tale that is, John. You must write that up in a book.'

'I am no author, Sally, but I do like a nice meal. Would you like a pudding?'

'No, thank you, John, that was delicious and made all the more delightful by your clever manipulation of money and the disagreeable people who tried to take advantage of pensioners. I hope the pensioners were grateful?'

'Hard to say. I don't think any of them realised what they had got themselves into.'

'Can you let me have their names and addresses, John? I want to write to them all and the Hamiltons, who now have a second chance in life.'

'I don't see why not.'

The two lawyers left the restaurant. John offered his taxi to Sally, but she insisted on walking, despite the drizzle.

'See you again, Sally, thanks.'

'No, thank you, John.' She gave him a peck on the cheek, then she walked away.

33

As soon as John returned to the penthouse, he went to his office and sent an email to Sally Moulton with the names and addresses of the four pensioners, as he had promised.

At midnight, John began to wonder what had happened to Fiona. He showered and read a new Lee Child murder mystery book in bed. He was about to turn the light out and go to sleep when he heard a commotion in the hall. He put his dressing gown on and went to investigate.

Fiona looked very frightened and was with a young man who John seemed to recognise.

'What the hell is going on?' demanded John.

'Don't fuck me up, mister. I know you smart lawyer types. I have a knife in my other hand, and I can sink it easily into the back of your girl here.'

'What is all this about? I am sure I have met you somewhere before.'

'You have, I am Toby, Toby Evans. I was going to work for Goose, but he died. So I didn't get any work.'

'That is not the whole truth, Toby. You killed Goose by going on board *Brave Goose* while we were at dinner in the yacht club. What you did is not clear to me, but we found Goose dead by the morning. His wounds were open, and he died from loss of blood. Why did you do that?' John tried to keep the conversation light but factual to attract Toby's attention away from Fiona.

'How do you know I went on board?'

'Because, Toby, we have CCTV covering the passerelle which clearly shows you entering and leaving the boat. I don't recall the time, but it was while we were ashore having dinner in the yacht club. Who paid you to do this, Toby?'

'No, you got this wrong. No one paid me.'

'Interesting. I think Brandon Phelan paid you. I have had Phelan's bank account investigated by the police. The most recent payment was to T Evans. That's you, Toby.'

'Ten grand is not enough for what I did. I need a lot more. That's why I am here. Pay me, or I will kill you both. I have nothing to lose now.'

'You will be caught whatever you do. You see this flat has CCTV everywhere and you have been filmed since you came in. Stop this nonsense. Give me the knife, and we can try and talk this thing through.'

'Don't give me that crap. I can't see any cameras.'

In a split second, Toby lunged at John, pushing Fiona to the floor as he did so.

'I will kill you, Mr Solicitor.'

'How will that help you get money from me?' John replied in a measured tone.

'Don't be so fucking clever. I am fed up with people like you in the world. All you do is take money from people and let the poor people starve.'

'If that's what you think, Toby, I feel sorry for you.' John was about to explain how he had just helped five families when Toby lunged at him with his knife. John felt at a disadvantage in pyjamas and dressing gown.

The knife ripped into his dressing gown but didn't find any flesh. Toby struggled to recover his knife from the folds of the dressing gown. John let fly with his elbow, hitting Toby in the throat. The blow to Toby's throat made him drop the knife. As he let go of the blade, John hit Toby full in the face, probably breaking his nose, which began to bleed.

'Now, you little shit, before you decide to take on someone in a fight, best to make sure you can win. You won't. If you want to continue, you will get hurt.'

'Fiona, here is the knife.' John kicked it over the floor towards Fiona. 'Run downstairs and get help. I will ring the police. Don't come back here until the police arrive. You can let them in. Take your card with you.'

John wished he had some bindings with which to truss Toby up, then realised he had something that would do the trick. John removed the cord from his dressing gown. While Toby was concussed, John bound his hands tight with one cord end. Pulling his legs up behind Toby, he secured his feet. He looked like a Christmas turkey.

John phoned 999 and asked for assistance, explaining what had happened. The controller on the phone promised a response as soon as possible.

John went into his bedroom and threw some clothes on, including a strong pair of shoes, just in case Toby decided to have another go at him.

'I wonder what Fiona did with the knife?'

As John pondered the issue and what he should do now, Fiona appeared with two police officers.

'Fiona, are you okay, darling?'

She rushed into John's arms. 'More to the point, are you okay, John?'

'I am fine. What did you do with the knife?'

'I put it on the little table outside the front door.'

On hearing this, one of the police officers went to find it.

'There is a knife here, Sarge.'

'Leave it there. We will bag it shortly.'

'Now, is this the intruder?'

'Yes, Sergeant, he held the knife first at the back of Fiona, then he decided I was more dangerous, so he came at me. I had only just got out of bed when I heard Fiona and Toby come in, so I just put on my dressing gown. It's the cord from the dressing gown that is restraining him.'

'Mr England, you called the intruder by name. Do you know him?'

'Yes, I have met him before in Mallorca.'

'There is quite a story behind this. I need to take some details. First, I will get this Toby character into our van and possibly the hospital. If you have hit him, that looks like excessive force to me.'

***

'Jon, it's John England. I know it's the middle of the night. I do, however, need some assistance. Just a word to a sergeant who has just taken away a young man who killed Goose and had a go at killing me a little while ago. If you get this message, please call me.'

The sergeant returned, notebook in hand. His constable had taken Toby to the police station.

'Now, sir, let's start at the beginning. Names first and addresses.'

'I am John England, a solicitor. This is my partner, Fiona Holmes. We both live here. This is a complex story, and I don't want to spend a few hours recalling every twist and turn. This man accosted Fiona as she was coming in from a night out. Normally no one could get to this floor without a special card. The lifts don't go beyond the twelfth floor. If you have a security lift pass, you can get there. Fiona, of course, has such a pass. The young man, Toby, held a very sharp knife to her ribs and forced her to let him in here. I was in bed and rushed up, putting on my dressing gown. It's the dressing gown cord I used to restrain Toby until you came with something a little more substantial.'

'You seem to know the assailant, sir?'

'I had met him only once when he applied for a job in Mallorca to look after an old gentleman friend of ours. We offered him the job.'

'So why was he coming after you and Fiona?'

'That, Sergeant, is a very long story. I will be happy to come to the station tomorrow and go through the whole story. However, DCI Jon Kim is very familiar with what has happened.'

'Bit unusual, sir, but I can go with it, as you seem to know people in high places.'

'I am not trying to pull rank, Sergeant. It's just the story is so convoluted going back many years, and Jon Kim has been involved with most of the story.'

'Please do not leave Manchester, sir, until we have the whole story. I will not be on duty tomorrow, but I will leave a message for the duty sergeant, who will deal with the interview.'

'Thank you for being so considerate, Sergeant. You don't need a card or anything to get out. It's just getting in that is tricky.'

34

On board *Brave Goose*, having left Sicily, the crew felt very traumatised.

'Noel, how far is it to the next port?'

'We have made a good start, Sally, we have covered about five miles, so it is about one hundred and ninety miles or so. Twenty-one hours. It's eight in the morning now, so we should be in Gallipoli by six tomorrow morning.'

'How are you feeling, Noel?'

'Not sure, Sally. I am delighted to be away from Sicily. It was a very stressful time, but it ended well. I just need to concentrate on what we are doing now. I hope Jock is getting some sleep. I will need him to take over by six this evening. Could you tell him for me, Sally?'

'Sure, Noel, I think he is sitting in the galley now.'

Sally was back to see Noel in ten minutes, bearing a cup of coffee and some biscuits.

'Thanks, Sal. Just what I need.'

'Jock and Jose are both fast asleep in their cabin. Not realising the stress we were all placed under, it has hit home once the ordeal was over.'

'Yes, I am feeling somewhat nervous. I don't understand that, but I don't feel as confident as I usually do. I will run the radar on 360 degrees, setting a three-mile warning zone, so an alarm will sound if another vessel comes within that zone. I will remain on the bridge in my chair, but I cannot guarantee I might not nod off now and again. The radar should warn me to pay attention.'

'Good idea, Noel. At least the sea is smooth.'

'True, but in a way, a rough sea would keep me more alert than the tranquil water just sweeping by, with a melodic swoosh.'

'I will sit in the saloon on the comfortable settee. If I drop off, I will be ready to help if you need me. Don't hesitate to wake me if you need help, Noel. Likewise, if I see you have dropped off and the alarm is ringing, I will wake you.'

***

It was half past ten when John and Fiona walked into the central police station in Manchester.

'Yes, sir, can you wait a moment? The officer dealing with this matter will be with you in a moment.'

John and Fiona sat on an uncomfortable bench, securely fixed to the floor. They were about to have a conversation when Jon Kim appeared.

'Jon, how good to see you.'

'And you, too. I gather there was a bit of trouble last night. Why don't you come through to an interview room where we can talk all about it?'

The grey interview room had two chairs on either side of the rectangular grey-topped table with a tape recorder at the wall end of the table. There was some natural light from a window high up in the wall.

'I can see you are taking in the lavish furnishings, Fiona. Sorry, it's the only room available at the moment. Do you mind if I record our conversation? It avoids me having to take notes. You can have a copy of the tape.'

'No problem, Jon, you do as you wish.'

'Tell me all about last night.'

'There is a lead-up to last night, Jon, which is important. I know you are familiar with the events that occurred in the sea between Mallorca and Barcelona, the involvement of the GEO.'

'Yes, I recall all that.'

'Do you recall Goose coming out of the hospital and a marksman who arrived on a noisy motorbike shooting Goose in the back when he stood for the first time in ages on the deck of *Brave Goose*?'

'I don't recall that bit of the story.'

'Cutting out the trivia, Goose made a recovery and was allowed home. I should say he was permitted to come onto *Brave Goose*. Once he was established on the boat, we left Barcelona and travelled to Puerto Pollenca in Mallorca. Goose managed to cope with the sea journey very well. Fiona and I went out for dinner with the four members of *Brave Goose*'s crew. Goose was in bed watching TV. He had already had a light supper, Sally, the cook, had made for him.'

'Yes, okay.'

'The intention was that Goose, who by now had sold *Brave Goose* to Fiona and me, would find an apartment close to the centre of Puerto Pollenca, which was wheelchair friendly. He needed help if he did that. A young man called Toby Evans had asked the yacht club office if they knew of any crewing jobs. The secretary recommended him to Goose. Toby came on board and was interviewed by Goose and us. He seemed to be ideal for the job.

'That night Toby returned and, as far as we can tell, beat Goose in his bed, splitting open his wounds. Goose bled to death overnight.'

'I see, so what did Toby do that for? He had a job. There must be some connection between Toby and the people who have been hounding you for money, John?'

'You are correct, Jon. As soon as we knew Toby had been on board that night, we were certain. We have CCTV on the gangplank, so we had a recording of all movements on and off the boat.'

'Okay, so how does all this lead up to Toby trying to kill you both last night?'

'Fiona went out last night with her girlfriends. You carry on, darling.'

'Yes, Jon, I was out late, coming back at about half past midnight, maybe a bit later. I was about to swipe my card to open the locked main doors of Peters Tower when a hooded man attacked me. He held a knife to my back. I could feel the cold steel on my back. He insisted we both come up to the penthouse. John must have heard the commotion. He was in pyjamas and was putting his dressing gown on.'

'That's correct, Jon. I had no shoes on, so I felt somewhat exposed to a fully dressed man with boots and a knife. He let Fiona go and came at me. He lunged at my midriff with his knife, which I managed to get tangled in my dressing gown. With my left hand, I held the knife where it was tangled. I then struck him with my right elbow. Then as he was hit, he let go of the knife. I hit him as hard as I could on his nose with my right hand. Down he went. I trussed him up with the cord from my dressing gown, feet and hands tied, like a turkey at Christmas.'

'What did Toby want, and was he being manipulated by someone else?' asked Jon.

'It is clear he wanted money. He expected me to pay him a considerable sum. I don't know for sure who is running him, but I suspect his boss is Brandon Phelan.'

'So why did he decide to try and get money from you directly, do you think?'

'I suppose, Jon, he realised money was available and wanted some. As to the issue with Brandon Phelan, the money for him has been paid, and I gather he has left Flat 803. I have no idea if he is still in the UK.'

'I think that makes it clear that Toby was acting on his own, John. If not, it would have involved Phelan for sure.'

'Yes, I see your point, Jon. Anyway, he is or should be, in custody. There should be sufficient information to charge him: knife crime, assault and attempted murder, as that was what came out of his mouth. 'I will kill you, Mr Solicitor', sounds like a threat to me.'

'Yes, John. I suppose the issue is, as it always is, did you use proportionate force?'

'That old chestnut. The police can prosecute me if they wish. You never know who you might meet in court,' John said, with a grin on his face, looking at Fiona.

'Toby is in hospital having his broken nose fixed. When he is discharged, we will put him before a magistrate. Will you be around next week, John?'

'No, we are flying to Corfu on Wednesday, and we shall be away for about six weeks.'

'Okay, I will keep you posted, John. The current magistrates seem to like people to be let out on bail. We can put a bet on that the accused never appears again unless we arrest them for something else.'

'Remove his passport, so at least he will have to remain in the UK.'

'We will try to get the magistrates to order that at least. Have a great holiday. I hope it is a peaceful one, John.'

'So do I, my friend. Thank you for sorting this out. I didn't fancy describing the whole back story to this issue.'

John and Fiona left the police station, relaxed and confident that Jon Kim would ensure Toby would at the very least be held in the UK.

***

As John and Fiona were entering the penthouse, John's mobile rang.

'Noel, how are you all, and where are you?'

'We have left Sicily and are twenty-five miles on our way to Gallipoli. We should be in port at six in the morning. We are now two hours ahead of UK time.'

'I will try and remember that, Noel. How is everyone after your ordeal?'

'Frankly, we were all somewhat strung out. The stress was terrible. Anyway, Sally's coffee and biscuits did the trick earlier. She and I are on watch with a guard ring on the radar. Jock and Jose are asleep. They will take over this afternoon. I will resume my watch at about five in the morning, ready to dock *Brave Goose* in Gallipoli.'

'Good sailing, Noel, looking forward to meeting you all again in Corfu. Have a good trip.'

'Fiona, I've just spoken to Noel. They are on their way. They left Sicily this morning. They hope to be in Corfu in three days, rest and refuel in Gallipoli. We need to start making plans. I need to get some euros.'

'Okay, John. I nearly said I would go shopping, but I bet you won't come with me?'

'I will; let's say tomorrow, we will go to a shop, and I will buy my euros.'

'Come on, Mrs Shopper, time to go and spend some money.'

The two left Peters Tower with a spring in their step. Fiona couldn't wait to visit all the boutiques down King Street, Deansgate and St Ann's Square.

'This is where all the best boutiques in Manchester are located, John.'

'What about lunch? Let's plan on going to Harvey Nichols for lunch either at twelve-thirty or one-thirty. Either way, we might miss the queues.'

'That sounds great, John. I have made a list of shops I would like to visit.'

'Okay, super shopper, what are they?'

'Diesel, Karen Millen, Polo and Harvey Nicks.'

'Well, that shouldn't take too long. What, in particular, are you hoping to find?'

'I need some shorts and T-shirts, a couple of bikinis and a smart dress that can be packed easily.'

'All right, I think all these shops are on King Street. You kick off in Diesel, then Karen Millen. By the time you have finished in those shops, I will have purchased my euros.'

'Sounds like a plan, John.' Fiona gave him a peck on the cheek and skipped off to Diesel.

John went to his bank and purchased five hundred pounds in euros in varying denominations. The bank was slightly anxious about his putting so much money in an envelope in his pocket. John was confident he would be fine.

Walking down King Street, he passed Diesel, just as Fiona was coming out with a bag which looked to be bulging.

'Looks like that shop was a success?'

Fiona turned round to find John. She had not noticed him.

'Yes, darling, sailing essentials.'

'Good thinking, where next?'

'I think it's Karen Millen. They should have a little number that will suit me.'

John wandered on, arriving at Boodles' window.

John muttered to himself, 'What would she like?' His thinking was that Fiona had endured so much during the last few months, and none of it was her fault.

'Hello. My girlfriend has endured several horrific situations in the last few months. I want to buy her a suitable present... diamonds, I think?'

'Of course, sir. May I suggest a pendant? They are always attractive and very wearable.' According to the badge he wore on his black jacket, the shop assistant or gemologist asked John to sit. 'I have a selection here. What sort of budget do you have in mind, sir?'

'I have no idea how much these things are, so I am unable to give you a figure.'

'Sir, we have a range of prices here starting at this end at six thousand and ending at the other end at forty-three thousand.'

David was pleased when John started at the expensive end.

'You have excellent taste, sir. You can always return with the item and receipt within a month, and we shall be delighted to change it if it doesn't quite hit the spot.'

'That's a good idea. I like this pendant with diamonds held on the chain as well as rubies and diamonds on the pendant itself.'

'I will just check the price on this one, sir. I shall only be a minute.'

David was back in a few minutes.

'David, forgive me for mentioning this. I am an honest person and a solicitor. You left a few thousand pounds worth of jewels in front of me. If I were not an honest person, they could pinch some or all of these.'

'Yes, sir, many people say that. You were under constant surveillance, sir. There is a CCTV camera over your head, hidden in the ceiling. The operator can lock all the doors and prevent anyone from leaving.'

'Good, I am pleased you have all this covered. What have you to tell me?'

'The list price of this item you have chosen is forty-three thousand pounds. I can do them for forty thousand for you. If, however, you were to purchase the matching earrings, then those cost twenty-five thousand pounds. I can do them for twenty-two thousand, sir.'

'Make it sixty thousand, and I will buy the pendant and the earrings.'

'Can I ask, sir, how you will be paying today?'

'Yes, I will use my debit card with my private bank.'

'Very well, sir, I will just get the machine. But as it concerns you, I will put the other items away, and I will get the pendant and earrings packed for you.'

'Julian, it's John England. I am about to buy some jewellery from Boodles on King Street, here in Manchester. I am about to use my debit card. Sixty thousand is the sum. I would be grateful if you would let the transaction proceed.'

David arrived with the card machine. 'Forgive me, sir. Banks usually like to be warned of large payments on cards.'

'I know, David. I have already spoken to my bank manager. It is all cleared.'

David offered the machine to John, with sixty thousand already set. John did what was required, and the transaction went straight through.

David realised this gentleman was a man of wealth.

'Mr England, here are your jewels all packed up.'

'Sorry, David, can you take it all back and have the box, which is so beautifully wrapped, covered in brown paper, so that it is not obvious what I have. I don't need the pink carrier bag either. It's a bit of an advert that I have something valuable.'

'Of course, sir. Would a plastic bag be helpful for you?'

'That would be excellent, thanks.'

David returned with the brown paper parcel and a Waitrose bag.

It wouldn't have been an Aldi or Tesco bag, would it? John mused to himself. David opened the shop door, and John walked up King Street to join Fiona.

They had a very relaxing lunch, after which Fiona did a little more shopping in Harvey Nicks.

'Hey, hun, I am tired now. Let's go back.'

A black cab returned them to Peters Tower.

35

'It's Jon Kim, John. I thought you would like to know that the duty sergeant does consider your defence of Toby Evans was proportionate.'

'Thanks, Jon. I wasn't losing sleep about that but thank you for letting me know.'

'John, Toby Evans has been remanded in custody so you can walk the streets in safety.'

'Fiona and I will go on holiday at the weekend with a clear conscience. I guess there will not be a trial for a while. I will be back at the end of September.'

'Okay, John, I will tell the CPS.'

'Jon, thank you so much for all your help. I can't tell you how reassuring it has been to know you were on our side and making all the appropriate arrangements. We are off to Greece now, flying into Corfu on Sunday.'

'You two lovely people have a wonderful holiday. You both deserve it.'

***

John and Fiona took a taxi and all Fiona's luggage and John's case to Terminal Two at Manchester Airport. In three and half hours, they would be landing in Corfu. Another taxi from Corfu took them to Gouvia Marina. Pontoon P could be accessed by a car.

The cabbie was out in a flash, realising his customers either owned the magnificent superyacht he had stopped by or were guests. Either way, he expected a tip. Twenty euros was his reward for being helpful and carrying some of the cases onto the quarterdeck. Jose did the rest.

'Hello everyone, how wonderful to see you all!'

It is wonderful to have you back on board, John and Fiona.'

The crew were dressed in *Brave Goose* polo shirts and navy-blue shorts. They looked so smart.

'Noel, you must tell us all about Sicily. And everyone, let's celebrate a restart of our ownership of *Brave Goose* and go out for dinner tonight. I saw that the last restaurant on the front looked the best. Jose, can you book a table for six at, say, eight-thirty? It will allow us all time to settle down and enjoy this warm sunshine for a while.'

'Thanks, John, we will look forward to it.'

John and Fiona opened the door to their cabin, and as they did so, Sally was behind them.

'No, that's the wrong cabin. You are the owners now, the owner's cabin for you.'

Sally swung open the owner's cabin door.

'This is now your cabin.'

Sally had decorated the cabin with flowers. The new bedding was pristine. All the cupboards, wardrobes and drawers had all been cleaned and lined. The bathroom was shining. The office had John's new computer.

'Sally, you have worked wonders! Thank you,' said Fiona.

'Oh, it's a new mattress and all new linen and pillows. If you don't like the pillows, it's my fault.'

'Gosh, Sally, it must have taken ages. What happened to the mattress and the sheets, etc.?'

'The police forensic team removed all the bedding. The mattress as well, which was a great help. All Goose's clothes went to charity. There was a charity shop in Puerto Pollenca.'

'You have done well, Sally. The cabin is beautiful.'

John and Fiona took some time to work out what would go where. Who would have which wardrobe?

'John, can I have these three wardrobes? It leaves a good-sized one for you.'

'Yes darling, I was expecting that division,' said John with a smile.

The pair enjoyed the afternoon and early evening sun on the boat deck for the next few hours.

It had been agreed that everyone would meet on the quarterdeck for a champagne reunion.

Fiona thought this would be an ideal opportunity to wear one of her new dresses.

'Wow, you look fabulous in your new pink dress. I love it. It will get to be even more beautiful as you turn brown.'

'Thank you, darling. I like the neckline. I thought it was quite sexy.'

'It is, darling. Something is missing. This is for you, my love, by way of some compensation for all the trauma you have had to endure.'

John handed Fiona a pink box tied up with a ribbon.

'Oh, John.' Fiona knew it was something sparkling. The Boodles ribbon printed with the shop's name gave the game away.

Fiona opened the box as quickly as she could. Her hands were trembling at the thought of what might lie within.

'John, how wonderful, you must have known about this dress!'

'No, darling, I had no idea, but as soon as I saw you in the dress, I knew I had done the right thing.'

'Can you please do the clasp for me, John? Oh, darling, this is just fabulous, thank you, thank you. My Prince Charming, I love you more than I can say.'

'You look fabulous in the dress. The diamonds make the outfit.'

'They will when I put these exquisite earrings in.'

They both made their way to the quarterdeck. John had picked up some envelopes on his way.

'Fiona, wow, you look absolutely fabulous. What a beautiful dress and pendant, and earrings to match. Just fantastic. Did you buy the diamonds with the dress in mind, or was it the other way round?'

'No, it was neither. I chose the dress. John has just given me the pendant and earrings, Sally.'

'That was very clever or lucky; whatever, they are just magnificent.'

'Let's have some champagne, Noel.'

'Certainly, John.'

'You all will not know that Toby Evans attacked us in Manchester. He held his knife to Fiona and made her open the door to the flat. He then attacked me. Luckily my Krav Maga training came back to help. He is now in custody, awaiting trial for assault on Fiona and me, and probably once the forensic reports from Spain are sent to Manchester, the ultimate murder of Goose.'

'Good heavens, do you think that this is the end of the matter, John?'

'I hope so, Noel. I have paid the money, so they can't want anything else. I will tell you why they were after Goose, but not now. Anyway, you have all had a traumatic experience in Sicily. I am so sorry you have been involved with all this. Here is a little extra compensation for the latest, and hopefully last, attack.'

'John, thank you so much. I think we are all going to have a wonderful time in Greece. Can't wait to get started.'

'Thank you, Noel. It's time we went for dinner.'

'Is *Brave Goose* all ready to go on a cruise, Noel?'

'Yes, John, everything is topped up. Fuel, wine, water, Sally has a large amount of frozen food in stock. Where would you like to go?'

'Fiona and I have discussed this. For the first week, we would like to wander around the Ionian, then perhaps we can go to Athens via the Corinth Canal, then into the Peloponnese and come back to the Ionian from the north.'

'Okay, John, I will work out a trip. I am looking forward to it.'

John's mobile rang.

'John, it's Jon Kim. I thought you would like to know that the Spanish police have arrested and charged the attempted kidnappers of you and Fiona with aggravated kidnapping and murder, as far as Goose was concerned. As a minimum, they are very likely to receive jail sentences of twenty-five years each.'

'That is excellent news, Jon. We can now have a holiday without the thought of any interruption.'

'Good, you two have a great time; you deserve it now.'

Out of habit, John went to his computer onboard *Brave Goose*. With the new satellite communication, he was always assured of a signal.

There was a call from Angela.

'John, we have had an application for Apartment 803. Brandon Phelan has gone. We will not be releasing his deposit as he didn't give notice and has left quite a bit of tidying up and cleaning to be done.'

'Good, he won't need the money. Who has applied for the apartment?'

'It's a Mr & Mrs Evans from London.'

'What does Mr Evans do?'

'Sorry, John, I don't know. They have paid six months plus a deposit upfront.'

'Why are they wanting to rent the flat?'

'Apparently, they have a son who is in trouble with the law, and they want to be in Manchester for when he is called for trial.'

'It just couldn't be, but it sounds like it to me, that they are the parents of Toby Evans, who tried to kill me. Okay, their money is as good as anyone else's. Let the letting continue.'

'That's good, John, they moved in yesterday.'

REFLECTIONS OF DEATH

PREVIEW CHAPTER

The next book in stories of John England will be published in 2023. The first chapter is attached to whet your appetite! Enjoy.

R A Jordan

1

The threat of further kidnappings was ringing in John's head. He was anxious not to let the news of the phone calls and emails he received from Georgios in Sicily become known. A quarter of a million pounds was now demanded. John had paid the two million eight hundred thousand of the three million demanded under duress. He had held back the two hundred thousand to pay the pensioners. Georgios had robbed them of their pensions using his fake finance company.

According to Georgios, further kidnappings would occur with the help of the Greek and Russian mafia. John was about to start a cruise around Greece onboard his super yacht *Brave Goose*. He was determined not to pay or tell Fiona. It would spoil the holiday.

It was three in the afternoon of Sunday 1st September 2019 when the plane touched down at Kerkira Airport, Corfu. A queue for the toilet was not helpful. The Greek toilets are, to say the least basic. There is a toilet pan in a cubicle without a seat or a door with no lock or catch. Greek drains will not cope with toilet paper. John was in stitches with laughter. Some wag had added to the warning notice about not dropping toilet paper in the toilet pan. 'No, just chuck it in!' By the time John had extracted himself from the loo, Fiona was in charge of the two bags and hand baggage by the carousel.

Leaving clothes, onboard *Brave Goose* has been a definite advantage. I guess the wardrobes will be packed by the time this current load of clothes has been stored.

'You are a tease, John.'

'Noel, it's John. Just to let you know, we are about to get a taxi. We should be with you within half an hour.'

'Okay, John, we are on pontoon D.'

The air-conditioned Mercedes taxi protected them from thirty-two degrees Celsius. It took about half an hour to reach the Gouvia Marina in Corfu. The taxi dropped them at the end of the passerelle attached to *Brave Goose*. John paid the man who had made a collection of their luggage on the quay. Jose welcomed John and Fiona and took the first load of bags to their cabin.

The whole crew of *Brave Goose* was in attendance to greet their owners. Noel the captain, Sally stewardess, Jock the engineer and Jose deckhand. Once they had dealt with the formalities, John and Fiona, remembering to go to the owner's stateroom, couldn't wait to change into shorts and polo shirts and enjoy a relaxing time on the quarterdeck. Sally had produced her iced lemonade, which was always a hit.

'Anything to report, Noel?' as the three sat around the quarterdeck table.

'Nothing more than you already know. We have just about recovered from the mafia invasion and were held hostage in the port of Catania in Sicily. Thank you for organising the payment of the ransom so quickly, John. We were all convinced we were in danger of being killed if the money didn't come through.'

'Well, I have some compensation for you all, so I hope that will be the end of the dangerous and frightening attempts to recover the three million which was paid back, despite the fact the Fitzallen and Phelan families were not entitled to it. The killing of Goose was unforgivable.'

John knew this was not true. He had only paid two million eight hundred thousand pounds. Georgios threatened to recover the total of three million. The two hundred thousand pound balance has been demanded plus fifty thousand to pay Georgios's troops. John had paid the pensioners back the money Georgios had stolen from them.

'There has been a man hanging around trying to discover who owned *Brave Goose*. I asked the marina not to divulge the information, and of course, we have not done so.'

'Oh, did this man have a name, Noel?' John had assumed it was a member of Georgios's mafia team.

'Yes, he said he was called Azmir. We didn't expect for a moment you would know him. He was trying to get to the island of Kalamos. He hoped we could give him a lift. I explained it could be at least two weeks before we went there. I told him there was a bus service from the mainland to Mitika. From there was a ferry to Kalamos. That would be the only way of getting there by public transport. I explained he would need to go to the port of Corfu and catch a ferry to Igoumenitsa, where he could catch a bus to Mitika,'

'Azmir, he said he was a Croatian? 'John suddenly felt uneasy. He began to feel sweat running down his back. He was sure his face had turned red. His heart started to beat faster. 'That is remarkable. Someone must have told him *Brave Goose* was my boat. I met Azmir when I was in the Army Legal Services in Bosnia. He was my interpreter.'

'Good heavens. I had no idea you were in the Army, John.'

'Neither did I', said Fiona.

'It's a long story, but I was in the Army for three years. Perhaps it would be appropriate if I explained my time in the Army.'

'Oh yes, tell us all about it, please', insisted Fiona.

'To go back even further, I read law at Balliol College Oxford. When I graduated, I studied at the College of Law in Chester. I then decided I would like some excitement in my life before settling down to become a solicitor. I joined the Army Legal Services. Once I had completed a six-month initiation course, including physical fitness, I was sent to Sandhurst. The Royal Military Academy. I was taught military skills, tactics, and legal skills required in conflict zones. Skills to lead and take command. I left Sandhurst with the rank of captain and re-joined the Legal Services Directorate.'

'Wow, that must have been quite an initiation, John? So what does a solicitor in the Army do?' Fiona was fascinated by what she had heard and desperate to know more. 'What happened next?'

'I was sent to Bosnia the year after the war had ended. I was involved in all sorts of issues. One of the more interesting ones was assisting the Bosnian government, such as it was, with preparing documents and voting arrangements for an election to their parliament.'

'Were you involved with the conflict John?' Fiona enquired.

'Yes, in fact, in Bosnia, not the conflict, but NATO troops had arrested one of the soldiers who had been a fighter involved in the massacre in Srebrenica. It was a nasty war. Ethnic cleansing, rape, torture and summary assassinations were commonplace. I had to interrogate this soldier with the assistance of Azmir. The Bosnian fighter had only just been captured. His gun and hand grenades had been taken from him. Azmir and I walked out of our office to cross the square. The fighter was ahead of us by a reasonable distance. He was being escorted to the interrogation suite by a NATO soldier. That's when it happened. The fighter exploded. He had been wearing a suicide vest under his clothes.

There were body parts all over the place. The ground turned red.

The NATO soldier escort was very severely injured.

Azmir and I were hit by shrapnel.

The Bosnia fighter was in pieces all over the square.

'I couldn't hear a thing. Blood was dripping from

my body. Azmir was in a similar state. I began to shake uncontrollably. It wasn't many minutes, but it seemed an age before medics came with a stretcher and took us to the first aid area. We had wounds dressed. I was taken by helicopter to Sarajevo airport. I am not sure where Azmir went.

That evening, I was operated on to remove numerous pieces of shrapnel.

The following day I was a casevac patient flown to the UK. Two injured soldiers were on the same flight. I couldn't talk to them as I wouldn't hear any response. I was deaf.'

'Oh, John, how terrible.'

'It could have been a great deal worse, darling. I could have been killed. I suspect that was the lot of the soldier.'

'So John, the opportunity to become a solicitor in Chester must have seemed so peaceful after the trauma of Bosnia?'

'You are so right, Noel. I left the Army about six months later. Despite my three year commitment at the outset. I only served just over two years. I took a long holiday, mainly in the Mediterranean, quite a bit of time here in Greece.'

'You never told me that, John?'

'You never asked. I have had a few injuries since, but my Krav Maga training on top of my Army training has been my saviour.'

'And mine', added Fiona.

Did Azmir say why he wanted to go to Kalamos? From my recollection, there is nothing much there?'

'No, John, I kept the conversation short, not knowing what he wanted.'

'Good, I guess when we get to Kalamos, we may discover what it is all about.'

'Gosh, John. I had no idea about all this.'

'Well, my love, you do now. I was in the Army Legal Services team. Does it make any difference to our relationship?'

'No, of course not. I don't know why I should even express surprise. It's just you don't think of the Army having solicitors.'

'Well, there you are. I might tell you all about it one day. Noel, what are the plans for this week?'

'Well, John and Fiona, I have a reservation in Lefkas Marina to moor *Brave Goose* for the evening of Friday 6th September. We are expected to leave by Monday 10th, and back again on Saturday15th September. This week is very casual. We can do anything you like.'

'That's a good plan, Noel. I guess Fiona would like to look at the shops in the marina. Perhaps we could eat ashore tonight. Would you all want to come? I will stroll over and book a table?

'We could then travel to Corfu town tomorrow, John, and moor under the castle. It's a lovely anchorage. We may be able to get on the outside of the mole so we could get access to the shore easily.'

I am sure Fiona would love a walk around the town, and we will eat out tomorrow evening.'

'That's all fine, John. We will be pleased to join you for dinner tonight. Thank you.'

John returned to the owner's cabin to find Fiona unpacking, hanging all her clothes in her allocated wardrobes.

'John, I am sorry if I upset you by asking about your time in the Army. I wasn't prying. It was a surprise, that's all.'

'Don't worry, darling. There is nothing to it. It is all behind me now. It is a closed book as far as I am concerned.'

'Will you let me into more of your secrets one day?'

'If you need to know. There is nothing important. So now let's get on with our holiday. I have booked a table for six at the restaurant opposite. The table will be available from eight-thirty. We can have drinks here before we go.'

'That's great, John. What are we going to do tomorrow?'

'Well, my love, I thought you would like to wander around the shops here. Then we would anchor in the bay under the castle near Corfu town. There are a great many interesting shops and buildings in town. You and I can have dinner in town, just the two of us.'

'Have you any more thoughts on what we do next?'

'Yes, but it will be a surprise.'

John asked Sally to bring some champagne flutes to the quarter deck. John opened a bottle of Goose's champagne with a loud bang as the cork flew into the harbour.

Once everyone had a glass of champagne, John toasted everyone's good health and looked forward to a happy and relaxed cruise.

'Now here are some envelopes, one each. My thanks go to you all. In the envelope is some compensation for the trauma you were subjected to on your way here. I am sure what happened was illegal—being held hostage by a group of mafia men with guns for a day. However, as it was in Sicily, I suspect the police have a different view. I hope the contents of the envelopes go a small way to compensate you for the outrageous events in Sicily. Possibly an island we may not have on our itinerary. Its cash, in euros, as I thought that would be the most useful. Everyone has the same amount. Enjoy it.'

A chorus of thanks erupted from the crew. They realised the crew's release, together with *Brave Goose*, must have cost John the three million pounds. The protagonists had been keen to collect. All of the crew had experienced a traumatic time one way or another, helping John avoid the fraudulent demands of the Irish families. The Irish were not entitled to the money but persisted with ever more dangerous stunts to recover what they believed was rightfully theirs.

It was eleven o'clock in the evening when they all returned to *Brave Goose*. Jose withdrew the passerelle. You know it is such a beautiful evening. I fancy sitting here for a while with a glass of brandy. Will you join me, darling?'

'Yes, I would love to, John. The brandy speaks of being on holiday in the Mediterranean.'

It was just gone midnight when John had finished explaining to Fiona what else he had done in the Army and why he had left. She gave him a huge kiss and suggested they go to bed.

'Will you tell me all about your exploits in the Army one day?'

'It was some time ago and not very interesting. Let's leave it.'

John knew that if he explained his activities in the Army, particularly his time in Bosnia in 1996 and 1997, he would regret it, as it was a most distressing time. Yes, he did have an interpreter called Azmir. He was a great guy, but it became problematic when Azmir's friend was arrested for laying an IED, killing a colleague and wounding two other soldiers. I had to prosecute the friend, which put Azmir in a difficult position. Azmir and the Russian mafia were to invade their holiday plans once again.

ABOUT THE AUTHOR

As a retired chartered surveyor and running my own business for forty-five years, many are the experiences I have encountered. Eleven years ago, shortly after selling my business, but working on a short-term contract for the purchasers, I was delayed on a train journey from London Euston to Macclesfield, Cheshire. The West Coast mainline was being 'improved', hence the delay. Wandering around Euston and Smiths newspaper shop, I paid what I considered a small fortune for a Moleskine notebook. My train was called as soon as I paid for it.

Sitting in my seat, a gin and tonic provided by Virgin, thank you, Richard Branson, I looked at what I had purchased. Why I bought it, I couldn't justify to myself. I found it a tactile book. Should I try writing that book? I had always promised to write. Leaving Euston slowly on the new Pendolino train, I noticed a Series two Land Rover, canvas hood, and all, parked in a lot near a warehouse.

Someone's pride and joy. I recalled the fantastic journey with three good friends to the South of France in just such a vehicle when we were all around twenty years old. I had so much fun with that vehicle. It also reminded me of a tragic event of a man committing suicide using his old Land Rover.

It wasn't long before I started to write. When I got off at Macclesfield, I had sketched out the story for the first novel, *Time's Up*.

I subsequently took myself off to Corpus Christi College, Oxford, to attend the *Sunday Times* creative writing course in consecutive years. Of the eighteen delegates who were all aspiring to write a book, I found I was the only person to have written a book! The bug had bitten, so I found myself penning some part of my next book, as I do most days.

I have a website on which this and all my other books are displayed and sold.

www.rajordan.uk

The follow-on book from this, *Failed Retribution*, is again a John England story –*Reflections of Death*

.

This book is printed on paper from sustainable sources managed under the Forest Stewardship Council (FSC) scheme.

It has been printed in the UK to reduce transportation miles and their impact upon the environment.

For every new title that Matador publishes, we plant a tree to offset CO_2, partnering with the More Trees scheme.

MORE TREES
LET'S PLANT A BILLION TREES

For more about how Matador offsets its environmental impact, see www.troubador.co.uk/about/